PENGUIN ⓟ CLASSICS

STRANGE TALES FROM A
CHINESE STUDIO

PU SONGLING (1640–1715) wrote his *Strange Tales from a
Chinese Studio* (*Liaozhai zhiyi*) over several decades, during a life
spent in obscurity in his home province of Shandong, in northern
China. The book amounted to nearly five hundred items of greatly
varying lengths, from short anecdotes and jottings to fully fledged
stories, on a wide variety of 'strange' themes. It was never published in his lifetime, and at first circulated in hand-copied versions. It was finally printed in 1766, in the southern city of
Hangzhou, and was reprinted countless times, attracting many
commentaries and imitations. It rapidly came to be considered the
supreme work of fiction in the classical Chinese language, just as
The Story of the Stone (also published in Penguin Classics, in five
volumes (1973–86)) came to be considered the pinnacle of fiction
in the vernacular. This new translation introduces a selection of
104 tales from the original work.

JOHN MINFORD studied Chinese at Oxford and at the Australian
National University and has taught in China, Hong Kong and
New Zealand. He edited (with Geremie Barmé) *Seeds of Fire:
Chinese Voices of Conscience* (1988) and (with Joseph S. M.
Lau) *Classical Chinese Literature: An Anthology of Translations*
(2000). He has translated numerous works from the Chinese,
including the last two volumes of Cao Xueqin's eighteenth-century
novel *The Story of the Stone* and Sunzi's *The Art of War*, both in
Penguin Classics. He has also translated *The Deer and the Cauldron* (2000–2003), a three-volume Martial Arts novel by the
contemporary Hong Kong writer Louis Cha. He is currently
Professor of Chinese at the Australian National University.

Acknowledgements

I was fortunate to receive a generous grant from the Taiwan Council for Cultural Construction and Development when I began this project, back in 1991. Without that three-year period of freedom I would never have been able to begin my journey into this strange and wonderful world, and write the first drafts from which these versions are descended. I wish to express my gratitude to the head of the Council, Kuo Wei-fan, and to my friends Joseph Lau, William Tay, Wang Ch'iu-kuei and Anthony Yu, for their loyal support over the years. Mark Elvin kindly invited me to spend the third year of this project (1993) as a Visiting Fellow at the Australian National University, and in Canberra Liu Ts'un-yan patiently answered several questions of mine. I am endebted once again to Richard Rigby, who sent me a copy from Japan of the invaluable *Liaozhai Dictionary*, compiled by Zhu Yixuan and his colleagues in 1991. Don Cohn gave me a beautiful old edition of the book, which he found in a bookshop in Tokyo. André Lévy, whose complete French translation is soon to be published by Picquier, has shared his knowledge and enthusiasm with me over the years. In Hong Kong, in the 1990s, Tong Man patiently went along with many a meandering train of thought as we read these stories together. More recently I have benefited, as always, from the acute comments of Rachel May, and from the shrewd emendations of David Hawkes, both of whom read the final drafts of this book in their entirety.

At Penguin, I am grateful to Paul Keegan for having so enthusiastically welcomed this book into the Classics series many years ago, and to Laura Barber for having waited so stoically during the intervening years for it to come to fruition. Caroline Pretty has been a wonderfully perceptive and discreet copy-editor, rescuing me from many careless errors and lazy omissions. She has been at all times a sympathetic collaborator, never an intruder.

These translations are dedicated to Günter and Barbara Wohlfart, dear friends, who shared good times 'in the green grove', and came when needed to 'the dark frontier'.

Introduction

Pu Songling, the author of these extraordinary tales, was born in the summer of 1640, four years before the final collapse of the Ming dynasty (1368–1644) and the arrival in Peking of the Manchu conquerors from the north. He died in February 1715, towards the end of the long reign of the second Manchu Emperor, Kangxi, having spent almost his entire life in the mountainous north-eastern province of Shandong.[1] His father was a well-to-do merchant from a village near the small town of Zichuan,[2] and Pu Songling grew up here during the unsettled times of the dynastic transition, as the old order was falling apart and the conquerors were taking charge of their new domain – the period referred to several times in these tales as the Troubles. Peasant rebellions and anti-Manchu uprisings erupted periodically in Shandong during his childhood, all of them brutally suppressed by the new rulers.

In the spring of 1658, by which time the dynasty was beginning to acquire a certain stability, Pu Songling sat for his first public examination and was placed first in all three stages of the highly competitive process. He was singled out for high praise by the eminent mandarin acting as Examiner, and looked set for a distinguished career as an official. But it was not to be. From 1660 onwards, every one of his many attempts at acquiring the vital second degree proved unsuccessful.[3] As a result, from the age of nineteen to the age of seventy-two he was to be a perpetual student, locked into the 'examination hell' of the Chinese civil service recruitment system,[4] supporting his family as a lowly private secretary and tutor in the households of one or another of the local wealthy families.

His failure as a mandarin was a source of deep personal disappointment, but it did at least leave him with ample leisure for reading and writing. Throughout his long life he wrote prolifically in a wide variety of literary genres: verse of all sorts, prose essays, practical reference works and handbooks, fiction, drama and ballads. It is, however, for his superb *Strange Tales*, on which he worked during most of his adult life, that he achieved immortality. While Cao Xueqin's *Story of the Stone*, that rambling and addictive novel of manners and sentiment, is regarded as the supreme novel written in the Chinese vernacular, the superb gallery of bizarre miniatures that constitute *Strange Tales* is seen as the pinnacle of fiction in the classical language.[5]

TRADITIONS

Pu Songling was enormously well read (all those years of studying paid off), and deeply conscious of writing in two long literary traditions of storytelling, two distinct genres, that of the *zhiguai*, which we may call the Weird Account, and that of the *chuanqi*, the Strange Story. Both used the highly elliptical classical language, as opposed to the vernacular favoured by many writers of fiction and drama ever since the Southern Song dynasty (1127–1278), and both were part of the broader realm of 'casual' belles-lettres (what the Chinese call *biji*, 'jottings').[6] A Weird Account might best be described as a pithy narrative of some strange event, a laconic record of some grotesque creature, of a haunting, a bizarre person, a peculiar phenomenon or coincidence. Here is a precursor of the genre, a strange little rudimentary myth, a fragment from *The Book of Hills and Seas*, one of the most ancient repositories of such things:

> Big Daddy chased the sun. As the sun went down he was thirsty and wanted a drink, so he drank from the Yellow and Wei rivers. They were not enough, so he started north to drink the Great Marsh, but on the way he died of thirst. He threw away his staff, and it became the Forest of Deng.[7]

Here is a later and more polished example, this time a thumb-nail sketch of a much-loved drunkard and eccentric, from the wonderful fifth-century collection of cameos *A New Account of Tales of the World*:

> On many occasions, under the influence of wine, Liu Ling would be completely free and unrestrained, sometimes even removing his clothes and sitting stark naked in the middle of his room. Some people once saw him in this state and chided him for it. Ling retorted, 'Heaven and earth are my pillars and roof, the rooms of my house are my jacket and trousers. What are you gentlemen doing in my trousers?'[8]

This sort of thing has fascinated Chinese readers since the dawn of literature, and still does. The Chinese press, both in the Mainland and in Hong Kong, regularly carries accounts of odd phenomena, sometimes human, sometimes not. In August 2004, for example, the Hong Kong press provided a piquant description of a man discovered in a remote part of the Chinese countryside, whose entire body was densely covered in hair.[9]

The Strange Stories are more artistically polished than the Weird Accounts. They are short works of fiction with fully developed plots and characterization. Some are romantic, some fantastical, some semi-historical, others are concerned with the exploits of magicians or Martial Arts adepts. These stories were first written during the Tang dynasty (618–907), more famous as a golden age for poetry, but the genre continued to be popular during the subsequent Song, Yuan (1279–1368) and Ming dynasties.[10]

Pu Songling brought these two traditions together in his *Strange Tales*, an achievement for which he has sometimes been criticized by purist literary critics. On the one hand we find in his collection longer stories with complex plots, often involving relationships between men, fox-spirits and ghosts, sometimes interweaving the events of several incarnations.[11] Then there are a large number of medium-length tales dealing with a variety of themes: the foibles of spiritual or alchemical pretension, both Buddhist and Taoist; the workings of illusion and enlightenment;

and the ways of human vanity and corruption in general.[12] These are interspersed with brief accounts of strange phenomena (earthquakes, hail-storms, mirages), of unusual abilities, pranks and preoccupations (rare sorts of kungfu, mediumistic skills – genuine or otherwise – strange performances with animals, obsessions with snakes); descriptions of unusual varieties of bird, fish, turtle and alligator, of magical stones, bags and swords; and tantalizing evocations of the transience of life, of strange tenants and abandoned halls. Pu Songling's collection ranges in style and form, as Anthony Yu writes, 'from gossipy anecdotes and ethnography-like fragments to polished compositions of exquisite language and superb control'.[13] I firmly believe that the richly heterogeneous nature of this book (to which I have tried to be faithful in this selection) was deliberate on the author's part. As we read we are offered the varied courses of a Chinese banquet. We are constantly being surprised and delighted, and yet nothing is there in excess. Pu Songling enjoyed breaking the rules, and he exploited to excellent effect the juxtaposition of contrasting elements, presenting his readers with, in the words of André Lévy, a 'full range of inconsistencies while at the same time providing a subtle, inimitable and elusive unity'.[14]

A CHINESE STORYTELLER'S STUDIO: SOURCES AND ALLUSION, HUMOUR AND MELANCHOLY

I recommend Pu Songling's own Preface (pp. 453–67) as by far the best guide to his sources, to his lineage as a writer and to his methods as a storyteller:

> Of tales told
> I have made a book.
> With time
> And my love of hoarding,
> The matter sent me by friends

> From the four corners
> Has grown into a pile.

A totally unreliable but nonetheless charming legend has our author collecting tales at the roadside, offering casual passers-by cups of tea and pipes of tobacco in exchange for strange or unusual anecdotes.[15] Scholars continue to debate to what extent his finished tales incorporate such 'popular' material. Certainly he received materials from others, but there is little to suggest that any of them were illiterate old women dropping by for a cup of tea. As we have just seen in his Preface, he thanks his far-flung friends for helping him, by sending him raw material which he then worked up into tales. In no less than seventeen of the stories in the present selection he names such sources. In eleven others historical people are mentioned in the story itself, and in at least six cases verifiable historical events are referred to. In Tale 12, 'Stealing a Peach', Pu Songling states clearly that the story is based on something he witnessed himself as a youth. After all, as he observes in his Preface, real experience can be stranger than mythology and fantasy:

> Here in the civilized world,
> Stranger events by far occur
> Than in the Country of Cropped Hair;
> Before our very eyes
> Weirder tales unfold
> Than in the Nation of Flying Heads.

Three tales (again from the present selection) are in some way related to his own family, and seven have some connection with his home town of Zichuan. Pu Songling also reworked stories that had been around for centuries. Examples of this are Tale 13, 'Growing Pears', based on a far shorter item from Gan Bao's fourth-century *In Search of Spirits*, and Tale 82, 'Princess Lotus', derived from two famous full-length Tang-dynasty tales.[16] And last but not least, in many cases he undoubtedly exercised his own fertile imagination. He was a creative artist. To quote his Preface once more:

> My irrepressible transports
> Are an unfettered rapture
> That cannot be gainsaid;
> My far-soaring ideas,
> An unbridled folly
> That cannot be denied.

So we are dealing with a collection of tales of diverse types, of diverse lengths, of diverse origins, and on equally diverse themes. But this diversity is brilliantly unified by a distinctive brand of lyricism and humour, and by a transcendent literary style. The French scholar and translator Jacques Dars has given a fine description of Pu Songling's art:

His tales are constructed and developed with consummate art, the episodes, transitions and surprises are cleverly handled, the descriptions lively, full of unexpected details. The depiction of character and the twists and turns in the plot testify to a rare imagination. The fantastic predominates, but it never wearies the reader, because here too the author knows how to vary his themes, his adventures, his tone, his style. It is to be noted too that despite his magisterial use of the classical language, which is that of a supreme master of Chinese, he enlivens his tales with a judicious admixture of popular expressions and well-turned idioms, which render the finished product less abstruse and add considerably to its charm. Over and above the exquisite formal beauty of the tales and the author's never-failing felicity of expression, there is a wonderful sense of proportion in the disposal of the elements within the whole, an overriding art such as one finds in the most beautiful Chinese jades: they are so perfectly carved and polished that one can caress them with one's eyes and gaze at them for ever in sheer wonder.[17]

These are the qualities that set Pu Songling apart from the many other tellers of strange tales of the seventeenth and eighteenth centuries.

Let us consider his prose style first. It needs to be stressed for readers of these translations that Pu Songling's original

language is somewhat daunting. Many a Chinese reader today
has a hard time making sense of it. Pu Songling was writing not
for the masses but for his fellow scholar-gentlemen, in their
secluded libraries or studios.[18] He could have chosen to write
in the vernacular, but he did not. His prose is extraordinarily
elegant and extremely demanding. The twentieth-century essayist Lu Xun, himself master of a crabbed semi-antique prose style,
once protested that Pu Songling used 'so many classical allusions
that ordinary readers find the language rather difficult'.[19] In that
sense the *Tales* are unashamedly highbrow.

But despite their apparent (and at first sight off-putting)
linguistic complexity, the *Tales* are never pedantic. On the contrary, one of their attractions for the Chinese connoisseur is the
lightness, and occasional disrespect, with which the author
wears his learning. Often he uses allusion as a straightforward
embellishment, a literary patina to the text. But sometimes
he will stand an allusion on its head and twist references,
subversively recycling the very material he had been obliged to
memorize and digest in his lifelong studies. Let me give one
example. In Tale 38, 'Fox Enchantment', the young man, who
is about to climb into bed with the fox-girl, recoils in terror
upon feeling her 'long bushy tail', and when she asks him what
the trouble is, he replies, 'It wasn't your face ... It was your
tail.' This phrase is one of countless throwaway allusions in
the *Tales*, the force and humour of which are utterly lost in
translation. The original expression (about 'face' and 'tail')
occurs in the *Zuo Commentary on the Spring and Autumn
Annals*, a venerable classic that Pu Songling (and every other
Chinese scholar) would have studied and memorized exten-
sively for his examinations. Lü Zhan'en, in his 1825 *Tales*
commentary, gives the exact wording in the original *Zuo Commentary* text: 'There is a saying of the ancients: "Fearing for its
head and fearing for its tail, there is little of the body left [not
to fear for]." '[20] As two other commentators, He Shouqi (1823)
and Dan Minglun (1842), point out, the author is teasing his
readers by playing with the classic text, giving it a mischievous
twist.[21] Pu Songling has, as he wrote in a poem, 'An idle jest to
share'.[22] It is a little as if John Cleland were to have put a

well-known line from Genesis into the mouth of a young rake
in the middle of a seduction scene in *Fanny Hill*. Pu Songling's
fellow literati, for whom he was writing, would all have understood. But for the translator this sort of 'scholar's studio' *jeu
d'esprit* poses almost insuperable problems.[23]

Ambivalence and wordplay, mellow humour coupled with
an irrepressible delight in the strange for its own sake, are
what give the book its personal flavour, its uniquely wry and
understated charm. It is a most individual voice. It is, as Pu
Songling suggests in his Preface, 'music that is what it is for
reasons of its own'. Pu Songling is essentially a *playful* author,
playful in his vision of the human condition, playful in the way
he uses language and tells his stories.[24] In this he resembles
Zhuangzi, the great Taoist philosopher and raconteur of the
fourth century BC. And like Zhuangzi, he enlightens as he
entertains, pushing at the boundaries of our everyday experience, stretching our vision in the tiniest of ways: a leaf blown
across a doorway, the trail of an insect as it makes its way
across a page. These things too are extraordinary, they can
open up new vistas of thought, help us to see things anew,
quicken strange intuitions.

Side by side with the humour, an unmistakable note of melancholy creeps in now and then. Once again, the Preface speaks
movingly of how the author has poured his soul, his spleen and
anguish, into his work:

> Midnight finds me
> Here in this desolate studio
> By the dim light
> Of my flickering lamp,
> Fashioning my tales
> At this ice-cold table,
> Vainly piecing together my sequel
> To *The Infernal Regions*.
> I drink to propel my pen,
> But succeed only in venting
> My spleen,
> My lonely anguish.

> Is it not a sad thing,
> To find expression thus?
> Alas! I am but
> A bird
> Trembling at the winter frost,
> Vainly seeking shelter in the tree;
> An insect
> Crying at the autumn moon,
> Feebly hugging the door for warmth.
> Those who know me
> Are in the green grove,
> They are
> At the dark frontier.

All of these elements, the elegant diction, the subtle humour, the pervasive melancholy, constitute the magic, what the Chinese call the *quwei* or 'flavour', of Pu Songling's work. It is a magic sadly absent from the many versions of the *Tales* retold in modern vernacular Chinese. The modern language is ill-equipped to evoke the peculiar ambience of the scholar-gentleman's world, the world of the traditional 'Chinese studio' (*zhai*), from which these tales emanate.

This 'studio world' was a very special space. It was a physical space, a pavilion set apart in the garden, screened perhaps by bamboos, a place of seclusion and privilege, where the literati could elaborate their fantasies, surrounded with their favourite knick-knacks (strangely carved inkstones, armrests for calligraphy, paperweights, brushes, seals, incense burners, weird roots and rocks, etc.). It is in just such a space as this that many of the experiences and encounters of *Strange Tales* take place. But the 'studio' was more than this: it was also a symbolic space, a gestalt. It denoted a whole cultural, spiritual, aesthetic and sensual world. Chinese writers and artists often encoded their own personal sense of identity in a 'studio name'. (Indeed they often had studio names without having an actual studio.) For example, the celebrated painter and calligrapher Zhao Mengfu (1254–1322) named his studio 'Pinetrees in the Snow'. Pu Songling's own studio name, *liao*, is virtually untranslatable. It contains several differing and yet interconnected senses: leisure, time on one's hands, a passing enthusiasm or whim, something ephemeral, chit-chat, a desolate feeling of helplessness or inadequacy. It also happens to be the ancient name for a place in Pu Songling's native province of Shandong. The little word is both nothing and everything. It is a mere trifle, a passing whim, but a trifle and a whim charged with poignant meaning. The studio that bears this name exists now as a collection of tales, a receptacle fashioned in the crucible of Pu Songling's imagination, a timeless prism affording a view into the inner world of the traditional Chinese scholar-gentleman.

THE EROTIC

These tales have also been prized (and sometimes frowned upon) for their discreetly and deliciously erotic flavour. The late-Ming period was noted for its voluminous production of pornographic and erotic fiction, designed for the tastes of the prosperous urban bourgeoisie of the Yangtze region. Pu Songling was catering for a mellower and more refined audience. His readers were not looking for the blow-by-blow accounts of sexual marathons that fill the pages of a crude late-Ming work such as *The Embroidered Couch*, nor were they looking for the subtler and more extended explorations of sexual mores to be found in higher-class novels such as *Golden Lotus* or *The Carnal Prayer Mat*.[25] That is not to say that his readers were genteel or prudish. On the contrary, they would have found their tastes well catered for by the strangely matter-of-fact manner in which sexuality is presented in *Strange Tales*. It is encountered quite explicitly, without prudery and without surprise, as part of everyday life. In a typical tale, a woman drifts into the studio of a young gentleman of leisure. Perhaps she is a local sing-song girl, or she may be a wife or concubine running away from an unhappy marriage. She may be a fox-spirit, or a ghost. The young man finds her extraordinarily beautiful, undresses her, and without delay they go to bed and make love. Then the story unfolds. Sex for Pu Songling is simply one arena in which human behaviour can be observed in its extraordinary intensity, richness and variety. It is intriguing insofar as it reveals human nature. *Strange Tales* is (among other things) a casebook of Chinese sexual pathology. A lonely woman, left too often alone at home by her merchant husband, couples with her dog. A young man with a roving eye is deluded by his neighbour's pretty wife into having sex with a rotten log and as a result has his penis fatally bitten by a scorpion. Another young man's impotence is miraculously cured by the administration of a large herbal bolus. A kungfu master bashes his penis with a mallet and feels no pain. We encounter aphrodisiacs, love potions and dildos. A troublesome fox-spirit is exterminated through more than usually vigorous and prolonged sexual intercourse. Extreme pain is inflicted on an innocent woman by the overly large sexual member of a visiting Wutong-spirit. Above all, again and again, we read of the seduction of an enervated young scholar by some fatally attractive woman-as-fox or woman-as-ghost, their sexual liaison leading to his eventual debilitation and premature death.

FOX-SPIRITS

The fox-spirit or *hulijing* has haunted the Chinese male imagination for centuries. When we read these stories today, what are we to make of them, these shape-shifting, irresistibly beautiful 'were-vixen'? What did they mean for Pu Songling? One moment they are sensual, seductive women, the next they are lying on the ground, no more than an animal pelt. They can be destructive and heartless, ruthless and vindictive. They can suck the life out of their young men, causing them to ejaculate to excess and robbing them of their precious Yang essence. They are seen as feeding on their victims, while prolonging their own span of life.[26] Such is the caricature of the fox-spirit. But they can also (especially in these tales) be tender and vulnerable, and capable of deep love and loyalty. For Pu Songling, the fox-spirit is a projection of the deeply ambivalent attitude of the Chinese male literati towards their women and towards the demands of physical and emotional love. He returns to this theme again and again. The power of feminine beauty and sexuality, the power of the Yin, as personified in the fox-spirit, inspires men and simultaneously incapacitates them, instilling in them a lethal mixture of infatuation, fascination and fear. It is above all the fear, the fear of being dominated in this way, that leads to the male response, to what Robert van Gulik has called the 'male sexual vampirism conducted under the guise of the so-called Taoist techniques of the bedchamber'. In this warlike scheme of things, man regards woman as the 'enemy' because by causing him to emit semen she 'robs' him of his precious Yang essence. 'A woman who has learned this secret [of nursing her own potency by absorbing the man's Yang] will feed on her copulations with men, so that she will prolong her span of life and not grow old, but always remain like a young girl.'[27] Men respond by evolving self-aggrandizing Taoist pseudo-alchemical sexual practices in effect to protect themselves against this threat, against the sexual predations of their women (fox-spirits). They are exorcizing their own fear. The same fear and the same need for sexual protection led to the extreme subjugation of women, to the openly sadistic practice of female mutilation known euphemistically as 'foot-binding'.[28]

But why did the fox take on these attributes, rather than any other animal? Van Gulik attributes the 'special sexual associations' of the fox-spirit to, first, 'the ancient belief in the [creature's] abundant vital essence', and second, to 'its proclivity to play pranks on man'. But I cannot help thinking that it is a lot simpler and more physical than this. The fox-spirit seems to me a powerful physical shorthand for feminine sexuality, for the woman's sex organs, for the object of male desire. To return to the example I have quoted above, from Tale 38, 'Fox Enchantment': 'Then he began to caress her and fondle her body, allowing his hand to stray to her nether regions, where to his great alarm he encountered a long bushy tail.' In a number of cases, fox-spirits are male, but then it is merely an extension of the same principle. They still represent the power of sexuality. One of the most striking male fox-spirits is the beautiful boy Huang, in the moving tale 'Cut Sleeve' (Tale 63). Huang, having

been at first the reluctant object of the obsessive sexual attentions of He Shican, ends up demonstrating his own genuine
affection by using his physical attractions to right an injustice
done to his lover in another lifetime.

In his observations on the 'Chinese fox', the British consular
official Thomas Watters was in many ways ahead of his time.
'Sometimes,' he observed in 1874, 'a man marries what he
thinks is a fine pretty woman, but finds that she is a genuine
fox – an experience I believe scarcely confined to China . . . The
poor unhappy prostitutes of Fuzhou and other places pray to
this demon to give them favour in the eyes of men.'[29] Watters
also quotes (with some reservations) the following passage
from a work entitled *Zoological Mythology* by one Professor
De Gubernatis (who was writing in a Western, not Chinese,
context):

> The fox is the reddish mediatrix between the luminous day and
> the gloomy night, the crepuscular phenomenon of the heavens
> taking an animal form. No form seemed more adapted to the
> purpose than that of the fox or the jackal, on account of their
> colour and some of their cunning habits. The hour of twilight is
> the time of uncertainties and deceits.

Watters himself testifies to the widespread fear of fox-spirits in
Fujian Province, and to the tendency to blame them for all sorts
of physical and psychic troubles:

> In several parts of Fujian, and in other places, vertigo, madness,
> melancholy, and other bodily and mental derangements, are
> ascribed to the action of this creature, in its capacity of sprite, or
> spiritual being, tormenting mankind . . . It is generally invisible
> to all, except the person afflicted, though occasionally it is seen
> by some friend or professional exorcist.

This sounds very much like Pu Songling writing, and Watters
goes on to tell (from firsthand sources of his own) a number of
fox stories worthy of *Strange Tales*, which for us have the
added interest of being told (not translated):

A countryman from a village in the neighbourhood of Fuzhou told me a few months ago of a relative whose son had been afflicted by this demon. The boy was pale and thin, and always unhappy: he did not care for his food or drink, and he enjoyed no amusement. His mother became distressed, seeing her darling child thus pining away miserably, and she called in a Taoist priest of local celebrity. The priest heard the child in his sleep cry out as if in fear of the fox, and he at once prescribed the usual remedy for possession by the [female fox-]elf. This is simply a charm called the Tian-si-fu and consists of a mystical character written by Zhang Tianshi, the hereditary head of the Taoists. One morning he brought the charm into the room where the mother and son were sitting, and at once proceeded to paste it up on the wall. At the very instant the charm was displayed the afflicted boy cried out: 'There goes the fox – catch him!' His eyes seemed to follow a form running out through the door and away to the hills, but he recovered his health and spirits and is now quite well.

GHOSTS AND THE SUPERNATURAL

Strange Tales is often referred to in Chinese as 'Tales of Foxes and Ghosts'. What of the ghosts in these pages? Relatively few of the tales selected here correspond to what we think of as spine-chilling stories of ghosts and the supernatural. We can point to Tale 3, 'Living Dead', Tale 4, 'Spitting Water', Tale 7, 'The Troll', and Tale 8, 'Biting a Ghost'. More usually, the ghosts are female revenants, exercising an attraction no less fatal than that of the fox-spirits and yet often capable of great love, as well as being deeply versed in the Arts of the Bedchamber. To quote van Gulik once more:

Sexual intercourse with a ghost was considered to be a source of extraordinary pleasure, and at the same time usually fatal. The Elected Girl asked: 'How do incubi originate?' To which [the ancient] Pengzu answered: 'If a person has an unbalanced sex life, his sexual desire will increase. Devils and goblins take advantage of this condition. They assume human shape and have sexual intercourse with such a person. They are much more skilled in this than human beings, so much so that their victim becomes completely enamoured of the ghostly lover. These persons will keep the relation secret and will not speak about its delights. In the end they will succumb alone, without anyone being the wiser. During sexual intercourse with such an incubus one will experience a pleasure that is greater than ever felt while copulating with an ordinary human being. But at the same time one will become subject to this disease which is difficult to cure.[30]

In Tale 54, 'Lotus Fragrance', the author gives us a lengthy description of a love triangle involving a young man, a fox-spirit and a ghost. In a series of almost metaphysical dialogues, the two female characters explore the workings of love 'between the species'. After an initial period of intense rivalry, the two of them, the fox-spirit Lotus Fragrance, and the ghost girl Li, become as devoted to each other as one can imagine a principal wife and a concubine might have been in a harmonious polygamous household. The reader is left at the end of the story with a powerful feeling of having glimpsed the inner workings of a characteristically Chinese domestic triangle. We are talking here, as so often in *Strange Tales*, not so much about strange supernatural entities as about subtle levels of human interaction. Many tales deal explicitly and powerfully with relationships between the sexes, with demons and psychic forces. Fox and ghost portray in striking symbolic terms the life-and-death struggle of the sexes, in which practices such as foot-binding and the Taoist 'coitus thesauratus', the obsessive practice of semen-retention, had evolved.

Often these tales are referred to as 'Tales of the Supernatural', and in a sense they are, in that they deal with the entire range of the Strange, stretching right across the spectrum of nature and supernature. In traditional Chinese thinking the boundary between 'this' world and the world 'beyond' is far more elastic than it is for Western readers today. I have always liked the philosopher-theologian Martin Buber's words in this context:

The spirits who come to woo or to take possession of mortals are not Incubi and Succubi surrounded by the vaguely terrifying aura of the other world, but beings of our own experience, only born into a deeper, darker plane of existence. [This is] natural magic operating in a familiar world. The order of Nature is not broken, its perceptible limits merely extend; the abundant flow of the life force is nowhere arrested, and all that lives bears the seed of the spirit.[31]

HOW TO READ *STRANGE TALES*

One of the best guides to reading *Strange Tales* remains the early-nineteenth-century commentator Feng Zhenluan. His words evoke perfectly the atmosphere of the scholar-gentleman's studio, the leisurely and culturally saturated ambience in which the tales were written, and in which Feng read them and wrote his commentary. A few of his jottings may serve to give an idea of this:

1. When wind and snow fill the sky and my fire has grown cold, my page-boy relights the coals and heats my wine. I dust my desk and turn up the wick of my lamp. When I come across a passage that catches my fancy, I quickly dash off a few lines.

2. Read these tales properly, and they will make you strong and brave; read them in the wrong way, and they will possess you. Cling to the details, and they will possess you; grasp the spirit, and you will be strong.

Appreciate the wonders of the style, see into the author's subtle intentions, grasp the human qualities of his characters and value his thoughts; then this book will be a unique guide to you in your own inner development. It will transform your character, and purify your heart.

3. All my life I have enjoyed reading the *Records of the Grand Historian* and the *History of the Han Dynasty*. But only the *Strange Tales* dispel oppression. After meals, after wine, after

dreaming, in rainy weather and in sunshine, after a conversation with good friends, upon returning from a distant journey, I may toss off a few comments. These merely reflect my personal feelings, and are never intended as serious commentary.

4. If one reads the *Strange Tales* just for the plot, and not for the style, one is a fool.

5. A man eager to climb famous mountains must have the patience to follow a winding path. A man eager to eat bear's paw must have the patience to simmer it slowly. A man eager to watch the moonlight must have the patience to wait until midnight. A man eager to see a beautiful woman must have the patience to let her finish her toilette. Reading requires patience too.

6. This book should be read as one reads the *Zuo Commentary*. The *Zuo* is huge, the *Strange Tales* are miniatures. Every narrative skill is there. Every description is perfect. It is a series of huge miniatures.

This book should be read as one reads the *Book of Zhuangzi*. The *Zhuangzi* is wild and abstract, the *Strange Tales* are dense and detailed. Although they treat of ghosts and foxes, the details make it very concrete and real. It is a series of wild details and concrete abstractions.

This book should be read as one reads the *Records of the Grand Historian*. The *Records* are bold and striking, the *Strange Tales* are dark and understated. One enters this book with a lantern, in the shadows of night. One comes out of it into the daylight, under a blue sky. Its few words evoke mighty landscapes and create magical realms. It is both bold and dark. It is both striking and understated.

This book should be read as one reads the *Epigrams* of the neo-Confucian philosophers. In the *Epigrams* the sense is pure; in the *Strange Tales* the sensibility is well tuned. Every time one thinks a situation weird, it is in fact very real and true to human nature. It contains both pure sense and pure sensibility.[32]

INTRODUCTION

I have tried to heed Feng's advice. But the more I have grown to love these tales myself, the more I have become aware of the limitations of my versions. Despite their shortcomings I still like to think of them as 'a pleasure to share with a few like-minded friends, to help the wine down after a meal or to while away the solitude of a rainy evening by a lamplit window . . . '.[33]

NOTES

1. Jaroslav Prúsek, Pu Songling's Czech translator, has evoked the Shandong landscape well:

> Fantastically wild mountain ranges rise straight from the plain, especially the Taishan massif, the holy mountain of the East, its gulleys thick with age-old cypresses and with coloured monasteries here and there on its sides; the capital of the province, Jinan, is famed for its great springs bursting from the ground like fountains and forming clear lakes in which the wooded hill-tops round the town are mirrored. It could even be said that Shandong is one of the most bizarre parts of China, the wild cliffs of the half-circle of mountains drop sheer to the sea . . .

From 'P'u Sung-ling and His Work', in *Chinese History and Literature* (Prague, 1970), pp. 111–12 (translated from the Preface to his 1962 anthology of *Liaozhai* translations).

2. Some scholars have argued that the Pu family may originally have been of either Arab or Turco-Mongolian origin, but certainly by the seventeenth century they seem to have become completely Chinese.

3. An apocryphal story attributes this repeated failure of his to a secret plot by fox-spirits and ghosts, anxious that official success might prevent him from immortalizing their exploits in writing. See Marlon K. Hom, *The Continuation of Tradition*, Ph.D. dissertation (University of Washington, 1979), p. 22.

4. The expression is taken from Ichisada Miyazaki's *China's Examination Hell: The Civil Service Examinations of Imperial China* (New Haven, 1981).

5. The authors of both works struggled in life and died in poverty and obscurity. (Cao Xueqin is thought to have been born in 1715, the year Pu Songling died.) Both of their creations circulated

at first in handwritten form, passing from one aficionado to another. And neither book was published until well after the author's death. *The Story of the Stone*, left unfinished by Cao Xueqin at his death in 1765, was completed and published in the last decade of the eighteenth century. *Strange Tales* was first printed in 1766, more than fifty years after the death of Pu Songling. It has a textual history almost as intricate as that of the *Stone*, which is well summarized by Allan Barr in his 1984 article 'The Textual Transmission of *Liaozhai zhiyi*', *Harvard Journal of Asiatic Studies* 44:2. For the *Stone*, see Cao Xueqin and Gao E, *The Story of the Stone*, trans. David Hawkes and John Minford, 5 vols. (Harmondsworth, 1973–86).

6. This vast domain of Chinese letters, neglected by translators, and largely unknown to Western readers, has always been trouble-some for historians of literature, precisely because it defies clear categorization. Apart from countless collections of short fiction, *biji* literature includes miscellaneous collections of memoirs, personal journals, contemplative essays, observations of nature and society, informal historical and antiquarian jottings and anecdotes, random philosophical musings, jokes and humorous sketches, geographical and epigraphic notes – and many other things besides. The only things that bind it together as a literary genre are that it was always written in the classical language and it was one of the favourite modes of self-expression of the traditional scholar-gentleman. It is a vast repository of the intimate outpourings of the Chinese literati through the ages.

7. John Minford and Joseph S. M. Lau (eds.), *Classical Chinese Literature: An Anthology of Translations* (New York and Hong Kong, 2000), I, p. 47. The Ming-dynasty critic Hu Yinglin described *The Book of Hills and Seas* (ed. Liu Xin (*c.* 50 BC– AD 23)) as the 'ancestor of ancient and modern works that discuss the strange'.

8. Adapted from Richard Mather's translation in Minford and Lau, *Classical Chinese Literature*, I, p. 669.

9. For further examples of these Weird Accounts, see Minford and Lau, *Classical Chinese Literature*, I, pp. 359–81 and 651–74.

10. Two of the most famous stories of this sort are 'A Lifetime in a Dream' by Li Gongzuo (*c.* 770–*c.* 848) and 'The World in a Pillow' by Shen Jiji (*c.* 740–*c.* 800), both of which lie behind Pu Songling's Tale 82, 'Princess Lotus'. For a selection of these stories from the Tang dynasty, see Minford and Lau, *Classical Chinese Literature*, I, pp. 1020–76. For a selection from later

dynasties, see Wolfgang Bauer and Herbert Franke (trans.), *The Golden Casket* (Harmondsworth, 1965).

11. See for example Tale 40, 'The Laughing Girl', Tale 41, 'The Magic Sword and the Magic Bag', Tale 54, 'Lotus Fragrance', and Tale 69, 'Butterfly'.

12. See for example Tale 1, 'Homunculus', Tale 13, 'Growing Pears', and Tale 14, 'The Taoist Priest of Mount Lao'.

13. Anthony Yu, ' "Rest, Rest Perturbed Spirit!": Ghosts in Traditional Chinese Fiction', *Harvard Journal of Asiatic Studies* 48:2 (December 1987).

14. André Lévy (trans.), *Chroniques de l'étrange* (Arles, 1996), p. 16.

15. Hom, *The Continuation of Tradition*, p. 23.

16. Altogether some thirty-seven of the 104 tales in this selection have precedents in the voluminous Chinese literature of fiction. See Zhu Yixuan, *Liaozhai zhiyi ziliao huibian* (Henan, 1986).

17. My translation from Jacques Dars and Chan Hingho, *Comment lire un roman Chinois* (Arles, 2001), pp. 197–8.

18. This has not prevented many of the tales from becoming enormously popular in easier retellings, or in ballad, stage and screen versions.

19. Lu Xun, *A History of Chinese Fiction*, trans. Gladys Yang and Yang Xianyi (Peking, 1976), p. 411.

20. Duke Wen 17th Year, in *The Chinese Classics*, trans. James Legge, 5 vols. (Hong Kong, 1861–72), V, p. 278. For the *Zuo Commentary*, see Minford and Lau, *Classical Chinese Literature*, I, pp. 165–77.

21. Both of these commentators are included in Zhang Youhe (ed.), *Liaozhai zhiyi huijiao huizhu huiping ben* (Beijing, 1962).

22. See the exchange between Pu and Wang Shizhen, translated in full in my commentary to Pu's Preface.

23. For a hilarious example of Pu Songling having fun with a *Zuo Commentary* allusion, see the Jesting Judgement' at the end of Tale 63, 'Cut Sleeve'.

24. For this playfulness, see for example Dan Minglun's comments on Tale 54, 'Lotus Fragrance'.

25. See Lü Tiancheng, attrib., *The Embroidered Couch*, trans. Lenny Hu (Vancouver, 2001). For *Golden Lotus*, there is the existing four-volume edition by Clement Egerton, *Golden Lotus* (London, 1939), and the ongoing (two volumes so far) work of David Roy, *The Plum in the Golden Vase* (Princeton, 1993–). For *The Carnal Prayer Mat* (attributed to Li Yu in the latter

half of the seventeenth century), see Patrick Hanan (trans.), *The Carnal Prayer Mat* (New York, 1991).

26. See Robert van Gulik, *Erotic Colour Prints of the Ming Period* (Tokyo, 1951), pp. 11 and 70.

27. Van Gulik, ibid.

28. See my introductory note to the Tang-dynasty tale 'Miss Ren', one of the earliest fox-tales, in Minford and Lau, *Classical Chinese Literature*, I, p. 1024. Of course, foot-binding was not considered 'strange' by Pu Songling; in his day it was an almost universally accepted practice.

29. Thomas Watters, 'Chinese Fox-Myths', *Journal of the North-China Branch of the Royal Asiatic Society* VIII (1874). Watters as a junior consular official had 'caused a stir in the British community by saying that he knew some Chinese whose word he would prefer to an Englishman's oath' (P. D. Coates, *The China Consuls* (Hong Kong, 1988), p. 213).

30. Van Gulik, *Erotic Colour Prints*, pp. 61–2.

31. From the introduction to Martin Buber, *Chinesische Geister und Liebesgeschichten* (Frankfurt, 1927), trans. into English by Alex Page, *Chinese Tales* (New Jersey, 1991). It was these German adaptations that so impressed Kafka. In a letter to his fiancée Felice Bauer dated 16 January 1913 he describes them as 'prachtvoll'. See *Briefe an Felice* (Frankfurt, 1967), p. 252.

32. My translation of Feng Zhenluan, 'Du Liaozhai zashuo', in *Liaozhai zhiyi huijiao huizhu huiping ben*, ed. Zhang Youhe, pp. 9–18.

33. Cao Xueqin, *The Story of the Stone*, V, p. 375.

Note on the Text, Translation and Illustrations

I began making these translations in the summer of 1991, in a dark cellar in the remote French mountain-village of Vingrau, by the light of a single bulb and with a large spider suspended above my head. The rugged range of the Corbières, into which Ezra Pound gazed from Quillan on his 1912 walking tour, remarking in his journal, 'Above Quillan the road leads into Chinese unreality',[1] is as strange a region in its own way as Shandong. Working on these tales has been inseparable from those mountains, and from the lonely spirit of the garrigue surrounding my studio at Fontmarty.

It will be evident to some readers that I owe a debt to Herbert Giles.[2] I first encountered these tales in his much reprinted late-Victorian versions, which have been retranslated into several languages, and have represented Pu Songling in the West for well over a century. In entitling this selection *Strange Tales from a Chinese Studio*, I am consciously paying homage to Giles and his *Strange Stories*, which I have always admired, even though a close reading of Giles's work certainly reveals the limitations of the taste of his time, which dictated what he thought he could permissibly do:

> I had originally determined to publish a full and complete translation of the whole of these sixteen volumes; but on a closer acquaintance many of the stories turned out to be quite unsuitable for the age in which we live, forcibly recalling the coarseness of our own writers of fiction in the eighteenth century. Others, again, were utterly pointless.[3]

One example will illustrate the ludicrous situation Giles found himself in, and in which he placed his reader. In Tale 6, 'The Painted Wall', the Provincial Graduate Zhu, who has been transported into the fairy realm of the temple mural, finds himself alone in the presence of the 'maiden with unbound hair'. '[W]ith no delay he embraced her and, finding her to be far from unreceptive, proceeded to make love to her.' This simple sexual encounter Giles transmogrifies into a formal wedding scene: 'Then they fell on their knees and worshipped heaven and earth together, and rose up as man and wife.' To this omission/interpolation Giles appends a footnote on Chinese wedding rites, a piece of pseudo-scholarship to authenticate his tampering with the text. His *Strange Stories* are filled with such things. But whatever his qualms about the content, Giles certainly appreciated 'the marvellously beautiful style of this gifted writer', and he brought a fine prose style of his own to the task of translation. I have not hesitated to borrow the occasional felicitous phrase of his.[4]

In my own translation I have decided not to use the many alternative names (literary sobriquets and flowery nicknames) which are often supplied by our Chinese author. For old-fashioned Chinese readers these were customary, in fact they revelled in the practice. There was a whole ritual surrounding the use of such fancy names. Men of letters would coin them at turning points in their lives, and would make a point of using them when referring to their friends. Pu Songling himself had several, including Liuxian (the Lingering Immortal) and Liu-quan (Mr Willow Spring). For English readers the transliterations are empty; they convey nothing, and amount to a meaningless burden. But to translate each fancy name fully would risk making the stories sound like something written by Ernest Bramah: 'O most honourable Master of the Bamboo Lodge, whither art thou wending thy weary steps?'

As for notes, in general I have provided the minimum of annotation, giving a few extracts from the commentators, old and new, when this seemed helpful, and providing information on specific details. The Glossary gives a number of broader explanations of some key terms that may seem a little daunting to the reader venturing into Chinese territory for the first time. One problem for the translator of these Chinese tales is that the Western reader is encountering two levels of strangeness at once. The culture itself is already 'other', a strange universe. And these tales are records of things found strange by a writer within that universe. In other words, certain things that were taken for granted by Pu Songling will be strange to some of his new readers – the Chinese degree and examination system, the tradition of binding feet. Taoism and alchemy, to name only a few.

I have followed two modern editions: that of Zhang Youhe (1962; many times reprinted), which adheres to what he considers to have been something close to the author's original order, collating a number of traditional texts and commentators; and the more recent edition of Zhu Qikai (1989), which paraphrases into modern Chinese the old glosses, adding valuable new matter from time to time. I have often found the traditional commentators helpful, not as literary critics but as informal 'reader's companions'. I believe that their voice occasionally helps the reader to re-create the 'studio environment' so essential for an enjoyment of these tales. In Tale 54, 'Lotus Fragrance', the reader will find some of the old commentaries inserted into the text. Listed chronologically they are:

Wang Shizhen (1634–1711)
Wang Jinfan (1767)
Feng Zhenluan (1818)
He Shouqi (1823)
Lü Zhan'en (1825)
He Yin (1839)
Dan Minglun (1842)

Readers wishing to consult the Chinese originals are directed to the Finding List at the back of the book, where they will find a corresponding number for each tale, enabling them to go to Zhang Youhe's edition.

The wonderful illustrations are taken from the late-nineteenth-century *Xiangzhu Liaozhai zhiyi tuyong*, first printed in Shanghai in 1886. Although coming over a hundred and seventy years after the author's death, these lithographs are a celebrated example of late-Imperial book illustration. The prominent scholar of Qing-dynasty (1644–1911) fiction and bibliography Qian Xingcun (Ah Ying) described them as the finest *Strange Tales* illustrations ever done. They help to visualize the setting, and are especially well observed in terms of details of interior decor, furniture, clothes, architectural environment and court-yard/garden layout. Because they were designed for an edition in sixteen chapters that lacked several items found in the author's original collection, there are a small number of tales without illustrations.

Of my selection of 104 tales, taken from a total of nearly five hundred, fifty-nine are from the first two chapters of the twelve-chapter edition.[5] In other words, more than half the tales here have been chosen from the first eighty-two in the Chinese, while the remaining forty-five are spread over the last ten chapters. Despite this fact, I hope that my selection gives a more or less representative idea of the extraordinary range of the book. I have tried to provide enough variety to demonstrate the huge diversity of the collection, but in the end I confess that the choice was often influenced by personal preference, and by the consideration of which pieces worked best in translation. I look forward to being able to provide more of these amazing tales one day.

NOTES

1. Ezra Pound, *A Walking Tour in Southern France: Ezra Pound among the Troubadours*, ed. Richard Sieburth (New York, 1992).
2. Herbert A. Giles (trans.), *Strange Stories from a Chinese Studio* (London, 1880). There were several subsequent editions. Of my 104 tales, thirty-one are also in Giles.
3. Giles, Introduction, pp. xx–xxi.
4. In this I am following J. M. Cohen, who openly incorporated

into his Penguin Classics editions of Rabelais and *Don Quixote* the occasional phrase pilfered from earlier classic translations.

5.   The exact figure depends on whether one includes a handful of tales whose authenticity has been questioned, and on whether certain items are counted singly or as multiple stories. For the purposes of the general reader it is sufficient to say that there are just under five hundred tales.

Note on Names and Pronunciation

In this book, Chinese names and place-names are in general spelled according to the Chinese system known as Hanyu Pinyin, which is now internationally accepted. (Occasional exceptions to this rule include well-established geographical names such as the Yangtze River, and the cities of Peking, Nanking and Canton.) It should be remembered that in Chinese the family name comes first, the personal name second. Our author's family name is Pu; his personal name is Songling.

The following short list may help readers with some of the more difficult sounds used in the Pinyin system:

c = *ts*   z = *dz*
q = *ch*   zh = *j*
x = *sh*

The following very rough equivalents may also be of help to readers:

Bo = *Boar* (wild pig)   Dang = *Darng* or *Dung* (as in
Cai = *Ts'eye* ('It's eye',   'cow *dung*')
   without the first vowel)   Dong = *Doong* (as in 'book')
Cang = *Ts'arng*   Emei = *Er-may*
Chen = *Churn*   Feng = *Ferng*
Cheng = *Churng*   Gui = *Gway*
Chong = *Choong* (as in   Guo = *Gwore*
   'book')   Jia = *Jeeyar*
Chuan = *Chwan*   Jiang = *Jeeyung*

Kong = *Koong* (as in 'book')

Li = *Lee*

Long = *Loong* (as in 'book')

Lü = *Lew* (as in French 'tu')

Qi = *Chee*

Qian = *Chee-yenne*

Qing = *Ching*

Rong = *Roong* (as in 'book')

Shi = *Shh!*

Shun = *Shoon* (as in 'sho*u*ld')

Si = *Szz!*

Song = *Soong* (as in 'book')

Wen = as in 'forgot*ten*'

Xi = *Shee*

Xiao = *Shee-ow* (as in 'shee-cow' without the 'c')

Xing = *Shing*

Xiong = *Sheeoong*

Xu = *Shyeu* (as in French 'tu')

Yan = *Yen*

Yi = *Yee*

You = *Yo*-heave-ho

Yu = *Yew* tree (as in French 'tu')

Yuan = *You, Anne!*

Zha = *Jar*

Zhe = *Jerr!* (as in French 'oeuf')

Zhen = *Jurn*

Zhi = *Jirr!* (a strangled sound somewhere between the 'u' of 'suppose' and a vocalized 'r')

Zhou = *Joe*

Zhu = *Jew*

Zhuang = *Jwarng*

Zi = *Dzz!*

Zong = *Dzoong* (as in 'book')

Zuo = *Dzore*

Strange Tales from a
Chinese Studio

I

HOMUNCULUS

Tan Jinxuan, a first-degree graduate of my home district of Zichuan, was a great believer in Taoist yoga. He practised it assiduously for several months, regardless of the weather, and seemed to be making some progress.

One day, he was sitting cross-legged in meditation when he heard a tiny voice inside his ear, buzzing like a fly and saying, 'I think I'm taking shape . . .'

He opened his eyes, but could see nothing, and the voice was no more to be heard. He closed his eyes, regulated his breathing once again, and the voice returned. This, he thought to himself with secret delight, must surely be the Alchemical Homunculus, the Inner Elixir of Immortality, speaking to him as it neared perfection in his Cinnabar Field.

From that day on, whenever he sat in meditation he heard the voice. He bided his time in silence, waiting for the right occasion, determined to see what the little fellow looked like. And then one day, when it spoke again, he replied, 'Most definitely taking shape . . .' Whereupon there came the strangest tingling in his ear, as if something was indeed making its way out. He took a peep, and there it was, a minuscule figure of a man twirling around on the ground, barely three inches tall, but in appearance as fierce as a yaksha-demon. Tan was still marvelling at this extraordinary apparition, and trying to compose himself so as to better observe its further metamorphosis, when a neighbour knocked at the door and called out, wanting to borrow something. The homunculus was thrown into a great fluster by the noise and went whirling around the room more frantically than ever, like a demented mouse desperately seeking its hole.

姹女嬰兒易結胎
成仙畢竟要仙才
小人三寸張皇甚
可是兜元國裡來

耳中人

A neighbour knocked at the door.

Finally the little man completely vanished from sight, leaving Tan in a state of utter desolation, as if his very soul had gone missing. He was taken with a violent fit and began howling hysterically. Nothing could induce him to be quiet. Physicians prescribed certain medicines, and eventually, after six months, he made a recovery.

2

AN OTHERWORLDLY
EXAMINATION

Song Tao was the grandfather of my elder sister's husband. He was a first-degree graduate and holder of an annual government stipend.

One day, he was lying ill in bed when he saw a messenger arrive at his door, bearing an official-looking document and leading a horse with white markings on its forehead.

'You are hereby summoned to the examination for the second degree.'

'But the Examiner has not arrived in town yet. They cannot be holding an examination!'

The messenger made no reply, but urged him to be on his way. So Song struggled out of bed, climbed on to the horse and was carried away down an unfamiliar road, which soon led to the outskirts of a city grand enough to be a royal capital. Presently they passed through the imposing buildings of a prefect's yamen and into a large hall, where, sitting up ahead, Song beheld a group of high-ranking mandarins, none of whom he could identify – with the exception of the God of War, Guan Yu. At the near end of the hall, beneath the eaves, stood a pair of low tables and round stools, and at one of these sat another man, evidently a first-degree graduate like himself. Song sat down at the other table, where brush and paper had been laid ready, and presently a strip of paper with the title of a formal essay topic came fluttering down from the blue and alighted in front of him. Song read the wording of the question: 'One man, two men; with intent, without intent.' The two 'candidates' proceeded to write their essays and, when they were completed, handed them in at the dais. Song's essay read in part: 'Virtue

Presently they called Song up.

pursued with intent deserves no reward; evil committed without intent merits no punishment.'

The Pantheon of Examiners passed his script along, and all of them praised it highly. Presently they called Song up to the dais and delivered the following judgement: 'There is a City God vacancy in Henan Province. You are the preferred candidate for the position.'

The truth suddenly dawned on Song. He kowtowed to the examiners, weeping and saying, 'How could I ever presume to decline such a great honour! But my aged mother is in her seventies and will have no one left to look after her. I beg to be allowed to nurse her until the end of her allotted span of life, when I will gladly take up the post.'

One of the examiners, who appeared to be the presiding deity, gave orders to check the mother's longevity file, and an attendant with a long beard brought out the registers and began leafing through them.

'The lady in question has nine years left on the Yang plane,' he reported.

The committee of deities was still debating the issue when the God of War made a proposal. 'Why do we not appoint the other candidate, Mr Zhang, to the post in an acting capacity for a period of nine years, after which time Candidate Song can take up his plenary appointment.'

This being agreed upon, he informed Song of the committee's decision in the following terms: 'In the normal course of events, you should proceed straight to this post. In view, however, of your laudable feelings of Benevolence and Filial Piety, we are approving a sabbatical leave of nine years. When that time has expired, you will be summoned again before this board.'

He ended by giving the other candidate a few well-chosen words of advice, whereupon both men bowed and withdrew from the hall. Zhang took Song companionably by the hand and accompanied him to the outskirts of the town, where he explained that he was from the town of Changshan and presented Song with a poem of farewell, the words of which have been lost, save for a couplet:

> With wine and flowers, the spring is ever present;
> With neither candle nor lamp, the night is still bright.

Song mounted his horse and went on his way. When he reached his village he awoke as if from a dream, to discover that he had been lying dead three whole days. His mother heard a groan emanating from within the coffin and immediately gave orders for her son's body to be lifted out of it. Half a day later, he had recovered sufficiently to be able to speak, and when he made inquiries in nearby Changshan, he learned that a Mr Zhang of the town had indeed breathed his last on the very same day as himself.

Nine years later, Song's mother passed away, as had been foretold. When her funeral rites were concluded, her son performed his ablutions, retired to his chamber, lay down and died. His wife's parents lived within the West Gate of the town, and at the moment of his death they saw him approaching their house, escorted by a large retinue and riding a richly caparisoned horse. He came walking into their main hall, made them a formal bow of farewell and went on his way. Not realizing that he was a departed spirit, they rushed out in great perplexity to inquire what it could mean, only to be informed that their son-in-law had just died.

Song wrote a short account of his experience, but alas, after the Troubles it was lost. I have given the gist of it.

3

LIVING DEAD

A certain old man of Yangxin came to live at Cai Village, a few miles from my home town. Here he and his son opened a roadside tavern, where travellers could put up for the night. It became a regular halt for the many carters and itinerant merchants who plied their trade on that route.

One evening, as dusk fell, four strangers arrived at the inn and asked for lodging, only to be told by the landlord that every bed was taken. They protested that it was too late for them to journey on, and pleaded with him to take them in. Finally, after much pondering and hesitation, he said that he could perhaps offer them a place for the night, but that he feared it would not meet with their liking. They replied that any lodging, even a mat in an outhouse, would suit them well – they were in no position to be choosy.

It so happened that the old man's daughter-in-law had only recently died, and her body was lying in one of the rooms of the inn. His son had gone away to buy the wood for the coffin, and had not yet returned. The landlord led the travellers to this room, which was set slightly apart from the main compound, on the other side of the thoroughfare. (It had been chosen as a 'lying-in' room for its relative seclusion.) When they entered, they saw a lamp burning on a small table, beyond which curtains were draped across the room. Through the curtains they caught a glimpse of the corpse itself, stretched out on a trestle-bed and covered with a paper shroud. In an alcove to one side of the room the men saw a row of four beds and exhausted from their day's journey, they threw themselves down and were soon snoring loudly – with the exception of one, and even he

was finally beginning to doze off when he heard a creaking
sound coming from the trestle-bed on which the dead body was
laid out. Opening his eyes, he was able by the light of the lamp
to distinguish the figure of the girl as she lifted off her paper
shroud, got down from the bed and started to move towards
the alcove where he and the other three were sleeping. Her face
gave off a golden glow, and she had a turban of raw silk
wrapped around her forehead. When she reached the beds, she
blew on each of the three sleeping men in turn, and the fourth
man, terrified that she would come to him next, stealthily drew
the bedclothes up over his face and lay there holding his breath
and listening. He heard her breathe on him just as she had done
on the others, and then he heard the sound of her footsteps as
she walked back from the alcove, and the rustling of the paper
shroud as she climbed back on to her trestle-bed. Poking out
his head, he saw her lying there, a rigid corpse once more. He
did not dare to make a sound, but stretched out a foot and
furtively kicked his companions, not one of whom made the
slightest movement in response.

His only hope of survival, he now decided, lay in getting
dressed and making a dash for it. He rose up in his bed and
was about to put on his clothes when he heard the creaking
sound again and dived back in terror under the covers. Once
more the girl walked over to the alcove, and once more she
breathed on him through the covers – this time several times –
before returning to her bed. He heard the trestles creak, and
knew she must be lying down again. This time he reached
slowly for his trousers, hardly stirring from his bed, then slipped
quickly into them and ran barefoot towards the door. The next
instant, the corpse rose from its bed and set off in hot pursuit
after him. He had already unbolted the door and was gone, but
she chased him through the village. All the while he ran ahead
of her, screaming. Not a single villager seemed to hear, and he
did not dare to stop and rouse the landlord by knocking at the
inn door, for fear that the slightest delay might result in his
capture by the fiend. Instead he kept running as fast as his legs
could carry him, out of the village and in the direction of the
county town. As he came to the eastern outskirts of the town,

he caught sight of a Buddhist temple and heard the *tok-tok* of the wooden fish that the monks were beating during their prayers. He ran up and knocked urgently at the temple gate, but the monks were too frightened to let in an unknown stranger in the middle of the night and turned him away. When he looked behind him, he saw the living corpse bearing down upon him. He had not a second to lose. Before the temple stood a poplar tree, some four or five feet in circumference. He darted behind it, dodging this way and that, always keeping the trunk between himself and the corpse, who now seemed to be growing increasingly fierce. They were both becoming more and more exhausted when all of a sudden the corpse stood stock-still. On his side of the tree trunk, the man was perspiring heavily from his exertions and quite out of breath. Suddenly he too froze, and the corpse lunged violently forward, reaching out both arms in a desperate and unsuccessful attempt to clutch at him around the tree. In utter terror, the man collapsed on the ground. The corpse remained there fixed in place, rigidly embracing the tree.

The monks had been following all of this from the safety of the temple precincts, and when the sound of the struggle died away, they came creeping out to find the man lying on the ground. They shone a lamp on him, and though at first he seemed dead, when they felt his heart they detected the faintest trace of a pulse. They carried him inside, and late that night when he finally regained consciousness they gave him some broth to drink and he told them the whole story. When the matin bell rang, they went out into the misty light to examine the tree, and found the girl's corpse still tightly clamped to it.

In great consternation, they reported this strange event to the County Magistrate, who came in person to investigate and conduct an inquest. He ordered his men to pull the girl's hands away from the tree, but this proved almost impossible and on closer inspection they could see that her fingers, which were curled like hooks, had penetrated into the trunk of the tree, burying her nails deep in the wood. It took the concerted efforts of several men to prise her away. The finger holes were long and narrow as if they had been bored by a carpenter's awl.

A messenger was sent to inform the old landlord, whose inn

4

SPITTING WATER

Song Wan of Laiyang was appointed Secretary to one of the Boards, and rented a very dilapidated house in the capital. One night, his mother, who was sleeping in the main hall, waited on by two maidservants, heard a strange sound coming from her courtyard outside, like the sound made by a tailor spitting on his cloth. She told her maids to poke a hole in the paper lattice and see what they could see. They beheld an old lady, short and hunchbacked, her white hair done up in a two-inch topknot, prancing around the courtyard like a crane. And as she pranced, an endless stream of water came spurting from her mouth. The maids, frightened by this strange sight, reported back at once to their lady, who was horrified. They helped her up to the window to see for herself, and at that very moment the old prancing crone came closer and spat a mouthful of water straight at them, splitting the paper and causing all three women to fall flat on the ground.

It was the middle of the night, and not a soul in the family was aware of what was happening. At sunrise the following morning, the household servants gathered outside as usual and knocked on the door. Receiving no reply, they grew alarmed, broke open the door and forced their way in, to find the lady and her two maids lying side by side on the floor, apparently dead. Upon closer inspection, one of the maids still had a slight trace of warmth in her chest. They sat her up, gave her water to drink, and in a little while she came round and was able to tell them everything she had witnessed.

When Mr Song arrived on the scene, he was devastated with grief and remorse. The spot where the strange old lady had been

噴水

莫道傳聞有異詞
茱陽宋母工仙時
何未噴水龍
鐘馗据地傷
心悔已遲

The old crone spat a mouthful of water straight at them.

seen before she vanished was examined minutely. Excavating to a depth of three feet, they uncovered white hair; digging still deeper, they found the remains of an entire corpse, an old woman exactly like the one the maid had described, her face still covered with flesh as if she were still alive. Mr Song ordered them to strike it, and when they did so the flesh and bones simply fell away. Beneath the skin the corpse was all rotten. It consisted of nothing but water.

5
TALKING PUPILS

In the city of Chang'an there lived a man by the name of Fang Dong, known as a gentleman of considerable accomplishments, while at the same time having a reputation as an unprincipled libertine. If ever a pretty woman caught his eye on the street, he would trail her and do his utmost to seduce her.

The day before the Qing Ming Festival, he happened to be out strolling in the countryside when he saw a small carriage pass by, with red curtains and embroidered blinds. It was followed by a train of servants and horses, including one particular maid on a pony, who struck Fang as being very good-looking. He went closer to get a better view of the girl on the pony and, as he did so, noticed through the slightly parted curtains of the carriage a young lady, about sixteen years old, gorgeously attired and of a beauty such as he had never witnessed in his life. He gazed at her dumbfounded, rooted to the spot, and then proceeded to keep up with the carriage for several miles, now walking slightly ahead, now trailing behind. Finally he heard the young lady command her maid to come to the side of her carriage.

'Let down the blinds, girl! Who does that wild young man think he is, the one who keeps ogling me in that insolent fashion!'

The maid let down the blinds and spoke angrily to Fang. 'My lady is the bride of the seventh young lord of Hibiscus Town, and she is on her way to visit her parents. She is no village lass for the likes of you to gawp at!'

So saying, she took a pinch of dust from the ground by the carriage wheel and threw it in his face. Fang was momentarily

瞳人語

目淫原自意淫來
眸子盲時萬念灰
友天視未遲從我
視轉移捷徑
在靈臺

Fang was momentarily blinded.

blinded and could not even open his eyes. He rubbed them, and when finally he did succeed in opening them, carriage and horses, young lady and maid, had all vanished into thin air! He returned home in great perplexity of spirit, all the time aware of a continuing discomfort in his eyes. He asked a friend to lift up his eyelids and take a look inside, and the friend told him that there was a clearly visible film over each of his eyeballs. The next morning, the condition was still more pronounced and there was an unstoppable flow of tears from each eye. The film continued to thicken, and after a few days it was as thick as a copper coin. In addition, a spiral-shaped protuberance began growing from the right eye, which resisted any treatment.

Fang was now totally blind, and his condition filled him with despair and remorse. Hearing that a Buddhist scripture, known as *The Sutra of Light*, had the power to cure ailments such as his, he acquired a copy and found a person to teach it to him so that he could recite it by heart. For a certain period of time, his physical discomfort and mental perplexity continued unabated, but after a while he began to find a certain peace of mind. Morning and evening, he sat cross-legged chanting the sutra and counting the beads of his rosary, and after a year of this he eventually succeeded in attaining a state of genuine detachment and serenity.

Then one day, out of the blue, he heard a voice, quiet as a fly, coming from within his left eye. This is what it said: 'It's pitch black in here! Unbearable!'

From his right eye came the reply 'Why don't we go out for a little stroll? It might help us shake off this gloom.'

Then he felt a slight irritation in both nostrils, as if two little creatures were wriggling down his nose. After a while he felt the creatures return and make their way back up his nostrils and into his eye sockets again.

'I hadn't seen the garden for ages!' said one voice. 'Aren't the Pearl Orchids looking withered!'

Now Fang had always been especially fond of orchids, and cultivated several varieties in his garden, which he had been in the habit of watering himself every day. But ever since losing his sight, he had lost all interest in them and had completely neglected them. Hearing this exchange, he promptly asked his wife why his orchids had been allowed to wither away. She in turn asked him how he even knew this to be the case, since he was blind, whereupon he told her about his strange experience. She went out into the garden, and sure enough, the flowers were quite dead. Greatly intrigued by what her husband had told her, she decided to hide herself in his room and keep watch. It was not long before she saw two little mannikins – neither of them any larger than a bean – emerge from his nose and fly buzzing out of the door. They were soon well out of sight, but were back again in next to no time, flying together up on to his face and in at his nostrils, like a pair of homing bees or ants.

They did the same thing two or three days running. Then Fang heard a voice speak from within his left eye.

'That tunnel is a dreadfully roundabout way of going in and out. Most inconvenient. We really should think of making ourselves a proper doorway.'

'The wall on my side is very thick,' replied the right eye. 'It won't be easy.'

'I'll try to make an opening on my side,' said the left eye. 'Then we can share my door.'

Presently Fang thought he felt a scratching and a splitting in his left eye socket, and an instant later, he could see! He could see everything around him with absolute clarity. Beside himself with delight, he promptly informed his wife, who inspected his eyes afresh and found that in the left eye a minute aperture had appeared in the film, a hole no larger than a cracked pepper-corn, through which gleamed the black globe of a pupil. By the next morning, the film in the left eye had disappeared alto-gether. But the strangest thing of all was that, on careful inspec-tion, there were now two pupils visible in that eye, while the right eye was still obscured by its spiral-shaped growth. Appar-ently both of the two eye-mannikins, his talking pupils, had now taken up residence in the left eye. So although Fang was still blind in one eye, he could see better with his one good eye than he had ever done with two.

From that day forth, he was a great deal more circumspect in his behaviour, and acquired an impeccable reputation in the district.

6

THE PAINTED WALL

Meng Longtan, a gentleman of Jiangxi Province, was staying in Peking with his friend the Provincial Graduate Zhu. One day, they went to visit a monastery together – not a particularly spacious establishment, with a modest hall of worship and a number of cells for Zen meditation. There was a single elderly monk in residence, who, seeing the visitors arrive, smartened himself up, went out to greet them and took them on a tour of the precincts.

In the main hall stood a statue of the Zen Master Baozhi, and there were superb murals on the two flanking walls, representations of men and animals that seemed to breathe with life. On the eastern wall was a painting of Apsaras Scattering Flowers, beautiful fairylike beings, among whom Zhu noticed one maiden with unbound hair, a flower in her hand and a magically smiling face. Her lips seemed to move, and the light in her eyes rippled like water. Zhu stared at this maiden like a man transfixed, and was soon utterly transported by the vision. He was wafted bodily up on to the wall and into the mural itself. He felt himself pillowed on clouds, and saw stretching before him a grand panorama of palaces and pavilions, a veritable fairy realm. He could see an aged abbot preaching the Dharma from a pulpit, surrounded by a throng of robed monks. Zhu was mingling with the crowd when presently he felt someone secretly tugging at his sleeve, turned to look, and saw the maiden with the unbound hair walking smilingly away from him. He followed her down curving balustraded pathways to the doorway of a small pavilion, where he hesitated. The maiden looked back and beckoned him on with the flower that she still held in her hand. So he followed her into the pavilion, where they found themselves alone, and where with no delay he embraced her and, finding her to be far from unreceptive, proceeded to make love to her. Afterwards she left him and went away, closing the door behind her and bidding him not to make the slightest sound. That same night she returned, and so their liaison continued for a further two days.

Her female companions perceived soon enough that there was something afoot, and discovered Zhu in his hiding place.

'Look at you!' they teased the girl. 'You've most probably got a baby on the way by now, and still you wear your hair like a little girl!'

They brought out hairpins and pendants, and helped her put up her hair like a grown woman, while all along she maintained a coy silence.

'Come, sisters, let's go!' cried one of them. 'We're spoiling their fun!'

And off they went, giggling among themselves.

Zhu gazed at her once more. With hair now piled high in a black cloudlike chignon and phoenix ornaments hanging down from it, she seemed even more adorably beautiful than before. They were alone again and soon fell to further sports of love, his senses suffused with the heady perfume that emanated from her body, a scent of orchid mingled with musk. Their raptures were, however, rudely interrupted by the clomping of boots, the clanking of chains, and a confused and raucous shouting outside. The fairy girl leaped up, and she and Zhu hurried to the door. Peeping through, they saw a guard standing there in full armour, with a face black as pitch, carrying chains and cudgels, and surrounded by a throng of maidens.

'Are you all present?' he barked.

'All present!' came the reply.

'Are you quite sure one of you is not harbouring a man from the world below in here?' cried the guard. 'If so, bring him out this instant! Don't go causing trouble for yourselves.'

'There's no one here!' they all protested.

The guard cast a piercing gaze around him, implying that he was about to search the place. Zhu's fairy went ashen pale.

'Hurry!' she whispered, turning breathlessly to her lover and trembling with fear. 'Hide under the bed!'

She herself opened a little side-door in the wall, through which she escaped, while Zhu took refuge beneath the bed, hardly daring to breath. The heavy boots came marching into the room, then left again, and as they stomped away into the distance, he heaved a sigh of relief. But he could still hear a great deal of coming and going and talking outside the door, and remained in a state of unbearable suspense, his eyes burning and his ears buzzing like crickets. He resigned himself to waiting quietly for his lady friend to return, barely remembering any more who he himself was or where he had come from in the first place.

Meanwhile his earthly friend Meng Longtan, who had been standing in the main hall of the monastery, suddenly noticed that Zhu was no longer by his side and asked the monk-guide where he had gone. The monk gave a wry smile.

'He is listening to the sermon.'

'Where?'

'Not far from here.'

Then, after a little while, the monk tapped on the wall with his fingers. 'What has kept you so long, sir?' he called out.

At that very instant the outline of Zhu became visible on the painted wall, standing there, his ears inclined as if he was listening to something.

'Your friend has been waiting for you all this time!' the monk called again.

All of a sudden Zhu drifted effortlessly down from the wall and stood there before them, dazed and deeply abstracted, like a lifeless block of wood, his legs swaying unsteadily from side to side, his eyes staring in front of him. Meng Longtan was absolutely flabbergasted and inquired, as nonchalantly as possible, what had happened to him. Zhu told him the whole story, concluding, 'So there I was waiting quietly under the bed when I heard a tapping noise like thunder, so I hurried out of the room to see what was going on.'

They all looked up at the maiden in the painting, the Apsara with the unbound hair. Sure enough, her hair was no longer

畫軸

微笑拈花座上
珠冠雲冠雨兩
模糊從來幻境
由心造試向黃
梁夢有無

They all looked up at the maiden in the painting.

hanging down but had been dressed in fine coils on her head. Zhu was utterly amazed. He bowed respectfully to the old monk and begged him for some sort of explanation. The monk chuckled.

'The source of illusion lies within man himself. Who am I to explain these things?'

Zhu seemed altogether downcast by his experience, while Meng was simply out of his depth, and heaved a sigh of incomprehension. The two men took their leave, walked down the monastery steps and went on their way.

7

THE TROLL

Sun Taibo told me this story.

His great-grandfather, also named Sun, had been studying at Willow Gully Temple on South Mountain, and came home for the autumn wheat harvest. He only stayed at home for ten days, but when he returned to the temple and opened the door of his lodgings, he saw that the table was thick with dust and the windows laced with cobwebs. He ordered his servant to clean the place, and by evening it was in sufficiently good order for him to be able to install himself comfortably again. He dusted off the bed, spread out his quilt, closed the door and lay his head down on the pillow. Moonlight came flooding in at the window.

He tossed and turned a long while, as silence descended on the temple. Then suddenly a wind got up and he heard the main temple door flapping noisily. Thinking to himself that one of the monks must have forgotten to close it, he lay there a while in some anxiety. The wind seemed to be coming closer and closer in the direction of his quarters, and the next thing he knew the door leading into his room blew open. He was now seriously alarmed, and quite unable to compose himself. His room filled with the roaring of the wind, and he heard the sound of clomping boots gradually approaching the alcove in which his bed was situated. By now he was utterly terrified. Then the door of the alcove itself flew open, and there it was, a great troll, stooping down at first as it approached, then suddenly looming up over his bed, its head grazing the ceiling, its face dark and blotchy like an old melon rind. Its blazing eyes scanned the room, and its cavernous mouth lolled open,

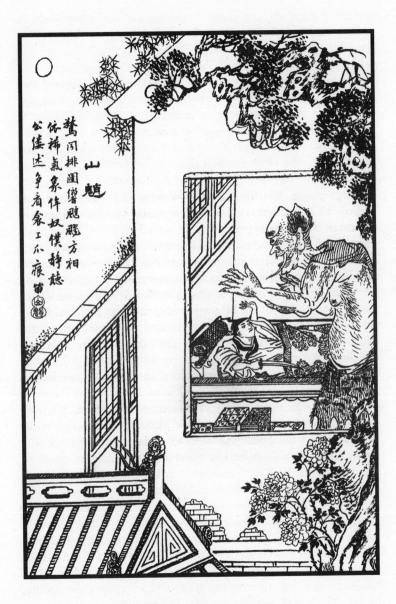

There it was, looming up over his bed.

revealing great shining fangs more than three inches long. Its tongue flickered from side to side, and from its throat there issued a terrible rasping sound that reverberated through the room.

Sun quaked in sheer terror. Thinking quickly to himself that the beast was already too close for him to have any chance of escape and that his only hope now lay in trying to kill it, he secretly drew his dagger from beneath his pillow, concealed it in his sleeve, then swiftly drew it out and stabbed the creature in the belly. The blade made a dull thud on impact, as if it had struck a stone mortar. The enraged troll flailed out at him with its huge claws, but Sun shrank back from it. The troll only succeeded in tearing at the bedcover, and pulled it down on to the ground as it stormed out.

Sun had been dragged to the ground with the bedcover, and he lay there howling. His servant came running with a lantern, and, finding the door locked, as it usually was during the night, he broke open the window and climbed in. Appalled at the state his master was in, he helped him back to bed and heard his tale. Afterwards they examined the room together and saw that the bedcover was still caught tight between the door and the door frame. As soon as they opened the door and the cover fell free, they saw great holes in the fabric, where the beast's claws had torn at it.

When dawn broke the next morning, they dared not stay there a moment longer but packed their things and returned home. On a subsequent occasion they questioned the resident monks, but there had been no further apparition.

8

BITING A GHOST

Shen Linsheng once told me this story.

A friend of his, an elderly man, was taking a nap one summer's day, and had drifted into a dreamlike state, when he perceived a woman raising his door-blind and entering his room, her head swathed in a length of white cotton and her body clothed in the hempen dress of mourning. She walked on into the inner apartments of the house, and he thought she must be his neighbour's wife come to pay his own wife a visit. On reflection he found it strange that she should be making a social call dressed in full mourning, and was still puzzling over this when the woman came out again. He looked at her more closely this time, and saw that she was a woman of some thirty years, with a sallow complexion, bloated features, a pronounced frown, and a strange expression on her face that struck fear into his heart. Instead of walking on and out of the room, she hesitated a while, and then slowly approached his bed. He feigned sleep, but secretly watched her every movement. The next second, she hoisted up her skirts, clambered on to his bed and pressed herself down on top of him with the force of a ton weight. His mind was still clear, but his hands when he tried to lift them seemed tied fast, and his feet when he tried to move them were paralysed. He would have cried out for help, but try as he might he found he could make no sound. The woman now began to sniff her way all over the old man's face, rubbing her nose in turn on his cheeks, his nose, his eyebrows, his forehead. Her nose was cold as ice, and her chill breath penetrated his very bones. He conceived a sort of desperate plan: he would let her work her way down to his jaw and then he would

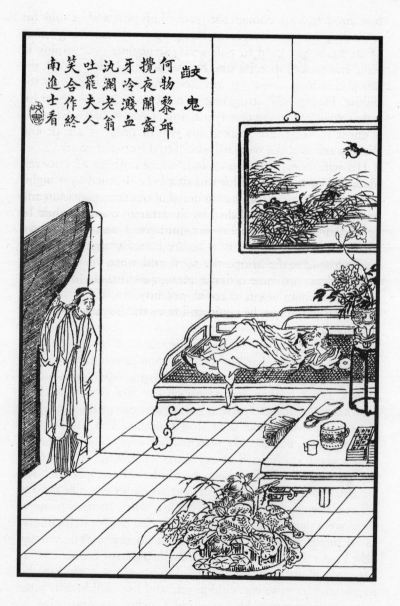

戲鬼

何物黎邱
攬夜闌齒
牙冷濺血
沈瀾老翁
吐罷夫人
笑合作終
南進士看

He perceived a woman raising his door-blind.

bite into her. Soon enough she reached his jaw, and he sunk his teeth deep into her face, summoning up every remaining ounce of strength. She tried to pull away, struggling and yelping in pain, but the old man bit into her harder than ever. He felt the blood dribbling down his jaw and dripping down on to the pillow. He was still struggling to hold on, when he heard his wife's voice out in the courtyard, and cried out, 'Help! There's a ghost in here!' He relaxed his jaw in order to speak and thereby released the woman, who flitted from the room.

His wife came hurrying in and, seeing nothing whatsoever, made fun of her husband for having been deluded by a nightmare. The old man told her in detail about the apparition and protested that the blood shed by the strange woman would be proof that it had been no mere nightmare. There was indeed a great wet stain on both pillow and bed, as if a large quantity of water had leaked through the roof, and when he bent down and smelled it, it gave off such an extraordinarily foul stench that the old man began to vomit violently.

Several days later, he could still taste the lingering stench in his mouth.

9

CATCHING A FOX

There was an elderly gentleman named Sun, who was the paternal uncle of a relation of mine by marriage, Sun Qingfu. This old man was an individual of great natural courage.

One day, he was taking a nap when he thought he saw something climb up on to his bed, and he began to experience a floating sensation in his body as if he were being carried aloft upon the clouds. Wondering secretly to himself if this was a case of fox-possession, he opened his eyes a slit and saw a creature the size of a cat, with yellow fur and a green mouth, working its way up from the end of the bed, wriggling along as if it was trying not to awaken him. Slowly it began clambering on to his body. It reached his feet, and they became numb; it reached his limbs, and they became limp. It was about to crawl on to his stomach when the old man managed to heave himself up and seize it tightly by the neck. The creature yelped frantically but was unable to free itself from his grip. Sun called out urgently to his wife to tie a sash around its middle. Then he pulled both ends of the sash.

'I have heard how clever you foxes are at changing shape!' he cried. 'Now show me what you can do!'

No sooner had he spoken than the creature retracted its stomach, shrinking to the size of a bamboo tube and almost succeeding in getting free. In terror the old man tightened the sash with all his might, whereupon the creature puffed out its stomach again until it was bloated and rigid and the size of a large bowl. Sun loosened his grip slightly, and it shrank again. The old man feared that it would escape, and he told his wife to kill it at once. She looked around her in great consternation

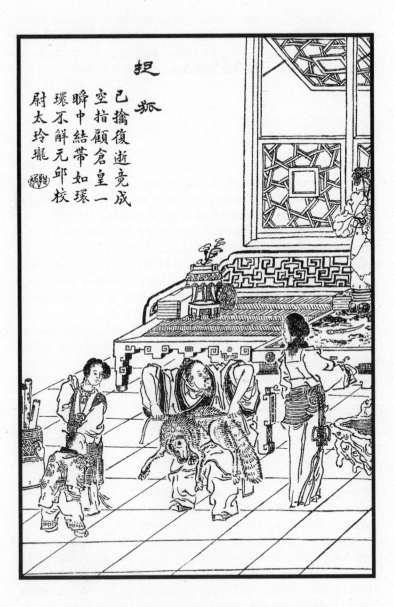

捉狐

已擒復逝竟成空
指顧倉皇一瞬中
結帶如環環不解
元郵校尉太玲瓏

The old man tightened the sash with all his might.

for a knife, and the old man turned to the left to indicate where one was to be found. By the time he turned back, all that remained in his hand was the sash, hanging in an empty loop. The creature had vanished without trace.

10

THE MONSTER IN
THE BUCKWHEAT

An old gentleman of Changshan County, by the name of An, enjoyed working on his land. One autumn, when his buckwheat was ripe, he went to supervise the harvest, cutting it and laying it out in stacks along the sides of the fields. At that time, someone was stealing the crops in the neighbouring village, so the old gentleman asked his men to load the cut buckwheat on to a cart that very night and push it to the threshing ground by the light of the moon. He himself stayed behind to keep watch over his remaining crops, lying in the open field with spear at hand as he waited for them to return. He had just begun to doze off, when he heard the sound of feet trampling on the buckwheat stalks, making a terrific crunching noise, and suspected that it might be the thief. But when he looked up, he saw a huge monster bearing down upon him, more than ten feet tall, with red hair and a big bushy beard. Leaping up in terror, he struck out at it with all his might, and the monster gave a great howl of pain and fled into the night.

Afraid that it might reappear at any moment, An shouldered his spear and headed home, telling his labourers, when he met them on the road, what he had seen, and warning them not to proceed any further. They were reluctant to believe him.

The next day, they were spreading out the buckwheat in the sun when suddenly they heard a strange sound in the air.

'It's the monster again!' cried old An in terror, and fled, as did all the others.

A little later that day, they gathered together again and An told them to arm themselves with bows and lie in wait. The following morning, sure enough, the monster returned a third

The creature knocked him back on to the rick.

time. They each shot several arrows at it, and it fled in fear. Then for two or three days it did not return. By now all the threshed buckwheat was safely stored in the granary, but the stalks of straw still lay higgledy-piggledy on the threshing floor. Old An gave orders for the straw to be bound together and piled into a rick, then he himself climbed up on to the rick, which was several feet high. He was treading it down firmly when suddenly he saw something in the distance.

'The monster is coming again!' he cried aghast.

Before his men could get to their bows, the creature had already jumped at him, and knocked him back on to the rick. It took a bite out of his forehead and went away again. The men climbed up and saw that a whole chunk of the old man's forehead, a piece the size of a man's palm, had been bitten off, bone and all. He had already lost consciousness, and they carried him home, where he died.

The monster was never seen again. Nobody could even agree on what sort of creature it was.

11

THE HAUNTED HOUSE

Mr Li of Changshan, the nephew of Li Huaxi, President of the Board of Justice, was the owner of a haunted house.

One day, he saw a long bench on his verandah, flesh-pink in colour, very smooth-looking and well finished. He did not recall possessing such a bench and went up to it and touched it, letting his hand run along its curves. The thing actually felt soft, like flesh, and he walked away from it in shock and revulsion. He had walked a few steps when he looked back and saw the bench move on its four feet and gradually vanish as it merged with the wall. Next he saw a long, shiny whitewood staff leaning against the wall. He took hold of it, and it too was so smooth that it slipped through his fingers, falling to the ground and wriggling away like a snake, until it too had vanished into the wall.

In the seventeenth year of the reign of the Emperor Kangxi, a scholar named Wang Junsheng took up residence in Mr Li's house – the very same house – as a family tutor. One evening, just when the lamps were lit, Wang was lying down on his couch with his shoes still on when suddenly he caught sight of a tiny man, some three inches tall, who entered the room, wandered around and then left again. A little while later, he returned carrying two small stools, which he placed in the room. They were tiny, like the miniature toys children make out of millet stalks. After another short interval two more little men came in, bearing a coffin about four inches long, which they placed on top of the two stools. As they were doing this, a lady entered the room with a bevy of maidservants. She was of the same minuscule proportions as the others, and was dressed in mourning, with a hempen cord tied around her waist

A *minuscule lady entered the room with a bevy of maidservants.*

and a length of white cotton wrapped round her head. She held her sleeve to her mouth and sobbed most piteously, making a sound a little like that of a giant fly.

Tutor Wang lay there quite some time watching all of this through narrowed eyes. As he watched, his hair stood on end and he felt himself enveloped in a layer of cold, like a coverlet of frost. Finally he gave out a great cry and leaped from his bed in an attempt to flee from the room, but as he went he tripped and landed with a crash on the floor, where he lay a gibbering wreck, quite incapable of rising to his feet.

The household heard the noise and came running, but saw no sign of anyone or anything out of the ordinary.

12

STEALING A PEACH

When I was a boy, I went up to the prefectural city of Ji'nan to take an examination. It was the time of the Spring Festival, and, according to custom, on the day before the festival all the merchants of the place processed with decorated banners and drums to the provincial yamen. This procession was called Bringing in the Spring. I went with a friend to watch the fun. There was a huge crowd milling about, and ahead of us, facing each other to the right and left of the raised hall, sat four mandarins in their crimson robes. I was too young at the time to know who they were. All I was aware of was the hum of voices and the crashing noise of the drums and other instruments.

In the middle of it all, a man led a boy with long unplaited hair into the space in front of the dais and knelt on the ground. The man had two baskets suspended from a carrying pole on his shoulders and seemed to be saying something, which I could not distinguish for the din of the crowd. I only saw the mandarins smile, and immediately afterwards an attendant came down and in a loud voice ordered the man to give his performance.

'What shall I perform?' said the man, rising to his feet.

The mandarins on the dais consulted among themselves, and then the attendant inquired of the man what he could do best.

'I can make the seasons go backwards, and turn the order of nature upside down.'

The attendant reported back to the mandarins, and after a moment returned and ordered the man to produce a peach. The man assented, taking off his coat and laying it on one of his baskets, at the same time complaining loudly that they had set him a very hard task.

'The winter frost has not melted – how can I possibly produce a peach? But if I fail, their worships will surely be angry with me. Alas! Woe is me!'

The boy, who was evidently his son, reminded him that he had already agreed to perform and was under an obligation to continue. After fretting and grumbling a while, the father cried out, 'I know what we must do! Here it is still early spring and there is snow on the ground – we shall never get a peach *here*. But up in heaven, in the garden of the Queen Mother of the West, they have peaches all the year round. *There* it is eternal summer! It is *there* we must try!'

'But how are we to get up there?' asked the boy.

'I have the means,' replied his father, and immediately proceeded to take from one of his baskets a cord some dozens of feet in length. He coiled it carefully and then threw one end of it high up into the air, where it remained suspended, as if somehow caught. He continued to pay out the rope, which kept rising higher and higher until the top end of it disappeared altogether into the clouds, while the other end remained in his hands.

'Come here, boy!' he called to his son. 'I am getting too old for this sort of thing, and anyway I am too heavy, I wouldn't be able to do it. It will have to be you.'

He handed the rope to the boy.

'Climb up on this.'

The boy took the rope, but as he did so he pulled a face. 'Father, have you gone mad?' he protested. 'You want me to climb all the way up into the sky on this flimsy thing? Suppose it breaks and I fall – I'll be killed!'

'I have given these gentlemen my word,' his father pleaded, 'and there's no backing out now. Please do this, I beg of you. Bring me a peach, and I am sure we will be rewarded with a hundred taels of silver. Then I promise to get you a pretty wife.'

So his son took hold of the rope and went scrambling up it, hand over foot, like a spider running up a thread, finally disappearing out of sight and into the clouds.

There was a long interval, and then down fell a large peach, the size of a soup bowl. The delighted father presented it to the

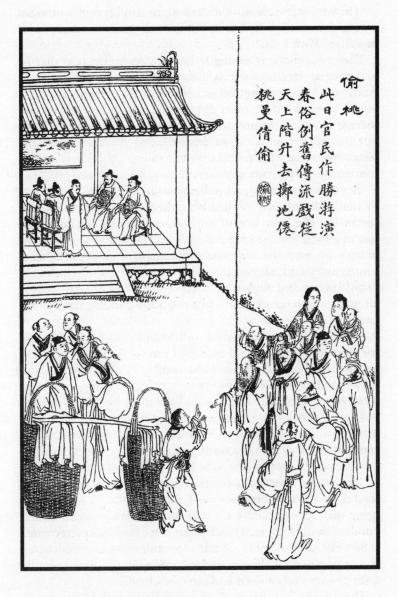

偷桃

此日官民作勝游演
春俗例舊傳流戲從
天上階升去擲地倈
桃曼倩偷

The top end of the rope disappeared into the clouds.

gentlemen on the dais, who passed it around and studied it carefully, unable to tell at first glance whether it was genuine or a fake. Then suddenly the rope came tumbling to the ground.

'The poor boy!' cried the father in alarm. 'He is done for! Someone up there must have cut my rope!'

The next moment something else fell to the ground, an object which was found on closer examination to be the boy's head. 'Ah me!' cried the father, weeping bitterly and holding the head up in both his hands. 'The heavenly watchman caught him stealing the peach! My son is no more!'

After that, one by one, the boy's feet, his arms and legs, and every single remaining part of his anatomy came tumbling down in a similar manner. The distraught father gathered all the pieces up and put them in one of his baskets, saying, 'This was my only son! He went with me everywhere I went. And now, at his own father's orders, he has met with this cruel fate. I must away and bury him.'

He approached the dais.

'Your peach, gentlemen,' he said, falling to his knees, 'was obtained at the cost of my boy's life. Help me, I beg you, to pay for his funeral expenses, and I will be ever grateful to you for your kindness.'

The mandarins, who had been watching the scene in utter horror and amazement, immediately collected a good purse for him. When the father had received the money and put it in his belt, he rapped on the basket.

'*Babar!*' he called out. 'Out you come now and thank the gentlemen! What are you waiting for?'

He had no sooner said this than there was a knock from within and a tousled head emerged from the basket. Out jumped the boy, and bowed to the dais. It was his son.

To this very day I have never forgotten this extraordinary performance. I later learned that this 'rope trick' was a speciality of the White Lotus sect. Surely this man must have learned it from them.

13
GROWING PEARS

A peasant was selling pears in the market. Sweet they were and fragrant – and exceedingly expensive. A Taoist monk in a tattered cap and robe came begging by the pear vendor's cart, and the man told him to be gone. When the monk lingered, the vendor began to abuse him angrily.

'But you have hundreds of pears in your cart,' returned the monk, 'and I am only asking for one. You would hardly notice it, sir. Why are you getting so angry?'

Onlookers urged the vendor to give the monk one of his less succulent pears, just to be rid of him, but the man obstinately refused. A waiter who was serving the customers at a nearby wine-stall, seeing that the scene was threatening to grow ugly, bought a pear and gave it to the monk, who bowed in thanks and turned to the assembled crowd.

'Meanness,' he declared, 'is something we monks find impossible to understand. I have some very fine pears of my own, which I should like to give you.'

'If you have such fine pears,' said one of the crowd, 'then why did you not eat them yourself? Why did you need to go begging?'

'I needed this one for the seed,' was the monk's reply.

So saying, he held the pear out in front of him and began munching it until all he had left was a single seed from its core, which he held in one hand while taking down a hoe from his shoulder and making a little hole in the ground. Here he placed the seed and covered it with earth. He now asked for some hot water to sprinkle on it, and one of the more enterprising members of the crowd went off and fetched him some from a

種黎

任教慳吝逼人寰天道原來
是好還頃刻花開頃刻實
神仙如戲譽貪頑

The water was scalding hot.

roadside tavern. The water was scalding hot, but the monk proceeded to pour it on the ground over his seed. The crowd watched riveted, as a tiny sprout began pushing its way up through the soil, growing and growing until soon it was a fully fledged tree, complete with branches and leaves. And then it flowered and bore fruit, great big, fragrant pears. Every branch was laden with them. The monk now climbed up into the tree and began picking the pears, handing them down to the crowd as he did so. Soon every single pear on the tree had been given away. When this was done, he started hacking at the tree with his hoe, and had soon felled it. Then, shouldering the tree, branches, leaves and all, he sauntered casually off.

Now, from the very beginning of this performance, the pear vendor had been standing in the crowd, straining his neck to see what the others were seeing, quite forgetting his trade and what he had come to market for. Only when the monk had gone did he turn and see that his own cart was empty. Then he knew that the pears the monk had just been handing out were all from his cart. And he noticed that his cart was missing one of its handles; it had been newly hacked away. The peasant flew into a rage and went in hot pursuit of the monk, following him the length of a wall, round a corner, and there was his cart-handle lying discarded on the ground. He knew at once that it had served as the monk's pear tree. As for the monk himself, he had vanished without trace, to the great amazement of the crowd.

14
THE TAOIST PRIEST
OF MOUNT LAO

In our town there lived a gentleman by the name of Wang, seventh son of his family, which was an old one. He had always been a fervent admirer of Taoism, and, hearing that there were a large number of Taoist adepts living up on Mount Lao, one day he shouldered his knapsack and set out on a trip in that direction.

He climbed one of the peaks and found himself before a monastery, tucked away in the middle of nowhere. He could see a Taoist sitting in meditation on his rush-mat, his long white hair down to his shoulders, his face ruddy with vitality. Wang knelt and engaged the monk in conversation, and, finding the old man's responses wonderfully deep, begged to be accepted as one of his disciples.

'You are too accustomed to a soft life,' replied the monk. 'I fear the hardship will be more than you can bear.'

Wang insisted that he could rise to the challenge, and took up residence in the monastery that very day. The priest had several disciples, and when they assembled towards evening, Wang bowed to each one of them in turn. Early the following morning, the priest summoned Wang, gave him an axe and told him to go and cut wood with the others. Wang promptly obeyed. After a month or so of this, his hands and feet were a mass of blisters. He decided he could bear it no longer and secretly began to long for home.

One evening, he returned from his chores to see two men sitting and drinking with the priest. It was already dusk, but the lamps had not yet been lit. Instead the priest cut out a circular piece of paper and stuck it on the wall like a round mirror, whereupon the room was instantly bathed in dazzling light. The mirror had become a veritable moon. The disciples stood around in a ring, coming and going at the priest's beck and call.

'On such a fine night as this,' remarked one of the guests, 'we should share our pleasure with one and all.'

So saying, he took a wine jug from the table and began pouring for all the disciples, bidding them drink their fill and be merry.

'How can that one jug possibly provide for all seven or eight of us?' thought Wang silently to himself.

The disciples went in search of more goblets, each eager to have a drink before the wine ran out. But, however often the wine was poured, to their amazement the supply never seemed to diminish.

'You have graciously provided us with this moonlight,' said one of the priest's guests. 'Should we not enliven the occasion by inviting the goddess Chang E to join us from her palace?'

With this he tossed one of his chopsticks at the 'moon', and a beautiful lady appeared in the middle of the circle of light, at first no more than a foot high, but attaining a full woman's height as she descended to the ground. Her slender waist and graceful arching neck were soon swaying to the steps of the centuries-old dance known as 'Rainbow Skirts'. And when the dance was finished, she began to sing:

> Lightly lightly
> Have I danced!
> Is this the world of men,
> Or am I still confined
> In my Cold Palace
> Of the moon?

Her voice was pure and thrilling, like the sound of the flute. When her song was done, she pirouetted up on to the table and, before her astonished audience knew what was happening, was once more transformed into a chopstick. The three men at the table laughed heartily.

'What a splendid evening this has been!' exclaimed one of them. 'But I don't think I can drink much more. Will you gentlemen accompany me for a last cup of farewell in the Palace of the Moon?'

The three of them rose, walked slowly towards the wall and entered the moon. The disciples watched them sitting up there drinking, perfectly visible down to the last whisker and eyebrow, as clear as a reflection in a mirror. Presently the moon began to fade, and when the disciples lit candles they beheld their Master sitting quite alone at the table. His companions were nowhere to be seen. The sweetmeats were still on the table, the moon no more than a mirror-shaped circle of paper on the wall.

'Have you all drunk your fill?' asked the priest of his disciples.

'Yes, Master,' was the reply.

'Then early to bed. Tomorrow there will be more wood to chop and grass to cut.'

The disciples retired obediently for the night.

Wang was thrilled by what he had witnessed, and his earlier thoughts of admitting defeat and abandoning his Taoist ordeal evaporated.

Another month went by, and again the hardship seemed more than he could bear. And still the Master had taught him no magical secret. He could wait no longer, and went to take his leave.

'I came here from a great distance to sit at your feet, Master. Even if I could not learn the Art of Immortality, I thought at least to acquire some minor accomplishment with which to nourish my spiritual aspirations. But alas, for these three months, I have done nothing but chop wood all day and return exhausted in the evening to sleep. Hardship such as this I have never known at home.'

The priest smiled. 'Did I not say it would be hard? See, you have proved me right. Tomorrow morning I will send you on your way.'

'Please, Master,' pleaded Wang, 'for all the days I have laboured, give me some trifling skill to take away with me, so that I will not go home empty-handed.'

'What skill do you desire?' asked the priest.

'I have noticed that wherever you go, walls are no obstruction to you. Teach me to walk through walls, Master. That will be enough.'

The priest smiled. 'Very well.'

He taught Wang a mantra, bade him recite it, then cried, 'Now go!'

Wang looked at the wall in front of him, but could not bring himself to walk into it.

'Try! Go!'

Wang started slowly, but when he reached the wall, there it was, as solid as ever in front of him.

'What are you waiting for? Head down and charge!' cried the priest. 'Don't procrastinate!'

This time, Wang took a few steps back from the wall, rushed at it full pelt and passed through it as if there were nothing there. Looking round him, he saw that he was indeed now on the other side of the wall. It had worked! He was delighted and returned at once to give thanks.

'When you are back at home,' said the monk, 'be sure to lead a pure life. If not, it will not work.'

The monk gave him something towards his travelling expenses and sent him on his way.

On his return, Wang boasted of his encounter with an Immortal, and claimed that he could walk through solid walls. His wife did not believe his tales, so he carried out the monk's instructions, took up a stance several feet away from a wall and rushed at it. This time his head made contact with some all too solid masonry and he crashed to the ground with a thud. His wife helped him up, looked at the egg-sized bump that was starting to emerge on his forehead and burst out laughing. Wang was bitterly angry, and cursed the old monk for a scoundrel.

笑道山士

顯學
念神仙一
薪癡椎
蘇枼苦難
撥祅求撥得寧
齋術似此居心
己可知

He rushed at the wall.

15
THE MONK OF CHANGQING

At Changqing there lived a monk of great spiritual attainment and virtue. He was over eighty years old but still hale and hearty. Then, one day, he fell to the ground and was unable to rise: the other monks came hurrying to his aid, but found him already lifeless. He had entered the state of nirvana. His soul meanwhile, unaware of his death, had gone drifting off to the south, to a place somewhere in the region of Henan Province.

The son of a noble Henan family was out that very same day with ten or so of his retainers, hunting hares with falcons, when his horse bolted and the young man was thrown to the ground and instantly killed. The wandering soul of the old monk from Changqing happened to be passing close by and in that very instant entered into his body. The young man gradually began to show signs of recovering consciousness. His retainers gathered round him and inquired how he was.

'What am I doing here?' he asked, opening his eyes wide.

They lifted him up and helped him home, where his women-folk in their many-coloured silks greeted him and inquired after his well-being.

'But I am a monk,' he exclaimed in amazement. 'What am I doing here?'

His family thought he must have taken leave of his senses and tried tweaking his ears to bring him round. The monk himself was quite unable to understand his own predicament, but resolved to close his eyes and say nothing further.

At mealtimes he would eat nothing but coarse rice, and refused to touch meat and wine. At night he slept alone, rejecting the attentions of his wife and concubines.

The wandering soul of the old monk entered into his body.

After a few days, he felt a sudden urge to go out for a stroll, to the delight of his family. The moment he stepped out of his room, his stewards thronged around him, with ledgers and accounts to be checked, but he told them he was still not feeling well and sent them all away.

'Do you know the village of Changqing, in Shandong Province?' he asked one of the household, who replied that he did.

'I feel so cooped up and bored here,' he said. 'I should like to go to Changqing and take a look around. Have my things made ready at once.'

They all protested that he was only just on the mend and that such a long journey seemed inadvisable. But he refused to heed their advice and set off the very next day, arriving at Changqing to find everything exactly as he remembered it. He made his way straight to the monastery, without needing to ask the way. When the junior monks (his erstwhile disciples) saw this young nobleman arrive, they greeted him respectfully.

'Where is your Master?' he asked them.

'He was transformed some time ago,' they replied.

He asked to see where they had buried him, and they took him to an isolated grave-site, the tomb itself some three feet high, the soil around it still bare, the grass having not yet had time to grow back. The monks were still trying to fathom the purpose of the 'young nobleman's' visit, when he sent for his horse and set off home again, instructing them as he left, 'Your Master was a monk of virtue. Guard with care whatever relics you have of his, let no harm come to them.'

They promised to do as he said, and he went on his way.

On his return home, from that day onwards he sat in a be-mused state, refusing to take the slightest part in family affairs. Several months went by like this, until finally one day he upped and left again, heading straight back to Changqing and his old monastery.

'I am your Master,' he announced to his former disciples.

This time they all thought he was raving, and looked at one another and laughed. But then he started telling them of how his soul had found a new body, and recounted in precise detail a number of events in his life as a monk, all of which tallied exactly with what they knew of their Master. They were obliged to believe him. He slept once more in his old bed, and they waited on him as they had done before.

The young nobleman's family came several times, with a great cortège of carriages and horses, and pleaded with him to go home with them, but he turned a deaf ear to their entreaties.

More than a year later, his wife sent a household steward with rich gifts of gold and silk, all of which he refused, except for a single plain cotton robe, which he kept for his own use. From time to time his friends from Henan Province would call on him if they were in the neighbourhood. They found a man of quiet dignity and sincerity, barely thirty years old but with the wisdom of a man fifty years his senior.

16
THE SNAKE-CHARMER

A certain man of Dongjun district made a living as a snake-charmer. He raised and trained two green snakes, the larger of which he called Big Green, and the smaller, Little Green. Little Green was his favourite. He had a red dot on the front of his head and was very quick to learn, writhing and coiling exactly in tune with his master's wishes.

After a year Big Green died, and the snake-charmer, although he meant to find a replacement, somehow never got round to doing so. Once, after spending the night in a temple in the hills, he awoke at dawn and opened his basket to find that Little Green had disappeared. He was utterly distraught, and went calling and searching everywhere in the half-light, without finding any trace of the snake.

Previously on his travels, whenever he came to a bosk or a stretch of dense undergrowth, he used to set Little Green free to roam as he pleased and the snake invariably returned of his own accord. So this time the snake-charmer hoped that he would do the same, and sat down to wait. But when the sun had climbed high in the sky and there was still no sign of the snake, he gave up hope and went disconsolately on his way.

He had walked only a little way from the temple when he heard a low rustling sound coming from a nearby thicket. He stood stock-still, gazing intently into the thicket, and out came Little Green. The snake-charmer was as overjoyed to see him as a man stumbling by chance upon some priceless gem. He continued on his way, and a little while later, when he put down his carrying pole and stopped to rest at a turn in the road, the snake stopped with him. When the snake-charmer looked back, he saw an even smaller snake following Little Green.

'I thought I'd lost you!' he said, stroking Little Green. 'So this is your little companion?'

He took out some food for them both. The smaller one made no attempt to escape, but coiled himself up and refused the food. Little Green fed him from his own mouth, with great solicitude. The second time the snake-charmer offered him something to eat, he took it, and when the meal was over, he followed Little Green into his basket.

The snake-charmer trained the newcomer, who mastered the tricks as perfectly as Little Green had done. He called him Baby Green, and went all round the country with his new act, making a great deal of money.

In general snake-charmers are obliged to change their snakes when they reach two feet in length. They simply become too heavy to handle. Little Green was different, because he was so exceptionally tame. But nonetheless, two or three years later, when he had grown to three feet and filled the entire basket, the snake-charmer finally decided it was time to let him go.

One fine day, he went out to the hills east of Zi County, gave Little Green something special to eat, then blessed him and set him free. The snake headed off but soon returned and began circling his basket. The snake-charmer pushed him away.

'Off you go! Sooner or later even the finest party has to end. Go and find yourself a hiding place down in the valley. Maybe one day you will turn into a magic dragon. Surely you don't want to stay cooped up in this basket all your life?'

Little Green wriggled away again, and the snake-charmer followed him with his eyes as he disappeared from view. But before too long he was back again, and this time when the snake-charmer pushed him away he flatly refused to leave and nudged the basket with his head. Baby Green was inside and becoming more and more fidgety and restless. Suddenly the truth dawned on the snake-charmer: Little Green wanted to say goodbye. He opened the basket and out shot Baby Green and wrapped himself around Little Green. Their tongues flickered as if they were talking to one another. Then they both went

Baby Green wrapped himself around Little Green.

wriggling off. The snake-charmer feared that Baby Green would never return, but after a while he came back all on his own, crawled sadly into his basket and lay down.

The snake-charmer never found another snake as perfect as Little Green. With time Baby Green grew larger and larger and became too difficult to handle. The snake-charmer eventually acquired another snake, one that also proved quick to learn. But he was not the equal of Baby Green, who by this time had grown as thick as a child's arm.

When Little Green first went off to live in the hills, the only people who saw him were the local woodcutters. The years went by and he continued to grow until he was almost the length of a man and as thick as a rice bowl. Then he started coming out and attacking travellers, who warned one another about this dangerous serpent, with the result that soon no one dared enter his territory. One day, the snake-charmer was passing through the area and a snake shot out at him fast as the wind. He fled in terror, but the snake kept coming after him. When the snake-charmer looked back and saw that he was almost upon him, in that same moment he recognized the red dot on the front of his head.

'Little Green! Little Green!' he cried, setting down his carrying pole. At once the snake stopped, lifted his head and gazed at the man for a long while, then wrapped himself around him, as he used to when they worked together. The snake-charmer knew that the snake meant him no harm, but Little Green was now so big and heavy that he brought the man to the ground. Hearing his cry of entreaty, the snake loosened his grip, then nudged the basket with his head, and the snake-charmer, knowing immediately this time what it was he wanted, opened the basket and let out Baby Green.

The two snakes twined around each other and clung together like a toffee twist, before finally separating. The snake-charmer gave Baby Green his blessing: 'I have been wanting to let you go for a long time. Now you have your old friend to keep you company.'

To Little Green he said, 'You brought him to me, you can take him away. One word: you can find food in plenty in the hills. Do not harm wayfarers. You will only make Heaven angry.'

The two snakes lowered their heads as if bowing in recognition of his wise admonition, then lifted their heads again and set off, the older one in front, the younger following, and wherever they went the branches of the trees parted to let them through. The snake-charmer watched them until he could see them no longer, then he continued on his way. From that day, travellers in that area went unmolested. As for the snakes, no one knows what became of them.

17

THE WOUNDED PYTHON

There were two brothers Hu, of Hu Village, both of them woodcutters, who went deep into a remote valley and there encountered a large python. The elder of the two brothers was walking in front, and the python started to swallow him. At first the younger brother was about to flee in terror, then the sight of his older brother taken in the snake's mouth threw him into such a fit of wild rage that he swung his woodcutter's axe and brought it down on the python's head, inflicting a severe injury. The snake continued nonetheless to swallow down its prey. The elder brother's head had already disappeared, but his shoulders were stuck in the snake's mouth. In desperation the younger brother seized the elder brother's feet and began tugging at them with all his might; he wrestled fiercely with the great snake and finally succeeded in dragging his brother free. The python went slithering away in great pain.

When he looked more closely at his brother, he saw that his nose and ears had already gone and he was barely breathing. He set off with him on his shoulders, and finally reached home having stopped ten times to rest along the way.

The wounded brother was tended for six months and eventually recovered. To this day his face still bears the scars of that terrible experience. Where others have a nose and ears, he has nothing.

Ah! To think that there are, in the peasant community, brothers as devoted as that!

A certain person has commented, 'The python did not harm the man any further because he was so touched by the younger brother's virtue and bravery.'

I believe this was the truth of the matter.

The elder brother's shoulders were stuck in the snake's mouth.

THE FORNICATING DOG

There was a merchant of Qingzhou who was much away on business, often for as long as an entire year. He had a white dog at home, and during her husband's absences his wife encouraged the dog to have sexual relations with her. The dog became quite accustomed to this.

One day, the merchant had just returned home and was in bed with his wife when suddenly the dog burst into the room, climbed up on to the bed and bit his master to death.

When the neighbours came to know of this, they were most indignant and reported the matter to the local Magistrate, who interrogated the woman under torture, and when she still refused to confess had her thrown into the county jail. He gave orders for the dog to be brought on a leash, and then summoned the woman into the tribunal. The moment the dog saw her he rushed forward, tore off her clothes with his teeth and leaped on top of her, adopting a posture that was unmistakably sexual. The woman could no longer deny the charge brought against her. The Magistrate sent them both, woman and dog, under guard to the higher court in the provincial capital.

On their way there, local inhabitants wishing to see them in the act of coupling bribed the escort, who dragged them out and forced them to perform in public. Wherever they stopped, this act attracted a crowd of several hundreds, and the yamen guards made a small fortune out of it.

Subsequently both woman and dog were sentenced to Lingering Death.

How many things are possible, in the immense universe of Heaven and Earth! This woman is certainly not the only creature with a human visage to have coupled with an animal.

THE GOD OF HAIL

Wang Yuncang, a gentleman of Shandong, was posted to the southern region of Hunan Province anciently known as Chu. En route he proposed to climb the famous Dragon and Tiger Peak and call upon the Taoist Heavenly Patriarch, who was resident there. He reached the lake, and just as he was boarding a boat, a man came rowing towards him in a little skiff, calling out to the boatman to introduce them. Even as Wang was sizing up the man's elegant and somewhat imposing appearance, he produced from his gown one of the Heavenly Patriarch's calling cards.

'My Master has learned of your imminent arrival and has sent me ahead to welcome you.'

Wang was astonished at their foreknowledge of his proposed visit, which only increased his sense of reverence towards the Taoist Patriarch and fortified his determination to wait upon him. He finally arrived at his destination, to find the Heavenly Patriarch surrounded by his retinue of strangely robed attendants, their hair and beards dressed in an antique manner. The Patriarch received him most cordially and treated him to a fine banquet. The man from the skiff also waited on him and, after a little while, Wang inquired who he was.

'He is a fellow countryman of yours,' replied the Heavenly Patriarch. 'Do you not know him?'

Wang begged to be enlightened.

'This is Li Zuoche, he whom men call the God of Hail.'

Wang's face fell in sheer astonishment.

'He has just informed me,' continued the Heavenly Patriarch, 'of a new rain-and-hail commission. He will soon have to take his leave of us.'

He hovered above the ground for a moment.

'Where is he going?' asked Wang.

'To Zhangqiu.'

Now Zhangqiu was right next to his own native town in Shandong, and Wang immediately got down from his seat and put in a plea for his neighbours, that they might be spared a violent hail-storm.

'Unfortunately this decree emanates from the Supreme Deity,' said the Patriarch. 'The quantity of hail to be dropped has been exactly predetermined and cannot be altered for personal reasons.'

The Patriarch could see, however, that Wang was deeply distressed, and after pondering the matter for a long while, he turned and instructed the God of Hail to discharge most of his hailstones on the hills and valleys, so as to spare the crops.

'And as you can see,' he went on, 'I have a guest, so would you mind making your departure a little more civilized than normal?'

The God left the hall and went out into the courtyard, where seconds later a cloud of mist could be seen billowing out from beneath his feet. He hovered above the ground for a moment, then lifted off with massive force, reaching first tree-top, then roof-top level. Finally there was an almighty crash of thunder, and as he soared up into the sky and northwards, plates rattled on the tables and the whole building quaked.

'You mean to say that every time he goes, it thunders like that!' gasped the awestruck Wang.

'Just now I asked him to tone it down,' said the Heavenly Patriarch, 'so he made it a leisurely take-off. Otherwise he would have zoomed straight up into the air – bang!'

When Wang eventually took his leave, he made a note of the date. Later he sent a man to Zhangqiu to make inquiries, and it transpired that on that exact day there had been a particularly heavy storm, with rain and hail filling the watercourses to overflowing. But strangely, only a few lumps of hail had landed on the fields.

20

THE GOLDEN GOBLET

Yin Shidan, who rose to be President of the Board of Civil Office, was a native of Licheng who grew up in circumstances of great poverty and had shown himself to be a young man of courage and resourcefulness.

In his home town there was a large estate that had once belonged to a long-established family, a rambling property consisting of a series of pavilions and other buildings that extended over several acres. Strange apparitions had often been witnessed on the estate, with the result that it had been abandoned and allowed to go to ruin. No one was willing to live there. With time the place grew so overgrown and desolate that no one would so much as enter it even in broad daylight.

One day, Yin was drinking with some young friends of his when one of them had a bright idea.

'If one of us dares to spend a night in that haunted place,' he proposed jokingly, 'let's all stand him a dinner!'

Yin leaped up at once. 'Why, what could be easier!'

And so saying he took his sleeping mat with him and went to the place, the others accompanying him as far as the entrance.

'We will wait here outside,' they said, smiling nervously. 'If you see anything out of the ordinary, be sure to raise the alarm.'

Yin laughed. 'If I find any ghosts or foxes, I'll catch one to show you.' And in he went.

The paths were overgrown with long grass and tangled weeds. It was the first quarter of the month, and the crescent moon gave off just enough light for him to make out the gateways and doors. He groped his way forwards until he found himself standing before the building that stood at the rear of the main compound. He climbed on to the terrace and thought it seemed a delightful place to take a little nap. The slender arc of the moon shining in the western sky seemed to hold the hills in its mouth. He sat there a long while without observing anything unusual, and began to smile to himself at the foolish rumours about the place being haunted. Spreading his mat, and choosing a stone for a pillow, he lay there gazing up at the constellations of the Cowherd and the Spinning Maid in the night sky.

By the end of the first watch, he was just beginning to doze off when he heard the patter of footsteps from below, and a servant-girl appeared, carrying a lotus-shaped lantern. The sight of Yin seemed to startle her and she made as if to flee, calling out to someone behind her, 'There's a strange-looking man here!'

'Who is it?' replied a voice.

'I don't know.'

Presently an old gentleman appeared and, approaching Yin, scrutinized him.

'Why, that is the future President Yin! He is fast asleep. We can carry on as planned. He is a broad-minded fellow and will not take offence.'

The old man led the maid on into the building, where they threw open all the doors. After a while a great many guests started arriving, and the upper rooms were as brightly lit as if it had been broad daylight.

Yin tossed and turned on the terrace where he lay. Then he sneezed. The old man, hearing that he was awake, came out and knelt down by his side.

'My daughter, sir, is being given in marriage tonight. I had no idea that Your Excellency would be here, and crave your indulgence.'

Yin rose to his feet and made the old man do likewise. 'I was not aware that a wedding was taking place tonight. I regret I have brought no gift with me.'

'Your very presence is gift enough,' replied the old man graciously, 'and will help to ward off noxious influences. Would you be so kind as to honour us further with your company now?'

Yin assented. Entering the building, he looked around him at the splendid feast that had been prepared. A woman of about forty, whom the old gentleman introduced as his wife, came out to welcome him, and Yin made her a bow. Then the sound of festive pipes was heard, and someone came rushing in, crying, 'He has arrived!'

The old man hurried out to receive his future son-in-law, and Yin remained standing where he was in expectation. After a little while, a bevy of servants bearing gauze lanterns ushered in the groom, a handsome young man of seventeen or eighteen, of a most distinguished appearance and prepossessing bearing. The old gentleman bade him pay his respects to the guest of honour, and the young man turned to Yin, whom he took to be some sort of Master of Ceremonies, and bowed to him in the appropriate fashion. Then the old man and the groom exchanged formal courtesies, and when these were completed, they took their seats. Presently a throng of finely attired serving-maids came forward, with choice wines and steaming dishes of meat. Jade bowls and golden goblets glistened on the tables. When the wine had been round several times, the old gentleman dispatched one of the maids to summon the bride. The maid departed on her errand, but when she had been gone a long while and still there was no sign of his daughter, the old man himself eventually rose from his seat and, lifting the portière, went into the inner apartments to chivvy her along. At last several maids and serving-women ushered in the bride, to the sound of tinkling jade pendants, and the scent of musk and orchid wafted through the room. Obedient to her father's instructions, she curtseyed to the senior guests and then took her seat by her mother's side. Yin could see from a glance that beneath the kingfisher-feather ornaments she was a young woman of extraordinary beauty.

They were drinking from large goblets of solid gold, each of which held well over a pint, and Yin thought to himself that one of these would be an ideal proof of his adventure that night. So he hid one in his sleeve, to show his friends on his return, then slumped across the table, pretending to have been over-powered by the wine.

'His Excellency is drunk,' they remarked.

A little later, Yin heard the groom take his leave, and as the pipes started up again, all the guests began trooping downstairs.

The old gentleman came to gather up his golden goblets, and noticed that one of them was missing. He searched for it to no avail. Someone suggested their sleeping guest as the culprit, but the old gentleman promptly bid him be silent, for fear that Yin might hear.

After a while, when all was still within and without, Yin rose from the table. The lamps had all been extinguished and it was dark, but the aroma of the food and the fumes of wine still lingered in the hall. As he made his way slowly out of the building, and felt inside his sleeve for the golden goblet, which was still safely hidden, the first light of dawn glimmered in the eastern sky.

He reached the entrance of the estate to find his friends still waiting outside. They had stayed there all night, in case he should try to trick them by coming out and going back in again early in the morning. He took the goblet from his sleeve and showed it to them. In utter amazement they asked him how he had come by it, whereupon he told them the whole story. They knew how poor he was, and that he was most unlikely to have owned such a valuable object himself, and so were obliged to believe him.

Some years later, Yin passed his final examination and obtained the degree of Doctor or *jinshi*, after which he was appointed to a post in Feiqiu. A wealthy gentleman of the district by the name of Zhu gave a banquet in his honour, and ordered his large golden goblets to be brought out for the occasion. They were a long time coming, and as the company waited a young servant came up and whispered something to the master of the household, who instantly flew into a rage. Presently the goblets were brought in, and Zhu urged his guests to drink. To his astonishment, Yin at once recognized the shape and pattern of the goblets as being identical with the one he had 'kept' from the fox wedding. He asked his host where they had been made.

'I had eight of them,' was the reply. 'An ancestor of mine was

狐嫁女

神儔攘飾埸
居也共人
間婚嫁如一
蘋笙歌雨
行燭夜深廈
爵笑尚書

Someone suggested their sleeping guest as the culprit.

a high-ranking mandarin in Peking and had them made by a master goldsmith of the time. They have been in my family for generations, but it is a long while since I last had them taken out of storage. When I knew we would have the honour of your company today, I told my man to open the box, and it turns out there are only seven left! I would have suspected one of my household of stealing it, but apparently there was ten years' dust on the seals and the box was untampered with. It baffles me how this can have happened.'

'The thing must have grown wings and flown away of its own accord!' quipped Yin with a laugh. 'But seeing that you have lost an heirloom, I feel I must help you replace it. I myself have a goblet, sir, very similar to this set of yours. Allow me to make you a present of it.'

When the meal was over, he returned to his official residence, and taking out his own goblet, sent it round straightaway to Zhu's house. When he inspected it, Zhu was absolutely amazed. He went to thank Yin in person, and when he asked him where he had acquired the goblet, Yin told him the whole story.

Which all goes to show that although foxes may be capable of getting hold of objects from a very long way away, they do not hold on to them for ever.

21

GRACE AND PINE

Kong Xueli, a descendant of the great sage Confucius, was a man of generous spirit and great refinement of character, and an accomplished poet. A close friend of his, who had been appointed Magistrate at Tiantai, wrote inviting him to come and stay, and Kong set off for Tiantai, only to find on arrival that his friend had died. Stranded without lodgings, and without the means to travel home, he put up in the Putuo Temple, where the monks gave him work as a copyist.

A hundred yards or so west of the temple stood the mansion of a gentleman named Shan, a member of a distinguished local family, who, having become involved in a protracted and ruinously expensive lawsuit, had taken his dependants to live in the country, leaving the place deserted.

One day Kong was out in a driving blizzard, the sort of weather in which everyone else decides to stay indoors, and happened to pass by the Shan mansion, where he saw an elegantly attired and handsome-looking young man emerge from the main entrance. The man also caught sight of Kong and, hurrying over to him, greeted him courteously and invited him to step inside out of the snow. Kong took an instant liking to the stranger and gladly followed him inside, looking around him with curiosity as he went. The various rooms of the mansion, though not particularly large, were hung with numerous fine embroidered hangings, antique calligraphic scrolls and paintings. Kong spotted a slim volume lying on a table entitled *Jottings from a Distant Realm* and, leafing through it, was a trifle puzzled to find that it was a work completely unknown to him. He assumed that the young man must be a member of the Shan family, since he was living in the Shan residence, and did not bother to inquire into his family background and connections. The young man, for his part, asked Kong in some detail about his own predicament and seemed most sympathetic to his plight. He encouraged him to set himself up as a tutor and start a little school.

'Alas,' sighed Kong, 'I am stranded far from home and can think of no one to act as my patron in such an enterprise.'

'If you would not consider it beneath you,' said the young man, 'I myself would be glad to be your first pupil and sit at your feet.'

Kong was touched by this gesture of friendship but modestly declined to assume the role of the young man's teacher, insisting instead that they should remain simply friends.

'Tell me,' he asked, 'why has this splendid house been closed for so long?'

'It used to belong to the Shan family,' replied the young man, 'but the young master went to live in the country, and ever since then it has been allowed to go to ruin. My own name is Huangfu. My ancestors hail from Shaanxi Province, far to the west. Our own home was burned down in a big fire, so we are lodging here temporarily at present.'

Kong now knew at least that the young man was not a member of the Shan family. The two continued to spend a most convivial evening together and ended up sharing the same bed that night.

At daybreak, a young pageboy came in to light a fire in their room, and Huangfu rose and went off to the inner apartments, while Kong sat up in bed with a quilt wrapped round him. Presently the pageboy returned to announce that the Master was coming, and Kong hurriedly rose from the bed, just as a white-haired old man entered the room.

'I must thank you, sir,' said the old man, speaking most courteously, 'for deigning to take my son in hand. At present he writes very indifferent prose, and I trust you will not allow considerations of friendship to interfere with whatever discipline you may consider necessary for his progress.'

He then presented Kong with an embroidered gown, a sable

hat, stockings and shoes. Kong washed himself and combed his hair, whereupon the old man called for wine and food to be served and a dazzling banquet was set before them. The food, the furniture, the clothes, were all of a rare quality, such as Kong had never witnessed in his life. After drinking several cups of wine with his guest the old man picked up his walking stick and went on his way in high spirits.

When the meal was over, young Huangfu came in to present some of his previous compositions, which were all written in an archaic style, quite unlike the elaborate Eight-Legged Essay required in the official examinations. When Kong questioned him about this, he smiled and replied, 'I have never had any particular ambition to sit for the examinations.'

That evening they drank again.

'Tonight let us enjoy ourselves to the full!' exclaimed Huangfu. 'Soon, alas, we must turn our minds to more serious matters.' He called for his pageboy. 'See if father is asleep yet. If he is, go quietly in to Fragrance and ask her to join us.'

The boy went, and returned carrying a piba-mandolin in an embroidered case. Presently a handsome young woman joined them, dressed in an exquisite gown, and Huangfu told her to play for them the air known as 'Bamboo Tears'. She plucked the strings with an ivory plectrum, and played with a strange vigour and passion, to rhythms subtler than any Kong had ever heard. Huangfu poured wine into large goblets, and they drank together into the early hours.

The next day, they rose early to begin their studies. Huangfu proved to be a gifted pupil, able to memorize texts at a single glance, and in no more than a couple of months he had perfected the required prose style. They arranged to have their drinking sessions every five days, making a point of always inviting Fragrance along to join them. Once, when Kong was somewhat the worse for wine, Huangfu noticed that his friend could not take his eyes off the girl.

'Fragrance is just a serving-maid, brought up by my father,' he commented, continuing in a friendly tone, 'I understand how lonely you must feel, so far away from home. In fact I have been meaning for some time now to find you a good-looking wife.'

'Then let it be someone like Fragrance!' said Kong, to which Huangfu replied with a smile, 'As the saying goes, "Little experience makes a man marvel at little!" If Fragrance is your ideal of beauty, then you are easily pleased.'

One day, when he had already been with them for half a year, Kong felt the urge to go out into the countryside for a stroll. He walked to the entrance of the mansion and tried the door, only to find it firmly locked from the outside. When he inquired why this was so, Huangfu told him that his father was anxious to discourage contact with strangers, who might disrupt the progress of his studies. Kong seemed to accept this explanation.

The summer was hot and muggy, and they decided to hold their lessons outside, in one of the garden pavilions. It was at about this time that Kong began to develop a strange swelling on his chest, which was at first the size of a peach, then overnight grew to the size of a large bowl. It gave him great pain and caused him to groan constantly. Huangfu came to visit him morning and night, but Kong slept and ate little, and soon began to waste away, his condition gradually deteriorating to the point where he ceased eating and drinking altogether. Huangfu's father came to call on him, and both he and his son lamented their guest's critical state.

'Last night I was thinking about Mr Kong's illness,' said young Huangfu to his father, 'and I felt sure that my sister Grace would be able to cure him. Just now I sent someone to grandmother's to fetch her. I wonder why she is so long coming.'

Just at that moment the pageboy came in. 'Miss Grace is here,' he announced, 'with her aunt and her cousin Miss Pine.'

Father and son hurried out to greet them, and in a little while returned accompanied by Huangfu's younger sister Grace, a girl of thirteen or fourteen years, with a bright sparkle in her eyes, and a figure as supple and lithe as a young willow. When Kong set eyes on her beauty, his spirits suddenly lifted. He at once forgot his pain and ceased his groans.

'This is my dear friend Kong,' said Huangfu. 'He is as a brother to me. Care for him well.'

A little coyly, Grace rolled back her sleeves, approached his bed and began taking Kong's pulse. As she held his wrist, he became aware of a perfume more fragrant than that of the rarest orchid.

'No wonder!' she concluded with a gentle smile. 'The heart meridian has been affected. His is a very serious illness but still curable. The swelling is already hardening, so we will have to cut it away.'

She took a golden bracelet from her arm and placed it on the diseased part, pressing it down gently. The swollen flesh rose an inch or more above the bracelet, but the base of the swelling was somehow contracted and contained, becoming considerably less extended than before. With her free hand she untied her sash and took from within her gown a knife with a razor-sharp blade as fine as a sheet of paper. Pressing the bracelet with one hand and holding the knife in the other, she cut lightly and deftly along the base of the swelling. Dark blood gushed from the wound, staining the mat on the bed beneath him. But Kong, who now craved nothing but the proximity of this beautiful girl, not only was oblivious to the pain but dreaded more than anything else the completion of the operation, since it threatened to bring with it her departure and a premature end to their short-lived intimacy.

Soon the diseased flesh had been excised in one piece, like a chunk of rotten wood cut from a tree. The girl called for water with which to bathe the wound, then from her mouth she spat out a red bolus, a pill the size of a large bullet, pressing it into the wound and turning it round and round. At the first turn, he felt a burning sensation; at the second, an insistent tingling; at the third, a lightness that permeated his body to the very marrow of his bones.

The girl put the bolus back into her mouth and swallowed it.

'There! You are cured!' she said, and hurried out. Kong leaped up to thank her, as if he had never been ill at all.

But his sufferings were not at an end. Now he found himself yearning more and more for her beauty, abandoning his books and sitting for hours musing on nothing, listless and dead to the world.

A little coyly, Grace began taking Kong's pulse.

'I think I may have found the right person for you, Brother Kong,' said Huangfu, perceiving his condition.

'And who is that, pray?' mumbled Kong.

'A cousin of mine.'

Kong brooded for a while, before replying, 'Do not trouble yourself for nothing.' He stared at the wall, and heaved a deep sigh:

> 'Speak not of lakes and streams to one
>   Who knows the splendour of the sea;
> The clouds around the magic peaks of Wu
>   Are the only clouds for me.'

Huangfu grasped his meaning at once (the cloud-wrapped peaks of Wu having once been the scene of a famous love encounter). 'My father admires your great accomplishments, and has long wanted to see you marry into our family. But Grace is my only sister, and she is still much too young to marry. My cousin Pine, on the other hand, is eighteen years old and a good-looking girl. If you don't believe me, see for yourself. She takes a walk every day in the garden; you can observe her from the front chamber.'

Kong did as his friend suggested, and watched Grace walking in the garden in the company of another young lady of great beauty, with dark, arched eyebrows and tiny feet encased in phoenix-patterned slippers. Kong observed to his great joy that she was every bit as beautiful as Grace, and he asked his friend to arrange the match at once.

The very next day, Huangfu emerged from the women's quarters and hailed his friend. 'Congratulations! Everything is settled!'

A separate courtyard was set apart for the wedding, and without further ado, that very night, the merry music of drums and pipes sounded in the house. Throughout the wedding ceremony Kong gazed blissfully at his bride, wondering if he was still on earth or had been transported to the Palace of the Moon. Once the ritual had been completed, their love was joyfully consummated.

Shortly after this, Huangfu came to Kong one evening and spoke to him in an unusually serious tone. 'I can never forget everything you have taught me. But since Lord Shan will shortly conclude his court case and urgently requires the use of his mansion, my family will be obliged to leave here and travel west. It is unlikely that you and I will meet again. It causes me great sorrow to have to say farewell.'

Kong wanted to go with them, but Huangfu urged him to return home to his own family. Kong protested that this would be hard for him to do.

'Don't worry,' said Huangfu, 'I shall take you there.'

Presently the father came with Pine and presented Kong with a gift of a hundred taels of silver. Huangfu led both Kong and his wife by the hand, ordering them to close their eyes and on no account to look, and presently they felt themselves soaring through space. They could hear nothing but the wind whistling in their ears. 'There, you are home now!' said Huangfu after a while, and they opened their eyes and beheld Kong's native village. This was the first time he knew for sure that Huangfu was no ordinary mortal.

He knocked happily on his family door, and his mother could not believe her eyes. But her happiness at seeing her son again was eclipsed by her delight at the beautiful wife he had brought home with him. As for Huangfu, when Kong turned to look for him, he had vanished.

Pine proved a devoted daughter-in-law, and her beauty and virtue became widely known in the district. In the course of time, Kong passed his third degree, qualified as a metropolitan graduate and was appointed a junior magistrate in the city of Yan'an. He proposed taking his whole family with him to his post, and although his mother thought the journey too long and resolved to stay at home, Pine went with him, having meanwhile borne him a son, whom they called Little Lord.

At his new post Kong fell foul of a visiting censor, and was relieved of his duties. He was temporarily confined to the Yan'an region and not allowed to travel home. Once, he was out hunting in the nearby fields when he saw a handsome young man ride towards him on a black horse, staring at him intently.

On closer inspection, who should it turn out to be but his dear friend, young Huangfu! They halted their horses, and the two friends laughed and wept at their reunion.

Huangfu invited Kong to go with him to his new home. They came to a village set in a thicket of trees whose leaves were so dense that they shut out the sun altogether. The doors of the house were embossed with great gilt studs, indicating an establishment of considerable distinction. Huangfu told him that his sister Grace was now married, and Kong also learned to his great sorrow that Pine's mother, his mother-in-law, had died. He spent the night there, and returned the following day with Pine and their son. Grace put her arms round their little boy and began playing with him.

'You have mingled our two species, cousin!' she teased Pine secretly.

Kong for his part expressed his heartfelt thanks to Grace for having saved his life.

'You are such an important man now,' she replied, 'and your old wound is completely healed! But you still remember the pain!'

Her own husband, whose name was Wu, also came to pay his respects and persuaded them to stay a second night.

In the morning, Huangfu came to speak to Kong, a woeful expression on his face. 'We are facing disaster! I beseech you to save us!'

Kong asked him to explain his trouble, and eagerly assured him that he would do whatever lay within his power. Huangfu hurried out, and assembled his whole family in the main hall, where they proceeded to kneel and give thanks to a bewildered Kong.

'The truth is,' explained Huangfu at last, 'we are not of human stock. We are all foxes. And today a terrible thunderstorm is about to strike us. If you are willing to risk your own life to protect us, we may yet be saved. If not, then take your child now and go; do not let yourself be caught up in our fate.'

When Kong swore to live or die with them, Huangfu told him to stand in the doorway sword in hand.

'When the thunder and lightning strike, stand firm, do not move!'

Kong followed his instructions and took up his stand. Soon black clouds obscured the midday sky, and it grew dark as night. When he looked around him, Huangfu's mansion had vanished, and in its place he saw a solitary earthen mound projecting into the sky, while beneath it a huge, bottomless chasm had opened up in the ground. As he looked aghast at this desolate sight, a crash of thunder shattered the heavens, shaking the hills to their foundations, followed by driving rain and a fierce gale which uprooted trees in its path. Dazzled and deafened by the tempest, Kong nonetheless continued to stand his ground firmly when suddenly, through the swirling dark-ness, he saw a gruesome monster, with great pointed beak and long claws, rise up from the depths of the chasm, bearing in its arms a human form. As it began to soar upwards through the mist, Kong knew at a glance that the body it was carrying was that of Grace. He leaped forward and struck out with his sword, whereupon the monster let Grace fall from its arms. Another great crack of thunder burst from the heavens, and Kong himself lay dead on the ground.

In a little while the storm passed, and Grace regained con-sciousness, only to see Kong dead by her side.

'How can I continue to live,' she sobbed bitterly, 'when he has given his life for me?'

Pine came forward, and the two cousins carried his body into the house. Grace bade Pine lift up Kong's head, while her brother Huangfu prised open his mouth with a golden hairpin. Grace then pinched his cheeks and pressed a red bolus into his mouth with her tongue, pressing her lips to his and pushing the bolus deep into his throat with her breath. There was a gurgling sound as it descended, and a minute later he regained conscious-ness and to his great joy saw his family gathered around him. It was as if he had awoken from a dream.

The place was too desolate for him to be able to settle there, and proposed instead that they should all return with him to his former home. They agreed to this, except for Grace. When Kong saw how downcast she was, he suggested that she should bring her husband with her, but that left the unresolved problem of his parents, who would be loth to be separated from their son. They had been discussing the matter all day, when suddenly a young servant came rushing in from the Wu household, breathless and drenched in perspiration, to announce that the entire Wu family had perished that very day in a natural calamity. Grace was beside herself with grief, and stamped the ground, sobbing inconsolably.

There was nothing now to prevent them from returning with Kong. He made all the necessary arrangements, while they spent several days packing their things. When they reached Kong's home, Huangfu and Grace were installed in a separate compound in the garden, where they kept their gate permanently shut, only opening it for Kong and Pine. Kong joined Huangfu and his sister for occasional games of chess, a cup of wine, a convivial conversation. They were like members of a single family. His son Little Lord grew up into a good-looking young man, always with a touch of the fox about him. Every time he went into town, folk knew he was the son of a fox.

22

A MOST
EXEMPLARY MONK

A man named Zhang died suddenly and was escorted at once by devil attendants into the presence of Yama, King of the Underworld. Yama checked his registers and turned angrily to the attendants, informing them that they had brought the wrong man and were to take him back immediately.

As they left, Zhang secretly entreated his devil guards to let him have a quick look at Hell and they led him all the way through the Nine Dark Places, past the Mountain of Knives and the Forest of Swords, pointing out the various sights one by one. By and by they reached a place where a Buddhist monk was hanging upside down in the air, suspended by a rope through a hole in his leg. He was crying out in excruciating pain. As Zhang approached, he saw to his great horror and distress that the man was his own brother. He asked his guards the reason for this appalling punishment, and they informed him that the monk had been condemned to this torment for having collected alms on behalf of his order, which he had then squandered on gambling and debauchery.

'Nor,' they added, 'will his punishment cease until he repents his misdeeds.'

When Zhang regained consciousness, fearing that his brother must already be dead, he hurried off to the Xingfu Monastery, where he had been in residence. As he went in at the door, he heard a loud shrieking and, on proceeding to his brother's cell, found him upside down, just as he had seen him in Hell, with his legs tied up above him to the wall, and an abscess oozing blood and pus between his thighs. Appalled, he asked him for an explanation, and his brother told him that he was in terrible

僧孽

倒懸觀痛
悲奇疾乾
浸金錢安
在我不生坐
僧能懺悔有
人觀歷九幽未

A Buddhist monk was hanging upside down in the air.

pain and that this was the only position in which the pain was at all bearable.

Zhang now described what he had seen in Hell, and the monk was so terrified that he at once gave up drinking liquor and eating meat, and devoted himself humbly to the recitation of the sutras and mantras of his religion. In a fortnight he was well again, and became known ever afterwards as a most exemplary monk.

23

MAGICAL ARTS

A gentleman by the name of Yu, in his youth a keen member of the sporting fraternity, delighted in boxing and feats of strength and was himself able to dance the whirligig while holding aloft a heavy metal jug in each hand.

During the Chongzhen reign of the former Ming dynasty, Yu was in the capital for the palace examinations when much to his distress his personal servant fell ill and took to his bed. At that time an expert fortune-teller frequented the marketplace, reputed to be capable of determining the span of a man's life with astonishing accuracy, and Yu decided to go and consult this man on his servant's behalf.

Before he had even spoken, the fortune-teller said to him, 'You wish to put a question concerning your servant's illness, do you not?'

'Why, yes!' exclaimed Yu in amazement.

'The servant's illness is nothing serious,' said the fortune-teller. 'But you, sir, are in grave peril.'

Yu asked to have his own fortune told, and the man proceeded to consult the hexagrams of the *Book of Changes*.

'Dear sir,' he exclaimed in a shocked voice, 'you are fated to die three days from now!'

Yu was dumbfounded.

'I do possess a trifling art in this connection,' the fortune-teller went on, unperturbed. 'For ten taels of silver I will undertake to intervene on your behalf.'

Yu, thinking to himself that if the time of one's death had already been determined by fate, such 'trifling' (and rather

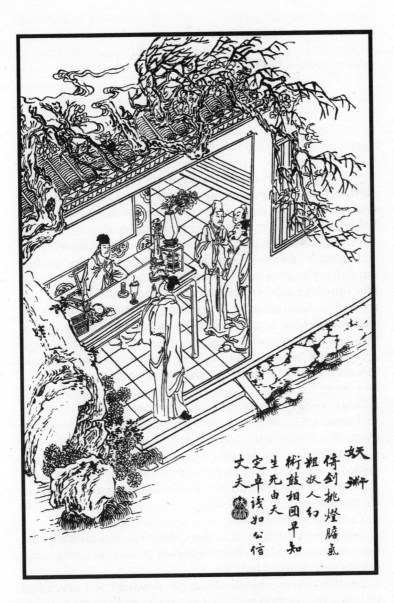

妖術

倚劍挑燈膽氣粗
妖人幻術敢相圖
早知生死由天定
卓詭如公信丈夫

The man consulted the hexagrams of the *Book of Changes.*

expensive) magical arts were probably of no use, rose silently to his feet and made to leave.

'You will regret having denied yourself this petty expense,' commented the fortune-teller.

Yu's friends were anxious on his behalf and urged him to pay whatever the fortune-teller asked, but he ignored their advice. The next two days passed uneventfully, and on the third he sat calmly in his room at the inn, waiting to see what would happen – and nothing did. Night fell, and he closed the door, trimmed his lamp and sat there quietly sword in hand, awaiting whatever fate held in store for him.

The first watch of the night was nearly ended, and there was still no sign of death's approach. He was about to lie down when he heard a rustling sound at the window and, hurriedly looking up, saw a tiny man with a spear on his back enter by the window and alight on the ground, where he grew to ordinary size. Grasping his own sword, Yu leaped to his feet and lunged out at the intruder, but his sword went swishing wide of the mark and meanwhile the man had shrunk in size again and headed for a crack in the window lattice, endeavouring to make good his escape. Yu hacked at him vigorously and finally brought him down. By the light of his lamp he saw the figure of a man cut out of paper, severed at the waist.

Yu now gave up all thought of sleep, and sat in wait. Presently another creature bored its way through a pane of the paper casement, a fearsome-looking, monstrous thing. The instant it touched the ground, Yu struck at it with force, splitting it in two halves, each of which went wriggling away. Fearing it might rise up a second time, he attacked it again and again, each time striking home, his sword ringing loudly with every stroke. Afterwards, looking closely, he saw a clay figure lying on the ground, broken into countless shattered shards.

He now moved his seat to beneath the window and kept his gaze fixed on the crack in the casement. After a while, he heard what sounded like an ox snorting outside, then the sound of something heaving against the window frame. The next thing he knew the whole wall of the room was shaking and seemed about to collapse. Afraid of being buried alive, Yu resolved to go out and fight. He threw open the door with a great swish and rushed out into the night. By the dim light of the moon he made out the figure of a huge ghoul, high as the eaves of the house, its face pitch-black and its eyes glowing with a sinister yellow light. It was naked to the midriff and barefoot, held a bow in its hand and had a clutch of arrows attached to its waist. Yu was still reeling from the shock of seeing this apparition when the ghoul let fly a shower of arrows. Yu fended them off with his sword and they fell to the ground, but when he tried to strike the creature directly, it counter-attacked by letting loose another arrow. Yu jumped to one side, and the arrow drove itself quivering into the wall – much to the fury of the ghoul, which now produced a sword and whirled it around, aiming at Yu's head. Yu ducked with monkey-like agility and the blade struck a stone, splitting it clean in two. Yu now darted between the ghoul's legs and slashed his own sword against its shins with a mighty whack. This enraged the ghoul more than ever, and it emitted a mighty thundering roar and began spinning round and chopping wildly at Yu, who ducked once more between its legs, so that when the monster's blade struck, it did no more than slice off a part of his robe. Yu now moved close up against the monster's ribs and dealt them a hefty thwack. The creature slumped to the ground and lay there. Yu continued to strike blow after blow at it, each one ringing into the night like a watchman's wooden clapper. Eventually he held high his lamp and beheld before him a man-sized wooden puppet, decorated in the most terrifying fashion, the arrows still tied at its waist. Blood was flowing from every place where his sword had struck.

Yu sat there until dawn, lamp in hand, knowing that each one of the three monsters had been sent against him by the fortune-teller, who was determined to prove his clairvoyant powers, even if it meant killing him in order to do so.

The next day, he told the story to all his friends, and some of them went with him to the fortune-teller's house. But the man had seen them coming, and had vanished into thin air.

'He is using a spell of invisibility,' said one of Yu's friends. 'But we can break it with dog's blood.'

Yu went again, armed this time with the blood of a dog, and when the fortune-teller vanished just as before, Yu acted quickly, smearing the dog's blood on the ground where the man had been standing. He saw him now, standing there, his head and face smeared with the dog's blood, his eyes blazing like those of some fearsome monster. They seized him and hauled him before the Magistrate, who had him put to death.

24
WILD DOG

During the rebellion led by Yu Qi, men died in countless numbers, mown down like fields of hemp. At this time, a peasant by the name of Li Hualong was trying to find his way home through the hills when he came across a detachment of government troops on a night march. Afraid of being rounded up indiscriminately as a bandit, and seeing nowhere to hide, he lay down in a heap of decapitated corpses, pretending to be dead himself and staying there until long after the troops had passed.

Then suddenly he saw the corpses, for the most part headless and armless, stand up in serried ranks like trees in a forest. One among them, his head still dangling from his shoulders, gasped, 'The wild dog is coming! We are done for!'

The others answered in a ragged chorus, 'Done for! Done for!'

The next instant, they all tumbled down again and lay there in motionless silence. Li was about to rise to his feet (trembling with fear though he was), when he saw a creature coming towards him, with the head of an animal and the body of a man. As the 'wild dog' came nearer, it bent down, sank its teeth into one after another of the heads and sucked out their brains. In terror, Li buried his own head under the nearest corpse. The monster tugged at Li's shoulder to get at his head, but Li burrowed down still further and succeeded for a while in staying out of its reach, until finally the monster pushed the corpse aside, thus exposing Li's head.

The terrified Li, groping around desperately on the ground beneath him, grabbed hold of a big stone the size of a bowl and

野狗

郊原殺氣慘陰霾
白骨縱橫孰掩埋
試聽同穀愁楚狗
可知鬼亦愛遺骸

Li buried his own head under the nearest corpse.

clutched it tightly in his hand. As the creature bent down to bite into him, he heaved himself up and with a great cry smashed the stone into its mouth. The thing made an odd hooting noise like an owl and ran off clutching its face and spitting mouthfuls of blood on to the road. In the blood, Li discovered, when he looked more closely, two fangs, curved and tapering to a sharp point, each over four inches long. He took them home with him to show his friends, none of whom had any idea what sort of a strange beast it might have been.

25

PAST LIVES

A certain Mr Liu, a second-degree graduate of the same year as my father's cousin Pu Wengui, had the ability to remember his various past lives, and was able to relate them in some detail.

In one of these lives, he had been born into a family of scholar-gentlemen, and had died at the age of sixty-two, having led a somewhat dissolute life. When he came face to face with the King of Hell, he was at first received with the normal respect due to a provincial notable, shown to a seat and offered a cup of tea. He noticed, however, that the tea in the King's cup was clear, while his own cup contained a cloudy liquid, like unstrained liquor. Was this, he wondered, the fabled Soup of Oblivion, the potion given to the spirits of the dead to render them oblivious of their past? While the King was looking the other way, he emptied his cup on the floor, pretending afterwards that he had drunk it all up. The next moment, the King, who had been perusing the record of the various misdeeds committed during Liu's life on earth, flew into a great rage and ordered his assembled demons to take Liu away, sentencing him to reincarnation as a horse. Liu was immediately seized and bound, and the demons carried him off to a building, the door-sill of which was so high that he was unable to step over it. He hesitated at the sill, and the demons behind him lashed him with all their might, causing him such pain that he stumbled forward and collapsed unconscious on the ground. When he came to, he saw that he was lying in a stable and heard a voice crying, 'The black mare has foaled!' Everything was clear to him, but he could say nothing. The next he knew he was dreadfully hungry, and for lack of any other source of food

六道輪迴
悲墮落三
生因果說
分明非閻
麥馬成奇
癖記浮前
身伏櫎情

三生

He emptied his cup on the floor.

began sucking at the mare's teats. Four or five years went by, and he grew into a fine strong horse but always remained at heart a fearful animal, terrified of the whip, the very sight of which sent him running away. His considerate master, when he rode him, always used a saddle-cloth, kept the reins loose and went at a leisurely pace, which he found more or less bearable. But the servants and grooms rode him bareback, squeezing his flanks and digging their heels into him, which caused him a searing pain in his insides. At length he could stand it no longer, refused all food, and three days later he was dead.

He duly reappeared before the King of Hell, who, upon discovering that he had deliberately tried to escape his fate before his time was due, had him flayed and condemned to reincarnation as a dog. He stood there looking most woebegone and refusing to move, whereupon the demons came behind him and lashed him until he was in such pain that he ran away from them and out into the open country. Thinking he would be better off dead, he jumped off a cliff and plunged to the ground, where he lay quite unable to move.

It was then he became aware that he was lying in a hole in the earth, one of a litter of puppies, and that an old bitch was licking and suckling him by turns. He was back in the world of the living. As he grew up, he knew in his mind that his own excrement was a foul thing, even though it somehow smelt fragrant to his senses. He made a firm resolve not to eat it. Several years he lived the life of a dog, always wishing he could find a way to die, but afraid that if he took his own life again he would be punished a second time for having cut his sentence short. Once again his master was kind to him, fed him well and was certainly not the type to think of ever putting him down. In the end he deliberately bit the man and tore off a piece of his leg, causing him to fly into a sudden rage and beat him to death.

This time, when the King of Hell checked the records and read of the dog's savage behaviour, he sentenced him angrily to several hundred strokes of the rattan and to reincarnation as a snake. At first he was confined in a dark room, from which it was impossible to see the sky. After a while he managed to climb his way up the wall, made a hole in the roof and escaped.

He found himself lying in the long grass, and it was then he knew that he was a snake. He took an oath not to harm a living thing, and to assuage his pangs of hunger with a diet of nothing but plants and fruits. A year went by, and many a time he thought of taking his own life, but knew he could not. Nor could he deliberately harm someone else in order to get himself killed. He had already suffered the consequences of these two stratagems. He spent his days longing for a good way to die, but nothing presented itself. And then one day he was sleeping in the grass, when he heard the noise of an oncoming cart, darted out into its path and was chopped in two by the wheels.

The King of Hell was astonished to see him back again so soon. But this time when he told his story, grovelling humbly on the ground, the King pardoned him, as an innocent creature that had lost its life by mischance, and permitted him to be reincarnated as a human being. And so he was born into the Liu family, and graduated in the same year as my father's cousin.

He was able to speak perfectly formed words the moment he came into the world, and as a child he was a prodigy, able to repeat anything by heart at a single reading – an essay, or an extract from one of the histories. He took his degree in the year *xinyou*. He was forever urging people to put proper saddle-cloths on their horses, and telling them how excruciatingly painful it was for a horse to have the rider dig in his knees, more painful by far than being whipped.

26

FOX IN THE BOTTLE

A woman of the Shi family in Wan Village was possessed by a fox-spirit. She suffered greatly, but was unable to get rid of it.

Behind the house was a bottle, and whenever the fox heard the woman's husband coming home, it would disappear and hide in this bottle. The woman made a note of this and formed a secret plan, which she mentioned to no one.

One day when the fox was hiding in the bottle, she plugged the mouth of the bottle with cotton wadding, then placed it in a big pot, poured in some water and brought it to the boil, fox and all.

'It's dreadfully hot in here!' cried the fox, as the temperature mounted. 'Stop this nonsense at once!'

The woman said nothing. The screams from within the bottle grew louder and louder, and then suddenly there was silence. She removed the stopper and looked inside the bottle. All she could see was a mess of fur and a few drops of blood.

狐入瓶

子避人何舍
婦翁避人常
斂形常小瓶中
豈知一旦罹
湯火入甕真
教酷吏同

She plugged the mouth of the bottle with cotton wadding.

27

WAILING GHOSTS

At the time of the Xie Qian troubles in Shandong, the great residences of the nobility were all commandeered by the rebels. The mansion of Education Commissioner Wang Qixiang accommodated a particularly large number of them. When the government troops eventually retook the town and massacred the rebels, every porch was strewn with corpses. Blood flowed from every doorway.

When Commissioner Wang returned, he gave orders that all the corpses were to be removed from his home and the blood washed away, so that he could once more take up residence. In the days that followed, he frequently saw ghosts in broad daylight, and during the night ghostly will-o'-the-wisp flickerings of light beneath his bed. He heard the voices of ghosts wailing in various corners of the house.

One day, a young gentleman by the name of Wang Gaodi who had come to stay with the Commissioner heard a little voice crying beneath his bed, 'Gaodi! Gaodi!'

Then the voice grew louder. 'I died a cruel death!'

The voice began sobbing, and was soon joined by ghosts throughout the house.

The Commissioner himself heard it and came with his sword.

'Do you not know who I am?' he declared loudly. 'I am Education Commissioner Wang.'

The ghostly voices merely sneered at this and laughed through their noses, whereupon the Commissioner gave orders for a lengthy ritual to be immediately performed for all departed souls on land and sea, in the course of which Buddhist bonzes and Taoist priests prayed for the liberation of his supernatural

妖宅

仗劍大呼互學院百聲
噬芙鬼揶揄榮。
燐火歸何求草道
瑜珈事從誣

The Commissioner came with his sword.

tenants from their torments. That night they put out food for the ghosts, and will-o'-the-wisp lights could be seen flickering across the ground.

Now before any of these events, a gate-man, also named Wang, had fallen gravely ill, and had been lying unconscious for several days. The night of the ritual he suddenly seemed to regain consciousness, and stretched his limbs. When his wife brought him some food, he said to her, 'The Master put some food out in the courtyard – I've no idea why! Anyway I was out there eating with the others, and I've only just finished, so I'm not that hungry.'

From that day, the hauntings ceased.

Does this mean that the banging of cymbals and gongs, the beating of bells and drums, and other esoteric practices for the release of wandering souls are necessarily efficacious?

28

THUMB AND THIMBLE

In the region of Zhending County, there lived an orphaned girl who at the age of six or seven was adopted into another family as a child-bride.

She had lived with them a year or two when her husband tricked her into having sexual relations with him and made her pregnant. Her stomach swelled up, and thinking she must be ill she went to see her foster-mother.

'Does it move?' the woman asked.

'It does,' was the girl's honest reply.

The foster-mother was greatly astonished, but considering how young the girl was, she was loth to jump to conclusions or pass judgement.

Not long afterwards the girl gave birth to a boy.

'Well I never!' sighed the foster-mother. 'A thumb-sized mother has brought a thimble-sized baby into the world!'

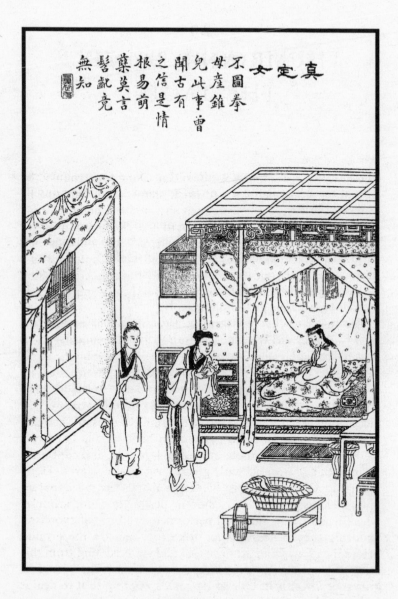

真定女

不圖拳
母產錐
兒此事曾
之信是情
聞古有
根易萌
藥莫言
鬢亂竟
醫無知

A thimble-sized baby!

29

SCORCHED MOTH
THE TAOIST

The household of Hanlin Academician Dong was troubled by fox-spirits. Tiles, pebbles and brick shards were liable to fly around the house like hailstones at any moment, and his family and household were forever having to take shelter and wait for the disturbances to abate before they dared carry on with their daily duties. Dong himself was so affected by this state of affairs that he rented a residence belonging to Under-Secretary Sun, and moved there to avoid his troubles. But the fox-spirits merely followed him.

One day when he was on duty at court and described this strange phenomenon to his colleagues, a senior minister mentioned a certain Taoist master from the north-east by the name of Jiao Ming – Scorched Moth – who lived in the Inner Manchu City and issued exorcist spells and talismans reputed for their efficacy. Dong paid the man a personal call and requested his aid, whereupon the Master wrote out some charms in cinnabar-red ink and told Dong to paste them on his wall. The foxes were unperturbed by these measures, however, and continued to hurl things around with greater vigour than ever. Dong reported back to the Taoist, who was angered by this apparent failure of his charms and came in person to Dong's house, where he set up an altar and performed a full rite of exorcism. Suddenly they beheld a huge fox crouching on the ground before the altar. Dong's household had suffered long from this creature's antics, and the servants felt a deep-seated sense of grievance towards it. One of the maids went up to it to deal it a blow, only to fall dead to the ground.

'This is a vicious beast!' exclaimed the Taoist. 'Even I could

焦螟

壇前狐已現真
形壇側奄奄然
婢未醒借口
鞠供良久得
閩東道士術
倡靈

The fox shrank back fearfully, indicating his submission.

not subdue it! This girl was very foolish to provoke it.' He continued, 'Nonetheless, we can now use *her* to question the fox.'

Pointing his index finger and middle finger at the maid, he
pronounced certain spells, and suddenly she rose from the
ground and knelt before him. The Taoist asked her where she
hailed from.

'I come from the Western Regions,' replied the maid, in a
voice that was clearly not her own but that of the fox. 'We have
been here in the capital for eighteen generations.'

'How dare creatures such as you dwell in the proximity of
His Imperial Majesty? Off with you at once!'

The fox-voice was silent, and the Taoist thumped the altar-
table angrily. 'How dare you disobey my orders? Delay a
moment longer, and my magic powers will work on you
harshly!'

The fox shrank back fearfully, indicating his submission, and
the Taoist urged him once more to be gone. Meanwhile the
maid had fallen to the ground again, dead to the world. It was
a long while before she regained consciousness.

All of a sudden they saw four or five white lumps of some
strange substance go bouncing like balls one after the other
along the eaves of the building, until they were all gone. Then
peace finally reigned in the Dong household.

30

FRIENDSHIP BEYOND
THE GRAVE

There was a gentleman of Huaiyang by the name of Ye. (His other names I cannot recall.) He was acknowledged by his contemporaries to be a master of prose and verse composition, but had been unlucky and had never yet succeeded in his first-degree examination.

Now a certain Ding Chenghe – Crane Rider – who hailed from the north-east was appointed Magistrate in Ye's district and, happening to read one of his essays, was most struck by the beauty of his prose. He summoned him and in the course of conversation found himself taking an immediate liking to him. He invited him to come and continue his studies in the official yamen, and provided him with a regular stipend and occasional gifts of money and grain to support his family. When it came to the time for the preliminary examination, Ding spoke highly of Ye to the Examiner, and as a result he was ranked among the most promising candidates.

After the first-degree examination proper, Magistrate Ding, who had entertained the highest hopes for Ye, obtained his draft essay and was ecstatic in its praise. But for some reason fate was against Ye yet again, however fine his essay may have been. When the results were posted, his name was nowhere to be seen on the list, and he made his way home a hugely disappointed man, full of remorse at having failed his friend and patron in this manner. He began to waste away and became as listless and dead to the world as a wooden puppet.

Magistrate Ding heard of this and summoned him to the yamen, where he did his best to console the young man, who wept without ceasing. Ding felt sorry for him and by way of consolation offered to take him along with him when he next went up to the capital for his own triennial review. Ye was most grateful to him for his solicitude, but bade him fare-well and returned home, where he shut himself away, refused to go out and in a short while fell seriously ill. Ding sent a string of messengers to inquire about his health, and pre-vailed upon Ye to take countless sorts of medicine, but all to no effect.

In the meantime, Ding himself was dismissed for some offence caused to a superior, and made up his mind to abandon his official career altogether and retire to the country. He wrote in a letter to Ye:

'I had already chosen a day to return to my home in the north-east, but shall postpone my departure to await your recovery. As soon as you are well, come to me, and we shall leave together the same evening.'

This message was brought to Ye's bedside, and when he read it, Ye wept profusely. His reply was brief, couched in the following terms:

'My illness is a serious and obstinate one. Please set off without me.'

The servant returned with this message, but Ding still refused to leave on his own, and waited. Several days later, his gate-man announced the arrival of Mr Ye, and Ding hurried out joyfully to greet him, asking anxiously after his health.

'Alas, this wretched ailment of mine has delayed you far too long, sir,' said Ye apologetically. 'But now at last I can accompany you.'

So Ding packed his bags and set off with Ye at first light the next morning.

When they reached Ding's native village, he instructed his own son to treat Ye with the greatest respect and to regard him as his teacher, waiting upon him and constantly keeping him company. The son's name was Zaichang, and he was at the time sixteen years old. He had not yet acquired a proficiency in the prevalent rhetorical techniques of the Eight-Legged Essay, although he was a youth of exceptional promise, and had only to read through a piece of prose a couple of times to memorize it perfectly. A year later, under Ye's expert tutelage, he was writing fluent compositions of his own and, thanks to his father's influence, was accepted into the District Academy. Ye copied out all his own best essays for young Ding to study, and the youth was able as a result to answer all of the seven questions in his examination papers and was listed second overall.

Ding the elder spoke to Ye. 'You have imparted to my son sufficient knowledge for him to succeed in his examinations. But you yourself, the fount of this knowledge, are still denied the success you deserve. This is indeed a sorry state of affairs!'

'It is simply the work of fate,' replied Ye. 'Thanks to our friendship and the good fortune it has brought me, I have at least been able to put my humble accomplishments to some good purpose. That is a consolation. And your son's success will at least show the world that my own dismal failure in life has not been due to a complete lack of talent. I am content with that. To have one true friend is enough for me. Why should I strive for worldly success?'

Ding was anxious that by keeping Ye too long a guest in his house he would prevent him from attending the next examination in his own home district, and urged him to return home for this purpose. Ye seemed most unhappy at the idea of leaving, and Ding did not insist but instead instructed his son to purchase for Ye the rank of membership in the Imperial College once he was in the capital, since this would entitle Ye to sit directly for the second degree. Ding junior duly succeeded in the metropolitan examinations, and immediately upon receiving the post of Secretary in one of the Boards, he arranged for Ye to be admitted to the Imperial College, and kept him company there day and night.

A year later, Ye himself finally sat the examinations in the capital and was awarded the full status of second-degree graduate. At the same time young Ding was ordered to go on a tour of duty to Henan Province.

'I shall be not far from your home town,' he said to Ye. 'This would surely be an excellent chance for you to return home and celebrate your own recent success.'

Ye was delighted at this idea, and together they selected a propitious day for the journey. On reaching the area of Huaiyang, young Ding sent servants and horses to escort Ye home. He arrived to find the house dilapidated and desolate, and, entering with some hesitation, encountered his wife just as she was coming out with her winnowing basket. When she set eyes on Ye, she dropped her basket and recoiled in horror.

'I am greatly changed, I know,' said Ye sadly. 'Now I have become a person of rank. But surely you recognize me, even if we have not seen each other for more than three years?'

'You have been dead this long while!' replied his wife from a safe distance. 'How can you talk of rank? We have not even been able to give you a proper burial! We were too poor to do so, and our little boy was too young to deal with such things. Now the boy is older and ready to take his place in the world. He will see to it that a grave-site is chosen in the proper way. I beseech you not to come and haunt us!'

This plea brought an expression of great sorrow to Ye's face. He walked hesitantly into the house, and there he saw his own coffin as plain as could be. He fell straight to the ground and melted into thin air before the eyes of his bewildered wife, leaving his gown, cap and shoes strewn on the ground like fragments of a discarded cocoon. Distraught with grief, the wife gathered the clothes up in her arms before abandoning herself to a fit of weeping. Presently their son came home from school, and seeing the horses tethered at the gate, inquired why they had come. Rushing in to tell his mother that they had a distinguished visitor, he found her brushing away her tears. She told him what she had just witnessed, and together they questioned the servants who had accompanied Ye, from whom they learned the full story.

The servants returned to their master, and when they told young Ding what had transpired he shed bitter tears and sent for a horse and carriage to take him to Ye's home, to mourn for him there. He provided money for the funeral expenses, and Ye was buried with the honours due to a second-degree graduate. Young Ding also provided generously for

She dropped her basket and recoiled in horror.

Ye's son, engaging a tutor for him and recommending him to the Examiner. A year later, he passed the first-degree examination.

31

KARMIC DEBTS

A prominent mandarin named Wang Xianqian, of Xincheng, had a steward who was very comfortably off. One day, this steward dreamed that a man rushed into the house and said to him, 'Today you must pay me back those forty strings of cash you owe me.'

The steward asked him who he was, but the man made no answer and hurried past him into the inner apartments.

The steward awoke, to learn that his wife had given birth to a son, and he knew at once that this child was a karmic retribution, his 'payment' of a debt contracted in a previous life. He duly set aside forty strings of cash, the sum specified in his dream, and used it to buy whatever food, clothes and medicines the baby might need.

By the time the boy was three or four years old, the steward found that of the forty strings (forty thousand coins all told), there remained no more than seven hundred coins. One day, when the wet-nurse came by and played with the child before his eyes, the steward merely looked at him and exclaimed, 'The forty strings are nearly spent. It is time you were on your way.'

The words were no sooner spoken than the child pulled a strange face, his head fell back and his eyes opened in a glassy stare. They tried to revive him, but without success. The father used the balance of the forty strings to pay for a coffin, and buried him.

This should be a warning to people with unpaid debts.

*

The wet-nurse came by with the child.

A childless old man once consulted an eminent monk on this same subject.

'You owe nothing,' said the monk, 'and are owed nothing: in such circumstances, how can you expect to have a child?'

A good son is the repayment of a debt due to his parents, the result of good karma; a bad, wilful child is a creditor come for his money, a bad karmic debt. The birth of a child should not be cause for joy, nor should the death of a child be cause for sorrow.

32

RITUAL CLEANSING

A certain Taoist priest who lived in the Chaotian Temple was an adept of the old breathing-yoga known as *tu-na*, 'breathing in the new, and breathing out the old'. An old gentleman also lodged in the same temple, and since the two of them shared the same interest in self-cultivation, they had become firm friends. The old man, who had lived there for several years, always went away ten days before the seasonal ceremonies to Heaven and Earth were due to be performed, and never returned until they were over. His regular absences puzzled the Taoist, and one day he asked him for an explanation.

'There should be no secrets between friends such as ourselves,' said the old man, 'so I will tell you the truth. I am a fox-spirit. When they hold those big ceremonies, unclean spirits like foxes are all exorcized. So I have to go somewhere else.'

The following year, he left as he always did, but this time there was a longer interval than usual before he returned. His Taoist friend thought it strange and questioned him again.

'This time you nearly saw the last of me!' replied the old man. 'I meant to get well away, but somehow I was feeling too lazy, so I thought I'd be safe sneaking under that big vat at the back, the one they use to cover the drain outlet. It seemed a good enough hiding place. But I was unlucky. One of the Spirit Guardians came to that very spot to cleanse it, and when he saw me he attacked me angrily with his whip. I fled in terror, but he chased me all the way to the Yellow River. He was just about to catch up with me, and in sheer desperation I threw myself into a cesspit. That was too disgusting for the Guardian, and he turned back. When I pulled myself out of the cesspit,

靈官

郊天鉅典軏
能干藩涸潛
踪膳尚寒
甲竟此孤
太分曉
乘興不
避避
靈官

'One of the Spirit Guardians attacked me with his whip.'

I absolutely stank, I was much too foul to return to humanity. First I jumped in some water to clean myself up, then I stayed underground for months, waiting for the filth and the stench to wear off. Today I have come to say goodbye, and to give you a warning. Leave this place. Take refuge somewhere else. A great disaster is on its way. This is not a good place to be.'

And with these words he left. The Taoist took his advice and went elsewhere. Sure enough, before long the troubles of the last days of the Ming dynasty began.

33

THE DOOR GOD
AND THE THIEF

The Temple of the Eastern Sacred Mountain is situated in the southern outskirts of the city of Ji'nan. On either side of the main entrance stand Door Gods over ten feet high, terrifying statues, popularly known as the Eagle and the Tiger.

There was a Taoist by the name of Ren living in the temple, who used to rise every morning at cockcrow and go to burn incense and recite his scriptures. Now, one day, a thief hid himself in the cloister and waited for the Taoist to rise before sneaking into his cell and rifling through his things. To his disappointment, there was nothing of value there, save three hundred copper coins that he found beneath the priest's mat. These he pocketed, loosened the door bar and made off, heading towards the slopes of Thousand Buddha Mountain. He had walked southward some way into the foothills, when he saw a strapping great fellow descending the mountain towards him, with a goshawk perched on his left shoulder. Coming closer, he observed the man's face, which was swarthy and dark as copper, and noticed a striking resemblance between him and one of the temple's Door Gods. He fell to his knees, trembling in terror. The spirit reproached him, 'Where are you off to with that stolen money?'

More terrified than ever, the thief kowtowed frantically. The Door God took hold of him and led him back to the temple, where he made him put the money on the floor of the monk's cell and left him there kneeling beside it. The Taoist, having finished his prayers, returned to his cell and was astonished to find the man there. The thief told him the whole story, and the Taoist took the money and sent him on his way.

鷹常神

神名鷹師竟何由解
使偷兒返自投三百
青錢原細事只惶
道士告焚修

A strapping fellow with a goshawk perched on his left shoulder.

34

THE PAINTED SKIN

A certain gentleman by the name of Wang, from the city of Tai-yuan, was out walking early one morning when a young woman passed him carrying a bundle, hurrying along on her own, though with considerable difficulty. He caught up with her, and saw at once that she was a girl of about sixteen, and very beautiful.

'What are you doing out here all alone at this early hour?' he asked, instantly smitten.

'Why do you bother to ask, since you are only a passer-by and can do nothing to ease my troubles?' was her reply.

'Tell me, what has caused this sorrow of yours? I will do anything I can to help you.'

'My parents were greedy for money,' she replied sadly, 'and sold me as a concubine into a rich man's household. The master's wife was jealous of me, and she was always screaming at me and beating me, until in the end I could bear it no longer and decided to run away.'

'Where are you going?'

'I am a fugitive. I have no place to go.'

'My own humble abode is not far from here,' said Wang. 'I should be honoured if you were to accompany me there.'

She seemed only too pleased at this suggestion and followed him home, Wang carrying her bundle for her. When they arrived, she observed that the house was empty.

'Do you have no family of your own?' she asked.

'This is my private study,' he replied.

'It seems an excellent place to me,' she said. 'But I must ask you to keep my presence here a secret and not to breathe a word of it to anyone. My very life depends on it.'

He swore to this.

That night they slept together, and for several days he kept her hidden in his study without anyone knowing that she was there. Then he decided to confide in his wife, the lady Chen. She feared the consequences if the girl should turn out to have escaped from some influential family, and advised him to send her away. But he paid no heed to her advice.

A few days later, in the marketplace, Wang ran into a Taoist priest, who studied his face with grave concern. 'What strange thing have you encountered?'

'Why, nothing!' replied Wang.

'Nothing? Your whole being is wrapped in an evil aura,' insisted the Taoist. 'I tell you, you are bewitched!'

Wang protested vehemently that he was speaking the truth.

'Bewitched!' muttered the Taoist, as he went on his way. 'Poor fool! Some men blind themselves to the truth even when death is staring them in the face!'

Something in the Taoist's strange words set Wang wondering, and he began to have serious misgivings about the young woman he had taken in. But he could not bring himself to believe that such a pretty young thing could have cast an evil spell on him. Instead he persuaded himself that the Taoist was making it all up, trying to put the wind up him in the hope of being retained for a costly rite of exorcism. And so he put the matter out of his mind and returned home.

He reached his study to find the outer door barred. He was unable to enter his own home. His suspicions now genuinely aroused, he clambered into the courtyard through a hole in the wall, only to find that the inner door was also closed. Creeping stealthily up to a window, he peeped through and saw the most hideous sight, a green-faced monster, a ghoul with great jagged teeth like a saw, leaning over a human pelt, the skin of an entire human body, spread on the bed – on *his* bed. The monster had a paintbrush in its hand and was in the process of touching up the skin in lifelike colour. When the painting was done, it threw down the brush, lifted up the skin, shook it out like a cloak and wrapped itself in it – whereupon it was instantly transformed into his pretty young 'fugitive' friend.

He peeped through and saw the most hideous sight.

Wang was absolutely terrified by what he had seen, and crept away on all fours. He went at once in search of the Taoist, but did not know where to find him. He looked for him everywhere and eventually found him out in the fields. Falling on his knees, he begged the priest to save him.

'I can drive her away for you,' said the Taoist. 'But I cannot bring myself to take her life. The poor creature must have suffered greatly and is clearly close to finding a substitute and thus ending her torment.'

He gave Wang a fly-whisk and told him to hang it outside his bedroom door, instructing him to come and find him again in the Temple of the Green Emperor.

Wang returned home. This time he did not dare to go into his study, but slept with his wife, hanging the fly-whisk outside their bedroom. Late that night he heard a faint sound at the door, and not having the courage to look himself, he asked his wife to go. It was the 'girl'. She had come, but had halted on seeing the fly-whisk and was standing there grinding her teeth. Eventually she went away, only to return after a little while.

'That priest thought to scare me!' she cried. 'I'll never give up! Not now, not when I am so close! Does he think I'm going to spit it out, when I'm so near to swallowing it!'

She tore down the fly-whisk and ripped it to pieces, then broke down the door and burst into the bedroom. Climbing straight up on to the bed, she tore open Wang's chest, plucked out his heart and made off with it into the night. Wang's wife began screaming, and a maid came hurrying with a lamp, to find her master lying dead on the bed, his chest a bloody pulp, and her mistress sobbing in silent horror beside him, incapable of uttering a word.

The next morning, they sent Wang's younger brother off at once to find the Taoist.

'To think that I took pity on her!' cried the priest angrily. 'Clearly that fiend will stop at nothing!'

He followed Wang's brother back to the house. By now, of course, there was no trace of the 'girl'. The Taoist gazed around him. 'Fortunately she is still close at hand.'

He went on to ask, 'Who lives in the house to the south?'

'That is my family compound,' replied Wang's brother.

'That is where she is now,' said the priest.

Wang's brother was appalled at the idea and could not bring himself to believe it.

'Has a stranger come to your house today?' asked the priest.

'How would I know?' replied the brother. 'I went out first thing to the Temple of the Green Emperor to fetch you. I shall have to go home and ask.'

Presently he returned to report that there had indeed been an old lady. 'She called first thing this morning, saying she wanted to work for us. My wife kept her on, and she is still there.'

'That's the very person we're looking for!' cried the Taoist. He strode next door immediately with the brother, and took up a stance in the middle of the courtyard, brandishing his wooden sword.

'Come out, evil one!' he cried. 'Give me back my fly-whisk!'

The old woman came hurtling out of the building, her face deathly pale, and made a frantic attempt to escape, but the Taoist pursued her and struck her down. As she fell to the ground the human pelt slipped from her, to reveal her as the vile fiend she really was, grovelling on the ground and grunting like a pig. The Taoist swung his wooden sword again and chopped off the monster's head, whereupon its body was transformed into a thick cloud of smoke hovering above the ground. The Taoist now took out a bottle-gourd, removed the stopper and placed it in the midst of the smoke. With a whooshing sound the smoke was sucked into the gourd, leaving no trace in the courtyard. He replaced the stopper and slipped the gourd back into his bag.

When they examined the pelt, it was complete in every human detail – the eyes, the hands and feet. The Taoist proceeded to roll it up like a scroll (it even made the same sound), placed it in his bag and set off. Wang's wife, who was waiting for him at the entrance, beseeched him to bring her husband back to life, and when the Taoist protested that he had already reached the limits of his powers, she became more and more hysterical and inconsolable, throwing herself on the ground and absolutely refusing to get up. The Taoist seemed to ponder the matter deeply.

'Truly, I cannot raise the dead,' he said eventually. 'But I can tell you of one who may be able to do so. Go to him, ask him, and I dare say he will be able to help you.'

Wang's wife asked him whom he was referring to.

'He is a madman who frequents the marketplace and sleeps on a dunghill. You must go down on your knees and beg him to help you. If he insults you, madam, you must on no account go against him or be angry with him.'

Wang's brother knew of this beggar. He took his leave of the Taoist, and accompanied his sister-in-law to the marketplace, where they found the man begging by the roadside, singing a crazy song. A good three inches of mucus trailed from his nose, and he was so foul it was unthinkable to go near him. But Wang's wife approached him on her knees.

'Do you love me, my pretty?' leered the mad beggar.

She told him her tale, and he laughed loudly.

'There's plenty of fine men in this world for you to marry! Why bother bringing *him* back to life?'

She pleaded with him.

'You're a strange one!' he said. 'You want me to raise the dead? Who do you take me for – the King of Hell?'

He struck her with his stick and she bore it without a murmur. By now quite a crowd had gathered around them. The beggar spat a great gob of phlegm into the palm of his hand and held it up to her mouth.

'Eat!'

She flushed deeply and could not bring herself to obey his order. Then she remembered what the Taoist had commanded and steeled herself to swallow the congealed phlegm. As it went down her throat it felt hard like a lump of cotton wadding, and even when, after several gulps, she managed to swallow it down, she could still feel it lodged in her chest. The madman guffawed.

'You really do love me then, don't you, my darling?'

And with those words, off he went. The meeting was clearly over, and he paid her no further attention. She followed him into the temple, determined to plead with him again, but though she searched every corner of the temple, she could find no trace of him. So she returned home, greatly downcast, filled with grief at her husband's appalling death, and overcome with shame and self-disgust at the treatment she had tolerated from the mad beggar. She wailed pathetically and for a time contemplated taking her own life.

When eventually she went to wash the blood from her husband's corpse and prepare it for the coffin, her women stood to one side watching, none of them having the stomach to approach their dead master's corpse. She lifted him up in her arms and started carefully replacing his internal organs, sobbing so fiercely that she began to choke and feel nauseous. Then she felt the lump of phlegm rising in her gullet and brought it up, so suddenly that she had no time to turn away, but spat it directly into the gaping wound in her husband's chest. She stared aghast: the phlegm had become a human heart and lay there throbbing, hot and steaming. In disbelief, she brought the sides of the wound together with both her hands, pressing with all her strength. If she relaxed her grip for an instant, she saw hot steam leaking from the wound. She tore a strip of silk from her dress and bound the wound tightly. In a little while, when she touched her husband's corpse, she felt the warmth returning. She drew the bedcovers fully over it. In the middle of the night when she lifted the covers, he was already breathing through his nose. By the next morning, he was fully alive.

'I was drifting,' he said. 'Everything was confused. It was like a dream. But all the time I felt this pain deep in my heart.'

The wound formed a scar the size of a coin, which disappeared with time.

35

THE MERCHANT'S SON

In the southern region of China known anciently as Chu, there lived a merchant who was often away from home on business, leaving his wife much on her own. During one of his absences she awoke from a dream of a sexual encounter, and feeling around her sure enough discovered a little man in her bed. There was something strange about him that betrayed him at once as a fox-spirit. After a little while, he climbed down from the bed and disappeared from sight, without even needing to open the door.

The next evening, when she went to bed, she asked her old cook to keep her company. She also asked her ten-year-old son, who usually slept in a separate bed, to come and sleep next to her. Late that night, when both cook and boy were fast asleep, the fox came again, and the merchant's wife mumbled something, as if she were talking in her sleep. This woke the cook, who called out to her mistress, whereupon the fox went away.

All the following day, the wife seemed somehow distracted, not her normal self at all. When night fell, she left her lamp alight and told her son to try not to sleep too soundly. Nonetheless, in the small hours, both cook and boy dozed off for a spell with their faces turned to the wall, and when they awoke the lady was nowhere to be seen. They imagined she must have gone out to relieve herself, but when they had waited a long while and there was still no sign of her, they began to have misgivings. The cook was too scared to go out and look, so the boy took the lamp and went searching everywhere for his mother. Eventually he found her lying stark naked on the floor in one of the other rooms of the house. When he went to help her up, she seemed not in the least ashamed of her nakedness.

From that day on, she became quite unhinged in her mind and took to singing, wailing, cursing and howling at all hours of the day and night. She now refused to have anyone with her at night. She insisted on sleeping apart from her son and sent the cook away as well. If her son heard laughter or voices coming from his mother's room, he would rise from his bed immediately and go in with a light. All he ever received for this was an angry scolding, which he accepted without a murmur. The members of the household thought him a plucky boy.

Then he started playing at being a builder, constructing piles of bricks and stones on the window-sills of his mother's room, which everyone thought was exceedingly naughty and strange. His elders tried to stop him, but he paid them no heed, and if anyone tried to take away one of his stones, he would hurl himself on the ground and scream like a baby – so they were reluctant to cross him.

After a few days of this, both his mother's windows were completely bricked up, and not a ray of sunlight could find its way into her bedroom. Next he plastered over the slightest chink in the walls with mud, working at it flat out all day. And when that job was finished, he busied himself sharpening the kitchen choppers, rubbing the blades noisily backwards and forwards, exasperating everyone in the process.

One night, the boy hid one of the choppers in his shirt and shaded his bedroom lamp with a gourd. He lay awake waiting for his mother's strange nocturnal mutterings to begin, and when they did, rushed in with his lamp uncovered, blocking the doorway and yelling at the top of his voice. A few minutes went by and nothing happened. Then just as he stepped away from the door and loudly announced his intention of searching the room, suddenly out rushed a creature resembling a fox and made straight for the open door. The boy struck it smartly with the chopper, and removed about two inches of its tail. He could see the blood dripping on to the floor. When he lifted his lamp to look around him more closely, his mother began abusing him, but he took no notice. He finally went back to his bed and fell asleep, his only regret being that he had not been able to hit the creature fair and square. But he reflected that, although he had failed to kill it, he had probably deterred it from coming again in a hurry.

The next morning, he followed the trail of blood, which led over the wall and into the garden of the neighbouring Ho family. That night, although to his great joy the fox did not reappear in his mother's room, his mother herself lay there prostrate, delirious and seemingly at death's door.

Shortly after this, her husband the merchant returned. Concerned at the terrible state his wife was in, he sat by her bedside asking questions, but she merely reviled him and treated him like some mortal enemy. The boy told his father everything that had happened during his absence, and the merchant, greatly alarmed, sent at once for a doctor to treat his wife. But she only threw the medicines prescribed by the doctor on the ground, and continued to assail her husband with abuse. He secretly included some of the prescribed herbs in her daily soups and tisanes, and at last she began to show signs of recovery, much to the relief of father and son. Then one night they woke up in the middle of the night to find her gone. They looked for her everywhere, and finally found her again in another room of the house. As the days went by she became more and more deranged, absolutely refusing to be in the same room as her husband, and in the evenings going off on her own to her separate room. If they tried to prevent her, she became abusive. Her husband tried locking the room, but she made her way there nonetheless and the door opened for her of its own accord. The merchant was deeply disturbed by all of this, and arranged for more than one rite of exorcism to be performed, to no avail.

One evening, the son went to the Ho garden next door and hid in the long grass, hoping to discover something about the trouble-making fox's whereabouts. As the moon rose, he heard the sound of voices and, pushing aside the grass, saw two men sitting there drinking, waited on by a servant with a long beard. The servant wore old clothes of a brownish hue. All three men spoke in hushed tones, and the boy could not make out much of what they said. He did, however, hear one of the two men say to the servant after a while, 'Tomorrow, be sure to bring us a jar of white liquor.' Shortly afterwards they both went away,

He saw two men sitting there drinking.

and only the long-bearded servant was left. He took off his robe and lay down to sleep on a rock, where the merchant's son was able to examine him carefully. He was like a man, but had an unmistakable tail. The boy would have gone home, but decided he had better spend the night in his hiding place for fear of being seen by the fox-servant. Just before dawn, he saw the two men return, one after the other, and disappear into the bushes.

When he returned home that morning, his father asked him where he had been all night.

'I spent the night at uncle's,' he lied.

Later that day, he went with his father to market, where he saw a fox's tail hanging in the hat shop and begged his father to buy it for him. His father would not, but the boy clung to his father's coat and after much wheedling talked him into making the purchase. The father was busy in the market, and the boy played around at his side. Then, when his father was not looking, he surreptitiously helped himself to some of his father's money and went off to buy a bottle of liquor with it, which he left behind in the shop, saying he would collect it later. His uncle on his mother's side – a hunter by profession – lived in town, and the boy hurried to his house, only to find the uncle out. His aunt asked how the boy's mother was.

'She's getting better, gradually,' he replied. 'But she's very upset by the way the rats keep nibbling at her clothes. She sent me to ask you if you have any rat poison.'

The aunt looked in her cupboard and took out about an ounce of poison, which she wrapped in a piece of paper and gave him. He thought this too small an amount for his purpose, so while she went out to make him a bowl of dumpling soup, he helped himself to another handful of the poison and slipped it into his pocket. Then he hurried in to tell his aunt not to bother cooking for him after all, as he had to go back and join his father in the market. He went off and secretly mixed the poison in with the liquor he had left behind in the shop, then loafed about in the market and finally made his way home in the evening. His father (who had left the market long before) asked where he had been all this time, and he said (truthfully this time) that he had called in at his uncle's.

From then on, he made a point of frequenting the market daily, until one day he spotted the long-bearded servant in the crowd. Marking him closely, he trailed him and eventually struck up a conversation with him, asking him where he was from.

'North Village,' was the man's reply. 'And yourself?'

'Oh, I'm from a cave in the hills,' said the boy.

Long Beard found his answer strange.

'We've lived in a cave for generations,' the boy continued. 'Haven't you too?'

Long Beard found this stranger still. He asked the boy his name.

'Hu,' he replied, which meant 'Fox'. 'Actually I was at the Ho garden the other day, and saw you with the other two. Don't you remember?'

Long Beard studied him a moment. He was almost ready to believe him, but not quite. Then the boy half-unbuttoned the lower part of his gown, enough to reveal a portion of his false tail.

'After all these years of living with men, I still can't do anything about *this*!'

'What are you doing here in the market?'

'My father sent me here to buy some liquor.'

Long Beard replied that he had come for the same purpose.

'And have you bought yours yet?' asked the boy.

'We are poor folk,' he replied. 'Usually I have to steal rather than buy.'

'That must be tricky,' said the boy. 'I'd be scared to steal.'

'My master sent me on this errand, so I have to go through with it,' said Long Beard.

'And who is your master?'

'I serve those two gentlemen you saw the other day. They are brothers. One of them is having an affair with the wife of a Mr Wang in North Village; the other is carrying on with the wife of an older man, a merchant from East Village. The merchant's son is a real villain! He chopped off part of my master's tail and it's taken all of ten days to heal. Today my master has plans to pay his lady friend another visit.'

With this, Long Beard took his leave. 'I must go and see to my business.'

'Stealing must be so much trouble,' objected the boy. 'It's much easier to buy. I've already bought some liquor, as a matter of fact; I've got it laid by in the shop. Why don't I make you a present of it? I still have some money left; I can easily buy myself some more.'

Long Beard protested that he would be unable to pay him back.

'Come, we belong to the same kind. Think nothing of it. Sometime when you are free we must get together for a drink.'

They set off together. When they reached the shop, he gave Long Beard the liquor, and then went home.

That night, his mother slept undisturbed and did not feel her usual urge to go rushing off to her separate room. The boy sensed that something must have happened. In the morning, he told his father part of the story, and the two of them went next door to the Ho garden, where they found two foxes lying dead in a pavilion and a third dead in the long grass. Blood was still trickling from their mouths. The liquor bottle was there, and when they shook it they found it was not empty. The merchant was greatly astonished when his son finally told him the whole story.

'Why did you not tell me about this earlier?' he asked.

'Foxes are such canny creatures,' replied the boy wisely. 'I had to keep it a secret or they would have found out.'

The merchant seemed extremely pleased with his son. 'When it comes to catching foxes,' he exclaimed, 'you are as crafty as Chen Ping!'

Father and son carried the foxes home. One of them was missing a chunk of its tail, and the scar (from the chopper wound) was clearly visible.

From that time on, they were all left in peace. The merchant's wife, although her mind gradually returned to normal, lost a great deal of weight. She developed a serious cough and brought up large quantities of phlegm, before finally making a good recovery.

Over in North Village, the wife of Mr Wang, who had been

possessed by the other fox, was, they discovered, also freed from her entanglements and she, too, made a complete recovery.

After this the merchant treasured his son more than ever. He taught him to ride and draw the bow, and in later life the boy rose to be a high-ranking military officer.

36

A PASSION FOR SNAKES

Wang Puling, a man of my home town of Zichuan, had a servant by the name of Lü Fengning, who had a passion for eating snakes. If he came upon a very small one, he munched it up whole and swallowed it like a spring onion. Larger ones he cut up into small pieces and ate with his hands, crunching them up loudly and vigorously, and letting the blood dribble all over his chin.

He had a very keen sense of smell. Once he sniffed out a snake through a wall and went rushing out to catch it. It was over a foot long. He had no knife with him at the time, so he bit into its head and ate it with the tail dangling and wriggling from his mouth.

37
A LATTER-DAY BUDDHA

Jin Shicheng, of Changshan, was all his life a man of extremes. He suddenly left home one day to become a *dhuta*, and wandered around like a crazy mendicant eating filth as if it were a delicacy. If he saw sheep droppings or dog excrement on the road in front of him, he would go down on all fours and start munching. He referred to himself as a Living Buddha, and attracted thousands of disciples from among the ignorant locals, men and women alike, who marvelled at his behaviour. If he ordered them to eat excrement by way of penance, not one of them dared disobey. So generous were the contributions that came his way, he was able to spend a fortune on the construction of lavish temple buildings.

The local Magistrate, Judge Nan, took exception to his strange ways, had him arrested and flogged, and ordered him to pay for repairs to the Confucian temple. Jin's disciples said one to another, 'Our Buddha is in trouble!' Contributions came pouring in, and the repairs were completed in less than a month. Far more money was raised than if some harsh magistrate had tried to extort it in the usual way.

38

FOX ENCHANTMENT

Dong Xiasi was a young gentleman who lived in the western-most part of Qingzhou prefecture. One winter evening, he spread the bedding on his couch, lit a good fire in the brazier and was just trimming his lamp when a friend called by to haul him off for a drink. He bolted his door and off they went.

Among the guests at his friend's house was a physician well-versed in the arcane art of fortune-telling known as the Tai Su, or Primordial, Method, performed by reading the pulse. The physician was demonstrating this skill of his for the benefit of all the guests present, and finally came to Dong and to another friend of his, by the name of Wang Jiusi.

'I have read many pulses in my time,' he pronounced. 'But you two gentlemen have the strangest and most contradictory con-figurations I have ever encountered. One of you shows Long Life, side by side with contraindications of Premature Demise; the other one shows Prosperity, but with contraindications of Poverty. Strange indeed! And quite beyond my competence, I fear. Yours, sir,' he said, turning to Dong, 'is the more extreme of the two.'

The two men were appalled, and requested some elucidation.

'I fear this has taken me to the very limit of my art. I simply can go no further. I can only beg you both to exercise the utmost caution.'

At first they were greatly distressed by the learned physician's remarks. But then they reflected on the almost too-carefully worded ambivalence of his prognosis and decided not to pay it undue attention.

Dong returned home late that same night and was exceed-ingly surprised to find the door to his study standing ajar. He

The physician was demonstrating this skill of his.

had drunk a great deal, and in his inebriated state he concluded that he must have forgotten to bolt the door earlier that evening. He had after all set off in rather a hurry. In he went and, without bothering to light the lamp, reached under the covers, to feel if there was any warmth left in the bed. His hand encountered the soft skin of a sleeping body, and he withdrew it in some trepidation. Hurriedly lighting the lamp, he beheld a young girl of extraordinary beauty lying there in his bed, and stood for a moment ecstatically contemplating her ethereal features. Then he began to caress her and fondle her body, allowing his hand to stray to her nether regions, where to his great alarm he encountered a long bushy tail. His attempt to effect a speedy escape was cut short by the girl, who was now wide awake and seized hold of him by the arm.

'Where are you going, sir?'

Dong stood there trembling in fear. 'Madam Fairy,' he pleaded with her, 'I beseech you, have mercy!'

'What have you seen to make you so afraid of me?' said the girl, with a smile.

'It wasn't your face . . .' Dong stammered. 'It was your tail.'

She laughed. 'What tail? You must have made some mistake.'

She guided Dong's hand down beneath the covers again, drawing it across the firm, smooth flesh of her buttocks, and resting it gently on the tip of her backbone, which this time was indeed quite hairless to the touch.

'See!' she said, smiling more sweetly than ever. 'You were just tipsy and letting your imagination run away with you. You really shouldn't say such unkind things.'

Dong drank in her beauty with his eyes, by now totally spellbound and greatly regretting his initial misgivings – though he still found himself vaguely wondering what she was doing in his room and in his bed. She seemed to divine his thoughts.

'Don't you remember the girl next door, with the brown hair? It must be ten years now since my family moved away. I was no more than a child then, and you were just a little boy.'

'Ah Suo!' cried Dong as the memory returned to him. 'You mean the Zhous' little girl!'

'That's right.'

'I do remember you! What a beautiful young lady you have become! But what are you doing here, in my bed?'

'For five long years I was wife to a simpleton. Both my parents-in-law passed away, and then my husband died, leaving me a widow and quite alone in the world. I thought of you, my childhood friend, and came here to seek you out. When I arrived it was already evening, and a moment later your friend called and invited you out, so I looked for a place where I could hide and wait for you to return. You were such a very long time, and I was beginning to shiver with cold, so I crept under your quilt to keep myself warm. You don't mind, do you?'

Ecstatically Dong stripped off his clothes and climbed under the quilt with her. His subsequent joy can well be imagined.

A month went by, and gradually Dong began to waste away. His family commented on his worsening condition, and expressed their concern, which he dismissed as groundless. But with time his features grew quite haggard and he himself began to take fright. He went to consult the same learned physician, who took his pulses again and declared, 'You are clearly bewitched. My earlier prognosis of Premature Demise has been borne out. I fear there is no cure for you.'

Dong burst into tears and refused to leave the physician, who performed acupuncture on his hand and moxibustion on his navel, and gave him certain herbal remedies to take.

'If anything untoward should cross your path, be sure to resist it with all your might.'

Dong went away fearing for his life.

When he reached home, the girl greeted him with sweet smiles and wanted him in bed with her at once. He protested vehemently, 'Leave me alone! Can't you see I am at death's door!'

He turned his back on her.

'Do you really think you can still live?' she cried bitterly, shame and anger mingling in her voice.

That night, Dong took his medicine and slept alone, but the moment he closed his eyes in sleep, he dreamed he was making love to the girl again, and when he awoke he found that he had ejaculated in his bed. He grew more afraid than ever, and went in to sleep with his wife, who lit a lamp and kept a close watch over him. Still the dreams continued, and yet every time he awoke the girl was nowhere to be seen. A few days later, he began to cough up large quantities of blood, and before long he was dead.

Now some while after this, Wang (the friend whose fortune had also been told on that fateful evening) was sitting in his own study one day when a young girl entered unannounced. He was immediately taken with her beauty, and made love to her without further ado. He asked her who she was and where she was from.

'I am a neighbour of your friend Dong, who was also a dear friend of mine,' she replied. 'Poor man! A fox cast a spell on him and he is with us no more! Foxes can cast powerful spells. Young gentlemen in particular, such as you and your friend, should guard against them.'

Wang was deeply moved by her words and loved her all the more. As the days went by, he too began to waste away and his reason started to wander. One night, in a dream, Dong came and spoke to him: 'Beware! Your lover is a fox. First she took my life, and now she wants yours. I have already laid charges against her before the courts of the Nether World, hoping to bring some comfort to my wounded spirit. On the night of the seventh day, you must burn some incense outside your room. On no account must you forget these words!'

Wang awoke and marvelled at his strange dream. He decided to speak to the girl.

'I am seriously ill,' he said, 'and it may soon be all up with me. It would be advisable for us never to make love again.'

'Do not worry,' she replied. 'All is destiny. If you are destined for a long life, then no amount of love-making is going to kill you. And if you are destined to die, no amount of abstinence will save you.'

She sat by him and toyed with him, smiling so sweetly the while that Wang was unable to restrain himself and soon found himself in her arms again. Every time they made love, he was filled with remorse. But he was incapable of resisting her advances.

The evening of the seventh day, he lit sticks of incense and stuck them in his door, but she pulled them out and threw them away. That same night, in a dream, Dong came to him again and reproached him for having failed to act on his advice. The next night, Wang secretly instructed his servants to wait until he was asleep and then to light the incense.

The girl was already in his bed.

'That incense again!' she cried, suddenly waking.

'What incense?' protested Wang, feigning ignorance.

She rose at once, and taking the sticks of incense, broke them into little pieces.

'Who told you to do this?' she said, as she returned to their room.

'My wife,' lied Wang. 'She is concerned at my illness, and believes that it can be exorcized.'

The girl paced up and down, greatly perturbed.

One of the servants, meanwhile, seeing that the incense sticks had been extinguished, lit some more.

'Ah!' cried the girl. 'Your aura of good luck is too strong for me. I shall have to tell you the truth. Yes, I did hurt your friend, and yes, then I came running after you next. I have done great wrong. I must go to the Nether World now and face your friend in the court of Yama. If you remember your love for me, I beg you, keep my body from harm.'

With these words she climbed slowly from the bed and then promptly lay down and died. When he lit the lamp, he saw the body of a fox on the ground. Fearing it might come to life again, he instructed his servants to skin it and hang up the pelt.

His illness now entered a critical phase. One day, he saw a fox come loping towards him.

'I have been before the court of the Nether World,' said the fox. 'Judgement was given against your friend Dong, whose death was reckoned to have been the consequence of his own lust. But I was still found guilty of enchantment. They took away my Golden Elixir, the fruit of all my years of toil. They have sent me back to be reborn. Where is my body?'

'My servants knew no better and skinned it.'

The fox was greatly distressed. 'It is true that I drove many men to their death. I deserved to die long ago. But nonetheless, what a heartless man you are!'

She took her leave, sadly, bitterly.

Wang all but died of his illness. But after six months he was restored to health.

39
EATING STONES

His Excellency Wang Qinwen, an old gentleman of Xincheng, had a groom also named Wang who, while still a youth, went off to Mount Lao to study the Tao. As time went by, he abstained from eating any cooked food and lived exclusively off pine kernels and white stones. He grew a shaggy coat of hair over his whole body.

He gradually started taking food again several years later, when, concerned for his ageing mother, he returned to live in his village. But he still continued to eat stones as before. He held them up to the sunlight to tell if they were sweet or bitter, sour or salty, then bit into them just as if they were yams.

When his mother died, he went back to the hills. That was some seventeen or eighteen years ago.

He held the stones up to the sunlight.

40

THE LAUGHING GIRL

Wang Zifu, a young man of Luodian Village in Ju County, lost his father at an early age. He was a brilliant youth, and successfully took his first degree at the age of fourteen. His mother doted on him and seldom allowed him to go on excursions out into the country. She betrothed him to a girl of the Xiao family, but the girl died before the marriage could be celebrated. He had looked for a suitable wife since that time, so far without success.

Our tale begins one Lantern Festival, on the first full moon of the year, when Wang's maternal cousin, a young man by the name of Wu, invited him out for a stroll. No sooner had they reached the outskirts of the village than a family servant came hurrying up to summon Wu home. Wang continued on his own. He had seen how many good-looking girls there were out taking the air, and felt in the mood for a promenade.

One young lady was out walking with her maid and had just picked a spray of plum-blossom. She had the prettiest face imaginable, with a great beaming smile. Wang stared at her utterly captivated, mindless of the usual rules of modesty and propriety. She walked a few steps past him and then turned to her maid: 'Who *is* that young man staring at me, with those burning burglar's eyes?'

She dropped the plum-blossom on the ground and walked on, talking and laughing animatedly as she went. Wang retrieved the blossom from the ground with a melancholy air and stood there a while musing abstractedly, before returning home in a mood of profound dejection.

When he reached home, he hid the plum-blossom beneath

his pillow, lay disconsolately down to sleep, and from that moment on would neither talk nor eat. As the days went by, his mother became very anxious about him. She had elaborate rituals of exorcism performed, but despite all her efforts her son grew thinner and thinner. Doctors examined him and prescribed herbal concoctions to bring out the disease, but his mind seemed to wander all the more feverishly. He was like a man possessed. When his mother tried asking, with great tenderness and concern, how it had all started, he refused to say anything.

One day, his cousin Wu came to the house, and Wang's mother secretly begged him to try to extract the truth from her son. Wu approached his bedside, and the minute he saw him, Wang burst into tears. Wu began by speaking words of comfort, and then gradually brought the conversation round to the subject of his cousin's illness and its origin. Wang confided in him, telling him the whole story of his hopeless infatuation with the smiling girl and begging him for his advice.

'Oh, you foolish fellow!' said Wu, laughing, but pleasantly. 'Your desire can easily be fulfilled. Let me seek the young lady out on your behalf. Since she was allowed to go out walking like that on her own, it is highly unlikely that she is from some grand family. So long as she is not yet betrothed, you can consider the match as good as settled! And even if she *is* betrothed, I am sure a generous gift in the right quarter will clear the way for you. You just concentrate on making a full recovery and leave the rest to me.'

Wang smiled wanly when he heard this, and Wu went out and informed his aunt, before himself setting off in search of the girl. Although, to the growing despair of Wang's mother, his exhaustive inquiries brought no results, Wang himself had been greatly cheered by his cousin's visit, and gradually recovered his appetite.

When Wu called round again several days later and Wang asked him how the matter was progressing, Wu felt obliged to invent a story. 'It's all settled! It turns out (would you believe it!) that the girl you saw that day is my own cousin – which makes her yours too, on your mother's side. She is still waiting to be betrothed. The two of you are a little more closely related than is usually thought proper, but that won't stop you from getting married. I'm sure I can explain everything to them, and the wedding can go ahead.'

Wang's joy knew no bounds. 'Where does she live?' he asked.

Wu improvised. 'In the hills south-west of here, ten miles or so away.'

Wang begged him again and again to be sure to take care of everything, and Wu went striding off, giving him every assurance that he would do so. Wang now began to eat and drink quite normally, and within a matter of days was quite restored to health. Frequently he reached beneath his pillow for the plum-blossom, which was withered but otherwise unchanged, held it in his hand and gazed at it in rapture, as if the blossom itself was his beloved.

Days went by, and when Wu still did not return, Wang began to wonder what was going on. He wrote to his cousin several times, pleading with him to come. Each time Wu procrastinated, giving one pretext or another, which filled Wang with resentment, then provoked him to bouts of anger and depression. His mother was afraid that he might suffer a relapse, but when she suggested to him that perhaps he should consider marrying someone else, he shook his head, rejecting the idea out of hand and continuing to wait day after day for his cousin to return.

Then, one day, he finally said to himself that ten miles was really not such a very great distance after all, that he needed no one's help to go that far, and placing the plum-blossom in his sleeve, he set off impulsively, without even informing his own family.

He walked alone, encountering no one on the road from whom he could ask the way. All he knew was that he should head for the hills to the south-west. After walking for ten miles or so, he found himself climbing into an enchanted landscape, range upon range of green hills stretching as far as the eye could see, with not a soul in sight and nothing but a tiny, steep mountain trail to follow. As he continued on his way, far away down in the valley below, hidden in an overgrown tangle of

flowers and trees, he caught sight of a little hamlet. He clambered down the hillside towards it and found a few simple
buildings, nothing more than a cluster of rustic thatched cottages, but nonetheless a place with a certain refinement and
charm. Before one of the cottages, situated towards the northern
end of the hamlet, was a stand of weeping willows, while inside
the cottage's garden walls could be seen a flourishing orchard of
peach and apricot, interspersed with delicate fronds of bamboo.
Birds sang in the branches. As this was clearly a private garden,
Wang did not venture in but sat down for a moment's rest on
a smooth boulder outside the house opposite. Presently he heard
a girl's voice from within the garden calling out, 'Petal! Are you
coming or not?'

It was a delicate voice, tender and vibrant with feeling. As he
sat there listening, a young girl walked out of the gate in the
wall opposite and began strolling along the road, with a sprig
of apricot-blossom in her hand. She lowered her head to fasten
it in her hair, but, chancing to look up and catch sight of him
sitting there, she ceased what she was doing, smiled and went
back inside with the blossom still in her hand. Wang recognized
her at once as the girl he had seen at the Lantern Festival, and
his heart leaped with joy. But what pretext could he find for
entering her home? And how should he address her? As his
cousin? They had never met before, and he was afraid of offend-
ing her in some way. There was no one at the door that he
could speak to, so he remained where he was, waiting restlessly,
now sitting on the stone, now lying down beside it, until the
sun had sunk low in the western sky. He quite forgot to think
whether he was hungry or thirsty, so desperate was he for
another glimpse of the girl. Every now and then she peeped out
through the door and seemed greatly surprised to find him still
there. Then finally an old woman emerged, leaning on a stick,
and addressed him. 'Where are you from, sir? I understand you
have been here ever since morning. I wonder what you want.
You must be hungry.'

He rose promptly to his feet and bowed. 'I was hoping to call
on my relations.'

The old woman was extremely deaf, and he had to repeat

himself much more loudly before she understood him. 'And what are they called, these relations of yours?' she asked.

He was unable to reply to this question.

'Strange!' replied the old woman with a smile. 'You say you were hoping to call on them, but you don't even know their names! I'd say by the look of you that you must be a bit absent-minded, a bookworm, a dreamer . . . Come on in with me. Eat some of our poor fare. We've a little spare bed you can sleep in. Tomorrow you can go home and find out what these relations of yours are called. Then you can come back another time and do things properly.'

Wang was just becoming aware of the pangs of hunger, and besides, this invitation to dinner was his perfect entrée into the precincts of the fair one! Without further delay he followed the old woman, and found himself walking through the gate and down a little white cobbled path, lined with trees, whose deep pink blossoms lay scattered on the stones. He was in a transport of delight. The path then wound its way to the left and through another gateway, into a courtyard embellished with flower-covered trellises and exquisite potted plants on stands. Wang was invited inside, into a room whose brilliantly painted white walls shone with the dazzling brightness of a mirror. A branch of flowering crab-apple reached through a window from the courtyard outside. Cushions, tables, couch – everything in the room was spotlessly clean. As he sat down, he became aware that someone was stealing a glance at him through the window.

'Petal!' called the old woman. 'Put some millet on to cook at once!'

A maid's voice answered from outside.

Wang told the old woman a bit about his family.

'So your mother's father was a Wu, then?' said the old woman.

'Indeed he was.'

'Why then, you must be my nephew!' she exclaimed in amazement. 'Your mother must be my younger sister! Over the years, our branch of the family has come down in the world, I'm afraid, and besides I never had a son of my own, so as a result we've quite lost touch with the rest of the family. Here you are, a fully grown man, my own nephew, and I didn't even recognize you!'

'It must have been you I came to see, Auntie,' said Wang, 'but in my confusion I forgot your name.'

'I married into the Qin family,' replied the old lady. 'I've no children at all of my own. There's just a girl who was born to my late husband's concubine. When my husband, Mr Qin, died, the girl's mother, the concubine, remarried and left the girl here for me to bring up. She's a bright cheerful child, but hasn't had much schooling, I'm afraid. She's forever playing! I'll call her in shortly, to come and pay you her respects.'

Presently the maid served dinner, the principal dish being a plump little home-grown fowl. The old woman kept helping him to more, and when he had finished eating, the maid came back to clear away the dishes.

'Call in Miss Ning,' said the old woman, and the maid hurried off to do her bidding. Shortly afterwards there was the sound of muffled laughter outside.

'Yingning,' called out the old woman, 'a cousin of yours is here.'

More laughter and spluttering could be heard outside. Then the maid ushered in the young lady of the beaming smile, who was hiding her face with her hand and seemed quite incapable of staunching her ever-flowing stream of laughter. The old woman looked at her angrily.

'We have a guest! What do you mean by all this silly noise?'

The girl managed a straight face for a moment, and Wang made her a bow.

'This is young Mr Wang,' said the old lady. 'He's your cousin, but we've never met before – isn't that strange?'

'And how old is the young lady my cousin?' asked Wang. The woman could not hear him, and Wang had to repeat the question, whereupon the girl started laughing again and looked down at the ground.

'I told you she lacked breeding,' commented the old woman. 'Now you can see for yourself. She is sixteen years old but silly as a child.'

'So she is one year younger than I am,' said Wang.

'If you are seventeen,' returned the old lady, 'then you must have been born in the Year of the Horse.'

'I was.'

'And who is your wife?'

'I am single.'

'I'm surprised that a good-looking young man of seventeen like yourself, with all your accomplishments, should still be single. Our Yingning is single too. Why, the two of you would make an excellent couple! It's a pity that you are cousins.'

Wang said nothing but kept staring at Yingning: he had eyes for nothing else.

The maid muttered to her young mistress, 'It's those burning burglar's eyes again!'

At this Yingning burst out laughing loudly. 'Come, let's go and look at the peach-blossom!' she said.

She rose at once and, hiding her mouth with her sleeve, made her way out with her maid, taking tiny little steps. Once outside the door, she immediately let out another of her loud laughs. The old lady now arose as well and gave orders for a second maid to prepare bedding and make sure the visitor was properly taken care of.

'This is such a rare honour for us,' she said. 'You must stay here for a few days and then we'll send you on your way home. If you are bored, there is a little garden at the back where you can take a walk, and there are books to read.'

The next day, he discovered the little garden – it was no more than a tenth of an acre, with a neat lawn, paths strewn with catkins and a three-roomed rustic summer-house, surrounded on all four sides with shrubs and flowers. He had walked a few paces through the flowers when he heard a whispering sound coming from up in one of the trees, looked up, and there was Yingning. When she saw him, she burst out laughing and it looked for a moment as if she might come tumbling down from the tree.

'Take care!' cried Wang. 'You might fall!'

She clambered down from the tree, laughing uncontrollably all the while, and was almost on the ground when her hand

嬰
寧

拈花微笑欲傾城
情到濃時轉不情
一味天真何爛漫
只宜呼作太慈生

He looked up, and there was Yingning.

slipped and she fell, which finally put a stop to her laughing.
Wang helped her up, gently squeezing her wrist as he did so,
whereupon she started laughing again at once and had to lean
against the tree, incapable of further movement. Wang waited
for her laughter to come to an end (which took quite some
time), and then he produced the withered plum-blossom from
his sleeve and showed it to her.

She took it in her hands. 'It's dead. Why have you kept it?'

'It is the blossom you dropped at the Lantern Festival,' he
replied. 'That is why I kept it.'

'But what for?'

'As a keepsake. To show that I have always loved you, that
I have never forgotten you. Since I saw you that day of the
Lanterns, my longing for you has made me ill. It has reduced
me to a shadow of my former self. I never thought I should
have this chance to see you again. Take pity on me. Be kind.'

'Of course I'll be kind, silly! Cousins are supposed to be kind,
aren't they? When you go, I shall tell one of the women to pick
you a whole bundle of flowers from the garden.'

'Are you out of your mind?'

'What do you mean, out of my mind?'

'It's not the *blossom* I love. It's the person who held it in her
hand.'

'We're not even that closely related. How can you talk about
loving me?'

'I don't love you as a *relation*. I love you as a man loves a
woman, as a husband loves a wife . . .'

'What difference is there?'

'Husband and wife share the same pillow and mat at night.
They sleep together.'

Yingning lowered her head in thought for a while. 'I am
certainly not used to sleeping with strange men.'

Imperceptibly, as she was speaking, her maid arrived, and
Wang made a somewhat confused departure.

A little later, they all met again in the old lady's presence.

'And where have you been?' she inquired.

'Talking together in the garden,' replied Yingning.

'The meal's been ready a long while,' said the old woman.

'What can you have been so busy talking about that kept you so long?'

'Cousin Wang says he wants to sleep with me,' she blurted out.

Wang was acutely embarrassed by this and cast her a disapproving glance. She smiled back at him and said no more. Luckily the old lady had not caught her words, and as she persisted with her questions, Wang hastily diverted her attention and changed the subject, at the same time whispering to Yingning that she had been indiscreet.

'Shouldn't I have said what I just said?' she protested.

'Not in front of others. It's a secret.'

'I don't have any secrets from Mother. And besides, where one chooses to sleep is not so special. There's no secret about that, surely?'

Wang found her naive way of speaking quite exasperating, but could think of no way to make her understand. When they had eaten, a number of his servants arrived from home with two mules, having been sent in search of their young master by his mother, who had become most anxious when he had failed to return. She had already sent out several search parties in the countryside immediately round their village, with no success. She had then called on his cousin Wu, to seek his advice, and Wu remembered the story he had improvised for Wang earlier and suggested to his aunt that she should search in the hills to the south-west. The servants had searched the villages one by one, and finally arrived at this one just as Wang was walking out of the cottage door. He went in to tell the old woman he was going home, and asked if Yingning could go back with him. She seemed only too delighted.

'I've been meaning to take her to meet her family for a long while. But I'm getting so old and weak these days, I can't travel far. It would be so nice if you could take her with you to meet her auntie!'

She called for Yingning, who came in, laughing.

'What are you so happy about,' grumbled the old woman, 'that you're forever laughing? If it were not for that, you'd be a fine young lady.' She looked at her crossly. 'Your cousin wants to take you home with him. Quickly now, go and get your things ready.'

She gave the Wang servants something to eat and drink, and then saw them all off, giving her daughter a few parting injunctions.

'Your aunt's family own a great deal of property and land. I'm sure they have enough to feed an extra mouth or two. You should stay there if you can, and try to get yourself some schooling and breeding, and then when you get married you'll know what it means to be a dutiful daughter-in-law. I shall ask Auntie to find you a nice husband.'

And so the two of them set out. When they reached the ridge to the north, they looked back and could just make out the form of the old woman leaning against the cottage doorway, gazing up at them.

Eventually they arrived at Wang's house, and his mother asked at once who the pretty girl was.

'She is your own niece,' replied Wang. 'Your sister's daughter.'

'That story of your cousin Wu's was made up,' his mother hastened to explain. 'I have no sisters, so how could I have such a niece?'

The girl, when questioned, replied, 'The old lady in the cottage *is* your sister. She is not my real mother. My father's name was Qin. He died when I was still a baby, and I can't remember him.'

'It is true,' said Wang's mother, 'that I did *once* have an elder sister who married a Mr Qin. But she died many years ago. She can't be this old woman you are talking about.'

She questioned Yingning about her foster-mother's facial features and asked her if she had certain birthmarks, and the girl's description accorded exactly with what she herself remembered about her dead sister.

'I suppose it must be her. And yet she died many years ago, so how can it be?'

She was still puzzling over this when cousin Wu arrived, and the girl retired to an inner room. When Wu learned what had happened, he stood there utterly dumbfounded for several minutes. Then something seemed to dawn on him.

'Is the girl's name by any chance Yingning?'

'Why, yes!' replied Wang.

'How extraordinary!' exclaimed Wu.

They asked him what he meant by this, and he went on to explain. 'After the death of our Aunt Wu, Uncle Qin was living on his own, and he was possessed by a fox-spirit. He fell ill and started to waste away. The fox-spirit gave birth to a baby girl called Yingning and left her in a bundle on the bed. The whole family saw it. After Uncle Qin finally died, the fox still used to come back occasionally. Later they pasted a Taoist charm on the wall, so the fox took her baby girl and went away for good. This girl must be the fox's daughter!'

They were puzzling over this between themselves when they heard Yingning burst out laughing from the inner room.

'She does seem such a very silly girl!' commented Wang's mother, going in at Wu's request to fetch her, and finding her still in the grip of one of her uncontrollable laughing fits. She urged her to come out, and Yingning finally succeeded in getting a grip on herself, sat quietly for a while with her face turned to the wall and then came out when she had fully composed herself. She managed to perform a single bow before turning promptly on her heel and retreating into the inner room again, where she let out a great peal of laughter. There were several other ladies present, all of whom found her behaviour highly comical.

Wu offered to go to the cottage and investigate, and at the same time to make inquiries about a possible marriage between the two young people. But when he reached the hamlet, all trace of the cottage had gone. There was nothing to be seen but a few blossoms strewn on a desolate hillside. He remembered that his Aunt Wu had been buried somewhere not far away, and found what he thought must be the place. But it was overgrown and the grave itself was no longer identifiable. He heaved a perplexed sigh and returned to the Wang family.

Wang's mother began to wonder if Yingning might herself be a ghost. She went in and repeated Wu's story about his dead uncle and aunt, Mr and Mrs Qin, but the girl exhibited no surprise whatsoever. When Mrs Wang condoled with her for being an orphan, she did not seem to take it at all tragically and instead kept on giggling in her silly way. The others did not know what to make of it at all.

Mrs Wang put Yingning to sleep in a room with one of the maids, and every morning she went in to see how the girl was getting on. Her needlework was certainly impeccable. It was only her incorrigible habit of laughing that detracted from her suitability as a future daughter-in-law. And yet somehow even that did not spoil her charm. However hysterically she laughed, people seemed to find pleasure in it, and the young women of the neighbourhood competed with each other for her company.

So Wang's mother (even though she was still unable to dismiss her fears of some ghostly influence at work) decided to go ahead and choose an auspicious day for the wedding. She spied on the girl during the day, but never detected anything untoward. She certainly had a shadow like a normal living human. On the wedding day, they dressed her up in a bridal gown and prepared her for the ceremony, but then she was taken with one of her laughing fits and became quite incapable of standing or kneeling properly, so in the end the usual formalities had to be dispensed with.

After the wedding, Wang, in view of his wife's complete naivety, was anxious that she might make some inappropriate reference to their private sexual relations. But she turned out to be particularly discreet in this regard, and never once said anything of the kind. Quite the contrary. She was in every way the very soul of discretion and sensitivity. If ever his mother was depressed or angry, all it needed was for Yingning to come and laugh, and the dark mood was at once dispelled. And if the maids were ever in any sort of trouble and feared a beating, they would ask Yingning to intercede on their behalf with the mistress and she always won them a free pardon.

She was passionately fond of flowers, and was always seeking to obtain new varieties from friends and relations. She even secretly pawned her own jewellery in order to buy more flowers, and after a few months every little corner of the house, every terrace, every fence, every shed, even the privy, had its floral display.

In the Wangs' back garden there was a banksia rose that had strayed from their neighbours' garden to the west, and was rambling all over a trellis. Yingning would often go there and climb the trellis to pick some of the fragrant blossoms for her hair. Mrs Wang reprimanded her for this, but she paid no heed. One day when she was up the trellis, the neighbour's son caught sight of her and was instantly smitten. He stared at her, and Yingning, with her usual directness, smiled back. He, thinking that she was leading him on, became more aroused than ever. Still with a broad smile on her face, Yingning pointed to a spot on his side of the wall, before climbing back down on to her own side. The young man was beside himself with joy at what he took to be an assignation, and returned to the same spot that very evening, to find her waiting for him.

He lost no time, and began to make love to her at once, only to feel a fierce shooting pain in his member, as if a sharp awl were boring into it. He fell with a great cry to the ground, and then, when he strained his eyes, saw before him not a beautiful woman but a rotten old log propped up against the wall. He had been making love to a dank hole worn in the log by the dripping rain. The young man's father heard him scream and came hurrying to his aid, but in reply to his questions the youth could only groan. It was only when his wife came to his side that he told the truth. They lit a lamp and shone it at the log, discovering in the hole a huge scorpion, the size of a small crab. The father, having chopped open the log and killed the scorpion, carried his son into the house, but later that night the young man died.

The family took young Wang to court, accusing his wife of sorcery. But the Magistrate, who had a high opinion of Wang and knew of his excellent reputation, dismissed the charge as false and would have had the dead youth's father caned had not Wang intervened on his behalf and procured his release.

Wang's mother spoke to Yingning afterwards. 'This time your silliness has really gone too far! I always knew there was something strange about your excessive cheerfulness, and that it would bring trouble and sorrow sooner or later. Luckily for you the Magistrate is a wise man, and the case will go no further. But if it had been some fool of a judge, he would have had you arrested and questioned in court, and my poor son would never have been able to hold his head up in public again!'

Yingning looked at her seriously for a moment and swore that she would never laugh again.

'There's nothing wrong with laughing,' said Mrs Wang. 'But it should be in the right place and at the right time.'

From that day forth, Yingning never laughed again. Even if someone tried to provoke her, she kept a straight face, though never an unpleasantly gloomy one.

One night, she was sitting with her husband when suddenly she began to weep. He was greatly puzzled.

'There's something I have never told you,' she sobbed. 'I haven't told you about it before, because we hadn't known each other very long and I didn't want to frighten you. But now that I know you better, and I know how much you and your mother love me, I must tell you the truth.

'I am the daughter of a fox. When my fox-mother went away, she entrusted me to a ghost-mother, who looked after me for ten years. I have no brothers. You are all I have in the world. Now my ghost-mother is lying out there all alone up in the hills, with no one to care for her and to bury her properly by her husband's side. Her soul is wandering unhappily beneath the Nine Springs.

'I beg you to do one thing for me, if you do not begrudge me the trouble or the expense: bury my ghost-mother properly, set her poor spirit at peace. Then she will cease to grieve, and will know that the child she reared bears her some gratitude, that daughters can be of some value. Perhaps my example may discourage parents from drowning their daughters.'

Wang agreed to do this for her. His only concern was that the old lady's temporary resting place would be too overgrown to find, but Yingning told him not to worry on that score.

Shortly afterwards, they both set out, pulling a decent coffin behind them in a cart. Deep in the midst of an overgrown thicket of brambles, Yingning pointed to the makeshift grave, and sure enough there they found the dead body of the old lady of the cottage, her skin still firm on its bones. Yingning took the body in her arms and wept bitterly as together they lifted it into the coffin and on to the cart and transported it to the grave of Mr Qin. And there they buried her next to her former husband.

That night, Wang dreamed that the old lady came to thank him. He awoke and told Yingning his dream.

'I also saw her tonight,' she said. 'She told me not to disturb you.'

Wang regretted that she had not detained the old lady.

'She is a ghost,' explained Yingning. 'There are too many living humans here, the aura surrounding us is too Yang. She could never have stayed long with us.'

Wang asked after the maid from the hamlet, the one called Petal.

'She is a fox too,' answered Yingning. 'And a very clever one. My fox-mother left her to keep an eye on me. She often brought me things to eat. I shall always be grateful to her for her goodness to me. My ghost-mother told me she is married now.'

Every year, at the Cold Food Festival, without fail, they went to the Qin grave, swept it, and paid their respects to the dead.

After a year had passed, Yingning gave birth to a son. Even when he was a babe in arms, he was never afraid of strangers, but always laughed in their presence – just like his mother.

41

THE MAGIC SWORD AND
THE MAGIC BAG

There was a gentleman of Zhejiang Province by the name of Ning Caichen, an open, generous person by nature, forthright and serious in his dealings. He always said that he had only ever loved one woman.

Once he passed through Jinhua on his travels and rested for a while at a temple in the northern outskirts of the city. The temple had once been rather grand, but now it was overgrown with weeds and seemed quite deserted. The doors leading into the monks' cells in the east and west wings stood ajar, and the only place that showed any sign of being inhabited was a single room on the south side, which, Ning observed, had been fitted with a new door-bar and lock. In the eastern corner of the main courtyard, below the main hall of worship, grew a stand of large bamboos, their stems two hands round, and below the steps leading up to the terrace stretched a vast pond, covered with a mass of water-lilies in full bloom. Ning was greatly taken with the quiet, rarefied charm of the place.

It was the time of one of the Provincial Education Commissioner's periodic visits, and since as a result accommodation in the town itself had become very expensive, Ning considered taking lodgings in the temple. He went for a stroll to await the return of the monks, if there were any.

Towards evening, seeing a gentleman arrive and open the newly fitted door on the south side of the main courtyard, Ning hastened to pay his respects and to announce his intention of staying.

'There is no one in charge here,' replied the gentleman. 'I too am only lodging here temporarily. If you think you might enjoy this lonely spot, I should be delighted to share it with you, sir.'

Ning was pleased at the man's friendly response. He made himself a pallet of straw and fashioned a little table out of wooden boards, clearly intending to stay for some time. That night the moon flooded the temple courtyard with its brilliant light, and the two men sat together in the portico of the main hall, conversing and becoming acquainted with each other. The gentleman introduced himself as Yan Chixia, and at first, even though he did not speak like a Zhejiang man, Ning imagined him to be a scholar up in town for the provincial examination. In due course Yan told Ning that he hailed from the western region of Qin. His way of talking seemed unusually blunt and unaffected. After chatting for a while, the two men bade each other goodnight with a bow and retired to bed.

It was Ning's first night in the temple, and he found it hard to fall asleep. He thought he could hear low voices outside, as if the members of a family were talking among themselves. Rising from his bed, he crouched against the northern wall of his cell, beneath the stone window-frame, and, peeping out, saw a small courtyard surrounded by a low wall, in which two women – one in her forties, the other an old lady in a faded red dress, with a long silver comb in her hair, humpbacked and unsteady on her feet – were talking in the moonlight.

'What has kept Little Beauty so long?' asked the younger of the two.

'She should be here any minute,' said the older.

'Has she been complaining to you, Granny?'

'No. But she does seem rather miserable.'

'Perhaps we are being too soft with her.'

Even as they were talking, a young girl of seventeen or eighteen, of an extraordinary personal beauty, entered the courtyard and the old lady laughed.

'One should never speak of people behind their backs! There we were talking about you, dear, when you come stealing in, silent as a little fairy. It's a good thing we weren't discussing your shortcomings.'

After a brief pause she continued, 'Why, you're looking pretty as a picture today! If I were a young man, I'd be head over heels in love with you!'

'And if *I* didn't have *you* to flatter me, Granny,' said the girl, 'I'm sure I'd starve for compliments . . .'

She and the middle-aged woman then exchanged a few words. Ning concluded to himself that they must be a family living next door, and went back to bed. He heard no further words spoken outside, and soon all was silent and he began to feel drowsy, but even as he was drifting off he became aware of someone coming into the room. He rose promptly from his bed and, peering into the gloom, to his astonishment recognized the girl from the courtyard outside. He asked her what it was she wanted, and she smiled.

'It is such a bright night and I couldn't get to sleep. I want to make love with you.'

'You really shouldn't say things like that!' replied Ning sternly. 'You must beware of what people might say. Gossip can be a terrible thing. A single false step can be a person's ruin.'

'It's the middle of the night, no one need ever know.'

Ning rebuked her again, but still she lingered, as if she had more to say, and finally he ordered her brusquely to leave.

'Go, or I shall call for the gentleman lodging in the south wing!'

This threat seemed to put the wind up her and she left. But just as she was walking out through the door, she turned back and placed a lump of gold on his quilt. Ning took the gold and threw it out on to the terrace.

'I will not be contaminated by evil stuff like this!'

The girl retrieved the gold and went away, looking greatly mortified and muttering to herself, 'That man has a heart of stone.'

The next day, a man from the nearby town of Lanxi, who was up in Jinhua for the examinations, came to lodge in the east wing of the temple. In the middle of the night, his servant found him dead, with blood dribbling from a small wound in the sole of his foot. The wound resembled a hole made by an awl. There seemed no obvious explanation for his sudden death. And then the very next night, his servant died in exactly the same manner. The following evening, when his fellow-lodger

聶小倩

阮具光明磊
落腸不達
劍俠六何傷
良宵自詫
奇緣者多
半青燁
注慕楊

Ning took the gold and threw it out on to the terrace.

Yan returned to the temple, Ning mentioned the two deaths and Yan commented that they seemed to him to be the work of evil spirits. Ning had always been a man of firm convictions and was not unduly disturbed by such strange goings-on.

That night, the girl came to visit him again.

'I've seen many men in my time,' she said, 'but never one as strong and unshakeable as you. You seem a saintly sort of person, and I can't bring myself to lie to you any longer – I must tell you the truth about myself. My family name is Nie, and I have always been known as Little Beauty. I died when I was eighteen years old, and they buried my body just outside this temple. Then an evil spirit took control of me, and ever since he has been forcing me against my will to cast spells on men, to seduce them and do all sorts of shameful things with them. Now there is no one left in the temple to kill apart from you, and I am afraid that the spirit will come looking for you. He will take the form of a yaksha-demon.'

Brave though he was, Ning found this prospect somewhat daunting. He asked her what precautions he should take.

'You must sleep in Mr Yan's room,' she replied. 'You will be safe there.'

'Why is he so special?'

'He is a strange one. Spirits don't dare go near him.'

'Tell me something,' he said. 'Tell me how you set about bewitching men.'

'I do it in one of two ways,' she replied. 'Either a man agrees to make love to me, in which case I secretly prick him in the foot with an awl so that he falls unconscious and his blood can be drawn off for the evil spirit to drink. Or else I tempt him with a piece of gold, which is really not gold at all but the spirit-bone of a raksha-demon. Once he has taken the gold, I can use it to cut out his heart and liver. I use whichever method seems most likely to work at the time.'

Ning thanked her for confiding in him like this, and asked her at which times he should be specially on his guard, to which she replied that the following night would be a dangerous one for him. As she left him she wept. 'I am sinking into a dark sea and cannot reach the further shore! But you are so strong! You are so bright and good, I know you can put an end to my pain. Take my bones back home with you, I beg you, and give them a decent burial. Set them at peace and bring me back to life!'

Ning gallantly agreed to her request and asked where he was to find her grave.

'At the foot of the white poplar tree, in which a crow has made its nest.'

With these words she went out through the door and vanished into the night.

Early the following day, afraid that Yan might decide to leave the temple, Ning invited him over, and later that morning set food and drink before him, anxious not to let him out of his sight. He broached the subject of spending the night with him in his cell, and at first Yan refused, saying that he was a creature of habit and much too accustomed to sleeping alone. In the end, Ning was so persistent (going so far as to carry his own bedding over to Yan's room) that Yan felt obliged to comply with his request, and made room for him.

'You are a true gentleman,' he said, with some vehemence. 'And I admire your courage greatly. But I have a secret that I cannot for the present divulge even to you. My secret is contained within this box of mine. I beg you not to pry. If you do, both of us will suffer the consequences.'

Ning gave his word. Yan placed the box to which he had been referring on the window-sill, and the minute his head touched his pillow he fell fast asleep and began snoring like thunder. Ning, by contrast, was unable to get to sleep at all. Around midnight he caught sight of a dim form outside, stealing up to the window, then a pair of blazing eyes peering into the room. Terrified, he was about to waken his room-mate, when a small bright object burst out of Yan's box and flew up into the air, cutting through the darkness like a strip of dazzling white silk, splitting in two the stone lintel above the window before flashing back into the box, swift as a bolt of lightning. By now, Yan was awake and on his feet, and Ning, pretending to be asleep, watched as he picked up the box and inspected it, then took something from it and held it up in the moonlight, smelling it and examining it with great care. The object was about two inches long and the width of a spring onion leaf. It shone with a crystalline white light. Yan wrapped it carefully in several layers of cloth and replaced it in the box, which was now broken.

'The brazen demon!' he muttered to himself, as he returned to his bed. 'To ruin my box like that!'

Ning, marvelling at the extraordinary event he had just witnessed, now rose from his bed and described to Yan all that he had seen.

'Since we have become close friends,' said Yan, 'I cannot keep the truth from you any longer. I am a swordsman with certain unusual powers. If it had not been for that stone lintel, the evil spirit would be dead by now. As it is, he is certainly wounded.'

'What was it that you were wrapping up just now?'

'A sword. I could smell the monster's evil aura on it.'

Ning expressed a wish to see this magic weapon, and Yan generously agreed to show it to him. Ning gazed in wonder at the dazzling little miniature sword, and from that moment on held his fellow-lodger in great awe.

The next day, he looked outside the window and saw traces of blood. He left the temple precinct and walked towards the north, where he saw rows of abandoned graves and above one of them a white poplar tree with a crow nesting in its topmost branches. Having concluded his business in Jinhua, he packed his bags in readiness to return home. Yan gave him a farewell banquet, at which he spoke warmly of their friendship and presented Ning with a scuffed old leather bag.

'This is a magical leather bag of mine. It was once used as a scabbard. Treasure it. It will ward off evil spirits.'

Ning expressed a desire to learn some of Yan's magical arts.

'You certainly have the virtue and the strength of character for such things,' said Yan. 'But you are a man destined for a great future in the world, not a man of the Tao like myself.'

Under the pretence that he was exhuming a younger sister of his who had been buried nearby, Ning dug up Little Beauty's bones, wrapped them in grave-clothes and hired a boat for the journey home. His family house was surrounded by fields, and he was able to dig a new grave and bury the bones just outside his studio. There he made a ritual offering and recited a prayer: 'In pity for your lonely spirit, I have buried you near my humble abode. Now I shall be able to hear your singing and weeping, and you will hear mine, and no demons can ever come to harm you again. This libation of mine is a poor one, but I pray that you will deign to accept it.'

He was making his way back to his studio, when a voice hailed him.

'Slowly! Let us walk together.'

He turned to look, and it was Little Beauty. She thanked him joyfully for what he had done.

'Ten deaths would not be enough to repay you for this kindness! Let me go in with you and show my respect to your parents. I would gladly serve them, even as a maid.'

Ning looked closely at her. Her complexion shimmered like a sunset cloud, her feet were as dainty as tiny upturned bamboo-shoots: he found her even more strikingly beautiful in the daylight than she had been at night. He led her to his studio and bid her stay there while he went in to speak to his mother. The old lady was appalled at what he had to say, the more so since Ning's wife had been ill a long time. She ordered him not to breathe a word of this ghost encounter to his wife, for fear the shock might be fatal.

Even as they were talking, Little Beauty flitted into the room and prostrated herself before the lady of the house.

'This is Little Beauty,' said Ning.

At first his mother was too shocked to do anything but stare. The girl spoke first: 'Madam, I am a wandering soul far from parents or family. I dearly wish to repay your son's great compassion towards me, by serving him faithfully.'

Ning's mother had to admit to herself that she was very charming.

'I am indeed delighted,' she replied at last, 'that you should be so attached to Ning. But he is my only son, the sole hope of our family. The continuation of our ancestral sacrifices depends on him. I cannot possibly have him marrying a ghost!'

'Truly I wish him no harm,' replied the girl. 'If you do not trust me, because I am a spirit from the Nether World, then let me serve him as a sister. That would also allow me to wait upon you, morning and evening, as a daughter.'

Ning's mother was moved by her obvious sincerity, and agreed to this unusual arrangement. Little Beauty also expressed a wish to call upon Ning's wife, but Ning's mother absolutely forbade this, on account of the wife's poor health. Little Beauty took herself off to the kitchen and supervised the cooking in the old lady's stead, seeming to know her way around every room of the house as if it were her own home.

At nightfall, Ning's mother began to feel afraid and sent Little Beauty off to sleep 'somewhere else', pointedly not preparing a bed for her. Little Beauty understood her meaning and went outside, making her way to the threshold of Ning's studio, where she stepped back and seemed to hesitate, as if afraid of something. Ning called out to her from inside, and she replied, 'There is something frightening in your room. I sense the aura of a sword. You were carrying it on your journey here. That's why I could not accompany you.'

Ning knew it must be the leather bag, and he took it down and hung it in another room. Now Little Beauty was able to enter the studio and sit down with him in the lamplight. For a while she said nothing, then at last she asked him, 'Do you ever study at night? When I was younger I used to be able to recite the Surangama Sutra, though I've forgotten a lot of it by now. If you could find a copy for me, I could recite it in the evenings and you could correct me.'

Ning was pleased with this idea. They sat silently together for some time, until the second watch of the night was almost ended. Still Little Beauty made no mention of leaving, and when Ning finally urged her to go, she spoke to him sadly: 'A lonely soul in a strange land dreads the desolation of the grave.'

'I have no second bed here,' said Ning. 'And we should observe decorum, as brother and sister.'

She rose, a slight frown on her face as if she might weep at any moment, and, moving slowly and fearfully, glided out of the door and on to the terrace, where she vanished from sight. In his heart Ning felt sorry for her, and would have let her stay and sleep in a separate bed, but was afraid of incurring his mother's displeasure.

Little Beauty waited on his mother morning and evening, bringing water for her to wash with, busying herself with house-hold chores, trying to please her in every way she could. When dusk fell, she always took her leave and made her way to the studio, where she would sit in the lamplight chanting the sutra until she could sense that Ning wanted to go to sleep, when she would leave him, always with the same sad expression on her face.

Now, Ning's wife had been ill of a consumption for a long while and his mother had, as a consequence, been weighed down with household work. Having Little Beauty to help took a great load off her, and with the passage of time she grew fond of her and gradually came to think of her as her own daughter. She ceased to regard her as a ghost. She no longer chased her out of the house at night, but insisted that she should stay and sleep with her in her own room. At first Little Beauty ate and drank nothing, but after six months had passed, she gradually began to take a little thin congee. Little by little, mother and son became extremely attached to her, and they would never have it mentioned in the house that she was a ghost. Indeed, strangers were unable to distinguish anything ghostly about her.

After a considerable interval of time, Ning's wife died. His mother now considered marrying her son to Little Beauty, but was still concerned that this might bring him harm. Little Beauty knew what was on her mind and spoke to her at an opportune moment.

'I have been here in your home for over a year now, so I think you know my true nature. I followed your son here because I wanted to put an end to my own evil-doing – I had nothing else in mind. Your son is a man of such shining virtue, admired by gods and men. All I want is to stay with him and help him for three years. When he achieves some noble rank, perhaps I too can win a little reflected honour in the Nether World.'

Ning's mother knew that she had no evil intent, but her

concern was that such a wife might never be able to bear her son a proper child and continue the family line. Little Beauty tried to reassure her on this score.

'Children are a predestined gift of Heaven. The Register of Destiny says that your son will have three sons, and that they will bring honour to his clan. This cannot be taken away from him simply because he has a spirit wife.'

The old lady believed her implicitly, and once she had discussed the match with her son (whose joy can be imagined), a wedding feast was held to which all the family members were invited. The guests naturally were agog to see the bride, and when she came into view, utterly poised and arrayed in her full bridal splendour, everyone in the hall was struck speechless with wonder. In their eyes she was a fairy, not a ghost, and from this time onwards Ning's relations contended with one another to give her presents and become her friend. Little Beauty turned out to be a talented painter of plum-blossom and orchids, and she gave them scrolls of her own painting in return, which the lucky recipients treasured.

One day, she was sitting by the window and seemed in an unusually melancholy mood. 'Where is that leather bag of yours?' she asked out of the blue.

'You were so afraid of it,' replied Ning, 'so I wrapped it up and put it away.'

'After all this time, I have absorbed a lot of your life force, so I am not afraid of it any more. Why not hang it up by our bed?'

Ning asked her what was really on her mind.

'For three days now,' she replied, 'my heart has been greatly troubled. It is the wicked demon of Jinhua! I know he resents me for having fled from the temple, and I sense that one day very soon he will come and find me.'

Ning took out the leather bag and she examined it closely, turning it over in her hands.

'This is where the magic swordsman used to put the heads of the men he killed! Look how old and worn it is! Who knows how many heads it has held in its time! It makes my flesh creep just to look at it!'

They hung the bag up in their room, and the next day moved it to outside their door. That night, Little Beauty warned Ning not to fall asleep and they sat together in the lamplight, waiting. Suddenly a creature dropped into the courtyard, like a bird alighting from the sky, and Little Beauty hid in terror behind the bed-curtains. Ning looked out: it was a little yaksha-demon, with blazing eyes and bloody tongue. It waved its claws menacingly in the air as it crawled towards the doorway, its eyes burning through the darkness. At the doorway it hesitated, went up to the leather bag and ripped at it with its claws. Suddenly a mighty noise erupted from the bag, which had meanwhile grown to the size of a huge basket of the sort used for moving earth, and something monstrous poked its head out and pulled the demon in. Then there was no sound, and the bag shrank back to its former size.

Ning stood there in open-mouthed astonishment, as Little Beauty came out from behind the bed-curtains.

'We are saved!' she cried happily.

They examined the bag together. All it contained was a quantity of colourless water.

Several years later, Ning succeeded at the doctoral examinations. Little Beauty bore him his first son, and then when he took a concubine, she and Little Beauty each gave him another son. In their lifetimes, all three sons became eminent mandarins.

42

THE DEVOTED MOUSE

Yang Tianyi told this story.

Once he saw two mice come out into his room. One of them was swallowed by a snake. The other mouse glared angrily from a safe distance, its little eyes like two round peppercorns. The snake, its belly full of mouse, went slithering back to its hole and was more than halfway in when the second mouse dashed forward and bit it hard on the tail. Furiously the snake backed out of the hole, and the mouse darted once more to safety. The snake gave chase but was unable to catch the mouse, and returned to its hole. As it entered the hole a second time, the mouse seized it by the tail again, exactly as before. Each time the snake went crawling in, the mouse struck; and each time it emerged, the mouse ran for cover. And so it continued for quite some time, until finally the snake came right out and spat the dead mouse on to the ground. The second mouse approached, sniffed at the corpse and began crying over its friend. Then, squeaking dolefully, it picked it up in its mouth and left.

My friend Mr Zhang Duqing wrote a poem on this subject, entitled 'The Ballad of the Devoted Mouse'.

義鼠

同類傷
殘恨莫
平復響有
銜仗身輕愧他
煮立烖其輩不及
幺麼義鼠情

The mouse bit it hard on the tail.

43

AN EARTHQUAKE

Between the hours of seven and nine in the evening of the
seventeenth day of the sixth month of the seventh year of the
Kangxi reign, a severe earthquake occurred. I happened to be
staying in Jixia, and was sitting in the lamplight drinking with
my cousin Li Duzhi. All of a sudden we heard a rumbling noise
like thunder, coming up towards us from the south-east. We
were both thrown into a great state of alarm, and had no idea
what the noise could be. The next moment, the table began to
rock violently from side to side, upsetting our wine cups, and
the very beams and pillars of the room began to creak as if they
would come crashing down on us at any minute. We looked at
each other aghast. It soon dawned on us that this must be an
earthquake, and we went hurrying out into the street, where
we saw buildings of every description – storeyed mansions,
pavilions, simple cottages – heaving up and down. The cries of
children and the wailing of women mingled with the sounds of
walls crashing and of whole buildings tumbling down. The
scene resembled nothing so much as the contents of a seething
cauldron. Men went tottering to the ground and sat there rolling
around with the movement of the earth, while great ten-foot
waves came surging down the course of the river. The town
echoed with the sounds of cocks crowing and dogs barking. It
was a full two hours before any semblance of calm returned.
And then we saw men and women gathering in the streets, stark
naked, anxious to speak to their neighbours, oblivious of the
fact that they were wearing nothing.
  I learned subsequently that in certain places the wells were
so disturbed that it was no longer possible to draw water from

It dawned on us that this must be an earthquake.

them, while in certain houses terraces that had once faced north now faced south. The mountain outside Qixia was split in two, while the River Yi near the town of Yishui flowed into a great depression to form a lake of several acres. Truly this was a most extraordinary phenomenon.

*

A woman of a certain town went out one night to relieve herself. On her way home she encountered a wolf and saw that it was holding her son in its mouth. She struggled bravely with the beast, and when the wolf loosened its grip, she was able to wrest away her child and take it in her arms. The wolf still crouched there motionless. The woman began to scream and her neighbours came hurrying on to the scene, whereupon the wolf finally ran off.

When the woman had recovered from the shock, she cried out for joy, and recounted the tale of her struggle with the wolf for the benefit of her neighbours, with many dramatic gestures. It was only when she had finished telling the tale that she became aware that she did not have a stitch of clothing on, and went running away.

This was rather like the naked townsfolk after the earthquake. How amusing, the way men panic and forget their normal inhibitions!

44
SNAKE ISLAND

On Guji Island – the Island of Antiquities – in the Eastern Sea, jasmine-flowers of every colour bloom throughout the four seasons of the year. But no one has ever lived on the island, and very few visitors make the crossing.

A gentleman named Zhang of Dengzhou, who was fond of hunting and adventure, heard tell of this island as an especially beautiful place, and, taking with him provisions and wine, he rowed out to it in a little boat. When he arrived, he saw the jasmine-flowers in full bloom. Their scent wafted several miles. Many of the trees he saw around him were huge, several arm-lengths in circumference. Zhang ambled here and there on the island, enjoying himself enormously, and eventually he sat down and poured himself a cup from his pitcher of wine. His one regret was that he had no companion with whom to share this pleasant moment.

Even as this thought entered his mind, a woman of a beauty beyond compare, wearing a dazzling crimson gown, appeared amid the flowers. She smiled when she saw Zhang.

'Here I was having such a lovely time all on my own. I had no idea that there was another flower-lover here on the island!'

'Who are you?' asked Zhang, greatly taken aback.

'I am a sing-song girl from Jiaozhou,' was her reply. 'I've come here with the Sea Prince, and he has gone off on a ramble, to visit some of the sites on the island. I stayed behind, because my little feet give me such trouble walking.'

Zhang, who had just been lamenting his lack of a companion, was overjoyed to find himself with this beautiful young lady and invited her to sit with him and share his wine. She spoke in a soft, entrancing voice, and soon had Zhang completely under her spell. Anxious that the Sea Prince might return at any moment and rob them of their pleasure, he threw his arms around her and began to make love to her. She seemed only too pleased to yield to his advances. Their passion had still not been fully consummated, however, when a sound was heard as of a rushing wind, bending the trees and plants to the ground. The young lady frantically pushed Zhang away from her and rose to her feet, crying, 'The Prince is coming!'

Zhang did up his clothes and looked around him in alarm. The young lady had already vanished. Turning a moment later, he saw a huge snake coming out of the bushes, its body thicker than a large bamboo bucket. In terror, Zhang took refuge behind a large tree, hoping the snake would not see him. But the snake advanced towards him and wrapped itself around both Zhang and the tree, enfolding them several times and pinning Zhang's arms tightly to his body so that he was unable to move. Then it raised its head, darted out its tongue and bit Zhang on the nose. Blood gushed from the bite and formed a pool on the ground, from which the snake, lowering its head, began licking. Zhang thought his last hour had come, when he remembered some fox-poison he had brought with him in a pouch at his waist. He succeeded in inserting two fingers into the pouch, broke open the paper wrapping and pressed some of the powder into the palm of his hand. Then he leaned over and looked down into his hand, so that the blood from his nose dripped on to the powder, forming a thick mixture of blood and poison in the palm of his hand, which sure enough the snake began to lick. It had still not finished drinking when it stretched its body, relaxing its grip, and began thrashing its tail with a thunderous sound against a nearby tree, bringing half the tree crashing down. Finally the thrashing ceased and the snake lay dead on the ground, straight and stiff as a log.

Zhang was for a long while too dazed to move, but eventually he recovered his wits and set off home with the dead snake. He

The snake wrapped itself around both Zhang and the tree.

was seriously ill for more than a month afterwards. It was widely suspected that the young lady was also a snake in human form.

45
GENEROSITY

Ding Qianxi of the town of Zhucheng was a wealthy gentleman of a chivalrous disposition, a staunch upholder of honour and a great admirer of the legendary brigand and knight errant Guo Xie. When a local censor began an investigation into Ding's affairs, he simply disappeared to the nearby town of Anqiu and, since it was raining, took shelter at an inn. By midday, when the rain had still not stopped, a young man came and provided him with an excellent meal. That evening Ding decided to stay the night, and his horse was fed with beans and fresh fodder, while he himself was served a hearty supper.

He asked the young man his name.

'The innkeeper is Mr Yang,' he replied. 'I am his nephew. My father is Mrs Yang's brother. My master normally makes a point of treating his guests well, but unfortunately he is away at present and my aunt is coping on her own. I'm afraid we are too poor to offer you proper service. I hope you will make allowances.'

Ding asked him how his uncle made ends meet, and the young man informed him that he was a man with neither land nor wealth of his own, who supplemented his meagre earnings from the inn by running a small gambling establishment on the premises.

The following day, the rain continued and once again Ding was well looked after. That evening he was puzzled to observe that the hay brought for his horse was in wet bundles of irregular lengths.

'To tell the truth,' explained the youth, 'we are too poor to store any proper hay. My aunt had to take some thatch off the roof.'

'My aunt had to take some thatch off the roof.'

Ding was more perplexed than ever. Were these folk expecting to be handsomely paid for the great pains they were taking? The following morning, before leaving, he offered the youth money, but he refused to accept it, only reluctantly agreeing (when Ding insisted) to take it in and offer it to his aunt. He reappeared shortly afterwards and handed it back.

'My aunt asks me to say that we are not in this business to rob people of their money. My uncle has been away from home and on the road for several days, penniless and relying on the generosity of others. How could we demand money from a traveller arriving at our inn?'

Ding let fall a sigh of admiration for this altruistic spirit of theirs.

'When your uncle returns,' he said, as he was leaving, 'please let him know that Mr Ding of Zhucheng stayed here, and ask him to call on me when he can. I should be honoured.'

Several years passed, and Ding had no news of the Yang family. Then came a year of terrible famine, during which the Yangs suffered greatly and were reduced to dire straits. Mrs Yang urged her husband to call on Ding, and he took her advice, making his way to Zhucheng and giving his name to Ding's gate-man. At first Ding hardly remembered who he was. But a few inquiries jogged his memory and he hurried out in his slippers to greet his guest and invite him in, bowing politely with hands clasped. Yang was wearing rags and worn-out shoes, and Ding at once showed him to a warm room, served him a veritable banquet and treated him with great respect and affection. The following day he had a thick, lined robe made for his guest. Yang was touched by Ding's generous hospitality, but his own family's survival was still in the forefront of his mind, and he could not help but hope for some more material aid. Several days went by without any mention of his being sent home with a parting gift, and finally Yang felt obliged to speak out.

'I cannot conceal this from you any longer, sir! When I came here to see you, we had less than a bushel of rice left at home. You have made me very comfortable here, and I thank you for your great generosity. But what of my wife and family?'

'Please do not concern yourself on their behalf,' replied Ding. 'I have already seen to their needs. Set your mind at ease, and stay here with us for a little longer. Naturally when you do leave I also wish to provide you with your travelling expenses.'

He invited gamblers from all over town to his house, put Yang in charge of the game in such a way that he would make a healthy profit, and by the end of the night Yang had earned himself the considerable sum of one hundred taels of silver. Now Ding accompanied him home. He arrived to find his wife decked out in fine new clothes, and a young maidservant waiting on her. Yang asked her in astonishment what had occurred.

'After you left,' she replied, 'the very next day, a carriage came laden with cloth and silk and grain, enough to fill a whole room. The man said it was a gift from a former lodger of ours, Mr Ding. And he presented me with this maidservant, to wait upon me.'

Yang was overwhelmed by this act of generosity. From that day he enjoyed a more comfortable life, and never again needed to struggle as he had done formerly.

46
THE GIANT FISH

There had never been mountains along the sea. Then one day
suddenly they appeared, a great range of them, peak upon peak,
stretching for miles, to the great astonishment of all who beheld
them. And then the following day, just as suddenly, the mountains moved away and there was nothing.

Legend had it that it was a huge sea-fish, which came every
Qing Ming Festival, along with all of its family, to worship at
their ancestral tomb. This was why it usually appeared on Cold
Food Day.

47

THE GIANT TURTLE

An elderly gentleman called Zhang, a native of the western region of Jin, was about to give away his daughter in marriage, and took his family with him by boat on a trip to the South, having decided to purchase there all that was necessary for her trousseau. When the boat arrived at Gold Mountain, he went ahead across the river, leaving his family on board and warning them not to fry any strong-smelling meat during his absence, for fear of provoking the turtle-demon that lurked in the river. This vicious creature would be sure to come out if it smelled meat cooking, and would destroy the boat and eat alive anyone on board. It had been wreaking havoc in the area for a long while.

Once the old man had left, his family quite forgot his words of caution, lit a fire on deck and began to cook meat on it. All of a sudden a great wave arose, overturning their boat and drowning both Zhang's wife and daughter. When Zhang returned, he was grief-stricken at their deaths. He climbed up to the monastery on Gold Mountain and called on the monks there, asking them for information about the turtle's strange ways, so that he could plan his revenge. The monks were appalled at his intentions.

'We live with the turtle every day, in constant fear of the devastation it is capable of causing. All we can do is worship it and pray to it not to fly into a rage. From time to time we slaughter animals, cut them in half and throw them into the river. The turtle jumps out of the water, gulps them down and disappears. No one would be so crazy as to try to seek revenge!'

As he listened to the monks' words, Zhang was already

forming his plan. He recruited a local blacksmith, who set up a furnace on the hillside above the river and smelted a large lump of iron, over a hundred catties in weight. Zhang then ascertained the turtle's exact hiding place and hired a number of strong men to lift up the red-hot molten iron with a great pair of tongs and hurl it into the river. True to form, the turtle leaped out of the water, gulped down the molten metal and plunged back into the river. Minutes later, mountainous waves came boiling to the water's surface. Then, in an instant, the river became calm and the turtle could be seen floating dead on the water.

Travellers and monks alike rejoiced at the turtle's death. They built a temple to old man Zhang, erected a statue of him inside it and worshipped him as a water god. When they prayed to him, their wishes were always fulfilled.

張老相公

譬電巧得鐵龜

計山羊鑄工治

鐵時行旅寺僧称快

日馨者長奉相公祠

They hurled the red-hot molten iron into the river.

48

MAKING ANIMALS

Many and various are the ways of bewitching folk. Sometimes sweet-tasting drugs are put in food, the eating of which sends the victim into a trance and causes him to follow blindly the person who has bewitched him. This is commonly known as 'hitting the wad'; south of the Yangtze it is known as 'dragging the wad'. It is young children who are most frequently bewitched and harmed in this way.

Then there is the art of turning men into animals, known for short as 'making animals'. This is less frequently encountered in the north, but is more common south of the Yellow River.

One day, a man came to an inn in Yangzhou, leading with him five donkeys. He tied them up near the stable, telling the landlord he would be gone a few minutes and giving him strict instructions to give them neither food nor water during his absence. He had not been gone long before the donkeys, which had been left to stand out in the glare of the sun, began to kick and bray and make a terrible racket. The landlord untied them and was about to tether them in the shade when suddenly they spotted water and made a rush to get at it. The landlord let them drink, and no sooner had the water touched their lips than they began rolling on the ground and were transformed into five women. The astonished landlord asked them what was going on, but they seemed incapable of speech, so he took them and hid them in one of his private apartments. Presently their owner returned to the courtyard of the inn, bringing with him five sheep. He asked the landlord at once what had become of his donkeys, and the landlord replied by showing him politely to a seat and offering him food and wine.

They were transformed into five women.

'Enjoy your meal, sir. Your donkeys will be brought to you in a moment.'

The landlord meanwhile went out into the yard and gave the sheep some water, on drinking which they were transformed into five young boys. He secretly reported the matter to the local yamen, and constables were sent to arrest the sorcerer, who died under torture.

49

THE LITTLE MANDARIN

A certain Hanlin Academician, whose name I can no longer remember, was dozing in his study during the daytime, when suddenly he saw a little procession filing through the room. There were horses the size of frogs, men less than finger-high, a retinue of several dozen insignia-bearers, and then a mandarin in a palanquin, wearing a black gauze cap and a ceremonial gown with an embroidered border, who was carried out through the doorway with great pomp.

The Academician marvelled greatly to himself at this extraordinary sight, and wondered if perhaps his sleepy eyes were playing a trick on him. Then one of the little men turned back into the room and came towards his bed, carrying a small fist-sized bundle, wrapped in felt.

'My master,' he declared, 'apologizes for seeming impolite, sir, and wishes to make you a present of this.'

The little man stood there but showed no sign of presenting either the bundle or anything else. A little later he chuckled to himself. 'Such a trifle – I didn't think you would have much use for it, sir! You might as well give it to me . . .'

The Academician nodded, and the little man set off happily once more, carrying the bundle on his back, and was soon lost to view.

And the shame of it was that the Academician had been too timid to ask him who they all were.

He saw a little procession filing through the room.

50

DYING TOGETHER

In a village near Jiyang, there was a man by the name of Zhu who at the age of fifty or so fell ill and died. His family had come into the dead man's room and were busy adjusting their mourning clothes when suddenly they heard him call out, loud and clear, and hurried over to the bed. Discovering to their delighted astonishment that he was indeed alive, they asked him to tell them something about his experience, but the only person he wanted to speak to was his wife.

'When I went, it never occurred to me to try and come back. But then, after a few miles, I kept thinking to myself: I'm leaving my wife behind! There'd be no joy left in life for an old body like you, having to depend on the children for everything, winter and summer, year in, year out. So I decided to come back and take you with me.'

At first they ignored this as the delirious raving of a man newly revived from the dead. But then he proceeded to repeat the exact same words.

'That's all very well and fine,' said his wife, 'but you've only this minute come back to life. How will you manage to die a second time?'

He waved aside this objection.

'That is not a problem. Just you go and see to any last-minute chores that need doing.'

At first she stood there motionless, smiling. Then she went out of the room, and returned a few minutes later.

'I've seen to everything,' she lied.

'Now dress yourself properly,' he said.

At first she refused to do this, but when he grew impatient

祝　翁

縫　綣　恩　私
悲　永　訣　由　來
怳　惚　寂　情　涘
從　今　白　首　不　歸
去　麻　縷　兮　香
賣　暖　心

The only person he wanted to speak to was his wife.

and urged her to hurry, she agreed to put on her best going-out gown, to humour him. All this time the ladies of the family were sniggering behind their hands.

Zhu now lay down with his head on the pillow and commanded his wife to do likewise, tapping on the bed beside him with his hand.

'Our children are all around us,' she protested. 'They will laugh at us if we lie down on the bed together like that in front of them.'

He thumped the bed.

'Dying together is no laughing matter!' he cried.

Seeing that he was in earnest and growing angrier by the minute, the family urged the lady to gratify this whim of his. She rested her head on the pillow and lay there next to him, stiff as a corpse. The members of the family were just beginning to snigger again, when they saw the smile fade from her face and her eyes close. A long silence ensued, and they thought she must have fallen asleep. But when they went up closer, to their horror they discovered that her skin was stone-cold and that she was no longer breathing. Her husband was dead too.

During the twenty-first year of the reign of Kangxi, I was given a detailed account of this event by the wife of old man Zhu's younger brother. She worked in the household of Judge Bi.

THE ALLIGATOR'S REVENGE

The alligator has its origins in the region to the west of the lower reaches of the Yangtze River. It is dragonlike in appearance, but shorter than a true dragon, and only able to fly sideways. From time to time, it emerges from the river and scours the banks for food – usually geese and ducks. Sometimes alligators are caught and these are sold to members of the Chen and Ke families (descendants of the Red Turban leader Chen Youliang), who have traditionally been eaters of alligator meat. People from other families never venture to eat it.

A traveller coming from west of the river captured one and kept it tied up with a rope in his boat. One day, he had moored in the Qiantang River when the rope worked its way loose and the creature suddenly leaped into the water. The next instant, great waves rose up and overturned the boat, which capsized and sank into the river.

SHEEP SKIN

A certain gentleman of Shaanxi Province, who passed the third degree in the year *xinchou*, was able to remember his previous incarnation. He said he had formerly been a scholar who had died in middle life and had appeared before Yama, the King of the Nether World, where he had seen with his own eyes the cauldrons and woks filled with boiling oil, the very instruments of torture he had read about on Earth. In the eastern corner of the hall stood a number of frames from which were suspended the skins of various animals – pigs, sheep, goats, dogs, horses. When the clerk of the court called out a name from his list, and the sentence specified into which animal form a certain person was to be reborn, the man referred to would be stripped naked, and an animal skin was taken down from the designated frame, for him to put on.

It soon came to the turn of the gentleman, and he heard the King pronounce his sentence: 'To be reborn as a sheep!'

One of the demon-assistants promptly took down a white sheep skin and was putting it on him, when the clerk remarked that the man had during his lifetime saved another man's life. The King consulted the files carefully.

'This man is to be spared!' he announced. 'His evil deeds were many, but this one good deed has redeemed them all!'

The demon-assistant then tried to remove the sheep skin, but it had already stuck fast. Two other demons came up, and by dint of much pulling, holding the man's arms tight and pressing against his chest, they finally succeeded in detaching it, causing him an indescribable agony in the process. The skin only came off in bits and pieces, however, and they were unable to remove

陝右某公

憑將善惡判陰曹
轉轂人羊數
莫逃賴有
救生功可贖
不曾戴角
祇披毛

They finally succeeded in detaching the sheep skin.

it cleanly. A piece the size of a man's hand remained stuck to the man's shoulder.

When he was reborn, he had a big white furry birthmark on his back, like a sheep-skin patch. However many times the hair was cut back, it always grew again.

53
SHARP SWORD

At the end of the Ming dynasty, the region around Ji'nan was overrun by bandits. Every township had its garrison of soldiers, and whenever a bandit was apprehended he was swiftly executed. The town of Zhangqiu had an especially large number of such bandits, and one of the government soldiers stationed there was known to possess a very sharp sword. His blade cut clean through anything, as though it were cleaving the air. One day, a group of a dozen bandits were caught and brought to the execution ground. One of them recognized the soldier with the sharp sword. 'Everyone says you've got the sharpest sword,' he mumbled. 'They say it can cut a head clean off in a single blow. I beg you, be the one to kill me!'

'Very well,' replied the soldier. 'Be careful to stay right next to me.'

The bandit followed the soldier closely to the execution ground. The soldier drew his sword and swung it once. The man's head tumbled to the ground and rolled a few feet. And as it rolled, it gasped, 'That *is* a sharp sword!'

快刀

尚殺原非弭盜法劇憐駢戮赴
西曹更無忍死須臾意但為
頭顱覓快刀

The man's head rolled a few feet.

54

LOTUS FRAGRANCE

Translator's note: In this longer story, I have incorporated some of the commentaries into the text, to show how this was normally done in the old Chinese editions of Strange Tales. *The commentators were constantly at one's side.*

There was a young man by the name of Sang Xiao, from the town of Yizhou. He was orphaned when still a young man, and went to live in Saffron Bank, a small country town nearby. His was a quiet, self-contained nature. He only set foot outside his lodgings twice a day, and then only to eat with his neighbour to the east. The rest of the time he spent alone at home in his studio.

Once his neighbour dropped by and said in jest, 'Living all on your own like this, are you never scared of ghosts and fox-spirits?'

Sang laughed. 'Why should a grown man fear such things? Supposing something of that sort does ever come to visit me, why, if it's male, I have a sharp sword at the ready; and if it's female, I shall simply open my door and invite the young lady in!'

The neighbour went home and plotted with his friends. They persuaded a local sing-song girl to lean a ladder up against Sang's wall and climb into his compound. She tapped her fingers on his door, and Sang peeped out and asked who was there.

'A ghost!' replied a woman's voice.

Sang had the fright of his life, and his teeth started chattering in his head. The sing-song girl lingered a little while, and then went away.

Dan Minglun: Game One – enter the sing-song girl.

The next morning, the neighbour called round again at Sang's lodgings, and Sang related his frightening encounter with a ghost, announcing his intention of quitting the place and returning directly to his home town. The neighbour clapped his hands: 'But I thought you said you would invite her in!'

Sang realized at once that they had played a trick on him, and his fears were allayed.

Dan Minglun: A clever, roundabout way of preparing for the next scene.

Six months went by uneventfully, and then one night there came another knock on his studio door, followed by a woman's voice again. This time Sang, confident that it was another of his neighbour's pranks, opened the door and invited the woman in. He gazed in wonder at the ravishing beauty who entered. When he asked her where she hailed from, she replied that her name was Lotus Fragrance, and that she was a sing-song girl from the Western District.

Dan Minglun: Game Two – enter the fox, as a consequence of Game One.

Sang was aware that there were quite a number of houses of pleasure in Saffron Bank, and he believed her tale. The lamp was soon extinguished, and the two of them climbed into bed, where they enjoyed to the full the sweet pleasures of love. From that day on, Lotus Fragrance returned to visit him every few nights.

Dan Minglun: The 'real' sing-song girl has prepared us for Lotus Fragrance [the false sing-song girl]. What subtlety, what skill! Li's subsequent appearance is linked to that of Lotus Fragrance. The whole story repeatedly links ghost and fox. They appear together, and the whole is in jest, it happens naturally, without the slightest trace of artifice. This scintillating text, with its strange transformations, grows entirely out of this word 'jest'. The essence of the writer's art lies in the playfulness of his conception.

One evening, Sang was sitting alone, lost in his thoughts, when he became vaguely aware of a woman's form flitting into the room. Thinking it must be Lotus Fragrance on one of her periodic visits, he rose to greet her – only to see before him a total stranger, a young girl of fifteen or sixteen, with long flowing sleeves and hair down to her shoulders. She was an exquisite vision, at one and the same time ethereally graceful and sensually alluring. When she moved, she seemed to drift through the air rather than walk. Sang at once had misgivings that she was a fox-spirit, and was greatly afraid.

Dan Minglun: Game Three – enter the ghost (as a consequence of Game Two).

'I am a daughter of the Li family,' she told him, as if divining his thoughts. 'My family are well-respected people. Your fame as a man of great refinement and culture has reached my ears, and I have long wished to make your acquaintance.'

Sang felt strongly drawn to her and took hold of her hand, which was cold as ice. 'Why are you so cold?'

'I'm only a young girl,' she replied, 'and extremely delicate by nature. It's a frosty night outside. Of course I am cold!'

She loosened her silken robe, and when they made love, he found her to be a virgin.

'This love of ours was destined to be,' she said to him. 'Tonight I have given you the flower of my purity. Take me in, and I will stay with you for ever and sleep by your side. But first you must tell me if you have some other lover.'

'There is no other,' replied Sang, adding, 'apart from a sing-song girl of the neighbourhood, and she does not come here often.'

'I must avoid her at all costs,' said the girl. 'I am not at all like those women from the houses of pleasure. And you, my love, must keep our secret and be sure never to mention me to her. Whenever she comes, I shall go; when she has gone, I shall return.'

The cock crowed, and she made to leave. But before going, she gave him a tiny embroidered slipper, saying, 'This is something intimate of mine. Touch it, turn it around in your hand, and your thoughts of love will reach me. But be careful never to touch it if there is anyone else present!'

He took the slipper. It was an exquisite thing, tapering to a fine point like a little bodkin for unpicking embroidery knots. The very next evening, when he was alone, he held it again and gazed at it, turning it round in his hand. Suddenly there she was, and soon they were making love. From that time forth, whenever he took out the slipper, there she would be, in answer to his desires.

He marvelled at this strange way she had of appearing, but whenever he asked her to explain, she would merely smile and say, 'I always arrive at the right moment!'

One night, Lotus Fragrance came to see him again. 'My dear!' she said in some alarm. 'You seem to be in very low spirits!'

'Not that I am aware of,' he replied.

That night, when she took her leave, Lotus Fragrance said she would be away for ten days. During this absence of hers, Li spent every night with Sang.

'Why has that lady-friend of yours not been to see you for such a long time?' she asked him one evening. He told her that Lotus Fragrance had gone away for ten days. Li smiled. 'Tell me, dearest, who is the prettier: myself, or this Lotus Fragrance?'

'Perhaps her skin is a little softer and warmer to the touch,' he replied. 'But you are both of you perfection!'

She pulled a face. 'You *say* that just to humour me! I am sure she's far prettier than I am – why, I dare say she is as beautiful as the Moon Goddess herself!'

She seemed most unhappy. Counting the days on her fingers, she calculated that it was already ten days since Lotus Fragrance had gone away. She told Sang that she had decided to spy on her rival, and that he must not breathe a word of it to Lotus Fragrance when she returned.

> *Dan Minglun: With the spying, the author brings ghost and fox into clear focus. The 'beauty contest' provides the context for the spying. What subtlety!*

True to her word, the very next night, Lotus Fragrance came to Sang. She talked and laughed gaily with him, but the moment they withdrew to bed she cried out in a shocked voice, 'Look at you! How dreadfully thin you have grown in these ten days! You must have been sleeping with someone else!'

Sang asked her why she said this.

'I can tell from your aura,' she replied. 'Your pulse is all broken, like a tangled skein of silk. You are possessed by a spirit.'

The following night, Li came and Sang asked her what impression she had formed of Lotus Fragrance.

'Oh, she's very beautiful all right. More beautiful than any woman on earth could ever be. That's the point. She is definitely a fox-spirit. When she went away, I followed her to her hole in the southern hills.'

Sang attributed this remark to jealousy and paid it no heed. But the next night he teased Lotus Fragrance, 'Someone's been saying that you're a fox-spirit. I don't believe it myself, but . . .'

'*Who's* been saying so?' snapped Lotus Fragrance, and pressed him for an answer.

Sang laughed awkwardly. 'Oh, I was only teasing . . .'

'And anyway, what makes fox-spirits so different from humans?' she asked.

'They cast spells on men, they make them fall ill, even die. That's why we are so frightened of them.'

'No!' protested Lotus Fragrance. 'It's not like that at all! A strong young man such as yourself can restore his vital energy three days after the act of love. Even a fox-spirit can do you no harm. But if you go indulging yourself day after day, then a human lover can do you more harm than a fox.

Feng Zhenluan: Wise counsel! Young people, take heed of this!

'You cannot blame everything on foxes! Someone must have been saying nasty things about me.'

Sang denied this, but she only pressed him the more, and in the end he told her all about his new lover, Li.

'I knew it! I could tell there was something strange about the rapid course of your illness! That girl is definitely not human. Don't breathe a word to her. Tomorrow night, *I* will spy on her . . .'

The next evening, Li came, but before she and Sang had exchanged more than a few words, they heard a cough outside the window and she fled. In came Lotus Fragrance.

'You are in grave danger! That new girl of yours is a ghost!

There is no doubt about it! Allow this infatuation of yours to continue, and you will be going to certain death!'

Sang thought to himself that she too was speaking out of jealousy, and said nothing in reply.

'I know you will find it hard to break with her,' Lotus Fragrance continued, 'but you must. I cannot stand by and watch you waste away and die. Tomorrow I shall bring you some herbs to help you purge this poison. Luckily it has not yet entered too deeply into your body. In ten days' time you should be cured. If you agree, I will stay here by your bedside and nurse you until then.'

The following evening, she came with a small quantity of medicine as promised, and gave it to Sang. The instant he swallowed the first dose, his bowels opened several times. He immediately felt a renewed lightness in his internal organs, and his whole sense of physical vitality was restored. He told her how grateful he was to her, but still he could not bring himself to believe that Li was a ghost. Lotus Fragrance slept by his side every night; but if he tried to make love to her, she refused him.

Dan Minglun: He knows that Li is a ghost, but he can't believe it.

Several days later, he began to put on weight and seemed to be growing stronger. Lotus Fragrance took her leave, earnestly beseeching him once more to break off relations with Li. He assured her – with apparent sincerity – that he would do so. But the moment she was gone and the door was closed, he trimmed his lamp, took the little slipper in his hand and thought of Li. The very next instant, there she was. She seemed resentful at their long separation (and at Lotus Fragrance's continued presence).

'She has just been caring for me these past few nights,' he protested. 'Surely you cannot hold that against her! You know I love you – that is what matters.'

She was somewhat mollified by his words. Sang lay down by her side and whispered, 'I love you deeply! But someone has said that you are a ghost . . .'

For a long while she was speechless. Then she burst out, 'It's her! It's that slut of a fox putting ideas into your head! You must break with her, or I shall go away and never see you again!'

She broke down and wept. Sang did everything he could to comfort and reassure her, and finally succeeded in calming her down.

The following evening, Lotus Fragrance returned. When she learned that Li had been with him again, she cried angrily, 'Do you *want* to die?'

Sang gave a little laugh. 'Why are you still so jealous, my darling?'

At this she grew angrier still. 'You were wasting away, you were on the verge of death, and I gave you back your health! If that's jealousy, then you're lucky I *was* jealous. If I hadn't been, what would have become of you?'

'*She* said that my illness was caused by a fox-spirit,' said Sang, deliberately goading her on. 'She said I was under a spell.'

'So you are!' sighed Lotus Fragrance. 'You are hopelessly blind! I can see now that something terrible will happen to you, and that whatever I say, you'll hold me to blame. Very well. I shall go away. This time I shall stay away for a hundred days. Then I shall come back to visit you on your sickbed.'

He pleaded with her to stay, but she went away in a fit of angry pique.

From then on, he and Li were inseparable day and night. After two months, he began to feel an overwhelming sense of fatigue, which he shrugged off at first. But he continued to grow thinner day by day, and could barely manage to drink even a cup of congee. He began to consider returning home and letting his own relations take care of him, but could not bear the thought of wrenching himself away from Li. He continued like this for several days, until he could no longer even rise from his bed. His neighbour could see that he was seriously ill, and sent his pageboy round every day with nourishing broths for the invalid.

Sang himself finally began to suspect Li, and one day he said to her, 'Now I regret not having heeded Lotus Fragrance's advice. Look at the state I am in!'

As he spoke, he closed his eyes and drifted into a semi-conscious state. A little while later, when he came round and looked about him, Li was nowhere to be seen. Days went by, and still she did not return. He lay there alone in his empty studio, emaciated, longing now for Lotus Fragrance's return with all his heart, just as a farmer longs for the time of his harvest. And then one day, just as he was thinking of her, the door-curtain was raised and in she came.

'My poor country fool!' she said, walking up to his bed with a tender smile. 'Was I telling the truth?'

Sang sobbed, confessing that he had been wrong and begging her to save him.

'This time the illness has entered deep into your vital organs,' said Lotus Fragrance. 'I know of no cure for it now. I have come to bid you adieu, and to prove to you that I was never jealous.'

Sang was overcome with grief.

'Under my pillow,' he said, 'you will find something. I want you to take it and destroy it.'

Lotus Fragrance found the slipper. But, rather than destroy it, she held it up to the lamplight, turning it over and toying with it. At once Li appeared. The instant she saw Lotus Fragrance she turned to flee, but Lotus Fragrance barred the doorway with her body. Sang began to reproach Li for the harm she had done him, and she stood there in silence.

Lotus Fragrance smiled. 'At last we meet face to face! You accused *me* of bringing this illness on him. Now what do you say?'

Li hung her head and begged forgiveness.

'How could you do this?' continued Lotus Fragrance. 'How could a beautiful girl like you use love as a weapon of hatred?'

Feng Zhenluan: These words – about using love as a
weapon of hatred – are a veritable Book of Life!

The girl flung herself on the ground and wept bitterly. Lotus Fragrance raised her, and asked her to tell her story.

'I am the daughter of Judge Li, the Deputy Prefect,' she began. 'I died when I was a young girl, and they buried me outside the wall of this house before my web of destiny was complete. I died like a silkworm in the spring, woven into its own cocoon, before it could finish making its thread. But my feelings of love

蓮香

七日沉痾遂
故我十年
儹約訂前
生閒中細
讀叕生傳
妖鬼爭妍
戲爲情

Li hung her head and begged forgiveness.

never died. It was always my heart's desire to be this young man's dearest companion. It was never my intention to cause his death.'

Dan Minglun: It is true that she had no intention of doing so, but with even the best intentions, love can lead to illness and death. Unbridled lust can kill even in a harmonious marriage.

'What I have heard,' said Lotus Fragrance, 'is that ghosts wish their man to die, because once he is dead he is with them for ever.'

'No!' cried the girl. 'Why, when two ghosts are together, there is no joy in it for either of them. If *that* were the sort of pleasure I wanted, there are dead young men aplenty in the Nether World!'

'What a silly girl you were,' retorted Lotus Fragrance, 'to make love with him like that night after night! Even a human lover would have endangered his health with such indulgence – let alone a ghost!'

'Foxes also drive men to their death,' said Li. 'What makes you so different?'

Dan Minglun: In truth it is neither foxes nor ghosts that hurt mortals; mortals hurt themselves. This sums up the entire preceding section. It also harks back to the original jest.

'You are speaking of the fox-spirits that feed themselves by sucking the life out of men. I am not that sort. You see, the truth is, there are harmless foxes, but never harmless ghosts. Ghosts are too dark, they belong for ever to the realm of Yin.'

Hearing this exchange, Sang could deny the truth no longer: Lotus Fragrance was a fox-spirit and Li a ghost. His long acquaintance with the two of them enabled him to accept this extraordinary fact with a certain equanimity. But even as they were talking, he felt his life force waning and gave a cry of pain.

'What are we going to do with our young man?' said Lotus Fragrance to Li. But Li merely blushed with shame and shrank from her despondently.

'I am afraid that even if he *were* to regain his health,' said Lotus Fragrance, with a wry smile, 'you would be more jealous than ever.'

At this, Li drew herself up, straightened her gown and bowed with some dignity. 'Find a skilled physician to heal him,' she said. 'Free me of my guilt, and I will gladly bury my head beneath the ground and never show my face here again.'

Lotus Fragrance took some medicine from her bag.

'I knew this day would come,' she said. 'When I left, I went searching on the three Fairy Hills. It took me three full months to bring together the necessary herbs. This special remedy of mine will restore any man afflicted with this wasting illness, even when it has reached such an advanced stage. But the cure must be administered by the person who caused the illness. So I must ask you to help me.'

'What must I do?' asked Li.

'All we need is a little saliva from your pretty mouth,' said Lotus Fragrance. 'I shall place one of my pills in his mouth, and then I want you to press your lips to his and spit.'

Li blushed fiercely and lowered her head, turning coyly from side to side and gazing at her embroidered slippers.

Lotus Fragrance laughed. 'One would think you were in love with your slippers . . .'

The girl was more embarrassed than ever and did not know which way to look.

'Come!' said Lotus Fragrance. 'There's nothing to it! You've done this sort of thing often enough – why so coy all of a sudden?'

She took a large bolus-like pill and held it to Sang's lips, then turned to Li and urged her on. Reluctantly Li did as she had been told, put her lips to Sang's and moistened the pill with her saliva.

'Again!' cried Lotus Fragrance, and again Li complied. Three or four times she repeated it, and finally the pill went down. In a little while, his belly began to rumble like thunder. Lotus Fragrance placed another pill between his lips and this time she herself pressed her lips to his and projected her own vital force into him. He felt his Cinnabar Field, the very centre of his being, take fire and his life force quicken within him.

'He is cured!' cried Lotus Fragrance.

Li heard the cock crow and, with some hesitation, departed,

leaving Lotus Fragrance to stay and take care of Sang. He remained at home, still too weak to go to his neighbour's for meals, and Lotus Fragrance locked the door from the outside, thereby creating the impression that he had gone home, and deterring any would-be callers. Meanwhile she continued to wait on him day and night, assisted in this by Li, who came every evening and looked up to her now like an elder sister. Lotus Fragrance for her part grew more and more fond of Li.

This ménage continued for three months, at the end of which time Sang was fully recovered. Then, for several evenings, there was no sign of Li. When she did finally appear, she stayed only a very short while, and from her face they could see that she was extremely downcast. Lotus Fragrance had often invited her to stay and share their bed, but she had always refused, and this evening was no exception. Later, when she took her leave, Sang went after her and carried her back in his arms, finding her as light as a straw burial-doll. She felt obliged to stay, and curled up on the bed as she was, fully clothed, occupying a space barely two feet long. Lotus Fragrance felt more affectionate towards her than ever, and secretly she urged Sang to embrace her. He tried to wake her, but in vain. Then he himself fell asleep. When he awoke, he reached for her but she had vanished. More than ten days passed by and still there was no sign of her. Sang missed her greatly, and often took out the slipper. Once he and Lotus Fragrance held it together.

'What a delightful creature she is!' said Lotus Fragrance. 'I've grown strangely fond of her myself! It's little wonder that you came to love her so!'

'In the past,' replied Sang, 'she came to me whenever I touched the slipper. I used to wonder what it meant, but I could never imagine that she was a ghost. Now whenever I see the slipper I see her face. It makes me feel so dreadfully sad.'

He wept as he spoke.

*

Now, just before this, in the Zhang family (a local household of some considerable means), a fifteen-year-old girl called Swallow had suddenly fallen ill, and when her illness was aggravated by an inability to perspire, she died. But the very next morning she appeared to come back to life, sat up in bed and wanted to be running around. Her father bolted the door to prevent her from going out. She began talking as if to herself: 'I am the spirit of the Judge's daughter. A young gentleman named Sang has been very good to me, and is always present in my thoughts. I left one of my slippers with him. I am a ghost, so you will achieve nothing by locking me up.'

> Dan Minglun: When she was a ghost, the slipper gave her such pleasure. In her new life, she is still unable to forget it. It is only after her rebirth that she can admit to being a ghost.

Her story seemed to make some sort of strange sense, but afterwards, when the Zhang family asked her how she had come to be where she was, and if she was truly who she said she was, she looked around her in a dazed fashion and was quite unable to provide an explanation. One of them told her that Sang was ill, and that he had left town and gone home. But she insisted that this was not true, which greatly perplexed them.

Sang's neighbour came to hear of this strange event in the Zhang family and of the various claims made by the girl, and he decided to climb his wall and investigate for himself whether his friend was still at home. He soon saw with his own eyes that Sang, so far from having gone away, was sitting in his studio talking to a beautiful lady. He was creeping in on them when, in the confusion of the moment, the beautiful lady vanished. In utter amazement, he asked Sang what was going on.

'Didn't I once say,' laughed Sang, 'that if a woman knocked, I would open the door and let her in!'

> Dan Minglun: He prevaricates by alluding to a true event in the past. And at the same time our author is able to remind us of the very beginning of his story.

The neighbour proceeded to tell him about the miraculous revival of Swallow Zhang and the strange things she had been saying. Sang unlocked his outer door at once, wanting to call on the Zhang family in order to learn more. But he could think of no acceptable pretext for doing so.

The girl's mother, Mrs Zhang, had herself meanwhile ascertained to her own great astonishment that the young gentleman named Sang had indeed (as Swallow insisted) never returned home, and she sent one of her serving-women to retrieve the slipper mentioned by Swallow in her deluded ramblings. Sang promptly handed it over, and Swallow was at first overjoyed to have it. But then, when she tried it on, she discovered to her dismay that it was a good inch too small for her. She looked at herself in the mirror, and suddenly to her horror the truth dawned on her: she had come back to life, but in a completely different body. Now she told her new family her entire story, and her mother believed that she was telling the truth.

'To think that I used to be so vain!' sobbed Swallow, continuing to look into the mirror. 'And even then I felt inferior beside Lotus Fragrance! Look at me now! I was prettier by far when I was a ghost!'

She held the slipper in her hand and wept inconsolably, lying there stiff and motionless under her covers from that day forth, and refusing all food. At first her body began to swell. For seven days, she continued to eat nothing and still she did not die. Gradually the swelling subsided, and she began to feel unbearably hungry and started to eat again. After a few days, her body began to itch and her skin fell away, and when she rose one morning, her bedsocks fell off her feet and on to the floor. Picking them up, she saw that they were much too large for her feet; so she tried one of the slippers on again and discovered to her delight that it was now a perfect fit. Looking once more in the mirror, she was overjoyed to see that her features had also been restored to their former beauty. She washed herself, combed her hair and went in to see her mother, everyone staring at her in amazement as she passed by.

Lotus Fragrance heard of this extraordinary transformation and encouraged Sang to send a matchmaker to the Zhangs. He was reluctant to take any such steps, since the Zhang family was so much wealthier than his own. Then, one day, an opportunity arose to make contact. It was old Mrs Zhang's birthday, and Sang went with some of her younger relations to offer his congratulations. When the old lady saw his name card among the others, she told Swallow to peep through the blind and take a look at the guests. Sang was the last to arrive. Swallow had no sooner set eyes on him than she went running out into the room, seized him by the sleeve and wanted to go home with him at once. Her mother reprimanded her, and she left the room in shame and confusion. But Sang himself had meanwhile recognized her as his former lover, and he fell weeping to his knees. The old lady raised him up, not in the least put out or offended. Sang took his leave and asked the girl's uncle to act as a go-between. Mrs Zhang duly selected an auspicious day and announced her intention of welcoming Sang into her family.

On returning to his lodgings, Sang told Lotus Fragrance what had happened and asked her what they should do. She maintained a long and melancholy silence, and then announced that she would have to leave.

'Now that you are getting married,' she said, paying no heed to Sang's tearful pleading, 'how can I possibly stay with you?'

But Sang would not hear of it. He had a plan. It was this. First they should return together as man and wife, he and Lotus Fragrance, to his native village, and then he could return and marry Swallow afterwards. Lotus Fragrance agreed to do this. On his return, Sang explained to the Zhangs how things stood, and although Mrs Zhang was angry to discover that he already had a wife and rebuked him for it, Swallow endeavoured to explain everything to her parents and finally succeeded in talking them round.

The day came for the wedding, and Sang went to fetch his new bride, having prepared his studio as best he could for the occasion. But when the two of them arrived, he found the whole place richly carpeted and ablaze with countless coloured lanterns. Lotus Fragrance accompanied the bride into the nuptial chamber, and when Swallow took off her veil, the two women were reunited in their happy friendship of former days. Lotus Fragrance was present when they drank the wedding cup, and then she asked Swallow to tell her the whole story of her rebirth.

Dan Minglun: What a darling Lotus Fragrance is!

Wang Shizhen: What a fine person was Lotus Fragrance!
I have seldom encountered a woman of such rare quality,
let alone a fox!

'That day,' began Swallow, 'when I left you both and went away, I was so miserable, I felt entirely lost. I was nothing but a ghost, a vile, strange creature. I was so wretched that I refused to return to my grave, but instead I drifted here and there on the wind, envying every living soul. In the daytime, I clung to the grasses and trees; by night, I roamed from one place to another. By chance I came to the Zhang home and saw a young girl lying dead on her bed. I went up to her, and somehow, without knowing how, I came back to life again – through her.'

Lotus Fragrance listened to her tale in silence, deep in thought.

Feng Zhenluan: Even a ghost needs will power!

Two months passed, and Lotus Fragrance bore Sang a son. After the birth, she fell suddenly ill and her condition grew more and more serious. She took Swallow by the hand one day. 'I wish to entrust my child – the fruit of my karma – to your care. My child is your child.'

Swallow wept to hear this and tried to comfort her. They called in doctors and clairvoyants, but Lotus Fragrance sent them all away. The illness reached its crisis, and her life hung by a thread. Sang and Swallow stood weeping at her bedside when suddenly she opened her eyes wide.

'Do not weep!' she said. 'You find your joy in life, I find mine in death. If it is our karma, we will see each other again ten years from now.'

And with these words she died.

When they lifted the bedcovers to prepare her for burial, they found the body of a fox. But Sang refused to regard her as a supernatural being, and buried her with all the usual ceremony.

Dan Minglun: Only after death does her body really
become that of a fox.

The boy was named Foxy (Hu-er), and Swallow reared him as if he were her own. On every Qing Ming Festival, she went to Lotus Fragrance's grave with the child in her arms and wept for her friend.

The years went by, and Foxy grew into a young man. He succeeded in the provincial examination, and the family prospered. But Swallow herself was never able to conceive. Foxy was highly intelligent, but he was always a frail boy and susceptible to illness, and Swallow was forever urging Sang to take a concubine in order to have another son.

One day, their maid came hurrying in. 'There's an old woman outside,' she announced, 'with a young girl for sale.'

Swallow invited the woman in, and the moment she saw the girl she let out a great cry. 'It's Lotus Fragrance returned from the grave!'

Sang studied the girl. She did indeed bear an astonishing resemblance to Lotus Fragrance. He asked the old lady the girl's age, and she told him that she was fourteen years old. When he asked her the price she wanted, she replied, 'The girl is all I have. But if she can find a good home and I can end up with enough to feed myself and save my old bones from the gutter, I'll be content.'

Sang paid her a generous price for the girl. Swallow took her by the hand and led her to her private apartment, where she pinched her cheek and laughed. 'Don't you recognize me?'

'No, I don't.'

When Swallow asked her her name, she replied, 'I am from the Wei family. My father used to sell soy milk in Xu City. He's been dead three years.'

Feng Zhenluan: How dull it would have been if the author had wasted a lot of ink explaining the details of Lotus Fragrance's reincarnation!

Swallow counted silently on her fingers. It was exactly fourteen years since the death of Lotus Fragrance. She looked again carefully at the girl: her features, her manner – they were all exactly those of Lotus Fragrance. She patted her on the head. 'Sister Lotus! Sister Lotus! You said we would meet again after ten years and you have kept your promise.'

The girl suddenly awoke as if from a dream and gave a great cry, staring fixedly at Swallow.

'She is the swallow of yesteryear,' put in Sang with a smile.

The girl wept. 'It is all true! It must be! I remember my

mother telling me that I was able to speak the day I was born. She thought it an ill omen and gave me dog's blood to drink, to make me forget my past life. Now I have woken from what seems like a dream. And you were once Miss Li who felt ashamed to be a ghost?'

They talked of their former lives, and there was joy and sorrow mingled in their words.

One day, at the Qing Ming Festival, Swallow said, 'This is the day my husband and I always go to weep at your grave.'

The three of them went together to the grave, which was completely overgrown, with a large tree above it casting a broad shade. The girl heaved a deep sigh, and Swallow turned to Sang: 'Sister Lotus and I have been close in two lifetimes. We never wish to be parted again. Take my bones and bury them with hers.'

> *Dan Minglun: Strange, that both ghost and fox should now be human beings! Stranger still that their bones from a previous existence should finally be buried together! If ghosts and foxes are like this, what harm can they possibly do?*

Sang did as she asked. He opened the Li family grave and took out the bones of the girl who had become first a wandering ghost and then Swallow, carried them home and buried them with those of Lotus Fragrance, who had died as a fox and been reborn as a soy-milk vendor's daughter.

When they heard this extraordinary tale, many of Sang's friends and relations dressed in respectful attire and came to pray at the grave of their own accord.

*

I was travelling south through Yizhou in the year *gengxu*, when I was detained by the rain and had to put up at the inn. A man named Liu Zijing, a cousin of Sang's, showed me an account of Sang's life written by a certain Wang Zizhang, a close friend of Liu's. It was well over ten thousand words long. What I have given here is merely the gist of it.

5 5
KING OF THE
NINE MOUNTAINS

There was a certain gentleman by the name of Li from the town of Caozhou, an official scholar of the town, whose family had always been well off, though their residence had never been extensive. The garden behind their house, of an acre or two, had been largely abandoned.

One day, an old man arrived at the house, inquiring about a place to rent. He said he was willing to spend as much as a hundred taels, but Li declined, arguing that he had insufficient space.

'Please accept my offer,' pleaded the old man. 'I will cause you no trouble whatsoever.'

Li did not quite understand what he meant by this, but finally agreed to accept the money and see what happened.

A day later, the local people saw carriages and horses and a throng of people streaming into the garden behind Li's residence. They found it hard to believe that the place could accommodate so many, and asked Li what was going on. He himself was quite at a loss to explain, and hurried in to investigate, but found no trace of anything.

A few days later, the old man called on him again.

'I have enjoyed your hospitality already for several days and nights,' he said. 'Things have been very hectic. We have been so busy settling in, I am afraid we simply have not had time to entertain you as we should have done. Today I have asked my daughters to prepare a little meal, and I hope you will honour us with your presence.'

Li accepted the invitation and followed the old man into the garden, where this time he beheld a newly constructed range of most splendid and imposing buildings. They entered one of these, the interior of which was most elegantly appointed. Wine was being heated in a cauldron out on the verandah, while the delicate aroma of tea emanated from the kitchen. Presently wine and food were served, all of the finest quality and savour. Li could hear and see countless young people coming and going in the courtyard, and he heard the voices of girls chattering and laughing behind gauze curtains. Altogether he estimated that, including family and servants, there must have been over a thousand people living in the garden.

Li knew they must all be foxes. When the meal was finished, he returned home and secretly resolved to find a way of killing them. Every time he went to market he bought a quantity of saltpetre, until he had accumulated several hundred catties of the stuff, which he put down everywhere in the garden. He set light to it, and the flames leaped up into the night sky, spreading a cloud of smoke like a great black mushroom. The pungent odour of the smoke and the choking particles of burning soot prevented anyone from getting close, and all that could be heard was the deafening din of a thousand screaming voices. When the fire had finally burned itself out and Li went into the garden, he saw the bodies of dead foxes lying everywhere, countless numbers of them, charred beyond recognition. He was still gazing at them when the old man came in from outside, an expression of utter devastation and grief on his face.

'What harm did we ever do you?' he reproached Li. 'We paid you a hundred taels – far more than it was worth – to rent your ruin of a garden. How could you be so cruel as to destroy every last member of my family? It is a terrible thing that you have done, and we will most certainly be revenged!'

And with those bitter words of anger, he took his leave.

Li was concerned that he would cause trouble. But a year went by without any strange or untoward occurrence.

It was the first year of the reign of the Manchu Emperor Shunzhi. There were hordes of bandits up in the hills, who formed huge roving companies which the authorities were quite powerless to apprehend. Li had numerous dependants and was especially concerned at the disturbances.

啸聚山林一念

九山王

癡老人不是帝

王師妻孥駢

戮東郊日記

召圍中縱火時

'What harm did we ever do you?'

Then, one day, a fortune-teller arrived in the town, calling himself the Old Man of the Southern Mountain. He claimed to be able to see into the future with the utmost accuracy, and soon became something of a local celebrity. Li sent for him and asked him to read his Eight Astrological Signs. The old man did so, and then rose hurriedly to his feet with a gesture of reverence.

'You, sir, are a true lord, an emperor among men!'

Li was flabbergasted and thought that perhaps the old man was making it all up. But he insisted that he was telling the truth, and Li was almost tempted to believe it himself.

'But I am a nobody,' he said. 'Tell me: when did a man ever receive the Mandate of Heaven and become Emperor in this way – with his own bare hands?'

'Why,' declared the old man, 'throughout history! Our Emperors have always come from the ranks of the common people. Which founder of a dynasty was ever *born* Son of Heaven?'

Now Li, who was beginning to get carried away, drew close to the fortune-teller and asked him for further guidance. The old man declared that he himself would be willing to serve as Li's Chief Marshal, just as the great wizard and strategist Zhuge Liang had once served the Pretender Liu Bei in the time of the Three Kingdoms. Li was to make ready large quantities of suits of armour and bows and crossbows. When Li expressed doubts that anyone would rally to his side, the old man replied, 'Allow me to work for you in the hills, sir. Let me forge links and win men over. Once word is out that you are indeed the true Son of Heaven, have no fear, the fighters of the hills will flock to you.'

Li was overjoyed, and instructed the old man to do as he proposed. He took out all the gold he had and gave orders for the necessary quantity of suits of armour to be made. Several days later, the old man was back.

'Thanks principally to Your Majesty's great aura of blessing, and in some negligible part to my own paltry abilities as an orator, on every hill the men are now thronging to join your cause and rallying to your banner.'

Sure enough, ten days later, a large body of men came in

person to swear their allegiance to the new Son of Heaven and to the Old Man of the Southern Mountain whom they acknowledged as their Supreme Marshal. They set up a great standard, with a forest of brightly coloured pennants fluttering in the breeze, and from their stockade on one of the hills they lorded it over the region.

The District Magistrate led out a force to quell this rebellion, and the rebels under the command of the old fortune-teller inflicted a crushing defeat on the government troops. The Magistrate took fright and sent for urgent reinforcements from the Prefect. The Old Marshal harassed these fresh troops, ambushing and overwhelming them, killing large numbers, including several of their commanding officers. The rebels were now more widely feared than ever. They numbered ten thousand, and Li formally proclaimed himself the King of the Nine Mountains, while his Marshal was given the honorific title of Lord Marshal Protector of the Realm. The old man now reckoned his troops were short of horses, and since it so happened that the authorities in the capital were sending some horses under escort to the south, he dispatched some men to intercept the convoy and seize the horses. The success of this operation increased the prestige of the King of the Nine Mountains still further. He took his ease in his mountain lair, well satisfied with himself and considering it now merely a matter of time before he was officially installed on the Dragon Throne.

The Governor of Shandong Province now decided, mainly on account of the seizure of the horses, to launch a large-scale expedition to quell the rebellion once and for all. He received a report from the Prefect of Yanzhou, and sent large numbers of crack troops, who were to co-ordinate with detachments from the six local circuits and converge on the rebel stronghold from all sides. The King of the Nine Mountains became alarmed and summoned his Marshal for a strategic consultation, only to find that the old man had vanished. The 'King' was truly at his wits' end. He climbed to the top of one of the mountains of his 'domain' and looked down on the government forces and their standards, which stretched along every valley and on every hilltop.

'Now I see,' he declared sombrely, 'how great is the might of the Emperor's court!'

His stronghold was destroyed, the King himself was captured, his wife and entire family were executed. Only then did Li understand that the Marshal was the old fox, taking his revenge for the destruction of his own fox-family.

56

THE FOX OF FENZHOU

There were a large number of fox-spirits in the residence of Judge Zhu, the Assistant Magistrate of Fenzhou. One night, when he was sitting alone, he saw a young lady pacing to and fro in the lamplight. At first he took her to be the wife of one of his servants and did not pay her much attention. But when he finally looked up at her, he saw that she was a woman unknown to him, and of the rarest beauty. He knew instinctively that she must be a fox-spirit and, finding himself greatly attracted to her, he ordered her to come over to him. She ceased her pacing.

'You speak to me so harshly, sir,' she said with a smile. 'I am not your servant!'

Zhu rose smiling to his feet, drew her down gently to sit by his side and apologized for his brusqueness. They soon became lovers, and with time grew to be as devoted to one another as husband and wife.

One day, she said to the Judge out of the blue, 'You will soon be promoted to a new post. The day of our parting is at hand.'

'When will that be?' asked Zhu.

'Any day now. But even as men come to your door to congratulate you, others will arrive in the alley to offer their condolences, and you will be prevented from taking up the new post.'

Three days later, he indeed received notification of his promotion; and the day after, this was followed by news of his mother's death. He was obliged to resign his post in order to observe the three-year mourning period, and planned to return to his family home in the company of the fox. But she refused to go.

汾州派

絕豔容光
一笑過汾州通
判奈愁何故人
情比桃潭水歇
說從來不渡河

'We can board the boat now.'

She saw him off as far as the river, where he begged her to board the boat with him.

'Surely you know that a fox cannot cross the river,' she said.

Zhu could not bear to part with her and lingered there on the riverbank, loth to see her go. Then somewhat abruptly she took her leave, saying that she needed to call on an old friend. She returned shortly afterwards, and presently a stranger appeared who said he wished to speak with her, and she took him aside into a little building. When the man had left, she came to Zhu and said, 'We can board the boat now. I shall accompany you across the river.'

'But only a moment ago you said you could not cross the water. What has happened to change things?'

'The man I went to call on just now is none other than the River God. I pleaded with him especially for your sake, and he has given me a dispensation for ten days. I must be back within that time. So I can stay with you a little longer.'

And so they crossed the river together. Ten days later, she made her final farewell and departed.

57
SILKWORM

Fu, a Cantonese gentleman in his sixties, had an only son named Lian, an extremely intelligent young man who had the misfortune to have been 'born a eunuch'. When our story commences he was seventeen years old, but his member was still tiny and shrivelled, no larger than a silkworm. This defect of his was common knowledge, and his marriage prospects were worse than poor.

The thought of the imminent extinction of his family line caused his father unremitting anguish. This, he would reflect wretchedly to himself, was his bitter but ineluctable fate.

Lian studied at home with a tutor, who one day happened to go out and leave the schoolroom unattended. During his absence, a man passed by the door with a performing monkey and Lian hurried out to watch, quite forgetting his studies. When he thought of what he might have to face on his tutor's return, he grew scared and ran away.

A few miles from home Lian caught sight of a young lady in a white dress ahead of him, accompanied by a maidservant. The lady turned to look at him and he saw at once that she was bewitchingly beautiful. She was hobbling along on her tiny bound feet, and he was soon able to catch up with her.

'I should like to ask that young man,' she said to her maid, 'if by any chance he is on his way to Hainan Island, to the port of Qiongzhou.'

The maid hailed Lian, and he asked her what she wanted.

'If you are going to Hainan Island,' replied the young lady, her mistress, 'to the port of Qiongzhou, I have a letter I would very much like you to take home for me. My mother will look after you when you get there.'

Young Lian had no particular destination in mind and was only too happy to take a trip out to sea, so he accepted the commission. The lady took out the letter and gave it to her maid, who handed it to Lian. He asked for the family name and address of her mistress.

'The family name is Hua, and they live in Qin-nü Village, a mile or so to the north of Qiongzhou.'

So the young man took a boat for Hainan and, reaching the northern outskirts of Qiongzhou when it was already dusk, asked the way to Qin-nü Village. But no one seemed to know where the place was. He continued to walk on northwards another couple of miles into the night, the moon and the stars shining brightly overhead. All around him lay open country and lush fields bathed in the luminous moonlight. There was no sign of anything resembling an inn, and he was wondering with some concern how he was going to pass the night, when he spied a tomb by the roadside and resolved to take shelter beside it and rest a while. To put himself out of reach of prowling tigers and wolves (the very thought of these creatures filled him with terror), he climbed up into a tree like a monkey and crouched there, clinging to one of the branches. He could hear the wind soughing in the pines, and the plaintive chirping of nocturnal insects, and was beginning to feel thoroughly miserable and to regret that he had ever undertaken this foolhardy errand, when suddenly he heard a voice beneath the tree and, looking down, beheld, not a tomb, but a courtyard house complete in every detail. In the courtyard, on a stone, sat a beautiful lady, waited on by two maidservants, one on each side of her, both of them holding brightly coloured lanterns. The lady turned to the maid on her left and said, 'Just look at the moon and the stars! What a beautiful sky it is tonight! We should celebrate the occasion and brew some tea from one of those special cakes of tea that Auntie Hua gave us.'

Lian sensed at once that the place was haunted and found himself trembling so badly with fear that he could hardly breathe. Suddenly one of the maids looked up.

'Look!' she cried. 'There's a man in the tree!'

'What shameless fellow thinks he can spy on us like that!' cried her mistress.

In his terror, Lian tumbled down from the tree and squatted on the ground, begging for mercy. The lady approached him, and his pleasing appearance seemed to mollify her anger. She drew him up and invited him to sit down beside her. He found himself gazing at a young lady of seventeen or eighteen, of a quite surpassing charm and beauty.

'Where would you be on your way to?' she asked him, speaking in the local Hainan brogue.

'I am delivering a letter for someone,' he replied.

'You never know what might happen out here in the wild. It is too dangerous to sleep out in the open. You are welcome to join us in our humble abode.'

She led the way into the house, where there was but one couch, on which she instructed the maids to place two quilts. Lian was very self-conscious about his physical handicap, and asked if he could sleep on the floor.

The lady smiled. 'It would be unpardonably rude of me to sleep alone up there and let my guest sleep on the floor!'

Lian felt obliged to sleep on the bed, but was so frightened that he curled up into a tight ball. After a little while, the lady slipped her dainty little hand under the cover and began softly fondling his body. Lian pretended to be asleep and not to notice what she was doing. A few minutes passed and she lifted the quilt and climbed in beside him, shaking him but eliciting no response. She slipped her hand further down to feel for his member. So crestfallen was she to discover the diminutive dimensions of what he had down there that she promptly withdrew her hand and crept disconsolately out from under the quilt. He heard the sound of her muffled sobbing and felt pangs of remorse, silently cursing the fate that had afflicted him so. The lady meanwhile called her maid to light a lamp. Seeing her mistress in tears, the maid became distressed herself and asked her what the trouble was.

'I am lamenting my wretched fate!' replied the lady.

The maid stood before the bed, looking into her mistress's

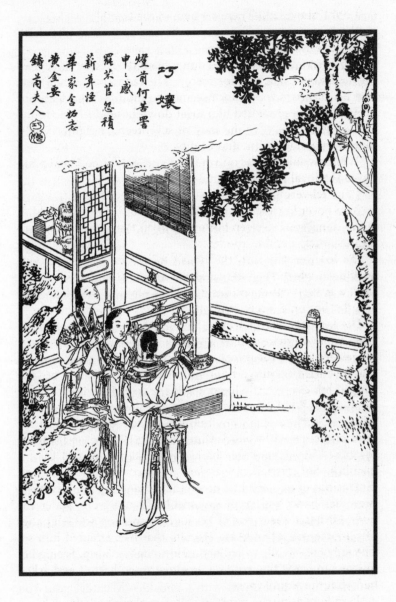

'Look! There's a man in the tree!'

face. 'You'd best wake the gentleman and send him on his way, ma'am.'

This made Lian feel more miserable than ever. Moreover it was the middle of the night, and outside all was dark and strange and he had nowhere to go. He was wrestling with his fear when the door opened and a woman entered the room.

'Auntie Hua is here!' announced the other maid.

Lian stole a glance at the woman, who was in her fifties, well-preserved and stylishly dressed. As she came in, she observed that the young lady was still awake and inquired why, but received no reply. Then she saw that there was a man in the bed and asked who had been sleeping with her. Clever (for such was the young lady's name) was silent.

'A young man arrived during the night,' said the maid, 'and stayed here.'

The woman laughed. 'So! I had no idea this was Clever's wedding night!' Then she noticed the tears still wet on her cheeks. 'What! Crying on your wedding night? That's not right. Has he been treating you roughly?'

The young lady said nothing, but looked more unhappy than ever. Auntie Hua went over and began undressing the stranger, in order to have a good look at him. As she did so she dislodged the letter, which fell on to the frame of the bed.

'Why, this is my daughter's handwriting!' she cried.

She opened it and read it through with many a sigh and cry of surprise. The girl inquired what the letter contained.

'It's from Tertia,' replied Auntie Hua. 'She says her husband Mr Wu is dead, and she has no one to turn to and is in a dreadful plight . . .'

'The young man told us he was delivering a letter,' said the young lady. 'It's a good thing we didn't send him on his way.'

Auntie Hua now roused Lian and questioned him closely about the letter. He told her the whole story.

'You've gone to a great deal of trouble on our behalf,' said Auntie Hua. 'I'd like to do something for you in return.' She looked him up and down with a chuckle. 'Whatever did you do to upset Clever?'

'I really don't know,' he mumbled pathetically.

She questioned Clever, who sighed and replied, 'I feel so wretched. In my lifetime I was married to *one* eunuch – and now, after death, I find myself in bed with *another*!'

Auntie Hua looked at Lian. 'So! You're more woman than man? Well, you are my guest, after all: I must treat you better than this. Let's see what we can do for you.'

She led Lian off to the eastern side of the house where she proceeded to feel around inside his trousers in order to verify Clever's verdict.

'No wonder the girl was so downcast!' she cried. 'But at least we've still got a bit of a stump to work on . . .'

She lit a lamp and started routing around among her boxes, eventually emerging with a large black bolus, which she instructed him to swallow at once, whispering in his ear that he must absolutely not take fright. Then she took her leave and Lian lay down alone, brooding on his strange predicament and wondering what cure it could be that the woman hoped to effect by means of the bolus. He fell asleep. It was the fifth watch of the night when he awoke, to feel a warmth travelling down towards his groin, then a stirring, followed by the beginnings of a wriggling and a tingling and a sensation of a definite something dangling in his crutch. He felt with his hand and lo! He was a real man! He was beside himself with joy, like a loyal minister presented with some rare decoration.

When dawn broke, Auntie Hua came in with some freshly baked cakes for him, telling him to be patient and wait there. She closed the door and went out again, taking Clever aside. 'That young man has done us a service. In return I want Tertia to adopt him as her brother. I've put him in the guest room and locked the door, so you won't have to see him and upset yourself again.' And with these words, Auntie Hua went on her way.

Lian, meanwhile, was growing bored and starting to fret. From time to time he went to a crack in the door and pressed himself up against it like a caged bird. Whenever he saw Clever passing by he wanted to call out to her and tell her his good news, but was always too coy to do so.

That evening Auntie Hua came back with her daughter Tertia

and pushed open the door. 'I fear we have cooped you up all day!' she exclaimed. 'Come, Tertia, say thank you to this kind gentleman.'

Her daughter came sidling into the room, brought her sleeves together and curtseyed to Lian. Auntie Hua told them to address each other thenceforth as brother and sister.

'Why doesn't *she* call *him* sister too . . .' sniggered Clever in the background.

Now they all went together to the main room, where they sat and drank a while. After a few cups of wine Clever began teasing him: 'Tell me, do eunuchs get excited too, when they see a beautiful woman?'

'The cripple,' replied Lian, 'can never forget the joy of walking. Nor the blind man forget the joy of sight.'

This brought a round of laughter. Clever could see that Tertia was tired, and urged her to go and rest, whereupon Auntie Hua gave her daughter a knowing look, clearly indicating that she was to go with Lian. The girl seemed a little bashful.

'Come,' urged her mother, a little untruthfully, 'he may seem a man, but really he's more of a woman. There's really nothing to fear!'

She chivvied them along, whispering conspiratorially to Lian as he went, 'Between ourselves, you are already as good as my son-in-law, even if to the outside world you are only her adopted brother.'

Lian was delighted and, taking Tertia by the arm, hurried with her to bed. There he set to in earnest, and since his was a newly honed blade, his joy in his newfound accomplishment can be readily imagined. Afterwards the two of them conversed intimately.

'Tell me something about Clever,' he asked her. 'What sort of a person is she?'

'She is a ghost,' replied Tertia, with a matter-of-fact air. 'Such a beautiful girl, but so unlucky! In her lifetime she was married to a Mr Mao, who turned out not to be a real man at all, and even when he was eighteen he was still incapable of – you know what . . . So the poor girl had a sad time of it. She carried her bitterness with her to the grave.'

Lian was astonished by this tale and wondered to himself if Tertia might not be a ghost too. She divined his thoughts.

'No, the truth is, I am a fox. Clever was living here in this tomb on her own and my mother and I had nowhere to go, so she let us move in with her.'

Now Lian was well and truly terrified.

'Don't be afraid,' said Tertia. 'We may be ghost and fox, but we will do you no harm.'

From that day forth, Lian spent his time with them both. They took their meals together and whiled away the days pleasantly in idle conversation. Although he now knew Clever to be a ghost, he was nonetheless greatly attracted to her. But somehow he never had an opportunity to show his feelings. Clever, for her part, found him a gentle, refined person and a witty conversationalist, and was herself drawn to him.

One day, Auntie Hua and her daughter Tertia went out, and as usual they locked Lian up in his room. He felt very much at a loose end and prowled restlessly round and round the room, occasionally calling Clever's name through the door. Clever told one of the maids to try out several keys, and in the end they succeeded in opening the door. Lian whispered something in Clever's ear, and she told the maid to leave them alone in the room, whereupon Lian took her in his arms, carried her over to the bed and embraced her passionately. She began to fondle his crutch, murmuring, 'My poor darling . . . To have nothing there at all . . .'

Even as she was speaking, she became aware that her hand had encountered something rather substantial. 'What's this!' she cried in surprise. 'The other day he was a midget – and now he's a giant!'

'The other day,' laughed Lian, 'when you first met him, he was just a bit shy. Today he's hurt by the horrid things you've been saying about him . . . He's angry and puffed up like a frog . . .'

They lost no time and were soon making love. Afterwards Clever said angrily, 'No wonder Auntie Hua kept you locked away! To think that when those foxes had nowhere to go, I took them in and gave them a home! I even taught Tertia to sew – I shared everything I had with them. And in return they wanted to keep *you* all to themselves!'

Lian comforted her, telling her exactly what had happened to him, but Clever was still resentful.

'You must keep this a secret,' urged Lian. 'Auntie Hua made me promise I would tell no one.'

They were still talking when in came Auntie Hua, and the two of them jumped up in a great fluster. Auntie Hua stood there glowering at them.

'Who opened the door?'

'I did,' confessed Clever, with an awkward smile.

Auntie Hua grew angrier and more voluble than ever.

'But Auntie,' retorted Clever smartly, 'if what you said is true and he's not really a man, then what's all the fuss about!'

Tertia was most distressed to see the two of them at each other's throats and tried her utmost to mediate, eventually succeeding in bringing them round and restoring the peace. Clever had spoken some harsh words, but from now on she did her best to humour Tertia, while Auntie Hua for her part continued to keep a close eye on young Lian, depriving him of any chance to be alone with Clever. All they could do when they encountered each other was to exchange soulful glances.

One day Auntie Hua said to Lian, 'Now that both Tertia and Clever are your wives, it seems to me that you cannot go on living here for ever. You should go home and tell your father and mother how things stand, so that they can make arrangements for a proper marriage.'

She packed a few things for him and urged him to leave. The two girls took a tearful farewell of Lian, especially Clever, who was in a dreadful state and could not stop weeping. Auntie Hua told them to dry their eyes, and hurried Lian on his way.

The moment he found himself out in the open again, the courtyard house had vanished entirely and there was nothing to be seen but a ruined tomb. Auntie Hua accompanied him on to the boat, saying as she left him, 'When you are gone, I shall bring the two girls and rent a house in your part of the world. If you still remember your love for them, come and claim your brides in the ruins of the Li garden.'

And so Lian set off home.

His father had in the meantime been sorely anxious at his son's disappearance and was overjoyed to welcome him home. Lian told him the story of his strange experiences, of Auntie Hua and of how she had promised him the two girls in marriage.

'Never trust the words of a spirit like that,' was the old man's response. 'It's your illness that has saved you. You mark my words. If you'd been a fully fledged man they'd never have let you go. You'd be dead by now.'

'They may not be human like us,' protested Lian, 'but they have true feelings. And they're so quick-witted and so beautiful. If I were truly married to wives such as them, then I'd be able to hold my head up and I'd no longer be a laughing stock.'

His father said nothing but smiled quizzically at his son.

Lian withdrew to his own quarters. In the days that followed he was unbearably frustrated at not having any opportunity to continue testing out his newly discovered virtuosity. Eventually, unable to contain himself any longer, he formed a secret liaison with one of the maids. One thing led to another, and soon they were indulging in full-blown intercourse in broad daylight. Lian was actually hoping in this way to bring his new-found skills to the attention of his parents. One day, a junior maid spied on the two of them while they were at it, and hurried off to inform her mistress. Mrs Fu could not believe her ears and insisted on going to have a peep herself. She was utterly amazed by what she saw, and summoned the maid involved to verify personally her son's newly acquired credentials. She was absolutely delighted by the turn of events, and let it be known to all and sundry that her son was now a properly qualified man and that families of suitable station might present proposals of marriage in the normal way. But Lian confided to his mother that he would marry none but the Hua girls, Tertia and Clever.

'There are so many beautiful women in *this* world,' complained his mother. 'Why pick a ghost and a fox?'

'If it were not for Auntie Hua, I still wouldn't know what it means to be a man,' replied Lian. 'If I break my word now, I'll only be bringing bad luck on myself.'

In the end his father agreed to go along with the idea, and

they sent a servant and a matchmaker to discuss the marriage with Auntie Hua. The two of them took a carriage and made their way a couple of miles east of the town, searching for the ruins of the Li family garden. In a bamboo grove, they saw a thread of smoke rising into the sky from a broken-down cottage. The old crone of a matchmaker stepped down from her carriage and went straight to the door, where she found Auntie Hua and her daughter sweeping and cleaning, as if they were expecting a visitor. The matchmaker introduced herself and explained her mission, and when she saw Tertia close to, gave a little cry of delighted surprise.

'So this is your daughter, the young master's wife-to-be! What a lovely young lady, to be sure! No wonder the young master dreams about her day and night!'

She asked about Clever, and Auntie Hua heaved a sigh. 'You must mean my foster-daughter. I'm sad to say that three days ago she suddenly fell ill and died.'

She served the old lady and her companion food and wine.

On her return, the matchmaker conveyed to Lian's parents her favourable impressions of Tertia, which pleased them greatly. Lian was heartbroken to learn the news of Clever's death.

On the day of the wedding, he questioned Auntie Hua himself, and she told him that Clever had been reborn somewhere far away in the North. Lian shed many tears of grief. He took Tertia home with him as his wife, but could never forget his love for Clever. If ever anyone came to Canton from Qiongzhou, he always asked if there was any news of her. One such traveller told him that the sound of a ghost weeping had been heard at the tomb near Qin-nü Village. Lian found this strange. When he spoke to Tertia about it, she heaved a great sigh. At length she began to speak, tears coursing down her cheeks. 'I have done Clever a great wrong!'

Lian asked her what she meant by this.

'When mother and I came here,' she replied, 'we didn't tell Clever we were coming. The weeping ghost near the tomb must be her. I would have told you the truth, but was afraid of revealing my mother's wrongdoing.'

When Lian learned that the ghost of Clever was still haunting the old tomb, he cast aside his sorrow, called for a carriage and, travelling through the night, hastened to the place. He knocked at the wooden entrance to the tomb.

'Clever!' he cried. 'Clever! It's me!'

Suddenly from within appeared a young woman with a baby in her arms. She looked up with a sad little cry and gazed at Lian with an expression of injured grief. He wept to see her thus, and, fondling the baby she held, he asked her whose child it was.

'This is the seed you left in my womb. He was born three months ago.'

Lian sighed. 'I should never have listened to Auntie Hua's words. You and the child must have suffered cruelly, abandoned here in your grave-home. I have done you wrong.'

He took them both back with him, and went in to show his mother the baby boy. She was delighted to see what a handsome, sturdy, human-looking sort of child it was – not at all the half-ghost she would have expected.

Despite everything that had happened, the two girls got along very well together and were both devoted to Lian's parents.

Some time afterwards, Lian's father fell ill. When the doctor was about to be summoned, Clever said, 'My father-in-law will not survive this illness. His soul has already left his body.'

They prepared his last things, and sure enough in a little while he died.

When Lian's son grew up, he greatly resembled his father. He was highly intelligent and passed his examinations at the age of fourteen.

Secretary Gao Zixia heard this story when he was visiting Canton. He could not remember the names of the places concerned, nor the outcome of the story.

58

VOCAL VIRTUOSITY

A woman, aged twenty-four or twenty-five, once arrived in the village with her medicine bag and set herself up as a physician. Patients wishing to consult her were informed that she could not make out a prescription herself but would have to wait till evening in order to communicate with the spirits. In the evening, she cleared out her little room and shut herself up inside it, while her patients waited outside, clustered around the door and window, trying their hardest to eavesdrop on what was going on inside, whispering among themselves and doing their best not to cough. It was eerily still and quiet both inside and outside the room.

Halfway through the first watch of the night, they heard the swishing of a door-curtain and the woman's voice inside, saying, 'Is that you, Ninth Aunt?'

'It is,' came another woman's voice.

'Has Winter Plum come with you?'

'I have,' answered yet another woman's voice, which sounded like that of a young maidservant.

The three women chattered on at great length, then the curtain hooks could be heard to move again.

'Sixth Aunt is here!' said one of the women.

'Has Spring Plum come and brought the young master?' cried a babble of voices all at once.

'He's been such a naughty boy!' This was yet another woman's voice. 'He's been screaming his head off and refusing to go to sleep! He had to come with his mother. I'd swear he weighs a hundred catties. I'm worn out!'

This was followed by a further exchange of greetings, Ninth

一技

紗窗月上夜迢迢
嘈雜珠喉
勝管簫
且是幻是真
莫辨簫
但聞嬌語
亦魂銷

Her patients waited outside trying to eavesdrop.

Aunt asking for news, Sixth Aunt chattering politely, the two maids grumbling, the child's happy laughter, the cat miaowing, all jumbled together. Then the voice of the young woman-physician herself could be heard, laughing as she said, 'What a sweet little boy, to bring the kitten all the way here!'

The voices faded away. Then the blind swished again, and there was a renewed hubbub.

'Why are you so late, Fourth Aunt?'

This time a young, dainty, lady's voice (evidently that of a third maid) replied, 'It was such a long way – hundreds of miles – Auntie and I hurried as best we could, but she's such a slow walker.'

There followed further desultory conversation, the sound of people moving chairs around and calling for more to sit on, voices of many kinds mingling in the general commotion that filled the room. After the length of time that it might have taken to eat a meal, quiet returned and the woman-physician could be heard asking for advice about a patient's illness. Ninth Aunt said she needed ginseng, Sixth Aunt recommended yellow vetch, Fourth Aunt atractylis root. After lengthy discussion, Ninth Aunt called for a brush and inkstone, and presently came the rustling sound of paper being folded and the tinkling sound of the brass brush-cap being pulled off and thrown on the table. This was followed by the grating sound of the inkstick being rubbed on the stone, and the click as the writing brush was placed back on the table. Then finally came the crunching sound as the herbs listed in the prescription were measured out and wrapped.

Presently the woman pushed aside the door-curtain and came out, calling for the patient to come forward and receive his written prescription and the herbs. As she turned back into the room they heard the three aunts making their farewells, the three maids, the little boy babbling, the cat miaowing – all at one and the same time. Ninth Aunt's voice was clear and piercing; Sixth Aunt's slow and coarse; Fourth Aunt's soft and enchanting. Each of the maidservants spoke with a different timbre too, and each voice could be clearly distinguished from the others. The amazed crowd outside were convinced that these were truly spirits. But it must be recorded that notwith-standing this elaborate rigmarole, the medicine prescribed had little beneficial effect.

This is what is known as 'vocal virtuosity'. It was no more than a ruse used by the young woman to sell her services as a physician. But it was an extraordinary performance all the same!

Years ago, Wang Xinyi told me that once, when he was in the capital and walking through the market, he heard the sound of a stringed instrument and a voice singing. The performance had attracted a large crowd. He went closer and observed a young man singing a song in long, drawn-out phrases. There was no musical instrument to be seen. He was simply rubbing his cheek with his finger as he sang, producing a sound just like that of a stringed instrument. This was another variation of vocal virtuosity.

59
FOX AS PROPHET

A certain Mr Li possessed a secondary residence in Wei County. One day, an old man appeared and offered to rent it, proposing an annual rental of fifty taels, to which Li agreed. The man left and nothing more was heard of him for some time, whereupon Li gave instructions to his servants to let the place to someone else. The very next day, the old man arrived and said to Li, 'I thought we already had an agreement that I would lease your house. Why have you let it to somebody else?'

Li explained the doubts occasioned by the old man's long absence.

'I was proposing a lengthy stay,' explained the old man, 'so I was obliged to consult the almanac for a propitious day on which to commence it, and this delayed me for ten days.' He then handed over a full year's rent. 'Even if the house stays empty for a whole year, do not ask me any questions about it.'

As he was leaving, Li asked him when he would be returning and the old man named the day. Several days after that date, when there was still no sign of him, Li went to inspect his villa and found the double doors bolted from the inside. Astonished to see smoke rising from a chimney and to hear voices coming from within, he sent in his visiting card, whereupon the old man came hurrying out and welcomed him very civilly, smiling and chattering in a most affable manner. When Li returned home, he sent one of his servants with presents for the old man, who gave the servant a most generous tip.

A few days later, Li gave a banquet for the old man and entertained him with great warmth and genuine pleasure. He asked him where he hailed from originally, and when the man gave the western province of Shaanxi as his native place, Li expressed some surprise at its remoteness from his present lodgings.

'This region of yours,' replied the old man, 'is a peaceful and harmonious one. My own province is not a good place to settle at present. Great disturbances will break out there.'

They were living in a time of great general calm and tranquillity, but Li did not inquire any further into the old man's meaning.

The very next day, the old man sent his card, inviting his landlord to a return banquet. Li was greatly astonished by the excellent food and lavish entertainment and wondered aloud if his lodger was perhaps some important official living incognito. The old man replied that, since they were now friends, he could tell him the truth: he was a fox-spirit in human form. Li was flabbergasted by this revelation.

He mentioned it to an acquaintance of his, and the local gentry soon came to know about his extraordinary lodger, which resulted in a constant flow of visitors at the old man's door, all of whom he received with the utmost civility. Soon even the local Prefect became a regular visitor. The one person who was not granted admission, however, was the local County Magistrate. The old man always fobbed him off with some excuse or other. The Magistrate even tried asking Li to plead on his behalf, but to no avail. When Li eventually asked the old man what his reasons were, the old man drew closer to him and whispered, 'You do not know this, but that Magistrate of yours was a mule in a previous life. He may seem a very distinguished gentleman, but really he is a person of shameless greed. I may not be human myself, but I consider it beneath my dignity to associate with the likes of him.'

Li made up some story to placate the Magistrate – that the old man was too much in awe of him to receive him – and the Magistrate believed him and ceased his entreaties.

濰水狐

浮朋重筵盞簪交燕
于離鄉攜別巢邑令
靡然徒自大竟難折
節訂狐交

The old man drew closer to him and whispered.

This all happened in the eleventh year of the reign of the Kangxi Emperor. The disastrous uprising of Wang Fuchen broke out shortly after this date in Shaanxi. The prophetic powers of foxes are to be believed.

60

THIS TRANSFORMATION

A certain monk (no one ever knew where he was originally from) lived in Ji'nan, and went every day to Hibiscus Street and Bright Lake, the entertainment quarter in the north-west part of the city. There, barefoot and wearing a tattered, patched cassock, he would frequent the various restaurants and tea-houses, chanting sutras and begging for alms wherever he went. He refused offerings of any kind, however – wine, food, money or grain – and when asked what it was he had need of, would give no reply. He was never seen to eat or drink anything.

'Reverend Master,' he was once politely advised, 'since you eat no meat and drink no wine, would it not be better to beg for alms in some lonely lane in a mountain village, rather than come here every day and endure the stench and clamour of the city?'

The monk continued his chanting unperturbed, his hands clasped, his long eyelashes motionless, as though he had heard nothing. A little later, the same advice was proffered again. This time the monk glared at his interlocutor.

'*This*,' he boomed, 'is the transformation I am seeking.'

He continued chanting and eventually went on his way. The man followed him, intent on knowing what '*this* transform-ation' could be, and why the monk was so set upon it. To his questioning the monk made no reply, but continued walking. When the man persisted, he bellowed again, 'You can know nothing! *This* is my transformation; *this* is what I am seeking.'

Several days later, the monk was seen outside the southern walls of the city, lying curled up beside the road, stiff as a corpse. He remained there motionless for three days. The local people, afraid that he would starve to death and that they would be held responsible, urged him to move on, promising him whatever food or money he needed. The monk said nothing and refused even to open his eyes, whereupon they began to shake him and berate him. The monk became angrier and angrier, until finally, producing a little knife from within his cassock, he slit open his stomach. He then reached in with one hand, pulled out his own innards and proceeded to lay them out on the roadside. Then he expired.

The locals were aghast. They informed the Prefect, and gave the corpse a hasty burial. Some time later, a dog dug up the shallow grave and exposed the prayer mat in which the monk had been wrapped when they buried him. It sounded hollow underfoot, and when they examined it more closely they found it still as tightly sealed as it had been at the burial. Inside, it was now as empty as a cocoon.

丐僧

誦任爾見梵修

苦剌刀與撞鐘

脱逃算怪老

任如此化老僧

原不欲人知

The monk slit open his stomach.

FOX CONTROL

A certain Academician was possessed by a fox-spirit, fell ill and began to waste away. All imaginable charms and prayers were resorted to, but to no avail. He begged for leave to return home, in the hope that he might thereby somehow escape the evil influence that was afflicting him. But the fox followed him on his journey. He now lived in mortal fear and knew not what to do.

One day he halted at Zhuo County, and there in the street he encountered a travelling quack who claimed to be able to subdue foxes. The Academician engaged his services, and the quack gave him a remedy, which was in point of fact a potent aphrodisiac. He urged him to swallow the medicine and then to have intercourse with the fox-spirit. He would be an invincible lover.

He followed the doctor's instructions. The fox-spirit sought to withdraw from his embrace, pleading with him to stop, but he ignored her entreaties and continued making love to her more fiercely than ever. She writhed and wriggled and struggled to escape, but he would not let her go. And then finally she fell silent. When he looked, he saw the body of a dead fox lying in his bed.

*

There was once a young gentleman of my home district who fancied himself greatly as a lover. He thought himself the equal of the legendary Lao Ai, whose enormous penis had given such satisfaction to the Empress Dowager of Qin. This gentleman claimed that he himself had never once been satisfied by any woman.

伏狐

珥筆丹墀称侍從
每因春恨欲途窮
鈴醫新授房中葯
玉碎花殘一瞬中

The quack gave him a remedy.

One night he was alone at an inn. It was an isolated building, and there were no neighbours. Suddenly a girl came hurrying into his room, through the closed door. He knew she must be a fox-spirit, and at once set about seducing her, stripping her naked and without further ado plunging his member straight in her up to the hilt. She felt a searing pain and screamed out loud, fleeing from the room and shooting into the night like a hawk loosed from the hand of a falconer.

He called out through the window, appealing to her with many words of lascivious endearment, in the hope of luring her back. But she had vanished without trace.

This man was a veritable Exterminator of Foxes! He could indeed have hung a sign up outside his door inscribed with the words 'Fox Control', and made a living that way.

62

DRAGON DORMANT

Commissioner Qu, of Wuling County, was reading in an upper room when a heavy rain began to fall. In the deepening gloom he caught sight of a little creature, bright as a glow-worm, wriggling its way on to his desk. It meandered across his scroll, scorching the paper as it went and leaving a trail behind it, like a slug. Somehow he formed the notion that it must be a dragon and, lifting up the scroll in both his hands, carried it outside. There he stood in the doorway for some time holding it solemnly aloft, but the creature simply coiled in on itself like a caterpillar and refused to budge.

'Have I caused you some offence?' pondered Qu aloud. He returned with the scroll and replaced it on the table. Donning full mandarin hat and girdle this time, he made a deep bow and carried it once more to the door. He stood beneath the eaves waiting, and finally the creature reared its head, stretched and took off into the air above the scroll, whirring and emitting a great stream of light. It flew a few yards, then wheeled round towards the Commissioner, its head now the size of a large earthenware jar, its huge trunk twenty or thirty hands in circumference. Round again it spun, and this time, with a rumbling roar, soared up into the heavens.

Qu returned to his desk and retraced its winding trail to one of the bamboo boxes in which he stored his books.

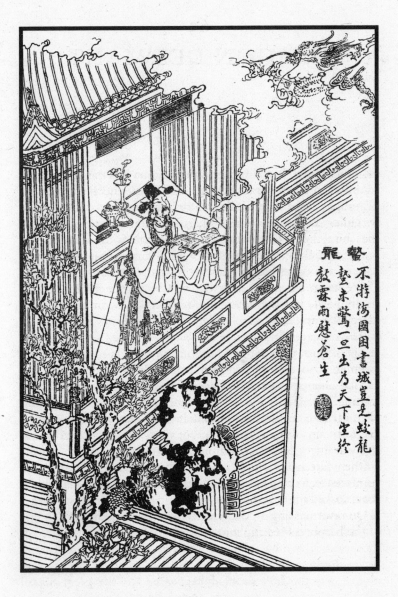

It soared up into the heavens.

63
CUT SLEEVE

He Shican had a studio out in the countryside east of Tiaoxi. One evening, he happened to go out doors, and saw a woman riding past on a mule, followed by a young man. The woman was in her fifties and seemed a person of some refinement, while the young man following her looked fifteen or sixteen, and possessed, so Shican observed, a quite extraordinary personal beauty. He was prettier than a girl. Shican was himself of the Cut Sleeve persuasion and had always had rather a predilection for boys. He gazed at the youth in breathless wonder, standing there on tiptoe and watching him disappear into the distance, before returning indoors.

The next day, he looked out for him from early morning till evening. It was sunset and growing dark by the time the boy finally came past again, and when Shican, in his most charming manner, asked him where he had been, he replied that he was visiting his grandfather. Shican invited him indoors, but he declined, saying he was pressed for time. Shican insisted, positively dragging him into the house, and the boy agreed to stay for a little while, after which he took his leave, saying that he could on no account be detained any further. Shican took him by the hand and saw him on his way, entreating him to drop by again if he was ever passing, to which the boy nodded and left.

From that day forth, Shican was unable to take his mind off the beautiful young stranger, and was forever pacing up and down, looking out for him. Then one day when the sun had almost set, the boy suddenly appeared, to the great joy of Shican, who invited him in at once, telling his servant to bring wine. He asked him his name.

'My name is Huang,' he replied, 'and I am the ninth in my family.'

'What brings you past here so often?'

'I am going to visit my mother. She is living at her father's and is often unwell.'

After a few cups of wine he stood to take his leave, but Shican held him by the arm, loth to let him go, and even resorted to locking the door. In the end Huang had no choice but to sit down again, his face flushed with embarrassment. Shican lit the lamps, and as they conversed he found Huang to be softly spoken and tender as a young girl. But the moment he spoke to him in an amorous fashion, the boy turned away coyly towards the wall. A little while later, he drew him up on to the bed, and at first Huang refused, pleading (rather feebly) that he was a poor sleeper. But Shican persisted, and in the end persuaded Huang to remove his shirt and gown and lie down on the bed in nothing but his silken trousers. Shican extinguished the lamp and was soon lying beside him, wrapping his arms and legs around him, hugging him and beseeching him to make love. Huang protested indignantly.

'I thought you a gallant gentleman, sir, and was happy to be your friend. But what you are suggesting is the way beasts in the wild behave!'

Presently the morning star began to shine, and Huang took his leave. Shican was now afraid that he would never see him again, and he was constantly on the lookout for him, pacing up and down in anxious expectation and gazing endlessly into the furthest distance.

And then, a few days later, the beautiful youth appeared. Shican welcomed him joyfully and craved his forgiveness, drawing him eagerly into his studio again, pressing him to be seated and engaging him in smiling conversation. He was hugely relieved to discover that Huang bore him no ill will from their last encounter, and in a little while he removed Huang's sandals and climbed on to the bed with him, fondling him and pleading with him once more.

'My affection for you is now deeply engraved on my heart,' said Huang. 'But surely this is not the only way in which we can show our feelings?'

Shican plied him with honeyed words, begging to be allowed just a single kiss of his jade-like body, to which Huang finally consented. And then Shican waited until he had fallen asleep to begin touching him in earnest. Huang awoke, reached for his clothes, rose from the bed and left at once, though it was still the middle of the night. From that day, Shican pined for him more and more. He ceased eating and sleeping, and began to waste away, and every day sent his pageboy out to scout for news of young Huang.

One day, Huang came past Shican's house and would have continued on his way, but the pageboy saw him and dragged him in. Huang was shocked to see how pale and thin his friend had become, and when he inquired with concern after his health, Shican told him the truth, sobbing and weeping as he spoke.

'I only meant it for the best,' said Huang gently. 'I thought that to love in that way would do me no good, and would bring you nothing but harm. That is why I refused you. But since you insist it will bring you happiness, perhaps I should not hold back any longer.'

Shican was overwhelmed with emotion when he heard this. That same day, when Huang left, he experienced a sudden recovery, and a few days later, when Huang returned to see him, he was quite restored to health. They were soon wrapped in each other's arms.

'Today I will let you have your way,' said Huang. 'But please do not expect this every time.'

Afterwards he said to Shican, 'Now I have a favour to ask of you.'

'Tell me what it is.'

'My mother has a heart ailment, and the only medicine that can cure it is the Primordial Bolus, a patent remedy prepared by the Imperial Physician Qi Yewang. I know you are on friendly terms with Dr Qi. Would you please ask him for one on my behalf?'

Shican agreed to do this, and before he left that morning, Huang reminded him of his promise. Shican went into town to procure some of the medicine, and he was able to give it to Huang when he returned that very evening. Huang was over-

joyed and clasped his hands together in a gesture of appreciation. Shican was eager to make love once more.

'Let us not become too deeply involved,' said Huang. 'I will find
you another lover, someone a thousand times better than me.'

Shican asked who this person was.

'A cousin of mine,' replied Huang, 'an extraordinarily beautiful young woman. If you agree, I will act as your go-between.'

Shican smiled, but said nothing in reply. Huang went away
with the medicine in his pocket, and returned after an interval
of three days, asking for more. Shican had missed him dreadfully in the meantime, and berated him for his long absence.

'I could not bear to hurt you,' said Huang, 'so I kept away.
If this is what I must do to win your approval, so be it. But I
beg you never to have regrets.'

From that day forth, they made love together every day.

Every three days, Huang asked for another dose of the medicine, and Qi the physician began to be puzzled by the frequency
of Shican's visits.

'This drug is one I never prescribe more than three times.
I fail to understand why the patient's condition has still not
improved.' He put three more doses in a packet and gave it to
Shican, adding, 'You yourself look extremely off-colour. Are
you sure you are not unwell?'

Shican said he was in perfectly good health, but when the physician took his pulses he exclaimed in alarm, 'Your pulse shows
a spirit possession! The illness is deep in the Shao-yin Meridian.
If you do not exercise the greatest caution, I fear for your life!'

On his return, Shican spoke of this to Huang.

'What a skilled physician he is!' said Huang with a sigh.
'What he says is true. You see, I am a fox-spirit. I have long
feared I would bring you unhappiness and suffering.'

Shican suspected that he was just making this all up, and
he kept some of the medicine back, in case he should never return. Then, as time went by, he fell seriously ill and asked the
physician to examine him.

'The other day,' said Dr Qi, 'you were not telling me the truth,
were you? Your soul is already roaming in the wilderness of death.
Even the best physician in the world would be of no avail now!'

Huang came to wait upon Shican every day, and every day his health declined still further.

'You would not heed my words!' protested Huang. 'And now it has come to this!'

Before long, Shican died, and Huang went away, weeping bitterly.

*

Now before any of this, a certain man, who also came from Tiaoxi and who had as a youth been a friend and fellow-student of Shican's, was selected at the exceptionally young age of seventeen as a Hanlin Academician and censor. At that time, the Provincial Treasurer of Shaanxi was a very corrupt individual who had so successfully bribed the officials at court that no one was willing to denounce his misdemeanours. The young, newly appointed Censor rashly submitted a memorial impeaching the Treasurer, and was promptly dismissed for having stepped beyond the bounds of his office. Meanwhile the corrupt Treasurer was promoted to Governor, and was constantly on the lookout for some means of avenging himself on his critic. The former Censor had as a youth enjoyed a bright reputation and had been much favoured by one of the rebel Princes. The Governor now purchased certain incriminating letters exchanged between the two of them and threatened him with them, whereupon the former Censor, in sheer terror, took his own life, and was soon followed in this by his wife.

The morning after his suicide, he suddenly awoke, seemingly arisen from the dead, and exclaimed, 'I am He Shican!'

He replied to questions exactly as if he were Shican. He had died at the exact same moment as He Shican, and Shican's spirit had clearly returned to life, borrowing the physical frame of his childhood friend, the unfortunate Censor. Nothing would induce him to stay where he was, but he insisted on hurrying off at once to his 'own' former abode.

The Governor got to hear of this strange event and, suspecting some sort of plot, resolved somehow to incriminate his newly resurrected enemy, sending one of his underlings to demand a 'squeeze' of a thousand taels. Shican (in his new life as the revived Censor) pretended to agree that he would pay up, but was deeply depressed at this turn of events. He was sinking further and further into despair, when to his utter astonishment it was announced that Huang was at the door. It was a reunion in which joy and sorrow were mingled. Shican wished to renew their former intimacy at once.

'How many lives do you think you have?' cried Huang.

'This second life of mine has so far been nothing but misery!' exclaimed Shican. 'Another death would be a welcome release.' He proceeded to tell the story of his (the Censor's) persecution at the hands of the man who was now Governor of Shaanxi. Huang brooded on it thoughtfully.

'Fate has been kind to us,' he said after a little while, 'by bringing us together again. You are still single, and that cousin of mine whom I mentioned before is just the person for you: she is beautiful and a resourceful girl, and I am sure she would be able to share and lighten your burden of sorrow.'

Shican expressed a desire to see her.

'That can be easily arranged,' said Huang. 'Tomorrow I shall fetch her to visit my old mother and we can pass this way. I will pretend that you are my sworn brother. I will say that I am thirsty and suggest stopping here for a drink. All you have to say is, "The donkey has bolted!", and I shall know that you agree to my suggestion.'

Once this plan had been made, Huang took his leave.

The following day, at noon, he came by with the girl, and Shican greeted them cordially with clasped hands. He sized up the girl at one glance: she was exquisite, truly a creature of unearthly beauty. Huang asked if they could drink some tea, and Shican invited them both in.

'Don't take it amiss, my dear,' said Huang to his pretty cousin. 'This gentleman is my sworn brother. It is quite proper for us to stop here briefly.'

He helped her down from her donkey, which he tethered outside the entrance. Shican produced tea and gave Huang a meaningful look.

'What you said was an understatement!' he said. 'For this I could happily die!'

休說狐綏事末妨何
生毛膽太猖狂坐間
儘有分桃癖盡使相
逢黃九郎

黃九郎

Shican greeted them cordially with clasped hands.

The girl seemed to understand that he was referring to her, and rose from her seat on the couch in an agitated flutter, saying, 'I really think we should be going now!'

Shican meanwhile glanced outside. 'The donkey has bolted!' he cried.

Huang rushed out, and the moment he was out of the room, Shican threw his arms round the girl and began making amorous overtures. She blushed fiercely and, seeming greatly put out, cried for her cousin, but received no reply.

'Surely you have a wife of your own, sir!' she wailed. 'And yet you would stain a maiden's honour in this way!'

Shican protested that he was in fact single, whereupon she changed her tune.

'Make an undying oath never to abandon me! Say that you will never discard me like a fan in autumn, and I will do as you command me.'

Shican swore by the light of the sun, and she resisted him no longer. Afterwards Huang returned, and she reproached him angrily for his conduct.

'This is He Shican,' said Huang, 'a gentleman of some renown, an Academician and a good friend of mine. I can vouch for his character. I am sure your mother would approve if she knew.'

Evening was drawing on, and Shican would not hear of her leaving. She for her part was afraid that Huang's mother would be shocked by their liaison, but Huang volunteered to shoulder the responsibility, and rode off on the donkey, leaving them alone.

Several days later, a lady of forty years or so came by with her maid. She seemed rather distinguished and bore a striking resemblance to Huang's cousin. Shican called to the girl to go out and take a look, and sure enough the woman was her mother.

'What a silly boy young Huang is!' she exclaimed. 'Why on earth didn't he talk to me about this before?'

The girl meanwhile had gone to prepare food in the kitchen, which she served to her mother. After eating the meal, the woman took her leave.

Shican was now happily married to a beautiful wife. But he still felt a cloud of danger looming over him. His wife asked him what was the matter, and he told her the whole story of his trouble with the Governor. She laughed.

'Cousin Huang can sort this out for you. Don't you fret.'

He asked her to explain her meaning.

'I happen to know,' she said, 'that the Governor has two obsessions: one is music, and the other is pretty boys. That's where Huang comes in. He can give the man what he wants most. In that way your danger can be averted, and you can have your revenge.'

Shican was concerned that Huang would refuse to act on his behalf.

'You just have to ask him nicely.'

The very next day, when Huang came, Shican went down on his knees before him. Huang seemed greatly taken aback. 'We have known each other in two lives! We would do anything for each other! Whatever it is you want of me, you don't need to grovel like this.'

Shican told him everything, and Huang looked a little put out by the proposal.

'You brought me here to be this man's wife,' argued his cousin. 'If you let him down now and he comes to grief, what will become of me?'

Huang could see he had no choice but to agree to his friend's request. Shican sent a letter to a friend of his, another censor, by the name of Wang, presenting Huang. Wang understood his purpose and laid on a special banquet for the Governor, telling Huang to dress up for the occasion in woman's clothes and to dance the Devil's Dance. The Governor was utterly captivated by Huang's ravishingly beautiful appearance and begged Censor Wang to let him have the boy, offering a high price, which Wang, after much haggling and show of reluctance, finally accepted. The Governor's joy was now such that he forgot all his previous grudges and quarrels (including his demand for a thousand taels from his enemy the former Censor). From the day Huang entered his household, the Governor could not tear himself away from him for a single moment. He lost all interest in his womenfolk. Huang was wined and dined like a king, gold was showered on him. And six months later, the Governor fell

ill and his health continued to deteriorate. When Huang knew
that his patron was about to set out on the dark road to death, he
bundled his wealth into a cart and took a day off to visit Shican.
By the time he returned, the Governor was dead. Huang now
spent the money setting himself up in a grand establishment of
his own, with maids and servants, and invited his mother and his
aunt to come and live with him. Whenever he went out, he did
so in great style, and no one knew him for a fox.

I have written a Jesting Judgement, which I here append, in
the light of the teaching of the great sage Mencius: 'The coming
together in sexual congress of man and woman is one of the
great natural bonds in human relations.'

> Light and dark,
> Hot and cool,
> Dry and moist,
> So it goes,
> True counterpoint
> Of Yin and Yang.
> Illicit trysts
> Twixt men and women
> Were once thought foul;
> How much the fouler reeks   10
> The passion of Cut Sleeve,
> Of Half-Eaten Peach,
> Of love twixt man and man!
> Only the mightiest warrior
> Can penetrate that tiny bird-track!
> That narrow grotto
> Leads to no Peach Blossom Spring:
> Surely the fisherman
> Poled up it by mistake!
> Our hero forsakes   20
> The play of Clouds and Rain,
> Turns away from
> The true way
> Of human consummation,
> Preferring the up and down

Of manual masturbation,
Yin and Yang
Widdershins,
Everything
30   Topsy-turvy.
He abandons the Flowery Pool,
For a phony tale
Of enlightened
Sublimation of desire.
On the Grassless Terrain
Of the Barbarian Grotto,
The One-Eyed Marshal
Leads the charge.
Tethering Red Hare
40   To the Rear Gate of the Barracks,
The General
Thrusts his halberd.
Seeking to steal the Great Bow
From the National Armoury,
He bursts the barrier.
In a slippery dream
A Yellow Eel wriggled
Between the student's thighs,
Omen of last night's union.
50   The plums sold by Wang Rong
Were juicy but sterile,
Their stones hollowed out
To put a stop to posterity.
Into the Black Pine Wood
Thunders the cavalry;
From the Yellow Dragon Palace
Surges the tide.
This nefarious pestle
Should be snapped off
60   At its root!
This wicked passage
Should be blocked up
For ever!

64

THE GIRL FROM NANKING

A youth by the name of Zhao, from Yishui, was on his way home from a commission in town when he caught sight of a girl in white standing by the side of the road, weeping and seemingly in great distress. One glance sufficed to convey her beauty, and his eyes lingered on her with delight.

'Alas sir!' sobbed the girl. 'Why do you not walk on? Why do you keep staring at me so?'

'I feel so sorry for you,' replied Zhao, 'seeing you here, all alone and weeping in this lonely place.'

'My husband is dead and I have nowhere to go! That is the cause of my distress.'

Zhao asked her why she did not try to find another husband.

'How can I hope to marry again?' she replied. 'I am so alone in the world and helpless. If I could only find a man to turn to, I would happily be his concubine.'

Zhao gladly offered to take her in himself, and she accepted his offer. It was still a long way to his home, and Zhao proposed hiring a carriage, but she declined, walking on ahead of him, flitting effortlessly along like a fairy. When they arrived at Zhao's house, she applied herself diligently to household tasks, fetching water and hulling rice.

Well over two years went by in this way, and then one day she addressed Zhao in the following words: 'I have been touched by your love for me. Soon we will have been together almost three years. Now I must go my own way.'

'But you said you had nowhere to go,' protested Zhao.

'I was not speaking in earnest. Of course I have a home. My father has a herbalist's shop in Nanking. If ever you want to

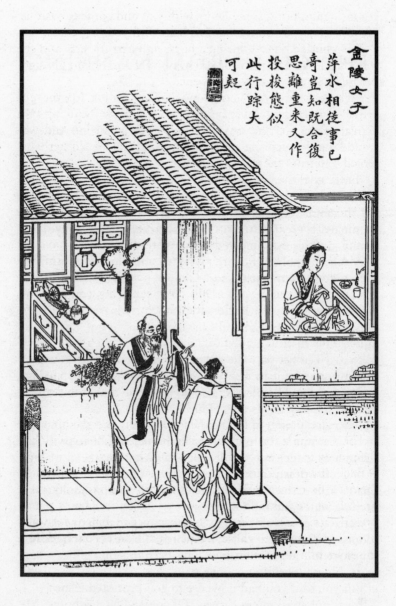

金陵女子

萍水相逢事已
奇豈知既合復
思離重來又作
投梭態似
此行踪大
可疑

The girl was out at the back, washing clothes.

see me again, bring some herbs with you and come to visit us. We will give you some money to help with your expenses.'

Zhao busied himself hiring a horse and cart for her, and she took her leave and went on her way, vanishing from his sight before he knew what had happened.

As time went by, Zhao found himself pining for the girl greatly. He bought some herbs and set off for Nanking. On arrival in the city, he deposited his herbs at an inn and was wandering through the streets when suddenly an old herbalist hailed him from the doorway of his shop.

'There goes my son-in-law!'

The old man invited him in. The girl was out at the back of the shop washing clothes, and even when she saw Zhao come in, she neither spoke to him nor smiled, but continued with her washing. Zhao was greatly put out by this and would have left at once had not the old man prevailed upon him to return. But even then the girl continued to ignore him. The old man told his servant to set the table and cook them a meal, and was about to give Zhao a handsome present, when the girl came out and stopped him.

'His luck is thin,' she said. 'Give him too much and he will never live to enjoy it. Give him a little money and write out ten prescriptions for him. That will be enough to set him up in life.'

The old man asked Zhao what herbs he had brought with him.

'They are already sold,' said the girl. 'Here is the money.'

The old man wrote out a number of prescriptions, gave Zhao the money for his herbs and saw him on his way.

Back at home, Zhao tried out the prescriptions and found them to be extraordinarily effective. To this very day there are folk at Yishui who know how to make up Zhao's patent prescriptions, one of which – a highly effective remedy for warts – consists of pounded garlic, steeped in rainwater collected from the eaves of a thatched roof.

65

TWENTY YEARS A DREAM

Yang Yuwei went to live on the banks of the Si River, in a studio out in the wilds. There were numerous old graves just beyond the wall of his property. At night he could hear the wind soughing in the poplars, like the sound of surging waves.

He sat up late one evening beside his lamp and was beginning to feel very lonely and forlorn when he heard a voice outside chanting some lines of verse:

> In the dark night the cool wind blows where it will;
> Fireflies alight on the grass, they settle on my gown . . .

Over and over again he heard the same plaintive, melancholy lines chanted by a delicate woman's voice. The sound intrigued him greatly. The following day, he searched outside but could find no trace of the singer, except for a length of purple ribbon caught in the brambles, which he took back with him and placed on the window-sill. Towards the middle of the second watch of that night, the chanting began again. He moved his stool across to the window, climbed on to it and looked out. The sound ceased immediately. He now knew for sure that this must be the chanting of a ghost. He felt himself strangely drawn to it.

The following night, he crouched inside the outer wall of the compound and lay in wait for the ghost. Towards the end of the first watch, he saw a young woman come walking, almost gliding, out of the tall grass, leaning on the trees for support as she came, head bowed, chanting her melancholy dirge. Yang gave a faint cough, and she vanished at once into the tall grass.

He continued to wait for her, and presently she reappeared. When her chanting was finished, Yang replied through the intervening wall:

> Who, alas, can know your heart's secret sorrow,
> As you stand at moonrise in your cold turquoise sleeves?

A long silence ensued, after which Yang retired to his room. He had been sitting there for a while when a beautiful young lady entered and, with a little shake of her sleeves, addressed him.

'You are indeed a gentleman of such refinement and cultivation, sir! It is a shame that I have shunned your company for so long.'

Yang helped her to a chair, scarcely able to contain his joy. She seemed so frail, and trembled, as if her body could barely support the weight of her own clothes.

'Where are you from?' he asked. 'Have you been long in these parts?'

'I am from the west, from the province of Gansu,' she replied. 'I followed my father here on his travels. When I was seventeen, I was taken with a sudden illness and died. That was twenty years ago or more. Since then I have haunted this desolate spot, lonely as a wild bird separated from its flock. The lines I was chanting I wrote myself, to give expression to my innermost feelings of grief. I have never been able to find lines to match them. You have completed the poem for me and brought me joy in the grave.'

Yang wished to make love to her without further ado, but she would not.

'I am a creature of the night,' she said, a slight frown crossing her brow. 'My dead bones are not like those of a living body. If we were to make love it would be an inauspicious union. It would only bring you an early death, and I could not bear to cause you harm.'

So Yang held back, merely toying with her breasts, which were as virginal and soft to the touch as freshly peeled lotus kernels. When he asked to see her little bound feet, her 'lotus-hooks', the tiny tips of which beckoned to him from beneath her skirt, she lowered her head and gave a little laugh.

'You're in a bit of a hurry, aren't you?'

Yang took her feet in his hands and caressed them, and, as he did, he noticed that one of her pale-green silk stockings was fastened with a purple ribbon, while the other was tied with coloured thread.

'Where is your other ribbon?' he asked.

'The other night you frightened me and I ran away – I must have dropped it somewhere.'

'Allow me to replace it for you,' said Yang.

He took the ribbon from where he had kept it on his window-sill and handed it to her. She was curious to know where he had found it, and he told her while she undid the coloured thread and in its place tied the ribbon round her stocking.

She started browsing through the books on his desk and came across Yuan Zhen's famous ballad, 'The Lianchang Palace'.

'When I was alive this was one of my favourite poems,' she said, heaving a sigh. 'I feel as if this is all a dream!'

They talked about their favourite works of literature together, and he found her remarks both perceptive and endearing. They 'trimmed the lamp at the west window', talking into the night like newfound bosom-friends. And, from then, the faint sound of chanting would announce her arrival every evening.

'Never mention me to any of your friends,' she enjoined him. 'I have always been timid by nature, and am nervous of being roughly treated.'

Yang gave her his word, and they were as happy together as two fish sporting in the water. They never made love, but were happier and more intimate than many a married couple. She would often copy out their favourite works for him by lamplight in her neat, elegant calligraphy, and she even compiled her own selection of one hundred poems on courtly themes, copying them out and reciting them for him. She asked him to set out the Go-board and to buy a piba-mandolin, and every evening she would teach him Go-moves or play him a new air on the piba. She played 'Rain Dripping on the Plantains by the

Window' but he found it unbearably melancholy, so she played him 'Oriole Singing in the Garden at Dawn' instead, which put him in a more cheerful mood. Thus they pleasantly whiled away the hours together well into the night and quite forgot the coming dawn. But the moment she saw first light at the window, she hurried away.

One day, a friend of Yang's by the name of Xue came to call and found him still asleep in bed. Xue was intrigued to see the piba and the Go-board in Yang's room, since to his knowledge his friend had never been fond of either. He started idly leafing through the books and papers on his desk and came across a handwritten scroll of poems on courtly themes, neatly written out in little characters. This intrigued him even more.

When Yang awoke, Xue asked him, 'Where do all these new hobbies of yours spring from?'

'Oh, I thought I'd try turning my hand to something new,' replied Yang, somewhat unconvincingly. Xue went on to inquire about the poems, which Yang pretended to have borrowed from a friend. Xue continued to glance through them, until he came to the very end, where he saw in minuscule characters the inscription: 'Written this . . . day of the . . . month, by Locket.'

He laughed. 'Locket – why, that's a lady's name! You can't fool me!'

Yang seemed most put out and quite at a loss for words. Xue kept plying him with questions but his friend refused to give away his secret, until finally, when Xue made as if to walk off with the scroll under his arm, Yang gave in and told him the truth. Xue begged to see this mysterious lady-friend of his at once, and when Yang told him that he had given her his word never to mention her existence to a soul, he only pleaded the more insistently. In the end, Yang could hold out no longer and agreed to arrange a meeting between them. That night, when she came, he told her what he had done, and she reproached him angrily.

'Did I not make you promise? And you have to go gossiping like this!'

He told her how it had happened.

'It is all over between us!' she cried. 'Our destiny has run its course.'

His entreaties were of no avail, and she rose to leave, saying, 'I shall have to stay away for a while.'

The following day when Xue called, Yang was obliged to tell him that the meeting could no longer take place. Xue suspected that he was being fobbed off and came back again that night with two of his friends. They stayed and stayed and showed no sign of wanting to leave, making quite a nuisance of themselves and creating a great din into the early hours. Yang was most put out by their behaviour, but could do nothing to stop it. This continued for several nights, until eventually, since there was still no sign of Locket, the men gradually began to lose interest and their antics became more subdued. Then one night, they were about to leave for good when they heard a faint chanting outside, a beautiful sound of indescribable melancholy. Xue inclined his ear to listen, enraptured. One of his friends by the name of Wang, a boorish fellow and something of a dab hand at the Martial Arts, picked up a large rock and hurled it through the window.

'Stop putting on such highfalutin airs!' he cried. 'Come out and show your face, or shut up! No one's interested in your dreary verses! That fancy wailing bores us to death!'

The chanting ceased abruptly. The others reproached Wang, and Yang was extremely upset with them all and expressed his displeasure in no uncertain terms. The following morning they finally took their leave of him, and that night he slept alone in his studio, hoping against hope that his lady-friend would return. But there was no sign of her.

And then two days later, she appeared.

'How could you invite all those nasty friends of yours!' she sobbed. 'You just about frightened the wits out of me!'

Yang offered her an abject apology, but she was inconsolable. 'I meant it when I said it was all over between us! Farewell.'

She hurried out, and even as he reached out for her she had vanished.

For more than a month she did not come again. Yang pined for her, wasting away to skin and bone, but what he had done could not be undone. And then one evening he was drinking alone when to his great joy she parted the door-blind and walked in.

'Have you forgiven me?' he cried.

She wept and hung her head in silence, while he kept repeating the question. It was as if she wanted to say something in reply but could not bring herself to do so. Finally she spoke.

'I walked out on you in such a temper, and yet here I am back again, begging you for a favour. I feel so ashamed of myself.'

Yang pressed her to tell him more.

'It has all happened so suddenly. A vile monster is bullying me into being his concubine! I come from a good family – how could I possibly stoop so low as to marry the ghost of a base-born slave! But I am too weak to resist him. I beg you to come to my rescue, if you still think of me as your wife! I know I can count on you . . .'

Yang was filled with angry indignation at her plight, and offered at once to lay down his very life for her sake if need be. His only concern was that he would be unable to cross the gulf between the living and the dead.

'Tomorrow night you must go to sleep early,' she said. 'I will come to fetch you in your dreams.'

They sat up together talking till dawn, and as she left she told him not to sleep during the following day and to be ready for their meeting in the evening. Yang promised to do as she said. Late that afternoon, he had a little to drink, climbed on to his bed a trifle tipsy and lay down fully clothed as he was. The next instant he saw her enter. She handed him a sword and led him into a building. They had closed the door and were talking together when they heard the sound of someone smashing the door down with a stone.

'He's coming!' she cried in a fearful voice. 'My enemy is coming!' Throwing open the door and rushing out, Yang saw before him a man with bristling moustaches, wearing a red hat and a black gown. He reproached him angrily for his behaviour and the man replied with a hostile glare and a torrent of abuse, whereupon Yang rushed at him in a mighty rage. The fellow with the moustaches picked up a handful of stones and hurled them in a shower at Yang, striking him on his wrist so that he could no longer hold his sword. At this critical juncture Yang saw a figure in the distance, a man with a bow and arrow slung round his waist, setting off on a hunting expedition. Looking more carefully, he recognized him as his friend Wang, the Martial Arts enthusiast, and yelled to him for help. Wang strung his bow and came running towards him, letting loose one arrow that struck the red-hatted fellow in the thigh and another that killed him outright. Yang thanked his friend profusely for his timely intervention, and Wang, having ascertained the details of the situation, was glad to have done something to atone for his earlier boorishness. He accompanied Yang into the young lady's room.

She stood there trembling and bashful, keeping her distance and not saying a word. On the table in front of her lay a little dagger about a foot or so long. The blade was inlaid with gold and jade, and it shone brilliantly in its case. Wang held it in his hand. He was ecstatic in its praise and loth to put it down. He chatted a little longer with his friend Yang, but, seeing the young lady still standing there so timid and bashful, he presently said goodbye and took his leave. Yang also made his way home and was climbing over the wall into the compound when he stumbled – and awoke with a start from his dream. The village roosters were already crowing. His wrist felt very painful, and by the light of dawn he could see that the skin was all red and swollen.

A little later that day, his friend Wang came to call on him and mentioned to Yang that he had dreamed a strange dream. 'Did you by any chance dream of shooting an arrow?' asked Yang. Wang was amazed that his friend should have known, and Yang showed him his bruised wrist and recounted his own dream. Wang for his part was still haunted by the beauty of the lady he had seen in his dream, his one regret being that it had not been a real encounter. He was pleased that he had been able to render some service to Yang's mysterious friend, and asked Yang to put in a word with her on his behalf.

That night she came to give thanks, and Yang gave all the credit for her rescue to Wang, at the same time conveying to her his friend's earnest desire to make her acquaintance.

'Such kindness should not be forgotten,' she said. 'But he is

連瑣

羨爾垂楊裊晚昏
吟懷悲楚
月無痕十年一覚
泉臺夢囘
必真無始返魂

Wang strung his bow and let loose an arrow.

such a big fellow, he does rather scare me.' She continued, 'He seemed to take a liking to that dagger of mine. My father bought it for a hundred taels of silver when he was in Canton, and I have always been fond of it. I had the handle bound with gold thread and set with pearls. My father was so saddened by my early death that he had it buried in the ground with me. I would like to give it to your friend as a memento.'

The next day, Yang passed this message on to Wang, who was overjoyed. And that very evening she came with the dagger.

'Tell your friend to treasure it. It is not Chinese: it comes from a foreign land.'

From that day forth, she and Yang continued to see each other as before.

Several months passed by, and one evening they were sitting in the lamplight when suddenly she smiled at Yang, as if there was something on her mind. She blushed, and hesitated three times. Yang took her in his arms and asked her what was troubling her.

'You have given me so much affection,' she began. 'I have received from you the breath of the living. I have eaten your food. All of a sudden my blanched bones seem to feel life stirring in them once more. But I need the seed and blood of a living man if I am to be truly born again.'

Yang laughed. 'But it was you who always said no. When have I ever denied you?'

'After we make love,' she said, 'you will be gravely ill for three weeks. But with the right medicine you can be cured.'

They made love, and afterwards she dressed herself and rose to her feet.

'I still need a little human blood. Can you bear the pain – for love's sake?'

Yang took a sharp knife and cut his arm, while she lay down on the bed and let the blood drip on to her navel. Then she stood up.

'I will not come again. Remember carefully what I am about to say. Count a hundred days from today, and go to my grave. You will see a blackbird singing in a tree. That is where you will find the grave. You must open it up.'

Yang noted all this carefully, and as she walked out through the doorway she said to him, 'Be neither a day early nor a day late. You must come on that exact day. Be sure not to forget.'

And so she left.

Ten days or so later, Yang fell gravely ill, his stomach becoming so swollen that he seemed close to death. A doctor gave him a remedy, which purged him of some vile stuff that resembled mud, and after another twelve days he had recovered.

On the hundredth day after Locket's departure, he duly made his way to the grave, sending one of his servants ahead with a shovel. As evening drew on, he saw two blackbirds in a tree.

'We can begin,' he ordered joyfully.

They hacked away the undergrowth and opened up the grave. The coffin boards had already rotted away, but the lady's body within the coffin was uncorrupted and still slightly warm to the touch. He wrapped her in a shroud and carried her home, laying her in a warm place. Her breathing was faint, tenuous like fine threads of silk. He fed her small portions of nourishing broth, and by midnight she was fully revived.

She always said to him afterwards, 'Those twenty years were like a dream.'

MYNAH BIRD

Wang Fenbin once told this story about a man in his native town who kept a mynah bird.

The man taught it to speak, and they became so intimate that the man took the bird with him every time he went travelling. A few years passed in this way. One day the man was passing through the town of Jiangzhou when he found that he had no money for the voyage home and became quite despondent.

'Why don't you sell me?' said the mynah. 'The Prince will pay a good price for me, and then you will not need to worry about the journey home.'

'I couldn't bear to part with you,' replied the man.

'Don't worry. Just leave as soon as you have the money. Wait for me under the big tree six miles west of the town.'

The man agreed to do this. He took the bird into the town, where they began talking to each other, gradually gathering quite a crowd. A eunuch from the Prince's court saw them and reported it to his master, who summoned them and expressed his desire to purchase the bird.

'But I have always depended on this bird for a living,' said the man. 'I do not want to part with him.'

The Prince addressed the mynah. 'Do *you* wish to live here?'

'Yes, I do,' replied the bird.

The Prince was delighted.

'Give him ten taels of silver,' continued the bird. 'Not an ounce more.'

The Prince was more delighted than ever, and immediately gave the man ten taels. The man took his leave, making a great show of how aggrieved he felt at the transaction.

雛　雛

客途賢鷺奈愁何
相伴依依祇八哥
賺得金來臣去也
能言畢竟慧心多

When the Prince spoke to the bird, it replied promptly.

When the Prince spoke to the bird, it replied promptly. The Prince ordered his servants to feed it some meat, and when the bird had eaten, it announced that it wished to take a bath. So the Prince ordered a gold basin to be filled with water and set before the bird. He freed the mynah from its cage, and it bathed and then flew up into the eaves, preening its feathers with its beak and shaking off the water, chattering all the while with the Prince. In a moment its feathers were dry, and it rose fluttering into the air, saying in a Shanxi accent, 'I must be on my way!'

The Prince and his courtiers looked around, but the bird had already disappeared. The Prince gazed long up into the air and heaved a sigh. The original owner was sought at once, but he had disappeared without trace.

Some time later, a traveller in Shaanxi Province to the west saw the man with the bird in the market at Xi'an town.

This story was recorded by Bi Jiyou.

67
LAMP DOG

His Excellency Han Daqian had a steward, who one night lay down to sleep in the lean-to scullery and saw a lamp shining in the building up above, bright as a star. After a little while, it floated twinkling down to the ground, where it was transformed into a dog. The steward saw the creature moving towards the rear of the house, and, leaping out of bed, he discreetly trailed it as it went slinking into the garden, where it was transformed into a young woman.

The steward knew now that it must be a fox-spirit. He went back to his bed and lay down, when all of a sudden he saw the woman coming towards him from the back of the house. He feigned sleep, intending to observe whatever transformation would take place next, but the woman merely bent over him and began to shake him. He went through the motions of waking, and asked her who she was. She was silent.

'Are you not the lamp that was burning up there?' he went on.

'Since you already know, why ask?'

So they spent the night together, and from then on she came to him every night and departed at dawn.

When the master came to know of this, he set two of his men to sleep with the steward, one on either side. But when they awoke they found themselves on the ground, without knowing how or when they had fallen there. The master flew into a rage and summoned his steward.

'The next time she comes, you must capture her. If you do not, I shall have you whipped!'

The steward dared not challenge his master, and withdrew

She covered her face with her sleeve.

without a word from his presence. To capture the girl would be hard, he thought to himself. But to fail to do so would mean a terrible fate! He was hesitating, unable to resolve upon any course of action, when suddenly he remembered that she always wore a tight little red blouse next to her body and never removed it. That might be her secret. If he could but lay hands on that, he might have power over her.

That night, when she came, she said to him, 'Your master has told you to capture me, has he not?'

'Indeed he has,' replied the steward. 'But how could I possibly betray you, when there is such love between us?'

As she slept that night, he surreptitiously took off her little blouse. She cried out and wrested herself away from him and was gone. She did not return thereafter.

Some time later, the steward was returning from an errand when he saw the woman in the distance, sitting by the roadside. As he approached, she covered her face with her sleeve. He dismounted.

'Why are you treating me thus?' he asked.

She rose to her feet and took his hand.

'I thought you had put all feeling for me out of your mind. If you still love me as you once did, I will forgive you. It was your master who ordered you to do what you did, after all. You are not to blame. But our affair is at an end. Fate has so decreed. Today I would like to hold a little farewell party.'

It was early autumn, and the sorghum was ripe and ready for harvesting. She led him by the hand into the field, and there in the very middle of the crop of sorghum stood a great mansion. He tethered his horse and went inside, and in the hall a feast had been spread. No sooner had he sat down than a host of maidservants appeared and began waiting on him.

Evening drew on and the steward took his leave, returning to report to his master. As he walked away he looked back. There was nothing to be seen in the field but the crop of sorghum and the raised pathways running through it.

68

DOCTOR FIVE HIDES

Chang Tiyuan of Hejin, when he was an official student, dreamed that he heard a voice speaking to him and addressing him as 'Doctor Five Hides'. He rejoiced at this propitious omen (the name having first been given to a legendary figure of the Spring and Autumn era).

When the Troubles came, Chang was stripped of all his clothes and left at night shut up in an empty room. It was midwinter and bitterly cold. He searched around in the dark and found a number of sheep-hides, which he wrapped around himself, thus managing to survive the night.

At dawn he looked more closely and saw that there were in fact exactly five hides. He burst out laughing at the joke played on him by the spirit of his dream. He later became a tribute student and was appointed Magistrate of Luonan County.

Bi Jiyou recorded this.

There were in fact exactly five hides.

69

BUTTERFLY

Luo Zifu was born in Bin County, and lost both his parents at an early age. When he was eight or nine years old he went to live with his Uncle Daye, a high official in the Imperial College and an immensely wealthy man. Daye had no sons of his own and came to love Luo as if he were his own child.

When the boy was fourteen, he fell in with bad company and became a regular frequenter of the local pleasure-houses. A famous Nanking courtesan happened to be in Bin County at the time, and the young Luo became hopelessly infatuated with her. When she returned to Nanking, he ran away with her and lived with her there in her establishment for a good six months – by which time his money was all gone and the other girls had begun to mock him mercilessly, though they still tolerated his presence.

Then he contracted syphilis and broke out in suppurating sores, which left stains on the bedding, and they finally drove him from the house. He took to begging in the streets, where the passers-by shunned him. He began to dread the thought of dying so far from home, and one day set off begging his way back to Shaanxi, covering ten or so miles a day, until eventually he came to the borders of Bin County. His filthy rags and foul, pus-covered body made him too ashamed to go any further into his old neighbourhood, and instead he hobbled about on the outskirts of town.

Towards evening, he was stumbling towards a temple in the hills, seeking shelter for the night, when he encountered a young woman of a quite unearthly beauty, who came up to him and asked him where he was going. He told her his whole story.

'I myself have renounced the world,' was her response. 'I live here in a cave in the hills. You are welcome to stay with me. Here at least you will be safe from tigers and wolves.'

Luo followed her joyfully, and together they walked deeper into the hills. Presently he found himself at the entrance to a grotto, inside which flowed a stream, with a stone bridge leading over it. A few steps further and they came to two chambers hollowed out of the rock, both of them brightly lit, but with no sign anywhere of either candle or lamp. The girl bid Luo remove his rags and bathe in the waters of the stream.

'Wash,' she said, 'and your sores will all be healed.'

She drew apart the bed-curtains and made up a bed for him, dusting off the quilt.

'Sleep now,' she said, 'and I will make you a pair of trousers.'

She brought in what looked like a large plantain leaf and began cutting it to shape. He lay there watching her, and in a very short while the trousers were made and placed folded on the bed.

'You can wear these in the morning.'

She lay down on a couch opposite.

After bathing in the stream, Luo felt all the pain go out of his sores, and when he awoke during the night and touched them, they had already dried and hardened into thick scabs. In the morning he rose, wondering if he would truly be able to wear the plantain-leaf trousers. When he took them in his hands, he found that they were wonderfully smooth, like green satin.

In a little while, breakfast was prepared. The young woman brought more leaves from the mountainside. She said that they were pancakes, and they ate them, and sure enough they were pancakes. She cut the shapes of poultry and fish from the leaves and cooked them, and they made a delicious meal. In the corner of the room stood a vat filled with fine wine, from which they drank, and when the supply ran out she merely replenished it with water from the stream.

In a few days, when all his sores and scabs were gone, he went up to her and begged her to share his bed.

'Silly boy!' she cried. 'No sooner cured than you go losing your head again!'

'I only want to repay your kindness . . .'

They had much pleasure together that night.

Time passed, and one day another young woman came into the grotto and greeted them with a broad grin.

'Why, my dear wicked little Butterfly!' (for such was the girl's name). 'You *do* seem to be having a good time! And when did this cosy little idyll of yours begin, pray?'

'It's been such an age since you last visited, dearest Sister Flower!' returned Butterfly, with a teasing smile. 'What Fair Wind of Love blows you here today? And have you had your little baby boy yet?'

'Actually I had a girl . . .'

'What a doll factory you are!' quipped Butterfly. 'Didn't you bring her with you?'

'She's only just this minute stopped crying and fallen asleep.'

Flower sat down with them and drank her fill of wine.

'This young man must have burned some very special incense to be so lucky,' she remarked, looking at Luo. He in turn studied her. She was a beautiful young woman in her early twenties, and the susceptible young man was instantly smitten. He peeled a fruit and 'accidentally' dropped it under the table. Bending down to retrieve it, he gave the tip of one of her tiny embroidered slippers a little pinch. She turned away and smiled, pretending not to have noticed. Luo, who was now totally entranced and more than a little aroused, noticed all of a sudden that his gown and trousers were growing cold, and when he looked down at them they had turned into withered leaves. Horrified, he sat primly upright for a moment, and slowly they reverted to their former soft, silken appearance. He was secretly relieved that neither of the girls seemed to have noticed anything.

A little later, they were still drinking together when he let his finger stray to the palm of Flower's dainty little hand. Flower carried on laughing and smiling, as if nothing had happened. And then suddenly, to his horror, it happened a second time: silk was transformed to leaf, and leaf back to silk. He had learned his lesson this time, and resolved to behave himself.

'Your young man is rather naughty!' said Flower, with a smile. 'If you weren't such a jealous jar of vinegar, he'd be roaming all over the place!'

Flower sat down with them and drank her fill.

'You faithless boy!' quipped Butterfly. 'You deserve to freeze to death!'

She and Flower both laughed and clapped their hands.

'My little girl's awake again,' said Flower, rising from her seat. 'She'll hurt herself crying like that.'

'Hark at you,' said Butterfly, 'leading strange men astray and neglecting your own child!' Flower left them, and Luo was afraid he would be subjected to mockery and recrimination from Butterfly. But she was as delightful as ever.

The days passed, and, as autumn turned to winter, the cold wind and frost stripped the trees bare. Butterfly gathered the fallen leaves and began storing them for food to see them through the winter. She noticed Luo shivering, and went to the entrance of the grotto, where she gathered white clouds with which to line a padded gown for him. When it was made, it was warm as silk, and the padding was light and soft as fresh cotton floss.

A year later, she gave birth to a son, a clever, handsome child with whom Luo loved to pass the days playing in the grotto. But, as time went by, he began to pine for home and begged Butterfly to return with him.

'I cannot go,' she told him. 'But you go if you must.'

A further two or three years went by. The boy grew, and they betrothed him to Flower's little daughter. Luo was now constantly thinking of his old uncle, Daye.

'The old man is strong and well,' Butterfly assured him. 'You do not need to worry on his behalf. Wait until your boy is married. Then you can go.'

She would sit in the grotto and write lessons on leaves for their son, who mastered them at a single glance.

'Our son has a happy destiny,' she said to Luo. 'If he goes into the human world, he will certainly rise to great heights.'

When the boy was fourteen, Flower came with her daughter, dressed in all her finery. She had grown into a radiantly beautiful young woman. She and Butterfly's son were very happy to be married, and the whole family held a feast to celebrate their union. Butterfly sang a song, tapping out the rhythm with her hairpin:

A fine son have I,
Why should I yearn
For pomp and splendour?
A fine daughter is mine,
Why should I long
For silken luxury?
Tonight we are gathered
To sing and be merry.
For you, dear lad, a parting cup!
For you, a plate of food!

Flower took her leave. The young couple made their home in the stone chamber opposite, and the young bride waited dutifully on Butterfly as if she were her own mother.

It was not long before Luo started talking again of returning home.

'You will always be a mortal,' said Butterfly. 'It is in your bones, and in our son's. He, too, belongs in the world of men. Take him with you. I do not wish to blight his days.'

The young bride wanted to say a last farewell to her mother, and Flower came to visit them. Both she and her husband were loth to leave their mothers, and their eyes brimmed with tears.

'Go for a while,' said the women, by way of comforting them. 'You can always come back later.'

Butterfly cut out a leaf and made a donkey, and the three of them, Luo and the young couple, climbed on to the beast and rode away upon it.

Luo's uncle, Daye, was by now an old man and retired from public life. He thought that his adopted son had died. And now, out of the blue, there he was, with a son of his own and a beautiful daughter-in-law! He rejoiced as if he had come upon some precious treasure. The moment they entered his house, their silken clothes all turned once more into crumbling plantain leaves, while the 'cotton padding' drifted up into the sky. They dressed themselves in new, more ordinary clothes.

As time went by, Luo pined for Butterfly, and he went in search of her with his son. But the path through the hills was strewn with yellow leaves, and the entrance to the grotto was lost in the mist. The two of them returned weeping from their quest.

70

THE BLACK BEAST

My friend's grandfather Li Jingyi once told the following story.

A certain gentleman was picnicking on a mountainside near the city of Shenyang when he looked down and saw a tiger come walking by, carrying something in its mouth. The tiger dug a hole and buried whatever it was in the ground. When he had gone, the gentleman told his men to find out what it was the tiger had buried. They came back to inform him that it was a deer, and he bade them retrieve the dead animal and fill up the hole.

Later the tiger returned, followed this time by a shaggy black beast. The tiger went in front as if it were politely escorting an esteemed guest. When the two animals reached the hole, the black beast squatted to one side and watched intently while the tiger felt in the earth with his paws, only to discover that the deer was no longer there. The tiger lay there prostrate and trembling, not daring to move. The black beast, thinking that the tiger had told a lie, flew into a fury and struck the tiger on the forehead with its paw. The tiger died immediately, and the black beast went away.

黑獸

鄭人舊底亮咸盧白額威

猶一擊殊奇歧由未猛柞

原石知此獸可除

The tiger returned, followed by a shaggy black beast.

71

THE STONE BOWL

A certain gentleman by the name of Yin Tu'nan, of Wuchang, possessed a villa that he rented out to a young scholar. Half a year passed and he never once had occasion to call on this young tenant of his. Then one day he chanced to see him outside the entrance to the compound, and observing that, despite the tenant's evident youth, he had the fastidious manner and elegant accoutrements of a person of refinement, Yin approached him and engaged him in conversation. He found him indeed to be a most charming and cultivated person. Clearly this was no ordinary lodger.

Returning home, Yin mentioned the encounter to his wife, who sent over one of her own maids to spy out the land, on the pretext of delivering a gift. The maid discovered a young lady in the young man's apartment, of a breathtaking beauty that surpassed (as she put it) that of a fairy, while the living quarters, she observed to her mistress, were furnished with an extraordinary variety of plants, ornamental stones, rare clothes and assorted curios, things such as she had never before set eyes on.

Yin was intrigued to find out exactly what sort of person this young man could be, and went himself to the villa to pay him a visit. It so happened the man was out, but the following day he returned Yin's visit and presented his name card. Yin read on the card that his name was Yu De, but when Yin pressed Yu De for further details of his background, he became extremely vague.

'I am happy to make your acquaintance, sir. Trust me, I am no robber, nor am I a fugitive from justice. But beyond that, I am surely not obliged to divulge further particulars of my identity.'

Yin apologized for his incivility and set wine and food before his guest, whereupon they dined together in a most convivial manner until late in the evening, when two dark-skinned servants came with horses and lanterns to fetch their young master home.

The following day, he sent Yin a note inviting him over to the villa for a return visit. When Yin arrived, he observed that the walls of the room in which he was received were lined with a glossy paper that shone like the surface of a mirror, while fumes of some exotic incense smouldered from a golden censer fashioned in the shape of a lion. Beside the censer stood a vase of dark-green jade containing four feathers – two phoenix feathers, two peacock – each of them over two feet in length. In another vase, made of pure crystal, was a branch of some flowering tree which he could not identify, also about two feet long, covered with pink blossoms and trailing down over the edge of the little table on which it stood. The densely clustered flowers, still in bud, were admirably set off by the sparsity of leaves. They resembled butterflies moistened by the morning dew, resting with closed wings on the branch, to which they were attached by delicate antenna-like tendrils.

The dinner served consisted of eight dishes, each one a gastronomic delicacy. After dinner, the host ordered his servant to 'sound the drum for the flowers' and to commence the drinking game. The drum duly sounded, and as it did so the flowers on the branch began to open tremulously, spreading their 'butterfly wings' very slowly one by one. And then as the drumming ceased, on the final solemn beat, the tendrils of one flower detached themselves from the branch and became a butterfly, fluttering through the air and alighting on Yin's gown. With a laugh, Yu poured his guest a large goblet of wine, and when Yin had drained the goblet dry, the butterfly flew away. An instant later the drumming recommenced, and this time when it ceased two butterflies flew up into the air and settled on Yu's cap. He laughed again.

'Serves me right! I must drink a double sconce myself!'

And he downed two goblets. At the third drumming, a veritable shower of butterfly-flowers began to fall through the air, fluttering here and there and eventually settling in large numbers on the gowns of both men. The pageboy drummer smiled and thrust out his fingers twice, in the manner of drinking games: once for Yin, and it came to nine fingers; once for Yu, and it came to four. Yin was already somewhat the worse for drink and was unable to down his quota. He managed to knock back three goblets, and then got down from the table, excused himself and stumbled home. His evening's entertainment had only served to intensify his curiosity. There was indeed something very unusual about his lodger.

Yu seldom socialized, and spent most of his time shut up at home in the villa, never going out into society even for occasions such as funerals or weddings. Yin told his friends of his own strange experience and word soon got around, with the result that many of them competed to make Yu's acquaintance, and the carriages of the local nobility were often to be seen at the doors of the villa. Yu found this attention more and more irksome, and one day he suddenly took his leave of Yin and went away altogether. After his departure, Yin inspected the villa and found the interior of the building quite empty. It had been left spotlessly clean and tidy. Outside, at the foot of the stone steps leading up to the terrace, was a pile of 'candle tears', the waxen accumulation, no doubt, of the revels of many evenings. Tattered curtains still hung in the windows, and there seemed to be the marks of fingers still visible on the fabric. Behind the villa, Yin found a white stone bowl, about a gallon in capacity, which he took home with him, filled with water and used for his goldfish. A year later, he was surprised to see that the water in the bowl was still as clear as it had been on the very first day. Then, one day, a servant was moving a rock and accidentally broke a piece out of the rim of the bowl. But somehow, despite the break, the water stayed intact within the bowl, and when Yin examined it, it seemed to all intents and purposes whole. He passed his hand along the edge of the break, which felt strangely soft. When he put his hand inside the bowl, water came trickling out along the crack, but when he withdrew his hand, water filled the bowl as before.

Throughout the winter months, the water in the bowl never

畫堂小飲報余德

居停蝶舞衣

飛醉不醒留

浮龍宮蓄水

器好從殘石

乞延齡

Despite the break, the water stayed intact within the bowl.

froze. And then one night it turned into a solid block of crystal. But the fish could still be seen swimming around inside it.

Yin was afraid that others might get to know of this strange bowl, and he kept it in a secret room, telling only his own children and their husbands and wives. But, with time, word got out and everyone was at his door wanting to see and touch this marvel.

The night before the festival of the winter solstice, the crystal block suddenly melted and water leaked from the bowl, leaving a large dark stain on the floor. Of the goldfish there was no sign whatsoever. Only the fragments of the broken bowl remained.

One day, a Taoist came knocking at the door and asked to see the bowl. Yin brought out the broken pieces to show him.

'This,' said the Taoist, 'was once a water vessel from the Dragon King's Underwater Palace.'

Yin told him how it had been broken, and how it had continued to hold water.

'That is the spirit of the bowl at work,' commented the Taoist, entreating Yin to give him a piece of it. Yin asked him why he wanted it.

'By pounding such a fragment into a powder,' he replied, 'I can make a drug that will give everlasting life.'

Yin gave him a piece, and the Taoist thanked him and went on his way.

72

A FATAL JOKE

The schoolmaster Sun Jingxia once told this story.

A certain fellow of the locality, let us call him 'X', was killed by bandits during one of their raids. His head flopped down on to his chest. When the bandits had gone and the family came to recover the corpse for burial, they detected the faintest trace of breathing, and on closer examination saw that the man's windpipe was not quite severed. A finger's breadth remained. So they carried him home, supporting the head carefully, and after a day and a night, he began to make a moaning noise. They fed him minute quantities of food with a spoon and chopsticks, and after six months he was fully recovered.

Ten years later, he was sitting talking with two or three of his friends when one of them cracked a hilarious joke and they all burst out laughing. 'X' was rocking backwards and forwards in a fit of hysterical laughter, when suddenly the old sword-wound burst open and his head fell to the ground in a pool of blood. His friends examined him, and this time he was well and truly dead.

His father decided to bring charges against the man who had told the joke. But the joker's friends collected some money together and succeeded in buying him off. The father buried his son and dropped the charges.

諸城
某巾

笑不
裏死
暗於
藏刀
刀死
旅於
交笑
上可
九知

某巾
上九占多驗先笑居然

霞隱識 [印][印]

Suddenly the old sword-wound burst open.

73
RAINING MONEY

There was a certain gentleman of Binzhou who was reading in his study one day when he heard a knock at the door. He opened the door and beheld a white-haired old man of a most antique appearance. He invited him in and asked his name.

'My name is Hu Yangzhen – Fox the Taoist Adept,' answered the old man. 'In truth I am a fox-spirit. I have heard of you as a gentleman of great erudition and refinement, and would like to make your acquaintance.'

Now this Binzhou gentleman was by temperament an open-minded sort of person, and quite happy to accept the old man for what he was. He soon entered into a lengthy conversation with him about matters ancient and modern, in the course of which his guest showed himself to be extraordinarily learned and eloquent, expressing himself most gracefully and expounding the classics with unusual insight. The gentleman was hugely impressed, and from that day forward he regularly invited the old man to stay for long periods of time.

During one of these visits, he pleaded confidentially with him. 'You and I are such good friends now. Look at the poverty that surrounds me. I know it would be the easiest thing in the world for you to come by some money. Won't you help me out?'

The old man fell silent for a while, appearing reluctant to comply with this request. Then he smiled. 'It would certainly be easy enough. But I shall need a dozen coins as seed.'

The gentleman provided the requisite number of coins, and the two of them adjourned to a separate room, where the old man began pacing up and down and chanting certain magical

Thousands of coins came clattering down from the ceiling.

incantations. After a short while, thousands of coins came clattering down from the ceiling in a great shower, and soon they were up to their knees in a veritable flood of money. They clambered on to the top of the pile, but the coins kept pouring down and covering their ankles, filling the entire room (which was about ten feet square) to a considerable depth.

'Satisfied yet?' asked the old man.

'Yes! That's quite enough!' cried the gentleman, whereupon the old man waved his hand and the 'rain' stopped. They both left the room and bolted the door from the outside. The gentleman was secretly delighted, thinking that he had suddenly become wealthy.

Some time later, he went back to contemplate his newly gained riches, but when he opened the door the money hill had vanished. All he could see on the ground were the dozen coins he had provided as 'seed' money. He was deeply disappointed, and accused the old man with some animosity of having cheated him.

'I was looking for a friend,' replied the old man angrily, 'someone to discuss books with, not a partner in crime! If what you want is money, then you'd better go and make friends with some petty thief! I'm afraid I cannot oblige.'

With these words, he shook his sleeves and was gone.

74

TWIN LANTERNS

Wei Yunwang was a native of Penquan Village in Yidu County. He came from a rich and influential family, but they had come down in the world and could no longer afford to support him in his studies. So while still a young man in his twenties, he was obliged to abandon studying and earn his living by working in his father-in-law's tavern.

One evening, he was lying alone in an upstairs room of the tavern when he heard footsteps below and sat up in alarm, listening with an increasing sense of apprehension as the sound came up the stairs, growing nearer and nearer and louder and louder. Then he saw two maidservants enter the room and walk over to his bedside, each bearing a lantern, while behind them walked a young gentleman, leading a smiling young lady in his direction. Wei grew more and more alarmed, knowing at once that these were fox-spirits. His flesh broke out in goosebumps and he lowered his head, not daring to so much as look at them.

The young gentleman laughed politely. 'Do not be afraid, sir. Allow me to present my younger sister. She has a predestined affinity with you, and has come to wait upon you.'

Wei finally looked up. Seeing that the young man was dressed in a splendid sable-lined robe, he blushed with shame at his own shabby appearance and struggled without success to find appropriate words to say in reply. Presently the young gentleman left the room, taking with him the two maidservants, who had meanwhile placed the twin lanterns on the floor.

Wei was now able to observe the young lady more closely. She had an ethereal, magical beauty, and he fell instantly in love with her, though he was still much too frightened to engage

雙鐙

双燈相對酒樓
居怀〳
姻緣半載條
羨熬病
鄰多鑑福溫
柔鄉味
定何如

Two maidservants entered the room, each bearing a lantern.

her in any sort of conversation. She looked at him and smiled.

'I can tell at once that you are not really the bookworm type, sir. So why are you behaving like this, like some helpless, stuffy scholar?'

And with these words she sidled up next to him on the bed and snuggled her hands inside his jacket. Wei's reserve very soon melted away, and he loosened her silken trousers. The two of them were soon smiling and exchanging intimate words, and it was not long before they were making love.

Before the morning bell rang, the two maidservants returned to collect their lady, who agreed before she departed to visit him again that very night. In the evening, true to her word, she came.

'My silly friend!' she said playfully to the ever bashful Wei. 'Look what a lucky man you are! You have a pretty girl coming to you all of her own accord every night – and it costs you nothing!'

Wei was delighted to have her to himself again. He gave her wine, and they drank together and played a guessing game. She won nine games out of ten.

'This time let me hold the coins in my hand,' she said with a laugh, 'and you guess. That way at least you stand a chance of winning. If you always let me do the guessing, you will never win.'

So they played happily all night and were about to go to bed, when the girl complained that the bedding had been too cold and uncomfortable the night before, and called for her maidservants to bring one of her own quilts, which they spread on the bed. It was deliciously soft and fragrant, made of silk and embroidered with flowers. In a little while, the two of them removed their clothes and went to bed together. When they made love, the heady scent of her lipstick transported him to a paradise of sensual pleasure.

Half a year passed in this way, and then Wei returned to his old family home. He was standing talking to his wife by the window one moonlit night, when suddenly he saw the girl of the twin lanterns, in a splendid dress, sitting on the wall outside and beckoning to him. He went out and walked towards her, whereupon she stretched out her hand and drew him effortlessly over the wall with her, holding his hand tightly in hers.

'Today I have come to bid you farewell. Please see me off a little way, as a token of the love we shared during all those months.'

Wei was taken aback and asked her what the reason was for her departure.

'In love,' she replied, 'everything is predestined. What more is there to say?'

Even as they were speaking, they had reached the outer limits of the village, and there they found the two maidservants, waiting with the twin lanterns. They all walked on together up Southern Mountain, to a high point on the mountainside, where the girl made her farewell. Wei knew that however deeply he wished her to stay, he had no choice but to let her go, and he stood there despondently, gazing at the twinkling lanterns as they gradually disappeared into the distance, before returning home in sorrow. That night, the villagers all saw lanterns shining up on the mountainside.

75

GHOST FOILED, FOX
PUT TO ROUT

Li Zhuming, the son of Li Jinzhuo, County Magistrate of Suining, was a man of a bold and fearless nature. His elder sister was married to Wang Jiliang of Xincheng, whose house contained several haunted upper rooms. Zhuming often stayed in this house during the summer, and always liked to sleep in one of these cooler upper rooms. On his first visit he was warned about the strange creatures that haunted the rooms, but he only smiled nonchalantly and insisted that his bed be prepared upstairs. His host, feeling it only polite to agree to his brother-in-law's request, suggested that one of his own servants should keep him company during the night, an offer which Zhuming firmly declined.

'I prefer to sleep alone,' he insisted. 'Nothing has ever frightened me in my life.'

His host nonetheless ordered his servants to light some sticks of a special incense (reported to have the power to calm evil spirits) in the incense burner, and to place the bed in whichever direction Zhuming preferred. Then they extinguished the light, closed the door and went out, leaving him alone in the room.

Zhuming had been lying there in bed for a while, when, by the light of the moon, he saw a teacup start to wobble from side to side on the table. The cup continued moving around and showed no sign either of falling to the ground or of coming to a standstill. He sat up and shouted at it, whereupon it stopped, with a sudden clattering sound. After this it was as if an invisible person picked the incense sticks out of the burner and started to wave them around in the room, creating a series of luminous criss-cross patterns in the air. Zhuming stood up and cried, 'What evil spirit has the effrontery to do this?'

He had risen naked from his bed, intending to seize hold of the offender, and now with one foot he felt under the bed for his slippers. Finding only one of them, and in too much of a hurry to bother searching for the other, he set out barefoot across the room, striking out at the still-waving incense sticks. In an instant they returned to the incense burner, the room reverted to normality, and quiet prevailed once more. Zhuming now went down on all fours and began groping for his missing slipper in every dark corner of the room when an object flew at him and struck him in the face. It felt remarkably like a slipper. He searched for it on the floor, but in vain. There was nothing there. He opened the door, went downstairs and called a servant to bring a lamp up to the room. Their search revealed nothing, and eventually he went to sleep again.

At daybreak the following morning, he asked several members of the household to help him continue the search for his missing slipper, and between them they turned everything – including the bed – upside down, without finding anything. In the end his host gave Zhuming a pair of his own slippers. Then, the very next day, Zhuming was gazing idly at the ceiling when he caught sight of a slipper stuck between two of the beams. He brought it down with a long stick and recognized it immediately as his.

Zhuming was originally a native of Yidu, and he had at one time taken up residence in the Sun mansion in nearby Zichuan, a very large property that had been left almost entirely uninhabited. Zhuming merely occupied half of it, the south compound, which looked out on to a tall, storeyed building, separated from it by no more than a wall. The upper-storey door of this building was often seen to open and close of its own accord, but Zhuming paid no special attention to this until one day, when he was chatting with members of his family in the courtyard, the door opened and a dwarf appeared and sat down facing towards them. He could not have been more than three feet in height, and wore a green robe and white stockings. He remained there motionless even as they watched him and

He took aim at the building.

pointed at him. Zhuming said out loud that he must certainly be a fox-spirit, and, fetching his bow and arrow at once, he took aim at the building. When the dwarf noticed what he was doing, he gave a mocking laugh and disappeared. Next Zhuming took his sword and went up into the building itself, cursing aloud and searching everywhere for the dwarf – but to no avail. Finally he returned to his own compound.

From then onwards, there were no further strange apparitions, and Zhuming continued to live there peacefully for several years.

Li Yousan, Zhuming's eldest son, was related to me by marriage. He witnessed these things with his own eyes.

76
FROG CHORUS

Wang Zisun once told me this story.

He was in the capital when he saw a man putting on a performance in the marketplace, with a wooden box divided into twelve sections, each of which contained a crouching frog. Whenever he tapped one of the frogs on the head with his little baton, it began to croak. If he was given money, he would start tapping the frogs' heads in earnest one after the other, producing an orchestral sound like a set of gong-chimes, every note perfectly pitched and clearly audible.

蛙曲

鼓吹曾經兩部詩池
塘青咋猶聽蛙
何人製就翻新曲韻
叶宮商了不差

Whenever he tapped one of the frogs, it began to croak.

77

PERFORMING MICE

The same Wang Zisun once told me this story as well.

There was a man in the city of Chang'an who earned a living by exhibiting his performing mice. He kept more than a dozen of them in a bag on his back. Wherever he found a crowd gathered, he would put together a little wooden frame and mount it on his back, just like a tiny makeshift stage. Then he would strike drum and clapper, and start singing a ballad from some old play. As soon as he started singing, the mice popped their heads out of the bag, wearing masks and full costume, climbed up his back and on to the little 'stage', where they stood on their hind legs and danced. The characterizations, male and female, corresponded exactly with the story he was telling, and their performance evoked all the pathos and comedy of human drama.

無儀祗合相

其皮都道長

安事窠奇莫

笑么麼鼯鼠

技居然也有

上場時

鼠戲

They stood on their hind legs and danced.

78

THE CLAY SCHOLAR

In Luo Family Village, there lived a young man named Chen Dai, who was not only ugly but a coarse oaf into the bargain. He had the undeservedly good fortune to marry an attractive wife who, although she had a low opinion of Chen and was extremely unhappy with her lot, remained faithful to him none-theless and got along well enough with her mother-in-law.

One night, she was sleeping alone when she heard the wind blow open a leaf of the door, and in came a young scholar, who took off his hat and clothes and climbed into bed with her. She was terrified and resisted with all her might, but found herself suddenly powerless to do anything but let him have his way with her. Then he departed. From then on he came to her every night.

After a month or so of this, she began to look haggard and worn. Her mother-in-law observed this and questioned her about it. At first she was too ashamed to say anything, but after persistent questioning, she finally broke down and told her the whole story.

'It must be a ghost!' exclaimed her mother-in-law in great alarm.

She did her best to conjure the spirit away with all manner of prayers and spells, but to no avail. Then they told the hus-band to hide in the room and lie in wait, cudgel in hand. At midnight, true to form, the young scholar appeared, placed his hat on the table, then took off his gown as usual and hung it on the rack. He was on the point of climbing into the wife's bed when suddenly he exclaimed, 'Ah! I detect the aura of a living being!'

泥書生

Dai came hurtling out of the shadows.

Hurriedly he threw on his gown again, just as Dai came hurtling out of the shadows and began battering him around his midriff and ribs. Then there was a sudden cracking sound, and though Dai looked everywhere in the room, he could see no sign whatsoever of the scholar. He lit a torch and saw a fragment of a scholar's gown fashioned out of clay lying on the floor, and a clay hat on the table.

79

FLOWERS OF ILLUSION

In Ji'nan, there lived a certain Taoist priest, about whose name or place of origin nothing was ever known. Winter and summer he wore an unlined robe, always the same one, tied with the same yellow sash, with neither trousers nor over-jacket. He always combed his hair with a broken comb, which he then stuck in his topknot like a hat. In the daytime he strolled barefoot in the marketplace, and at night he slept in the street. In a circle several feet around him, the ice and snow would melt. When he first came to Ji'nan, he used to perform conjuring tricks, and the residents competed with each other to give him alms.

One day, a local layabout plied him with wine and begged to learn something of his magical arts. The Taoist refused to divulge any of his secrets, and later, when he went to bathe in the river, the man made off with his clothes (such as they were), planning thereby to extract what he wanted from him. The Taoist called out to him to bring them back and promised this time to share a secret with him, but the man did not believe him and refused to hand over the clothes.

'Are you quite sure you won't give them back to me?' asked the Taoist.

'Quite sure.'

The Taoist said nothing. But then all of a sudden his yellow sash (which the man still had in his hands) turned into a huge snake, several hands thick, coiled itself six or seven times around the man's body, and then rose up into the air, glaring and hissing and spitting at him. The man fell terrified to his knees, his face drained of colour, and begged the Taoist to spare his life. The Taoist took hold of the snake, which immediately became his sash again, while on the ground a snake could be seen slithering off into the city.

This episode made the Taoist more of a celebrity than ever. The local gentry, hearing of his extraordinary abilities, invited him to join them on their excursions and he became quite a society favourite. Even the highest-ranking local mandarins such as the Provincial Administration Commissioner and the Provincial Censor heard of him and took him along with them to official junkets. One day, the Taoist sent invitations to these various dignitaries to join him in the Water Pavilion on Daming Lake in the centre of Ji'nan. When the day came, they all found formal written reminders on their desks, without the slightest sign of how these had been delivered. They duly made their way to the Water Pavilion, where the Taoist came out to greet them, bowing politely. They entered the pavilion, to find it completely empty and bare. There was no sign of tables or chairs, and they thought the Taoist was trifling with them.

'I regret that I have no servants of my own,' announced the Taoist to his guests. 'I shall be obliged to ask you for the loan of some of your officers, to wait on us.'

They agreed to this, whereupon the Taoist painted a double door on the wall and proceeded to knock at it. A voice answered from within, there was the sound of a lock turning, and the doors opened. The guests hurried forward to look through the opening, and saw within a flurry of busy activity and a room filled with screens, curtains, tables and chairs. Attendants carried all these things to the door, and the Taoist instructed his guests' men to take them and set them out in the pavilion but on no account to speak to the men from the other side of the door. The exchange took place silently, with the two parties doing no more than looking at each other and smiling and laughing. In a matter of moments, the pavilion was sumptuously furnished, and the tables laid with jugs of the finest and most fragrant wines and plates of the richest and most succulent meats, all of them brought out from the room on the other side. The guests were utterly amazed.

The pavilion looked out over Daming Lake, which in the height of summer was always covered with flowering lotuses.

This banquet was taking place in the depths of winter, and all that could be seen outside was the cold, mist-covered water of the lake.

One of the mandarins exclaimed with a sigh, 'What a pity there are no lotuses to add lustre to this splendid gathering!'

The other guests all echoed his sentiment. Seconds later, one of their men came hurrying in to announce: 'Sirs, the lake is covered with lotus leaves!'

They all leaped to their feet and hurried to the window to look out. Sure enough, they beheld a great expanse of green, dotted with lotus buds. And then, in a matter of seconds, thousands upon thousands of lotus buds opened fully and their heady scent was wafted to them on the breeze. They marvelled at this extraordinary spectacle and ordered the man to row out on to the lake and pick some of the flowers. Presently they could see him in his boat disappearing into the lotuses, only to return minutes later empty-handed. When questioned, he replied, 'I rowed out towards the flowers. I could see them in the distance, but as I rowed closer to the northern shore of the lake they somehow vanished and then I saw them over by the southern shore . . .'

The Taoist smiled. 'These are dream-lotuses, empty flowers of illusion . . .'

Later, when the banquet drew to a close and they had drunk their fill, the flowers faded and a brisk northerly breeze sprung up, sweeping away the leaves and leaving the lake wintry and bare once more.

The Ji'nan Circuit Intendant was much taken with the Taoist, and invited him to take up residence in his yamen, so that he could enjoy his company on a regular basis. One day this Intendant was drinking with a number of guests. He kept a rare vintage wine in his cellar, which he occasionally shared with his friends in small quantities, and on this particular day his friends were enthusiastically appreciating this fine wine and clamouring for their cups to be refilled. The Intendant apologized but insisted that his supplies were limited and that he was unable to provide them with any more. The Taoist smiled.

'Gentlemen,' he said, addressing the guests, 'I can see that

結將幻術驚
官宰頃刻花
鬧術六神拍
衆大家齊叫
絶叟荊人是
灌荊人

寒月笑聲聲

'Sirs, the lake is covered with lotus leaves!'

you are eager to drink your fill. If you will allow me to play host for a moment, I will be happy to oblige.'

They were of course delighted for him to do so, and the Taoist slipped a wine jug into his sleeve, bringing it out again seconds later and proceeding to fill everyone's glass from it. The wine was first-class, indeed it was identical to the Intendant's special vintage, and the guests were able to continue drinking to their hearts' content. The Intendant, greatly perplexed, went to his cellar to examine his wine vat, and found that although the seal had not been tampered with in any way, the precious vat was completely empty. He was secretly both angry and ashamed, angry with the Taoist for playing this trick on him, and ashamed at his own meanness. He gave orders for the Taoist to be arrested for sorcery and given a good caning. But no sooner had the cane touched the Taoist's flesh than the Intendant himself felt a stinging pain on his own buttocks; and as the blows continued to rain down, so the Intendant's own skin was lacerated. The Taoist made a great show of screaming with pain down below in the tribunal, but up on the dais the Intendant's buttocks were already staining his chair of office red with blood. He gave orders for the caning to cease immediately, and told the Taoist to quit the city forthwith.

The Taoist went away, no one knows where. He was subsequently sighted in Nanking, wearing the same old, unlined robe, tied with the same yellow sash. But if anyone ever spoke to him, he merely smiled.

80

DWARF

During the reign of the Emperor Kangxi, there was a professional magician who used to take around with him a box in which he kept a dwarf, only a little more than one foot in height. For a fee, he would open the box and tell the dwarf to come out and sing. The performance over, the dwarf would return to the box.

This magician came one day to Ye County, where the local Magistrate impounded the box and questioned the dwarf in some detail as to his place of origin and his background. At first the dwarf did not dare to speak, but when the Magistrate persisted, he gave the details of his family and home village. It transpired that as a young boy he had been kidnapped on his way home from school by the magician, who had given him certain drugs, as a result of which his limbs had shrunk permanently. Subsequently the man had taken him around with him and used him for public performances.

The Magistrate was extremely indignant and had the magician put to death. He himself kept the dwarf, with a view to curing him of his condition, but was never able to find an effective remedy.

小人

肢體矯揉供
裁具由來兒
蛾僞江湖試聽
訴供言如繪
左道應嚴兩
觀誅

At first the dwarf did not dare to speak.

81

BIRD

Wang Wen was a gentleman of Dongchang, a holder of the first degree, by nature a straightforward and honest young man. He went on a trip to the south, through the twin provinces of Hunan and Hubei, and on his way put up at an inn in the village of Six Rivers. Taking a stroll through the village, he encountered a neighbour of his from Dongchang, a wealthy merchant by the name of Zhao Donglou, who was often away from home for years on end. Zhao took Wang warmly by the hand and invited him to the house where he was staying. As they went in, Wang caught sight of a beautiful woman sitting in the room, and, greatly shocked at this breach of Confucian decorum, he made to leave. But Zhao followed him outside, took his hand and drew him back, calling through the window to the young woman, whose name was Maid, to be off. Wang agreed to go back inside, and Zhao set wine and food before him.

'Tell me,' inquired Wang, as the two of them settled down to a friendly conversation, 'what sort of a place *is* this that you are living in?'

'It is a house of pleasure,' admitted Zhao. 'I have been away from home so long and have taken lodgings here.'

As they spoke, the girl kept coming in and out, and Wang, feeling increasingly ill at ease, stood to take his leave again. But once more Zhao pressed him to stay. Then, the next minute, another young woman passed fleetingly by the doorway and catching sight of Wang cast him a bewitching glance, full of the strangest tenderness and passion. To Wang's eyes she resembled a being from some fairy realm. He was an upright fellow, but this vision quite unmanned him.

'Who is *that* beautiful creature?' he asked.

'That,' replied Zhao, 'is the second daughter of the Madame of this establishment. She goes by the name of Bird and is fourteen years old. A number of clients have offered her mother huge sums of money to spend the night with her, but the girl always says no. Sometimes the old bawd even beats her, but she insists that she is too young and pleads to be let off. So to this day she is still a virgin.'

Wang sat there listening, his head hung in silence, nodding in such a dazed way that he must have seemed almost uncivil.

'If you are so struck by her,' said Zhao playfully, 'why not allow me to negotiate on your behalf?'

'I could never dare to entertain such hopes,' said Wang abstractedly. But as evening drew on and he still showed no sign of leaving, Zhao repeated his offer, in the same playful tone.

'I deeply appreciate your kindness,' said Wang, this time adding, on a more practical note, 'but, alas, I simply don't have the money!'

Zhao was familiar enough with Bird's proud and obstinate temperament. Confident that she would never agree to the proposal, he thought it safe to offer to help Wang out to the tune of ten taels of silver. Wang bowed in thanks and hurried out, returning with every penny of his own he could muster (it amounted to some five taels), which he gave to Zhao, bidding him make haste to approach the bawd on his behalf. Just as the old woman was insisting that the sum offered was far too small, to her great surprise Bird spoke up.

'Mother, you are forever complaining that I never earn you any money. Well, today I've finally decided to do what you've always wanted of me. And this will only be my first assignment, remember. Don't turn good money down just because you think it's not enough! In the end I'm sure I'll bring you in plenty!'

Her mother knew how difficult her daughter could be, and was so pleased to hear her agree to anything that in the end she gave her approval and sent one of the maids to fetch Wang. Zhao was greatly taken aback by this unexpected outcome, but he could hardly back out of the negotiations at this juncture, and handed over the money to the bawd. And so Wang and the young lady were able to enjoy the fruits of their passion.

'I am just an ordinary sing-song girl,' she said to him afterwards, 'and no fit match for a gentleman such as you! I feel so honoured that you should have wanted to give me your love. But now you have spent your last penny for this one night of bliss. How will you manage tomorrow?'

Wang sobbed inconsolably, unable to reply.

'Come, do not lose heart,' said the girl. 'I have always wanted to give up this wretched way of life. But until now I'd never met a man like you, someone I felt I could truly trust. My mind is made up. We should run away together this very night . . .'

Ecstatically, Wang rose to his feet, and the girl with him, as they prepared for their departure. The third watch of the night sounded from the bell-tower as she hastily changed into men's clothes and the two of them hurried out together to the inn where Wang was staying. They knocked at the door and asked to be let in. Wang had brought two mules with him on his travels. He now roused his servant and told him to make ready to leave at once, inventing some urgent business that necessitated an immediate departure. The girl tied good-luck charms to the servant's legs and to the ears of the two mules, then they untethered the animals and off they galloped, the three of them, so fast that Wang could hardly see where they were going. He only heard the wind whistling past them, and then it was morning and they had reached the city of Hankou, where they stopped and rented lodgings. Wang was lost in amazement at the speed of their journey.

'If I tell you the truth,' said Bird, 'you must promise not be frightened. I am not an ordinary human: I am a fox. That mother of mine has always wanted to squeeze every penny she can out of me. She has been horribly cruel to me and has made my life an endless misery. Now at last I have escaped from that sea of woe! We are more than thirty miles from that terrible place, and they can never find us now. I am saved!'

Wang was too much in love to have any doubts or misgivings.

'Here I am with you, my flower,' he said simply. 'But we have nothing to our name but these four bare walls. We are paupers. I only fear that one day you will forsake me . . .'

'How can you think such thoughts? We can open a market stall and earn enough to get by, the three of us. The first thing we should do is sell the mules to raise some money.'

Wang did as she suggested, and they set up a small stall outside their lodgings, where he and the servant worked hard together selling wine and tea, while Bird made capes and embroidered purses. They were able to earn enough each day to live quite well, and after a year or so they could even afford to take on a maid and an old serving-woman of their own. Now Wang no longer needed to don an apron himself, but became the manager of their little family enterprise.

One day, all of a sudden, Bird seemed very downcast. 'Alas!' she cried. 'I know that something terrible will happen tonight!'

He asked her to explain.

'My mother has found out where I am. She will be after my blood for sure. She may send my elder sister, in which case all will be well. But I'm afraid she may come herself.'

At midnight, she suddenly became more cheerful. 'All is well! It's my sister Maid who is coming.'

Sure enough, shortly afterwards her sister pushed open the door and walked in. Bird greeted her with a smile, but her sister scolded her harshly.

'Weren't you ashamed, to run away like that? Mother has sent me to find you and bring you home.'

With these words she took out a rope and tied it round Bird's neck. Bird cried out indignantly, 'And why should I not stay faithful to one man?'

Maid grew angrier and angrier and seized hold of her sister, tearing her dress. By now the servants had come to witness the spectacle, and eventually Maid took fright and hurried away.

'Now that she's gone,' said Bird, 'it will be mother's turn. She is sure to come herself. Disaster is nigh! We must act quickly.'

They packed their things in haste and made ready to move on, but before they could get away the bawd was at the door, her face dark with anger.

'I knew you would disobey your sister and that I would have to come and get you myself!'

Bird fell to her knees and pleaded tearfully, but the bawd paid her no heed, seizing her by the hair and marching her off, leaving Wang to brood in misery, unable to sleep or eat. He hastened back to Six Rivers, willing to pay money to redeem her, but though he found the house, there was no sign of the ladies and the neighbours had no idea where they might have gone to. Wang returned to Hankou in despair, and finally he disbanded his household and returned east to Shandong with what money he still had.

Several years later, he happened to be in Peking on his travels and was walking past a Foundlings Home when he caught sight of a boy of seven or eight. His servant stared at the child, thinking that he bore a striking resemblance to his master.

'Why are you staring at that boy?' asked Wang. The servant smiled as he mentioned the likeness that he had observed, and Wang seemed to find the idea strangely pleasing. He looked at the boy more closely. He was a handsome child, and reflecting that he himself had no male heir and that this foundling did indeed resemble him in some strange way, he decided on the spot to buy him and adopt him as his son. When he asked the boy his name, he replied, 'Little Wang.'

'If you were abandoned as a baby,' asked Wang, 'how do you come to know your name?'

'My teacher told me that when I was found I had the words "Son of Wang Wen of Shandong" written on my chest.'

'But that is my name!' cried Wang in astonishment. 'And I don't have a son . . .'

The only explanation he could think of was that this was the son of some other man with the same name as himself. And yet something about the boy had taken his fancy, and he already felt a growing sense of attachment. When they returned home to Shandong, all who saw them assumed that they were father and son.

As Little Wang grew up he showed a great liking for physical activities, especially hunting and combat of all sorts, and was not in the least squeamish when it came to taking life. In fact he positively relished it, and there was nothing his father could do to curb him. The family business was of no interest to him whatsoever. The boy also claimed to be able to detect the presence of ghosts and fox-spirits, a claim the locals at first refused to credit. But then a villager was possessed by a fox-spirit and when they asked Little Wang to go and find it, he went to the man's house, pointed immediately to the place where the fox was hiding and told them to attack it where it was. They did so, and they heard the fox howling, and then a mess of blood and fur came tumbling to the ground and the villager was never again troubled. From then on, the locals all agreed that the boy was a 'strange one'.

One day, Wang Wen was strolling in the marketplace when he ran into his old friend Zhao Donglou, the wealthy merchant, now greatly changed, dishevelled and haggard, a shadow of his former self. Wang inquired, in some alarm, where he had been all this time and what had happened to him. Zhao asked him gloomily if they could find somewhere private to talk, and Wang took him off and bought him a cup of wine.

'As soon as the bawd got hold of Bird again,' began Zhao, 'she beat her and abused her horribly. Then she moved north and tried again to break the girl's will, but Bird vowed she would rather die than have another man, so the old woman locked her up. Bird gave birth to a baby boy, and was forced to abandon it in a little alley. The child was taken to the Foundlings Home. He must be a big boy by now. He is your own flesh and blood!'

'Heaven sent him to me!' wept Wang, and told his friend the story of finding the boy. 'But how do you yourself come to be in such a dreadful state?'

'I have finally learned for myself,' said the other, 'the perils of the pleasure-houses and their life of "love and joy". What more can I say?'

It emerged that he had followed the bawd north to Peking, taking his wares with him. They were heavy and awkward to transport, and in the end he was obliged to sell them at a loss. And what with the assorted expenses of travelling – not to mention Maid, who expected him to provide her with every luxury – as time went by he ruined himself and the bawd began to treat him with the open contempt she reserved for the impecunious. Sometimes Maid was sent out to sleep with wealthy customers and would not return for several days in a row. Zhao would be seething with rage, but could do nothing.

One day, when the bawd was away, Bird called to him from a window, 'In a place like this there is no such thing as love! The only thing they know how to love is money. You must get away from here, or you will come to a terrible end.'

These words filled Zhao with a sudden sense of fear and foreboding. For him it was as if he had awoken from a dream. He decided to leave and return home to Shandong, but before he left he went secretly to see Bird, who gave him a letter for Wang. After he had told his tale, he handed Wang the letter, which read in part:

'. . . I know that our boy is with you now. Zhao can tell you of my troubles. This is all the working of karma! What is there left to say! I am kept locked in a dark room and never see the light of day. I am beaten till my flesh breaks out in sores. Hunger gnaws at my heart. A single day seems to last a year. If you still remember that first night we spent together, when we held each other close and kept each other warm, with nothing but a thin quilt against the cold and the snow, then for our love's sake I beg you and our son to find a way to rescue me from this torment. I beg you to spare my mother and sister. They are cruel and heartless, it is true, but they are my flesh and blood, so please tell the boy not to harm them. That is my earnest wish . . .'

As Wang read the letter, tears streamed down his face. He gave Zhao a generous gift of money and went on his way.

His son, Little Wang, was by now eighteen years old. When he told him all about his mother and showed him the letter, the youth's eyes blazed with anger, and that very day he went to the capital and ascertained the whereabouts of the bawd Wu (for that was her name). Arriving at her establishment, he walked directly in through the throng of customers and found Maid sitting drinking with a client. When she set eyes on him, she stood up with a look of sheer terror on her face. He pounced on her and killed her outright, to the great alarm of the other guests, who took him for a common thief – until they saw the woman's corpse change into that of a dead fox before their very eyes. Little Wang hurried on in, sword in hand, and found the bawd in a back room supervising one of the women who was making soup. As he ran into the room, the bawd vanished from sight in an instant. Casting a quick glance around the room, he drew his bow and shot an arrow up towards one of the beams. A fox fell to the ground transfixed, and instantly he decapitated it. Then he discovered the place where his own mother was being held and threw a stone to break the casement of her window. Mother and son called out to one another, and the first question she asked was what had become of her mother.

'I have already killed her!' cried the impetuous youth.

'Why did you not listen to my words?' she cried in anguish. She told him to bury the old bawd-fox out in the fields. He pretended to agree to this, but instead skinned both foxes and put their pelts away in his bag. He went through the bawd's coffers and took all the money he could find, before setting off home with his mother.

Mother and father were reunited in a touching scene. Wang asked his son what he had done with the bawd.

'She is here,' replied the son. 'In my bag.'

And he produced two fox pelts, to the great consternation of his mother.

'You are a disobedient son!' she reproached him angrily. 'Why was this necessary?'

She wailed and beat herself and wanted only to die. Wang did his utmost to console her, and told their son to bury the pelts.

'Now that you are safe and happy,' protested Little Wang, 'suddenly you forget all the beatings and hardships you once endured!'

This provoked another outburst of anger from Bird, after which she broke down in a fit of weeping. The son went off and buried the pelts, and when he reported to her that it had been done, she became calmer.

With Bird's return, Wang prospered. He greatly appreciated the part played by his friend Zhao in all of this, and rewarded him handsomely, telling him the whole story of the bawd and her daughters, and that they were all foxes.

雅頭

宵遁匆匆到
漢皋平康樂
藉獄同操鄴前
有子姓神武洗
隨還期更伐毛

The woman's corpse turned into that of a dead fox.

Little Wang was an extremely devoted son, but subject to the
direst rages and tantrums if crossed.

'We must deal with our son's wild streak,' said Bird to Wang
one day. 'If we do not, I am afraid he will commit further
murders and ruin us all.'

So that night she crept up on Little Wang while he was asleep
and secretly bound him hand and foot.

'I have done nothing wrong!' he cried as he awoke.

'I am only going to cure you of your wild streak,' said his
mother. 'It won't hurt.'

He yelled and screamed but could not break loose. Taking a
large needle, she drove it into the side of his ankle, to a depth
of about half an inch, then she wrenched it out with all her
might. There was a sharp, cracking sound. She repeated the
procedure on his arm and on the top of his head. Then she
untied him and patted him gently until he fell asleep. The
following morning, he hurried straight in to see his father and
mother, with tears on his face.

'All night I've been remembering the dreadful things I've
done, things no man ought ever to do!'

They were both delighted at his change of heart. From that
day forth, he was gentle as a young girl, and regarded in the
district as the very model of virtue.

82

PRINCESS LOTUS

At Jiaozhou, there lived a man by the name of Dou Xu. One afternoon, he had just dozed off when he saw a man dressed in rough servant's clothing standing beside his bed, looking around nervously as if he wished to say something. He asked him what he wanted, and the man replied, 'My master invites you to call on him.'

'And who, pray, is your master?'

'He lives close by,' was all the old man would say.

So the two of them set off. After turning a corner, they came to a place where pavilion rose above storeyed pavilion in a succession of elaborately roofed buildings, and as they wound their way through this unending maze, it seemed to Dou that he was entering a world utterly different from the world of men. A stream of maids and ladies-in-waiting kept passing by, calling out 'Has Mr Dou arrived?', to which the servant answered in the affirmative. Presently a distinguished-looking mandarin came forward to meet them, greeting Dou very politely and escorting him up into a reception hall.

'This is most kind of you,' said Dou. 'But I do not have the honour of knowing who you are, and have never called on you before, so I cannot help but feel somewhat ill at ease.'

'My lord and master,' replied the mandarin, 'has long heard of you as a man of excellent family and the highest principles. He is most anxious to make your acquaintance.'

'And who is this lord of yours?' asked Dou, with growing puzzlement.

'That you will see for yourself in just a moment.'

Two maids-in-waiting then appeared carrying banners, and

led Dou on through doorway after doorway until finally they came to a great hall where Dou saw a person who was clearly a king, sitting on a throne. The King came down to greet him at once, insisting that Dou should occupy the place of honour on his left, and as soon as the formalities were over and they were both seated, he gave orders that a fine banquet should be set before them. Dou gazed tongue-tied at the wall above them, where he observed a calligraphic panel hanging, inscribed with the words 'Cassia Palace'. The King spoke first.

'I am honoured to have you as a neighbour, and greatly value the bond of affinity that exists between us. Please let us put aside all constraint, all suspicion and fear, and enjoy ourselves to the full!'

Dou expressed his agreement with this proposal. When the wine had gone round several times, he heard a sound in the distance, of pipes and singing, an ethereal, delicate music unaccompanied by any beating of the drum. After a minute or two, the King looked about him and cried out to his assembled courtiers, 'I am going to give you all a line of verse, and would trouble one of you gentlemen to give me a line in response. My first line is this:

A genius enters the Cassia Palace.'

Even as the courtiers were busy racking their brains for an answering line, Dou sang out:

'*A gentleman cherishes the lotus flower.*'

'How strange!' exclaimed the King. 'Lotus is my daughter's name. What a coincidence! There must surely be a predestined affinity between the two of you. Send word to the Princess to come in and meet our guest!'

In a few moments, the tinkling of jade ornaments was heard, and a delicious fragrance of orchid and musk wafted through the hall, announcing the arrival of a young lady of sixteen or seventeen years, of peerless beauty. The King instructed her to curtsey to their guest, and introduced her as his daughter the Princess Lotus. Once these formalities were completed, the Princess withdrew once more to her chamber.

As Dou watched her leave, his soul was utterly transported. He sat there entranced, and when the King raised his goblet and urged him to drink, he simply stared into space. The King seemed to understand what was going on in his mind.

'You and my daughter certainly seem a perfect match – if it were not for the problem posed by the difference of species. What do you say?'

It was as if Dou had not even heard the King speak. He continued gazing into the distance like a man deranged, until finally one of the courtiers sitting next to him nudged his foot.

'Didn't you see His Majesty raise his goblet? Didn't you hear His Majesty speak?'

Dou started and, recovering himself at once, rose from the table and apologized abjectly to the King for his rudeness.

'Your hospitality has been so generous, and without being aware of it I am afraid I must have drunk to excess. Please forgive my boorish behaviour. It is growing late, and you must be tired, sire. I should take my leave.'

'I am most delighted to have met you,' replied the King, rising to his feet, 'and I am only sorry that you are in such a hurry to leave. But I will not detain you. If you care to remember us, I shall be very glad to invite you here again.'

He instructed some of his eunuchs to escort Dou home. On the way one of them asked him, 'Just now when His Majesty said that you and the Princess were a perfect match, he seemed to be offering you her hand in marriage. Why did you say nothing?'

Dou stamped his foot in frustration at the thought of his missed opportunity, and all the way home his mind was filled with a painful sense of regret.

And then suddenly he awoke, to find that the sun had almost set. He sat there on his bed in the evening light, brooding on everything that had happened to him in his dream. After his evening meal he put out his candle, hoping to revisit the Cassia Palace once more. But it was beyond recall, and he heaved a sigh of bitter disappointment.

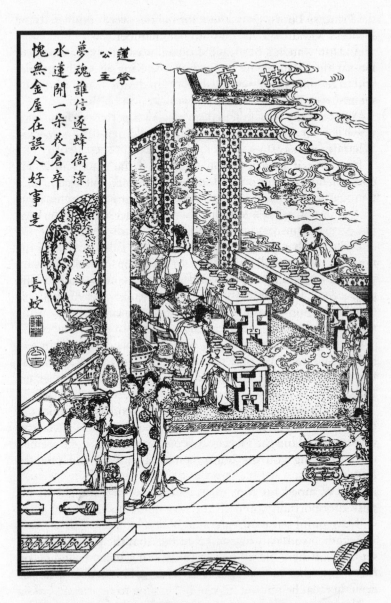

蓮學公主

夢魂誰信逐蜂衙渌
水蓮開一朶花倉卒
愧無金屋在誤人好事是

長蛟

The King introduced her as his daughter the Princess Lotus.

One evening, he was lounging on his couch with a friend when he saw before him the very same servant who had come on the previous occasion, summoning him once again to appear before the King. Up he jumped and hurried off to the palace, where he prostrated himself before the King, who raised him up and once more offered him a seat beside his throne.

'Since we last met,' began the King, 'I know that we have been much in your thoughts. I have a mind to offer you my daughter in marriage. I trust you will not disdain to accept such an offer . . .'

Dou rose to his feet and thanked the King, who gave orders to his chamberlains and officers of state to join them for a banquet. When they had finished their wine it was announced by one of the ladies-in-waiting that the Princess had completed her preparations, and immediately afterwards a bevy of young ladies accompanied her into the hall, a red silken veil covering her face. She glided forwards with tiny steps and stood, supported by her maids, on a woollen carpet, where she and Dou proceeded to perform the rites of marriage. When this was concluded they were escorted to their residence, to the exquisite warmth and heady sweet fragrance of the nuptial chamber.

'Having you by my side, my dearest,' he said to the Princess, 'brings me such joy that I could forget death itself. My only fear is that today's meeting will turn out to be no more than a dream.'

'But here we are together, you and I!' replied the Princess, holding her hand to her mouth to stifle a little laugh. 'It is clear as anything. How could it be a dream?'

In the morning, Dou rose and amused himself by helping the Princess to apply her make-up, and then with a sash he carefully measured the size of her waist, and with his fingers the length of her feet.

'Have you gone mad?' she said with a laugh.

'I have so often been deceived by dreams in the past,' he replied. 'So I am making a careful record of everything. If this turns out to be a dream, at least these details will help me to remember it.'

They were still happily chatting when a maid came rushing into the room.

'A monster has broken into the palace!' she cried. 'The King has fled to one of the side halls. All is lost!'

Dou ran off in great alarm to find the King, who grasped his hand and spoke to him with tears in his eyes.

'You have been so kind as to accept my daughter's hand. I was looking forward to a long and happy friendship – and now this calamity has befallen us, and the very fate of my kingdom hangs in the balance! I fear all is lost!'

Dou begged to know the nature of the calamity, and the King handed him a dispatch that was lying on the table.

'Read this!'

The document began:

From the Grand Secretary of State, Black Wings, of the Hall of Contained Fragrance, to His Royal Majesty, announcing the arrival of a most strange monster. We advise the immediate evacuation of the Court in order to ensure the very survival of your kingdom. A report has just been received from the Eunuch Officer at the Yellow Gate, stating that ever since the sixth day of the fifth moon, a huge monster resembling a python, ten thousand feet in length, has been lying coiled up outside the entrance to the palace. It has already devoured more than 13,800 of Your Majesty's subjects and is reducing every hall in your palace to ruins. Learning of this state of affairs, I decided to brave the danger and take stock of the situation myself. I have seen the beast with my own eyes, an evil-looking monster with a head as big as a mountain and great eyes that gleam like rivers and seas. Every time it raises its head, it swallows whole halls and pavilions, and when it stretches itself, walls and houses are brought tumbling down. Never in the whole of history has there been such a scourge, such a fearful calamity! The continued existence of our ancestral temples and altars is threatened! We therefore beseech Your Royal Majesty to depart at once with the royal family and seek a safer and happier abode elsewhere . . .

Just as Dou finished reading the dispatch, and his face turned ashen pale, another messenger came rushing in.

'The monster is coming!' he cried.

The whole Court burst into cries of lamentation, as if their last hour was at hand. The King himself was paralysed by fear.

'I entrust my daughter to your care!' he cried, turning tearfully to Dou, who ran back breathlessly to his chamber, where he found the Princess and her maids clinging together, weeping and lamenting their fate. She clutched at his gown.

'Oh husband,' she cried, 'what will become of me now?'

Dou was himself on the very brink of despair. He took her hand. 'I am poor,' he mused aloud, 'and have no golden house fit for a princess. But my humble abode can perhaps serve as a refuge for a while . . .'

'In this desperate hour, we have no choice!' wept the Princess. 'I beg you, take me there at once!'

Dou gave her his arm, and in no time they were at his house.

'Why, this is a delightful home!' said the Princess. 'It is better by far than my old kingdom. But what of my father and mother? I must ask you to build a home for them, so that they can live here with all their subjects.'

Dou protested that this would be an extremely difficult undertaking.

'If you cannot help me in my hour of need,' wailed the Princess, 'what use are you as a husband?'

Dou comforted her as best he could, but she went into their chamber, threw herself down on the bed and abandoned herself to a fit of weeping from which he could not arouse her. He was still racking his brains for some course of action, when he awoke and found that the whole thing had been a dream. And yet there was a constant buzzing in his ears, which he knew did not emanate from any human being. Looking around him more carefully, he discovered that the sound was coming from two or three bees that were flying around his pillow. Dou cried out aloud in astonishment. When his friend questioned him, he told him the whole story of his latest dream and the friend was equally amazed. Together they looked more closely at the bees, which were now clustered around the sleeve of Dou's gown and would not be brushed off. The friend urged him to make a hive for them, which he saw to without delay, supervising the construction himself. As soon as the first two of its walls were completed, a swarm of bees came streaming in from outside and installed themselves within it, and before the roof was even on the hive a mass of bees had already established itself within. Dou and his friend traced them back to the old garden of an elderly neighbour, who had kept a hive for over thirty years, from which he had always obtained an abundant supply of honey.

When the old bee-keeper heard Dou's story, he went to examine his hive and discovered that there was not a single bee left inside it. He opened it up and found a large snake, ten feet long, which he caught and killed. So this was the huge python-like monster that had swallowed whole halls and pavilions . . . As for the bees, they remained with Dou and thrived. And nothing else of a strange nature occurred.

83

THE GIRL IN GREEN

In Yidu County, there lived a young man by the name of Yu Jing. He had taken his books with him to lodgings at the Temple of Sweet Springs, and one night he was sitting there chanting a text when he heard a woman's voice at his window.

'Oh Mr Yu, what a very serious student you are!'

He was still wondering what a woman could possibly be doing up there in the hills, when in she came, pushing the door open with a disarming smile.

'So very serious!'

He jumped up in alarm, and found himself standing before a young lady of the most incomparable delicacy and the most exquisite beauty, clad in a green tunic and a long skirt. He knew at once that this was no ordinary mortal and asked her, perhaps a trifle emphatically, where she was from.

'I'm hardly going to bite you!' she replied. 'Why the inquisition?'

He was instantly captivated, and they shared his bed that very night. When he came to loosen her silken tunic, it revealed a waist so slender that his hands could encircle it with ease.

The last watch sounded and she slipped away, returning to him the following, and every subsequent, night. On one such night, they were drinking together when she made a remark which betrayed an unusual understanding of music.

'I love the sound of your voice,' he said. 'It is so fine and soft. Sing me a song. I am sure it will quite carry my soul away . . .'

'I'd rather not,' she replied, smiling as ever. 'I wouldn't want to carry you too far away . . .'

He pleaded with her all the more.

'I am not trying to be unkind,' she said. 'It is just that I do not want others to hear. Oh, if you really insist, I'll sing a song. But quietly, just for you.'

She tapped her 'Golden Lotuses', her tiny bound feet, lightly on the edge of the bed and began to sing:

> Jackdaw singing in the tree
> Tricks me away before the light;
> I'll gladly wet my pretty shoes,
> If I can stay with you tonight.

Her voice was light as silk, and barely audible. Yu Jing listened intently, and his whole being vibrated to the haunting, lilting melody.

The song ended. She opened the door and peeped outside.

'I must make sure there is no one at the window.'

She searched the whole length of the building.

'You seem so frightened. What is the matter?' asked Yu Jing, when she returned.

'There is an old saying,' replied the girl, with her ever-present smile. 'A ghost that steals life must forever live in fear. Such is my fate.'

She lay down to sleep, but she seemed restless and ill at ease.

'This idyll of ours is fated to end,' she finally said to Yu Jing. He begged her to explain.

'My heart beats strangely. I know my end is close at hand.'

'Strange movements of the heart, flutterings of the eyes, such things happen to us all from time to time,' he protested. 'You must not be so gloomy!'

She seemed a little comforted by this, and they united once more in tender passion. As the last watch of the night came to an end, she threw on her dress, descended from the bed, and walked as far as the door. There, instead of undoing the bolt, she began pacing back and forth.

'I do not know why, but something fills me with dread. Come outside with me, I beseech you.'

Yu rose and went out with her.

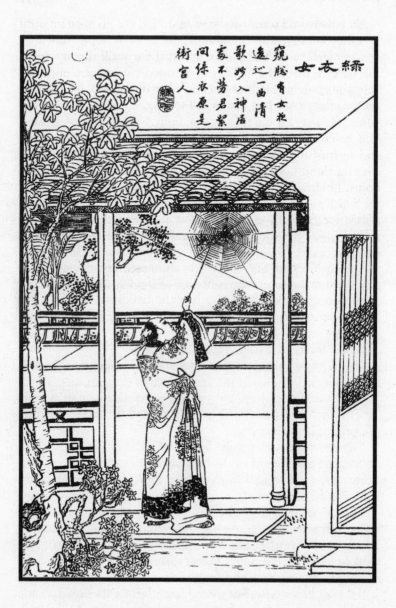

綠衣女

窺朕有女妝
遠迩一曲清
歌妙入神居
家不芳君紫
問綠衣原是
衛宮人

It was a green hornet, in the throes of death.

'Stay there and watch me,' she said. 'Do not go in again until I am beyond that wall.'

'Very well,' said Yu, and he watched her walk silently down the outer wall of the cloister and round the corner, until she was out of sight. He had already turned and was on his way back to bed, when he heard a desperate cry for help. It was her voice. He hurried out again, but though he gazed all around him he could see no trace of her. The voice was still audible and seemed to be coming from up above him, from the eaves over the door. Looking up he saw a huge spider, like a big black bolus, holding in its clutches a little creature that was making the most pitiful noise: it was a green hornet, in the throes of death. He carefully disentangled it and carried it back to his room, where he placed it on the table. Soon it recovered sufficient strength to move, crawled slowly up on to his inkstone and down into the ink. Presently it emerged again, clambered down from the inkstone and began dragging itself across the table, tracing the words

thank you

on the wooden surface. Then it shook its wings several times and flew out of the window. He never saw it again.

84

DUCK JUSTICE

A peasant living in Bai Family Village to the west of our county town stole one of his neighbour's ducks, cooked it and ate it. That night, his entire body was consumed by an intense itching, and when he looked at himself at first light he saw a fine layer of eiderdown all over his body. If he so much as touched it, it caused him considerable pain. He was appalled, but no remedy he tried was of any avail.

That night, he dreamed that a man came to him and said, 'Your illness is Heaven's punishment. Only if the duck's rightful owner shouts abuse at you will the down fall away.'

Unfortunately his neighbour was a very forgiving old man who, when he had been robbed previously, had shown not the slightest animosity. The peasant went down on his knees and begged him: 'Someone stole one of your ducks. Let's just call him Mr "X". The one thing he's really frightened of is being shouted at, so give "X" a good telling-off, shout at him, call him all sorts of names, and he will never do it again.'

The old man merely smiled. 'Why should I waste my breath on such a worthless fellow?'

And he did nothing. In the end, the peasant had no other recourse but to tell the old man the whole truth. Whereupon the old man showered him with abuse, and his affliction was cured.

罵鴨

盜得隣翁廚下烹肌膚一
夜鴨毛生從知世上穿窬
輩不罵無由減罪名

He dreamed that a man came to him.

85

BIG SNEEZE

There was a man of Xuzhou by the name of Liang Yan, who for a long time suffered from a chronic sneezing condition.

One day, he was lying down when he felt a strange itching in his nose. He jumped up and gave a large sneeze. A creature jumped out and landed on the ground, no bigger than the tip of a finger, in appearance somewhat like a tiny clay figurine of a dog. He sneezed again, and another creature fell to the ground. Four times this happened, by which stage there were four little creatures wriggling around on the floor, sniffing at each other. Then all of a sudden the strongest of them devoured the weakest and grew at once noticeably larger. In a trice it had consumed the other two as well. It was now the sole survivor and had grown larger than a squirrel. It stuck out its tongue and licked its lips.

Liang was greatly alarmed and tried to trample on the thing. But the creature jumped on to his stocking and began making its way up his leg. Liang took hold of his gown and shook it, but it clung on and would not be moved. It edged its way up the embroidered fastenings of his gown and began digging its claws into his flesh, whereupon Liang, in sheer terror, tore off the gown altogether and threw it on the ground. But when he felt his midriff, the creature was still firmly attached, and when he tried to push it off he was unable to dislodge it. He pinched it, and when he did so, he felt the pain himself. It had become a growth, a part of him, its mouth and eyes permanently closed, like a dormouse.

梁彥

滅臭無端更
噬齧突末切
近竟何事世間
不少強吞弱
莫走橫心
感召夫

It began digging its claws into his flesh.

86

STEEL SHIRT

Sha Huizi was a master of the powerful form of kungfu known as Steel Shirt. He could hack through the neck of an ox with the flat of his hand. He could thrust his hand directly into the animal's belly.

Once he was at Qiu Pengsan's house. A large block of wood was suspended in midair, and he ordered two strapping great fellows to hoist it up and let it fall. He took the full impact, but the block merely smacked loudly against his naked belly and bounced away across the room. Then he took out his penis, laid it on a stone and began hammering away at it with a wooden mallet, without causing himself the least injury. But he refused to try using a knife.

He took the full impact on his naked belly.

87

FOX TROUBLE

Zhang Taihua, a wealthy clerk of Tai'an, was experiencing fox trouble. All his attempts to contain the fox-spirits or exorcize them had proved fruitless. He even reported the matter to the local Magistrate, who proved powerless to do anything.

At the same time as this, in a village to the east of Tai'an, a fox had taken up residence in a certain peasant's home, and was witnessed by the villagers in the form of a white-haired old man who took part in all the village ceremonies, just like other folk. He claimed to be the second in his generation, and they all called him Old Mr Fox the Second.

It so happened that a young scholar called on the Magistrate of Tai'an and in the course of conversation mentioned the existence of this Old Mr Fox the Second. The Magistrate thought he saw in this a way of helping Clerk Zhang out of his predicament, and he advised Zhang to go and call upon the old fox-gentleman. One of the Magistrate's yamen-runners, who happened to be from the village in question, confirmed the story and invited Zhang to return with him to the village, where he arranged a banquet and invited Old Mr Fox along.

At the banquet Old Mr Fox was most civil, behaving just like a regular gentleman.

'I know all about this trouble of yours,' he said to Zhang, when he explained his problem. 'I regret to say I am unable to deal with it for you myself. But I have a friend by the name of Zhou the Third, who has lodgings at the foot of Mount Tai, in the Temple of the Eastern Sacred Mountain. He should certainly be able to control these foxes for you, and I will ask him to do so.'

Zhang was delighted to hear this, and expressed his gratitude. As he was leaving, Old Mr Fox said he would prepare a banquet for the very next day and that they should all meet to the east of the temple. Zhang agreed to this.

The following day, Old Mr Fox brought along his friend Zhou the Third, who turned out to be another foxy-looking fellow with bristly moustaches and a complexion dark as steel, dressed in cavalryman's breeches. The three of them drank several rounds together.

'My good friend Old Mr Fox here,' said moustachioed Zhou to Zhang, 'has already spoken to me of your problem, and I know of it in every detail. These particular trouble-making creatures are numerous and a difficult bunch, unlikely to listen to mere words of persuasion. I'm afraid it may have to come to a fight, and for this purpose I shall be obliged to lodge at your house. I am certainly willing to undertake this little commission for you, if you so wish.'

Zhang pondered this proposal for a while. He would in effect be ridding himself of one set of fox problems and gaining another, exchanging an old evil for a new one. Zhou understood his hesitation.

'Do not fear. I am not at all like the other foxes. And besides, you and I have a predestined affinity. Please have no misgivings on my account.'

Zhang finally consented, and Zhou gave him his instructions: 'Tomorrow I want your entire household to shut themselves up in a single room and not to make the slightest noise. Just leave the rest to me.'

Zhang returned home, and the following morning he did exactly as he had been instructed. Presently the sound of violent fighting broke out in the courtyard and continued for some time, before it was replaced by complete silence. Then the members of Zhang's household opened the door and, peeping out, saw blood all over the steps and several little fox heads, no bigger than rice bowls, strewn on the terrace. In the middle of the room beyond, which had been swept clean specially for the occasion, sat the moustachioed Zhou the Third, bolt upright. He greeted Zhang with clasped hands and a smile on his face.

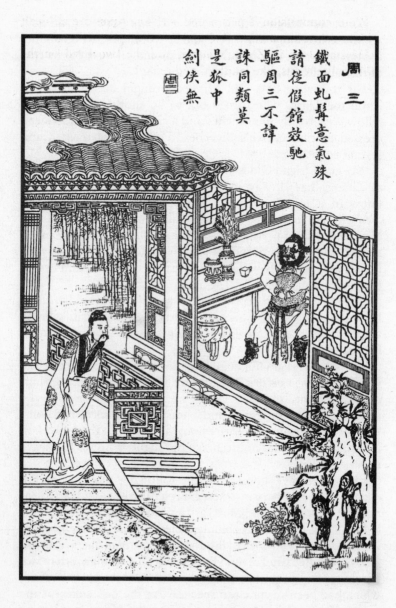

鐵面虬髯意氣殊
請從假館效馳驅
周三不諱
誅同類莫
是狐中
劍俠無

周三

'Your commission is performed, sir.'

'Your commission is performed, sir. The foxes are all dealt with and exterminated.'

He stayed on in Zhang's home, and the two lived on the most polite terms, like landlord and tenant.

88

LUST PUNISHED BY FOXES

A certain man bought a new house, only to discover that it was haunted by fox-spirits, who constantly spoiled his clothes and other belongings and dropped dirt into his noodles.

One day, one of this gentleman's friends dropped by to visit him. Unfortunately he was not at home, and that evening, since her husband had still not returned, his wife prepared dinner for the guest, before eating separately with her maid.

Now, her husband was a somewhat dissolute character who made a hobby of collecting aphrodisiacs of one sort or another. At some time or other that day the resident fox-spirits had secretly slipped one of the drugs from his collection into the congee. While the wife was eating her dinner she noticed a strange taste that resembled camphor and musk and asked her maid what it might be, but the maid said she knew of nothing. After dinner, the wife began to experience an overwhelming feeling of sexual arousal, and the more she tried to suppress it, the stronger and the more urgent it became. There was no available man in the house other than the guest, her husband's friend, and so she made her way to the guest-room and knocked at the door.

The guest asked who it was, and the woman gave her name. He asked her what she wanted, and when she remained silent, he guessed her intentions.

'Your husband and I are friends and treat one another decently. I could never behave in such a bestial manner with my friend's wife.'

The wife remained there standing at the door and refused to leave.

狐懲淫

疑雨疑雲思
不禁隔窓未
歡逗琴心勸
君休蓄房中
藥猶恐真成
蕩婦唫

She made her way to the guest-room and knocked at the door.

'Your husband,' he protested angrily, 'is a man with a reputation in the community! Are you determined to destroy it?'

With these words he spat at her through the window-lattice,
and finally in great embarrassment she left. As she went she
began asking herself how she could have done such a thing.
Then she recalled the strange taste in her congee bowl at dinner.
It entered her mind that it might have been caused by one of
the aphrodisiacs from her husband's collection, and when she
went to look, she found that one of the packages had indeed
been tampered with, and the contents scattered all over the
cups and bowls on the kitchen table. She remembered having
once heard that cold water acted as an antidote in such cases,
so she drank some water immediately and soon came round.
She awoke from her state of drugged confusion to a feeling of
intense remorse and shame. All that night she lay there brooding
restlessly, and as dawn was almost breaking, unable to face the
world, she threw her sash over a beam and hanged herself. Her
maid found her and untied her in the nick of time. Although
by this time she was all but dead, she gradually recovered
consciousness.

The guest meanwhile had left during the night. The following
day at dawn, the master of the house returned to find his wife
in bed and plainly unwell. No matter how many times he asked
her what the matter was, she lay there in complete silence and
would do nothing but weep. When the maid informed her
master that her mistress had tried to hang herself in the early
hours, he pressed his wife with more and more questions, and
finally she sent her maid away and told him the whole story.

The husband heaved a sigh. 'It is *my* lust that is being punished! This is no fault of yours. Fortunately, this friend of mine
is a good man, or I would never be able to hold my head up in
the world again.'

After this experience, he became a reformed character, and
the foxes disappeared completely.

89

MOUNTAIN CITY

The Mountain City of Mount Huan is acknowledged to be one of the wonders of my home district, even though many a year goes by when it is not seen at all. Sun Yu'nian was drinking with his friends on a terrace when suddenly they beheld a lone pagoda on the mountainside opposite, rising up far into the deep blue sky. They looked at one another in sheer disbelief, since they knew of no Zen monastery in that vicinity. Then a host of palaces and halls sprang into view, with roofs and flying eaves of bright green-glazed tiles, and it dawned on them that this was the Mountain City of Mount Huan.

Presently two or three miles of high walls and crenellated battlements, the city's mighty fortifications, became visible, and within the walls they could distinguish countless storeyed buildings and residential districts. Then suddenly a great wind arose, the air grew thick with dust, and the city could scarcely be seen any longer. By and by the wind subsided, the air cleared, and the city had vanished, save for one tall tower, reaching up high into the sky. Each storey of this tower was pierced by a row of five shuttered windows, all of which had been thrown open and let through the light from the sky on the other side. One could count the storeys of the tower by the rows of bright dots. The higher they were, the smaller they became, until by the eighth storey they resembled tiny stars, and above that they became an indistinguishable blur of twinkling lights disappearing into the heavens. It was just possible to make out figures on the tower, some hurrying about, coming and going, others leaning and standing in a variety of postures.

A little while longer, and the tower began to diminish in size,

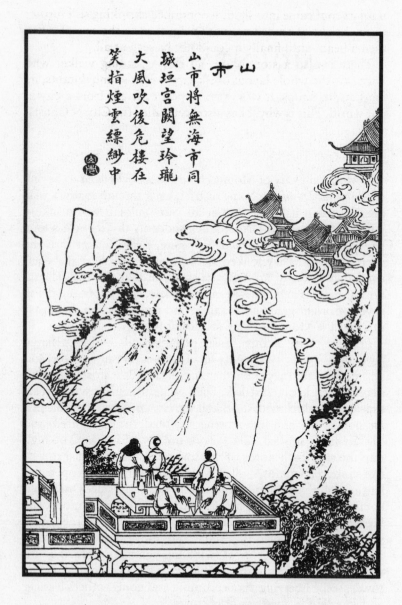

山市

山市將無海市同
城垣宮闕望玲瓏
大風吹後危樓在
笑指煙雲縹緲中

It dawned on them that this was the Mountain City.

until its roof came into sight. It continued shrinking still further to the height of an ordinary building, then to the size of a fist, then a bean, until finally it could not be seen at all.

There is also a story about an early morning walker who once saw the whole layout of the city – with its inhabitants, its markets, its shops. It was in no respect different from a city in our world. This is why it has also been called the City of Ghosts.

90

A CURE FOR
MARITAL STRIFE

A certain young gentleman named Sun married a young lady of good family named Xin. From the day she became his wife, she wore a pair of chastity-trousers fastened with several sashes and presented to her husband an impregnable fortress, repulsing his every advance and absolutely refusing to make love to him. On their marital bed, she kept a supply of sharpened awls and hairpins ready for use in self-defence.

Having sustained several painful injuries, in the end Sun resigned himself to sleeping in a separate bed, and a month later abandoned all attempts at intimacy with her. As the saying goes, he did not 'venture near the tripod'. Even when they met during the day, she did not grace him with a word or a smile.

One of Sun's friends came to know of this and said to him in private, 'Does your wife ever drink?'

'A little,' was Sun's reply.

The friend went on, jokingly, 'Why then, I know how to bring the two of you together. It is an excellent method, guaranteed to succeed.'

Sun inquired what he had in mind.

'First you must give her a cup of drugged wine. That will knock her out, and then she will let you have your way.'

Sun laughed at the crudity of the idea, but secretly thought to himself that it might just work. He consulted a doctor and carefully mixed up a concoction of wine and the potent herbal root known as monkshood (a well-known narcotic and anaesthetic), which he left on the table in their room. That night, he warmed himself a separate, untainted wine and drank several cups of it before retiring to bed. Three nights he followed this same procedure, but his wife showed no signs whatsoever of taking the bait. Then, one night, when he had been lying in his bed for some time, he noticed that his wife was still sitting up in bed on her own. He deliberately began to snore, whereupon she climbed down from her bed, took the drugged wine from the table and went to warm it on the stove. Sun watched with secret delight as she drank a whole cup, then poured herself a second, drank about half, tipped the rest back into the wine kettle, straightened out her bedding and lay down to sleep. A long silence ensued. Her lamp was still burning, and Sun suspected that she was still awake.

'The lamp will catch fire!' he called out.

There was no reply. Again he called, and again there was no reply. He got down naked from his bed and went over to look at her. He could see that her senses had indeed been completely numbed by the drug. He lifted the coverlet, lay down beside her and began untying her numerous protective wrappings one by one. She was perfectly aware of what he was doing, but could neither move nor utter a word. She could only let him have his way with her, whereupon he returned to his own bed.

When eventually she recovered the full use of her faculties, she was overwhelmed with such feelings of disgust and self-loathing that she tied a sash to a beam and hanged herself without further ado. In the midst of his dreams, Sun heard a strange gasping and groaning, and when he rose from his bed and went hurrying over, he found his wife hanging there, her tongue already protruding two inches from her mouth. Aghast, he cut her down and carried her to her bed, where in time she regained consciousness.

Sun himself now began to feel an intense physical repugnance towards his wife. They avoided each other as much as was humanly possible, and if they were obliged to be in each other's company would hang their heads and ignore one another. Four or five years passed in this gloomy fashion, during which time they barely exchanged a single word. She might be in a room talking and laughing with someone else; but the moment she saw her husband come in, her face would harden and she would grow cold as ice. Sun moved into his study and slept there the whole year round. On the rare occasion when he yielded to parental pressure and allowed himself to be dragged back to the conjugal bedroom, he would sit there sullenly facing the wall, then climb into bed and go to sleep without a word. His parents were most disconsolate about the turn things had taken.

One day, an elderly nun came to visit the household. She met the wife and spoke highly of her to Sun's mother, who said nothing but heaved a deep sigh. Later the nun asked her in private what was troubling her, and was told the whole story.

'This is an easy matter,' she said.

'Bring my daughter-in-law around,' said Mrs Sun, 'and I will reward you handsomely.'

The nun looked about them to ensure that they were alone, and lowered her voice.

'I want you to go out and buy one of those erotic scrolls, and in three days' time I will be able to deal with this for you.'

With these words the nun went on her way. Mrs Sun purchased a scroll as instructed and awaited the nun's return, which duly occurred three days later.

'We must preserve the utmost secrecy about this,' said the nun. 'Neither of the young people must know what we are planning.'

She proceeded to cut out the figures of the two lovers in one of the paintings, then asked for three needles and a pinch of moxa. All of this she wrapped up in a white paper bundle, on the outside of which she wrote some strange wriggly lines that looked like the traces of an earthworm. Then she told Mrs Sun to find a way of getting her daughter-in-law out of the way while she herself went into the bedroom, removed the young woman's pillow, slit a hole in it and inserted her package, stitching it up again and putting it back in its original place. Having done this, the nun departed.

That evening, full of hope, Mrs Sun prevailed on her son to sleep in his nuptial bed and posted an old serving-woman outside to spy on the couple. Late into the night, the woman heard Sun's wife call her husband by his intimate name (a rare event), but Sun did not so much as reply. After a little while, the wife spoke to him again and this time Sun uttered an audible groan of disgust.

孤生

獨向蘭閨望
月明春宵
韋負太無情
何人為置
迴心院雙宿
雙飛過
一生

She cut out the figures of the two lovers.

Mrs Sun went into the room herself at dawn to find husband and wife sleeping with their backs to each other, and she knew that the nun's magic had been ineffective. She called her son aside and tried to talk him around, but the mere mention of his wife's name threw him into a temper and made him gnash his teeth. His mother scolded him angrily for this, and walked off in great displeasure.

The next day, the nun returned and was greatly puzzled when she was told that her magic had failed. The old serving-woman who had spied on the couple gave her a full account of what she had seen and heard. The nun smiled.

'No wonder! You told me it was the *wife* who had grown cold towards her husband, so I was working on her. Now it seems that the wife's feelings have changed for the better, and it is the husband who is in need of my assistance. Allow me to perform the magic again, for the two of them. I assure you that we will be successful this time.'

The mother agreed to this. She procured her son's pillow, they repeated the procedure, and yet again she made her son promise to sleep in his wife's room. Late that night, a great deal of tossing and turning could be heard from their separate beds, followed by the recurring sound of coughing, as if neither of them could sleep. After some time, they could be heard whispering to each other in one bed, but it was impossible to make out exactly what they were saying. Finally, as dawn was breaking, there was a lot of audible giggling and murmuring of sweet endearments. The old serving-woman reported all of this to Mrs Sun, who was delighted. The nun came and was handsomely rewarded.

From that day forth, the Suns were a happily married couple, as harmonious as the proverbial lute and zither. They are now in their thirties, have a son and two daughters, and for over ten years have not had a single disagreement. If ever their friends ask them what it was that wrought the change, they laugh and say, 'Who knows! Things changed! Before the change, the merest sight of a shadow of the other would bring on a fit of temper. Since the change, the slightest sound of the other's voice fills us with joy! We ourselves have no idea what happened!'

91

A PRANK

A certain fellow of my home district, a well-known prankster and libertine, was out one day strolling in the countryside when he saw a young girl approaching on a pony.

'I'll get a laugh out of her, see if I don't!' he called out to his companions.

They were sceptical of his chances of success and wagered a banquet on it, even as he hurried forward in front of the girl's pony and cried out loudly, 'I want to die! I want to die . . .'

He took hold of a tall millet stalk that was growing over a nearby wall and, bending it so that it projected a foot into the road, untied the sash of his gown and threw it over the stalk, making a noose in it and slipping it round his neck, as if to hang himself. As she came closer, the girl laughed at him, and by now his friends were also in fits. The girl then rode on into the distance, but the man still did not move, which caused his friends to laugh all the more. Presently they went up and looked at him: his tongue was protruding from his mouth, his eyes were closed. He was quite lifeless.

Strange that a man could succeed in hanging himself from a millet stalk. Let this be a warning to libertines and pranksters.

戲纜

抽蘊舒弗太
無端賦浔紅
頳一笑看鑄
錯料應心不悔
一魂雅善傍
雕鞍

The man still did not move.

92

ADULTERY AND ENLIGHTENMENT

The Patriarch Luo was from the town of Jimo. He had passed his childhood in great poverty, and when it fell to his family to provide an able-bodied male for guard service on the northern frontier, he was the one chosen. There he lived for several years, during which time a son was born to him. The frontier-post commandant had always been extremely kind to him, and when he was transferred as Colonel to the western province of Shaanxi, he wanted to take Luo with him. Luo entrusted his wife and son to the care of his good friend Li and travelled west with his superior.

It was three years before he had an opportunity to see his family again. The Colonel wanted a letter delivered to the northern frontier and Luo volunteered to go, requesting leave to visit his wife and children at the same time, which the Colonel readily granted.

Luo was greatly relieved to find his wife and son in good health, but was somewhat bemused to see a pair of men's shoes beneath the bed. He went to give thanks to his friend Li, who entertained him cordially with wine. His wife insisted how wonderfully kind Li had been, and Luo was profuse in his expressions of gratitude.

The next day, he said to his wife, 'I have to deliver my commanding officer's letter today, and won't be back this evening. Don't bother to wait up for me.'

He went out, mounted his horse and rode away. But instead of delivering the letter, he hid nearby and in the dead of night returned home. He heard his wife and Li talking together in bed, flew into a great rage and broke down the door. The two of them fell to their knees and begged him to spare their lives. Luo had already drawn his sword, but he put it back in its sheath and addressed the following words to his friend: 'I took you for a decent man, but now I have seen the truth for myself. Why, your blood would sully my sword! I will make you an offer: take my wife, take my son, take my military position and duties too. I shall leave you my horse with all its trappings, I shall leave you my weapons, and go my own way.'

And off he went.

The local people reported the strange facts of the case to the Magistrate, who had Li flogged and extracted from him a full confession of adultery. But since there were no witnesses, no one to testify to the truth of his story in any way, and since Luo himself had in the meantime vanished entirely and remained unfindable despite an extensive search, the Magistrate suspected the adulterers of having murdered him and subjected the pair of them to a prolonged inquisition. A year later, they both died from the ill effects of severe torture, and the son was sent back to the family home in Jimo under official escort.

Some time later, a woodcutter from the garrison town of Stone Casket was up in the hills when he came upon a Taoist hermit sitting in a cave. This hermit was never seen to beg for alms, and he soon came to be regarded by the local people, who brought him offerings of food, as a holy man and a living marvel. Someone eventually recognized him as Luo, the Colonel's former aide. Devotees started coming in droves and gifts of food filled the cave, but he refused to touch any of it and seemed to find the clamour of humanity offensive. With time his visitors became fewer and fewer, and as the years went by, the tangled bushes outside the cave grew into a thicket so dense that passers-by could only peep through and catch a glimpse of the hermit, who always sat immobile in the exact same spot.

A long interval of time elapsed, and he was seen to leave his cave and go wandering on the mountainside. But the minute someone approached him, he disappeared. And when the locals looked inside the cave, they were amazed to see him sitting there as formerly, his clothes covered with layers of dust. Going

妻孥久別幸平安
決絕如何一旦
拌檀鉞絲將刀
放下便成佛祖
勾死雞
羅　祖

He put his sword back in its sheath.

back a few days later to have another look, they saw him still sitting there, with two Jade Icicles hanging from his nose. They knew from this venerable sign that he had indeed finally been 'transformed'. They built a temple in his honour, and during the third month of every year the place was thronged with pilgrims coming to burn joss at his shrine. His son came, and they honoured him with the title 'Little Patriarch' and presented him with all the offerings brought by pilgrims. To this day, Patriarch Luo's descendants come to the temple once a year and are given the offerings.

When Liu Zongyu of Yishui told me this story in detail, I laughed and said, 'Nowadays believers are not interested in leading saintly lives, they all want to become Instant Buddhas! Tell them from me that this is one true path to Instantaneous Buddhahood: put down your swords!'

93
UP HIS SLEEVE

A certain Taoist named Gong (he had no other names and no one knew where he was from) once requested an audience with the Prince of Lu, but the Prince's gate-men refused to announce his presence. One of the Prince's senior eunuchs came out, and when the Taoist made him a bow and begged him to hear his plea, the eunuch, seeing how wretchedly tattered his clothes were, sent him curtly about his business. When he returned, the eunuch flew into a rage and had him forcibly escorted away, instructing one of his underlings to follow the man and give him a good beating. When they came to a deserted spot, the Taoist took out two hundred taels of gold.

'Take this gold to your master,' he said, smiling to himself, 'and tell him that I do not really want to see the Prince at all. It is just that I have heard what a wonderful park he has at the back of the palace, full of the most beautiful plants and trees, exquisite pavilions and galleries, among the finest anywhere in the world. Truly I should count myself a happy man if he would agree to show me round the park.'

He gave the servant a few taels of silver, and the man gladly transmitted his request (and the bribe). His master, the senior eunuch, was now only too delighted to receive the Taoist at the rear gate of the palace and show him around the Prince's garden. They climbed to the upper storey of one of the pavilions, and the eunuch was leaning out over the window-sill when suddenly the Taoist gave him a little push and the eunuch felt himself first falling and then hanging in midair, suspended from the waist by nothing more than the flimsiest tendril of some clinging vine. When he looked down he saw beneath him a giddy height, and hearing the faintest sound as of the vine beginning to snap, he let out a terrified scream. In a matter of seconds, several of his fellow eunuchs arrived on the scene in a state of extreme consternation to find him dangling at a great height from the window. Climbing up into the pavilion, they discovered the end of the vine attached to the window-sill. They would have lowered him down to the ground but the vine seemed too weak, and although they searched everywhere for the Taoist, he had vanished without trace. At their wits' end they went in to report the matter to the Prince, who came to investigate for himself. He was utterly perplexed by what he saw, and gave orders to spread rushes and wads of cotton floss on the ground and then to cut the vine. Everything was prepared, when suddenly the vine snapped of its own accord and they saw that the eunuch had never been more than a foot off the ground. A titter of incredulous laughter broke from the assembled eunuchs.

The Prince now gave orders that the whereabouts of the Taoist should be ascertained. It was eventually discovered that he was lodging in the residence of a gentleman named Shang, but when one of the Prince's men went there to have words with him, he found that the Taoist had gone out and had not yet returned. He encountered him on his way back, and took him to see the Prince, who entertained him and asked him to give a demonstration of his powers.

'I am nothing but a country bumpkin, sire,' said the Taoist. 'I have no special skills. But since you have been so kind as to entertain me, allow me to present a little dancer. Let this be my humble offering.'

So saying, he produced a beautiful lady from within his sleeve and placed her on the ground, where she kowtowed to the Prince. The Taoist asked her to perform the piece known as 'The Banquet at Jasper Pool', in honour of His Highness. After a brief introductory monologue from the lady, the Taoist produced a second figure, who introduced herself as the Queen Mother. And then, one after another, he produced all the Queen's fairy attendants – ending with a weaving maid, who showed the Prince a celestial robe, a dazzling garment woven in golden brocade. The Prince could not believe that it was genuine and wanted to inspect it.

'You must on no account touch it!' cried the Taoist. But the Prince paid him no heed and held it up to take a closer look. Sure enough, he saw that it was of a seamless weave such as could never have been woven by mortal hands.

'I wished to show you my humble devotion, sire,' said the Taoist sadly, 'and was able to borrow this treasure for a while from the heavenly realm. Now it has been sullied, and I shall never be able to return it to its rightful owner.'

The Prince, thinking the performers must be celestial maidens, wished to detain some of them. But the moment he looked at them more closely he saw that they were all in fact singing girls from his own harem. Then it occurred to him that the song they had just been singing was one he was not familiar with. Sure enough, when he asked them about it they replied that they themselves had not known what it was they were singing.

The Taoist put the celestial garment on the fire and whisked the charred remains into his sleeve. On further inspection, his sleeve proved to be quite empty. The Prince came to feel a deep respect for the Taoist, and wanted to install him in his palace.

'I am a creature of the wilds,' replied the Taoist. 'For me, your palace would be a cage. I have more freedom in Scholar Shang's residence.'

The Taoist regularly left the palace at midnight and returned to his lodgings, although from time to time the Prince was able to prevail upon him to stay overnight. At the Prince's banquets, the Taoist would make flowers bloom out of season. Once the Prince asked him, 'I have heard it said that Immortals still have a need for human attachment. Is this true?'

'This may be true of Immortals. But I am not one of their kind. As for me, my own heart is like a block of lifeless wood.'

Once when the Taoist stayed overnight in the palace, the Prince sent a woman from his harem to test him out. She went into his room and called to him several times, without eliciting any response. She lit a candle and saw him sitting cross-legged on the couch, his eyes closed. She shook him, whereupon one of his eyes opened a slit and then closed again. She shook him again, and he started snoring. She pushed him with some force, and this time he tumbled down on to the ground, but remained sound asleep, snoring like thunder. She rapped him on the forehead, but merely hurt her own finger, while his head made a hollow sound like a metal cauldron.

She went in to report all of this to the Prince, who told her to try pricking the Taoist with a needle, which she did. But the needle would not enter his flesh. She tried pushing him again, and by now he had become so heavy she could not shift him at all. A dozen men were sent with orders to lift him up and throw him back down on to the ground. He was like a stone weighing a ton, and they were scarcely able to move him. In the morning, they found him lying there on the ground, still fast asleep. When he awoke, he smiled and said, 'I must have had a nightmare and fallen on the ground, without even knowing it.'

From then on, if ever he was sitting or lying down, the ladies of the palace would prod him for fun. The first time they did so, he would be soft, but gradually his flesh grew hard to the touch, like iron or stone.

Often the Taoist would not return to his lodgings in Scholar Shang's house until after midnight, by which time his host would already have locked the door. And yet in the morning, when he came to open it again, the Taoist would be asleep in his room.

Now, this Scholar Shang had once had a close liaison with a sing-song girl by the name of Mercy, and the two had sworn to marry one day. Mercy had a beautiful voice and was widely acclaimed as an instrumentalist. The Prince of Lu came to hear of her and had her brought to his palace to become part of his harem, thus tearing her away from the heartbroken Shang. Shang asked the Taoist one evening if he had ever set eyes on Mercy during his visits to the palace.

'I have seen all of the Prince's ladies,' was the Taoist's reply. 'But I don't know which one of them is Mercy.'

Shang described her in some detail, enough for the Taoist to be able to identify her. Then he begged him to take her a message.

'I am a man of religion,' joked the Taoist. 'I can hardly be a carrier of love letters.'

Shang continued to plead with him, until finally the Taoist held out the capacious sleeve of his gown and said, 'Very well then, if you really want to see her, hop in!'

Shang peeped inside the sleeve and, beholding a space as large as a room, went down on his hands and knees and crept in, finding himself in a luminous chamber, as spacious as the reception hall of a mansion, fully furnished with tables and couches. Somehow the space caused him to experience no sense of confinement or oppression. The Taoist made his way to the palace and sat down for a game of Go with the Prince. When he saw Mercy come into the room, he made as if to brush away a speck of dust with his gown and – hey presto! – she was whisked into his sleeve without anyone having noticed the slightest thing. Shang was sitting there lost in idle reverie when suddenly he saw a beautiful lady float down from the eaves of his 'room'. He recognized her at once as Mercy, and the two of them were soon wrapped in the ecstasy of reunion.

'This is a very special occasion,' said Shang, 'and we must commemorate it in verse.'

He began to improvise the first line of a poem, as he did so inscribing it calligraphically on the wall of their room:

Deep in the Prince's palace, you were lost for so long without trace;

Mercy continued:

Today in wonder I behold again my loved one's face.

Shang wrote the third line:

The world within the magic sleeve is great indeed;

And Mercy concluded:

It nourishes our love, it feeds our deepest need.

Just as they finished the poem, five men burst in upon them, wearing eight-cornered hats and pink robes. Neither of the

袖裏乾坤大若何曠夫怨
女盡色羅還君佳麗繇君
祀煞費倦心一片婆

肇傳

The Taoist sat down for a game of Go with the Prince.

lovers knew who these men were. Without a word they seized Mercy and led her away, while Shang watched in stupefied amazement.

When the Taoist returned to his lodgings, he called Shang to come out and inquired how their meeting had passed off. Shang did not tell him the whole story. The Taoist smiled and turned his sleeve inside out for him to see. There, barely discernible, in tiny characters the size of louse eggs, were the four lines of verse they had written.

Ten days later, Shang asked if he could go again to the palace. In all he went three times. On his third visit, Mercy said to him, 'I can feel a child moving in my womb, and am most concerned. I keep my waist tightly confined with a sash, but in the palace people are quick to notice and there is nowhere for me to give birth unobserved. They will hear the baby cry. Talk to the Taoist, tell him to come and rescue me when he sees that my time is near.'

Shang promised to do this, and on his return he went to see the Taoist and fell on his knees before him. The Taoist raised him and said, 'I already know what has happened. Do not be distressed. Your family line depends on this child, and I shall do all that I can. But from now on, you will not be able to enter the palace again. I told you I could not act as a go-between for your private love affairs . . .'

Several months went by, and one day the Taoist came in and announced to his friend, with a smile, 'I have brought your son with me! Quickly, bring out his swaddling clothes!'

Shang's wife was a very worthy and understanding sort. She was nearly thirty years old, and though she had given birth several times, only one son had survived. She had recently given birth to a daughter, who had died when she was barely one month old. When Shang told her about this infant son of his, she was overcome with joy and came hurrying out. The Taoist dipped his hand into his sleeve and produced the baby, who was sound asleep and still had the umbilical cord trailing from its stomach. Shang's wife took it in her arms, and it began crying at once.

The Taoist took off his own gown. 'The blood of childbirth

has stained my robe, a thing we Taoists abhor. I have done this for your sake. Now I am obliged to discard this old friend of twenty years.'

Shang presented him with a change of clothes, and the Taoist enjoined him, 'Do not throw away this old robe of mine. Burn a tiny amount of it and the ashes will help in cases of difficult birth, or bring down a stillborn child.'

Shang followed the Taoist's instructions and put the old robe safely away.

One day, a long time later, the Taoist said to Shang out of the blue, 'Be sure to keep a piece of that old robe I gave you for yourself. You may need it. When I am dead and gone, do not forget!'

Shang sensed something ill-omened about this remark. The Taoist walked off without saying anything further, and made his way to the palace to see the Prince.

'Your subject wishes to die!' he announced, and when the distraught Prince protested, he replied, 'This is fated. There is nothing more to be said about it.'

The Prince refused to believe this, and begged him to stay. They played a game of Go, after which the Taoist rose abruptly to his feet. The Prince tried to detain him yet again, but he asked to be allowed to withdraw to an outer room. Eventually the Prince gave him leave to go and the Taoist hurried out to the room, where he lay down, and when the Prince went to find him he was already dead. The Prince bought him a coffin and buried him with due ceremony. Shang, for his part, mourned his departed friend with bitter tears, understanding now that his earlier words had indeed been a prophecy.

The tattered robe turned out to be most efficacious in hastening birth, and many came to ask for a piece of it. At first Shang gave out strips from the bloodstained sleeve, then from the collar, which proved every bit as potent. Heeding the Taoist's parting injunction, and thinking that his own wife might one day have a difficult birth, he had torn off a blood-stained patch the size of a hand, which he carefully put away.

Now, one of the Prince's most beloved consorts had a prolonged and difficult labour, and after three days, the doctors having done all they could for her, someone mentioned Shang's remedy. Shang was sent for at once, and after one dose of the miraculous ash-potion, the baby was safely born. The Prince was ecstatic and rewarded Shang with silver and bolts of brocaded silk – all of which he declined. The Prince asked him what it was he desired.

'I dare not say, sire,' replied Shang.

Once more the Prince asked, and this time Shang prostrated himself before him. 'If truly you wish to show me a favour, then what I desire above all else is Mercy, who was once a singing girl before entering your palace.'

The Prince sent for Mercy and, when she arrived, asked her age.

'I entered your palace when I was eighteen, sire, and have been here fourteen years.'

The Prince thought her too old for what Shang had in mind, and summoned his entire harem, parading them before Shang and telling him to take his pick. But Shang insisted that Mercy was the one he wanted.

'Why, you lovesick scholar!' jested the Prince. 'I'll wager the two of you were betrothed years ago!'

Shang finally told him the truth, and the Prince prepared a fine carriage and horses, presenting Mercy with the bolts of brocade that Shang had declined, as her trousseau, and saw her off in person.

Mercy's son had been named Xiusheng – Sleeveborn – and he was by this time already eleven years old. They never forgot the Taoist's kindness, and visited his grave every Qing Ming Festival.

A frequent visitor to Sichuan Province once encountered the Taoist on the road, carrying a scroll.

'This scroll,' he said, 'comes from the Prince of Lu's palace. I left in such haste, I never had time to return it to the Prince. Would you be so kind as to do so for me?'

When the traveller returned and learned that the Taoist was in fact already dead, he decided not to trouble the Prince with the scroll. It was Shang who told the Prince about the encounter and returned the scroll. The Prince opened it, and sure enough, it was something he had once lent the Taoist. He was intrigued by this strange turn of events and gave orders for the Taoist's grave to be opened. The coffin was found to be empty.

The son born to Scholar Shang's wife died young, and it fell to Sleeveborn to continue the family line, as had been foreseen by the Taoist.

94

SILVER ABOVE BEAUTY

A certain scholar of Yishui was studying in the mountains when one night two beautiful women came into his room and sat down side by side on his bed, smiling quietly, their light silken sleeves brushing silently against the bedstead.

Presently one of them rose and spread a white silk scarf on the table, inscribed with three or four lines of fine grass-script calligraphy, which the young scholar did not bother to study closely. Beside it the other lady placed a lump of silver, three or four taels in weight, which he took at once and placed in the sleeve of his gown.

The first lady picked up the scarf and took the other lady by the hand. They went out, laughing, 'What an unbearably vulgar fellow!'

The scholar felt for his silver, and it was gone.

Two beautiful women had sat beside him and offered him a thing of beauty, and he had paid it no heed but instead had pocketed the silver, like the unbearable beggar that he was!

As for the foxes, what charming creatures they must have been! One can just imagine their enchanting appearance!

何來長袖態翩翩小摺無
塵坐並肩不愛綾巾愛金
鏈書生俗狀亦堪憐

沂水晉卡

He took the silver at once.

95

THE ANTIQUE LUTE

A gentleman of Jiaxiang named Li, an accomplished player of the Chinese lute, was out strolling one day in the eastern out-skirts of the town when he saw a workman dig out of the ground what was clearly a lute of considerable antiquity. He bought the instrument from him very cheaply and took it home. When he dusted it clean, it gave off a strange light. He fitted it with strings and played it, and it produced an unusually clear, full tone. He was as delighted with it as if he had acquired a rare and precious piece of jade, and stored it away in a secret place, wrapped in a brocade bag, showing it to no one, not even his closest relations.

One day, the newly appointed Deputy Magistrate of Jiaxiang, a man named Cheng, sent his card and called on Li. Li had never been one for socializing, but since the man had taken the first step he reciprocated and went to call on him. A few days later, the Deputy Magistrate invited Li over again for a drink, and persisted until finally Li accepted. This Cheng turned out to be a cultivated man of a debonair disposition, spirited in his conversation, and Li found himself enjoying his company. The very next day, he sent over his card and an invitation, and the two of them spent another pleasant evening in each other's company. From that day forward, they never missed a chance to celebrate some special occasion together – the blooming of a flower, a moonlit night.

A year or more later, Li was at Cheng's residence when he noticed a lute lying in a brocade bag on a table. He took it out of its bag and began playing it.

'So you are a lute-player too!' exclaimed Cheng.

'It is what I have always loved most in life,' replied Li.

'In all the time we have known each other,' said Cheng in some amazement, 'you have never once spoken of this accomplishment of yours!'

He poked the brazier and threw some fragrant sandalwood on the coals, and as he did so he asked Li to give him a little recital. Li obliged.

'You are a master!' exclaimed Cheng when it was finished. 'I should like to play a little something too, but you must promise not to laugh at me.'

He played the piece known as 'Riding the Wind'. His performance had a crystalline quality about it, and conveyed to perfection a transcendental sense of leaving the world and its dust behind. Li was overwhelmed and begged Cheng to accept him as a pupil.

The two men, having discovered this shared passion, became the closest of friends, and over the course of the following year Cheng taught Li everything he knew of the art of the lute. But every time he went to visit Li, Li always offered him his ordinary lute to play on. He never once let him see the treasure he had hidden away.

One night, they had both been drinking and were a little tipsy.

'I have been learning a new air,' said Cheng. 'Would you like to hear it?'

He played him 'The Lament of the Fairy of the River Xiang', interpreting it with a sadness that brought tears to the eyes of Li, who waxed lyrical in his praise.

'Ah,' said Cheng, 'if I only had a really fine old instrument to play it on! Then you might hear some true beauty in the music.'

'I have a lute put away,' said Li, on a sudden impulse. 'It is a most unusual instrument. By now it is clear beyond a doubt that we are soul-brothers. We "know each other's sound". How can I keep this wonderful instrument of mine a secret from you any longer?'

He opened the cupboard and took out the lute, removing it from its bag. Cheng dusted it with the sleeve of his gown, sat up at the little lute table and played the lament once more. This time the music was sheer perfection. It blended strength and tenderness to a rare degree. Li was profoundly moved and found himself tapping his fingers ecstatically in time to the notes.

'Alas, this superb instrument merely draws attention to my inadequate technique,' mused Cheng aloud. 'Now if my wife could play on it, *then* you would hear some real music.'

'Is she also a skilled lute-player?' asked Li in surprise.

'The melody I played just now,' replied Cheng, 'is something I learned from her.'

'A pity that she resides in your inner apartments,' said Li, 'and that I shall never have the good fortune to hear her play.'

'Surely good friends such as ourselves need not be confined by such conventions,' said Cheng. 'Tomorrow, come to my house with this instrument of yours. I will ask my wife to play, and we can listen through a blind.'

Li was delighted at the idea and went the following day with his lute. Cheng set a fine meal and excellent wine before him, and after a while he carried the lute through to the inner apartment, returning to sit down again with Li. Presently through the blind they distinguished the outline of a beautiful form, and then a subtle fragrance emanated from behind the blind, followed by the sound of the lute. Li listened, and although he did not recognize the melody, he felt his senses ravished and his soul transported to another realm. When the music ceased, he peeped through the blind and saw a young woman, some twenty years old, of a striking beauty. Cheng now poured him a large goblet of wine, and from behind the blind the lady struck up another melody, this time the piece known as 'All My Heart's Care'. Once again Li was ravished by the sheer beauty of the sound. He was quite carried away by the experience and began drinking recklessly. Finally he rose to take his leave and asked for his lute.

'You are drunk,' protested Cheng. 'Imagine what would happen to the lute if you were to stumble on your way home? Come back tomorrow, and I will bid my wife show you the full extent of her skill.'

局註

三

一曲湘妃惬素心秘
藏不惜示知音人
琴一吉無消息流
高山何處尋

Li was ravished by the sheer beauty of the sound.

So Li went home and called again the next day, only to find Cheng's residence quite deserted. An old concierge answered the door, and in answer to his inquiries she told him that the entire household had gone away that very morning.

'I have no idea where or why. They said they might be away three days.'

Three days later, Li returned and waited, but evening came and still there was no sign of them. The yamen staff themselves were beginning to have misgivings and reported the disappearance to the Chief Magistrate, who gave orders for the doors to be broken down and the premises searched. The place was completely empty. There was nothing left but a few sticks of furniture. The strange affair was reported to the senior authorities, who were unable to unearth any clues.

The loss of his lute utterly devastated Li, so much so that he could neither eat nor sleep. He travelled hundreds of miles seeking information about Cheng, but succeeded only in ascertaining that his home was in the southern region of Chu, and that he had been transferred from there to Jiaxiang some three years before, having paid a handsome bribe for the posting. Li searched throughout Chu, inquiring everywhere, but nowhere could he find a man of that name, until eventually someone mentioned a Taoist recluse named Cheng, who was reputed to be a very fine lute-player.

'This Cheng was said to possess certain magical arts, and to be able to turn base metals into gold. Three years ago he disappeared, and has not been seen since.'

That must be the man, thought Li. Further inquiries confirmed that the ages and physical appearances of Cheng the Taoist recluse and Cheng the Deputy Magistrate tallied perfectly. So it became clear that the hermit had purchased the office in Jiaxiang simply in order to obtain the antique lute. Li recalled that during the first year of their friendship he had not once mentioned his interest in music, but little by little had brought out his own lute, then demonstrated his musical skill, then cast a spell on him with the woman's beauty. The whole process had taken three years, at the end of which time he had succeeded in his goal, which was to make off with the lute. The

Taoist's passionate craving for the rare instrument had turned out to be stronger even than Li's!

This Taoist was surely one of the most subtle and refined swindlers the world has ever seen!

WAITING ROOM
FOR DEATH

A gentleman named Li of Shang River County was a devotee of the Tao. Half a mile or so outside his village stood a temple, where he built himself a little hermitage and used to sit performing his meditations. Itinerant Buddhist and Taoist monks would sometimes pass by and put up for the night, and Li would enter into conversation with them and extend to them whatever hospitality he could.

One day, during a sharp cold spell following a heavy fall of snow, an old monk came by with his bag, asking for shelter. The man's speech struck Li as being full of the most unexpected and marvellous insights. He stayed a couple of nights and was about to go on his way again, but Li prevailed upon him to stay a few days longer.

It so happened that Li was obliged to make a visit home, and as he left, the old monk begged him to lose no time in coming back, saying that he wished to be sure to bid him a proper farewell. Li hurried back at cockcrow the very next morning, knocked at the gate and, when there was no reply, climbed in over the wall. He saw a lamp burning in the room and, thinking there must be something strange going on, stood there secretly observing.

The old monk was packing his bag. He had a skinny ass with him in the room, tethered to the lampstand. On closer inspection, it was not a real beast but one of the effigies buried with the dead. Its ears and its tail twitched from time to time, however, and it was quite visibly breathing.

Soon the monk's bag was packed and he opened the door of the hermitage and led the ass out through it, Li following them

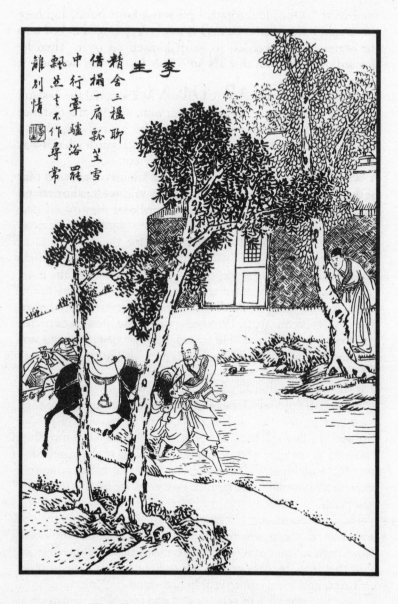

Outside the gate there was a large pond.

unobserved. Outside the gate there was a large pond, and here the monk, having tethered his ass to a tree, plunged naked into the water and proceeded to wash himself all over. Then he dressed himself, led the ass into the water and washed it likewise.

When these ablutions were finished, he mounted the ass and set off at a smart pace. Li called after him, and from a distance the monk turned to salute him, clasping both hands together in a polite gesture of farewell. Li could not distinguish what it was he said, and the monk was soon lost to view.

Wang Meiwu said that this Li was a friend of his, and that he had once visited his little hermitage and seen a horizontal scroll hanging in the entrance hall, inscribed:

Waiting Room for Death.

The wording testified to the unusually deep nature of the man.

97
ROUGE

In the city of Dongchang there lived a veterinarian named Bian, whose daughter Rouge was a girl of exceptional beauty and intelligence. Her father doted on her and wanted to find her a husband from a good family, but none of the local families of standing would consider an alliance with such a humbly born young lady, and as a result, when she came of age, she was still single.

Across the street from the Bians lived a family by the name of Gong. Mr Gong's wife, Madame Wang, was a somewhat loose woman, fond of having a bit of fun, especially at the expense of others. She used to come over regularly and chat with Rouge in the women's quarters of the Bian household, and the two became quite friendly.

One day, Rouge was seeing Madame Wang to the door when she caught sight of a man passing by in the street, dressed all in white. She was struck by the man's appearance and took an immediate fancy to him, staring at him with her bright glistening eyes. The young man for his part lowered his head and strode on down the street, but Rouge continued gazing after him as he walked away.

Madame Wang guessed at once what was going through Rouge's mind, and said playfully, 'What a fine pair the two of you would make, you with your brains and beauty, and a handsome young man like that!'

Rouge flushed coyly and said not a word.

'Do you know who he is?' asked Madame Wang.

'No, I don't.'

'Well I do. He's Li Qiusun, a promising young first-degree

scholar, who lives in South Lane. His late father was a well-respected mandarin, and we used to be neighbours, so I know him quite well. There is not a man more gentle and considerate than he is. He is wearing white today because his wife has died and he is still in mourning. If you fancy him, I'll drop a hint or two for him to send over a matchmaker.'

Rouge said nothing in reply, and Madame Wang went away with a smile on her face.

Days went by without any news, and Rouge supposed either that Madame Wang had not had the leisure to drop her 'hint', or that the man himself was too proud to marry beneath him. She brooded about it miserably, gradually ceasing to eat and sleep, and lying on her bed listless and depressed day and night. After several days, Madame Wang called on her again and, seeing the state she was in, inquired as to its cause.

'I really can't say for sure,' replied Rouge weakly. 'I just know that ever since we last met, I have been utterly miserable. I only feel half alive.'

'My husband has been away on business and he still hasn't returned,' whispered Madame Wang conspiratorially. 'That's why I haven't been able to get word to the young man yet. This indisposition of yours wouldn't be on account of him, would it, my dear?'

Rouge flushed deeply.

'If things are as bad as that,' said Madame Wang, with a laugh, 'for goodness' sake do something about it! Don't go making yourself ill! Don't be coy! Take the plunge – invite him over tonight. I am sure he won't refuse.'

Rouge sighed. 'It's true, I am in a bad way. And I know there's no sense in being coy. I'm sure you're right. If only he were to think of marrying me and sent a matchmaker, my illness would be cured at once. But I could *never* be so forward as to see him secretly before we were married.'

Madame Wang nodded and went on her way.

Now, when she had been a young woman, Madame Wang had had intimate relations with her neighbour, a man by the name of Su Jie, from an educated family. Since her marriage to Mr Gong, this Su had been taking advantage of her husband's frequent absences to revive their earlier intimacy. That very evening, he chanced to come over to visit his old flame, and Madame Wang thought to entertain him by telling him about Rouge's predicament, even jestingly suggesting that *he* might be the one to communicate the girl's infatuation to handsome young Mr Li. But Su immediately formed other plans of his own. He had himself long been aware of Rouge's good looks, and he now secretly rejoiced at this new amorous opportunity that had come his way. He even half thought of confiding in Madame Wang, but he reflected that she was bound to be jealous, and in the end affected indifference towards the young girl's plight, while at the same time casually extracting from his lover detailed information concerning the layout of Rouge's living quarters.

The very next evening, he climbed over the wall of the Bian compound, made his way directly to Rouge's apartment and tapped with his finger on the window.

'Who's there?' she asked.

'It's me – Li Qiusun!' he replied.

'My heart yearns for a loving union with you,' replied Rouge, 'one that will endure a lifetime, not a single night. If you truly love me, then send a matchmaker to ask for my hand. If you are asking me to sleep with you tonight, then the answer is no.'

Su pretended to respect her scruples but pleaded with her to vouchsafe him one touch of her slender wrist as a sign of their love. She had not the heart to refuse him this request. Struggling feebly from her bed, with some considerable effort she opened the door. Su hurried into the darkened room, threw his arms around her and without further ado attempted to have his way with her. Rouge was far too weak to resist and fell to the ground, gasping for breath. Su pulled her forcefully towards him.

'You are so rough and cruel!' she cried. 'Not at all how I imagined you to be! I thought you would be kind and caring! I never thought you would treat me violently – knowing I have been poorly! Stop this minute, or I shall raise the alarm and both of us will be ruined!'

Su was afraid of being exposed and pressed her no further. But he did ask her for another assignation, to which Rouge replied that the next time they met would be on their wedding day. Su protested that this was unbearably far in the future and insisted on something sooner, whereupon Rouge, finding his pestering most disagreeable, eventually relented and agreed to see him again once she was fully recovered. Su asked for a token of her consent, and when she flatly refused, he seized hold of her foot, pulled off one of her embroidered slippers and went away with it.

'I have promised myself to you, body and soul!' she called after him. 'You know I would happily give you anything. The one thing I fear is that your family will think me too humble to be your wife, and that I will end up a laughing stock. Whatever happens, I know you will never give me back my slipper. I beg you, do not abandon me now. If you do it will be the death of me!'

After leaving the Bian house, Su went straight to Madame Wang's to spend the night. He was already in bed when his thoughts turned to the slipper and he reached into his sleeve to feel for it, only to discover that it was gone. He jumped up and lit a lamp, then shook his clothes and searched for it everywhere. When Madame Wang asked him what he was looking for, he made no reply, suspecting her of having hidden it. She laughed at him, and this only strengthened his suspicions. In the end he could conceal the truth no longer and confessed to what he had done. He went outside with his lamp and looked for the slipper everywhere, but it was nowhere to be found. He returned to bed greatly dismayed, comforting himself as best he could with the thought that it must be somewhere in the neighbourhood and that nobody else would have seen it or picked it up at such a late hour. The next morning, he rose early and went out looking for it again, but in vain.

Now, there lived in the district a disreputable character by the name of Big Mao, who had already made several fruitless attempts to seduce Madame Wang. Aware of Su's greater success in this connection, he had wanted to catch the two of them at it, thinking that he could thereby put pressure on Madame Wang to let him have his share. Going past her house that very night, he tried the gate and, finding it unbolted, was sneaking his way in on tiptoe towards the window of her room when his feet encountered something soft and silky. He picked the object up from the ground and found it to be an embroidered slipper wrapped in a silk handkerchief. Putting his ear closer to the window he overheard Su's confession – his detailed account of his frustrating encounter with the delectable Rouge. Beside himself with delight and excitement, Big Mao crept back out again.

Several days later, it was Big Mao's turn to climb over the wall of the Bian compound and into the courtyard. But unlike Su he had not been briefed on the topography of the house, and ended up making his way towards the father's room by mistake. Old Bian saw a silhouette through his window and, guessing from the suspicious way he was behaving that the man must have come to do some harm to his daughter, he angrily snatched up a knife and ran outside. Big Mao took to his heels in terror, but Old Bian caught up with him just as he was about to scale the wall. In desperation, Big Mao turned around and snatched the knife from the old man. By this time Rouge's mother was also awake and had raised the alarm, and Big Mao, unable to extricate himself from Old Bian's grasp, struck him down with the knife.

Rouge, who was by now somewhat recovered from her earlier indisposition, had also been roused by all the noise, and mother and daughter came hurrying together into the courtyard bearing lanterns, to find Old Bian lying there on the ground unconscious, bleeding profusely from a great gash on his head. The old man died before he could utter a single word. At the foot of the wall, they found an embroidered slipper, which the mother soon recognized as belonging to her daughter. She questioned the girl sternly, and Rouge tearfully told her how several nights earlier a young man had broken into the house. She did not want to implicate her neighbour Madame Wang, and insisted that young Li (for she was still under the impression that it was he who had assaulted her) had come to see her on his own initiative.

At daybreak the following day, the Bian family brought charges against Li, who was duly arrested by the Magistrate. Li was not an eloquent person and, though he was nineteen

胭脂

小劫情天

又煩明辨冤枉

謝良媒五花妙判駕

鴛鰈東國爭傳折獄才

He overheard Su's confession.

years old, in the presence of strangers he became as tongue-tied and awkward as a child. He was terrified at being arrested, and when he appeared before the Magistrate he began trembling and was utterly at a loss for words. The Magistrate was all the more convinced that he must be guilty of the killing of Old Bian, and had him tortured on the rack. The extreme pain drove him to make a false confession of guilt, whereupon he was sent under escort to the local Prefectural Yamen and tortured all over again. Throughout this ordeal his heart was filled with indignation at the injustice he was suffering, and he wanted more than anything else to confront Rouge (whom he himself had never met) and tell her of his innocence. As it was, every time they were brought together in court she denounced him angrily, as a result of which he became more tongue-tied than ever and even less able to vindicate himself. He was sentenced to death, and although his case was reviewed several times, each successive judge confirmed his guilt.

The matter finally came before the Prefect of the provincial capital Ji'nan, who happened at that time to be a gentleman by the name of Wu Nandai. Wu observed to himself straightaway that this young prisoner did not look at all like a murderer, and secretly sent one of his assistants to have a private talk with him, thereby presenting him with an opportunity to put his own case. The assistant's report convinced Wu more than ever that Li had been wronged and that there had been a miscarriage of justice. He deliberated for several days before proceeding to hear the case formally.

First he questioned Rouge.

'Did anyone else know about your secret encounter with the young man?'

'No one,' she replied.

'Was there anyone with you the very first time, when you saw young Mr Li passing by in the street?'

Again she insisted that there had been no one else present. The Prefect now summoned the young man and, speaking in a measured and reassuring tone of voice, asked him for his account of the facts.

'One day,' Li finally began, 'I was walking past the Bian

residence when I saw my old neighbour Madame Wang and a young girl standing in the doorway. I hurried away and did not exchange a single word with either of them.'

On hearing this, Prefect Wu immediately berated Rouge. 'A moment ago you said there was no one with you. What was this neighbour of yours, Madame Wang, doing there?'

He threatened her with torture, and the girl was too frightened to stick to her story.

'It's true, Madame Wang was with me. But honestly, she had nothing to do with what happened.'

The Prefect adjourned the case and ordered the arrest of Madame Wang, who was brought in a few days later and questioned upon her arrival, before she had a chance to talk to Rouge.

'Who murdered this girl's father?' asked the Prefect.

'I don't know.'

'Rouge has told me that you know who the murderer is. How dare you try to conceal anything from this court?'

'She's lying!' cried Madame Wang. 'That little slut is obsessed with men. Perhaps I once said something about acting as a matchmaker for her, but it was all just a joke. How was I to know she would try and get the man in bed with her?'

Prefect Wu went on to cross-examine her in minute detail, and Madame Wang gave him a full account of what she had said in jest. He summoned Rouge.

'You told me that Madame Wang had nothing to do with the case!' he declared angrily. 'And yet now she herself has confessed to offering you her services as a matchmaker!'

Rouge burst into tears. 'I have been a bad daughter! I've already been responsible for my father's death, and now I've caused this court case, which is dragging on endlessly! I couldn't bear to involve her too.'

Prefect Wu turned to Madame Wang. 'Did you speak to anyone else about this little joke of yours?'

'I spoke to no one,' she replied.

'Surely husband and wife have no secrets from each other!' exclaimed Wu angrily. 'Are you saying you didn't even tell your husband about it?'

'My husband has been away from home for a long time and has still not returned,' she replied.

'Nevertheless,' said the perceptive Prefect, 'human nature being what it is, when people like yourself have their little jokes, more often than not they like to make fun of the stupidity of others and to parade their own cleverness. Don't expect me to believe that you did not tell a soul.'

He gave orders for Madame Wang to be tortured with the ten-finger rack. The prospect of this was too much for the poor woman, and she finally confessed that she had indeed mentioned Rouge's infatuation to Su Jie. The Prefect at once set young Li free and ordered the arrest of Su Jie.

When Su came before the court, he denied any knowledge of the murder or the events leading up to it.

'Do you expect me to believe the word of a known frequenter of brothels such as yourself!' declared the Prefect. He had him severely tortured, and Su made a confession.

'Yes, I did take advantage of Rouge. But when I lost the slipper, I never dared to go there again. I know nothing about the murder.'

'A man who scales the walls of other men's houses and abuses a young woman as you did will stop at nothing!' said the Prefect angrily. Further torture reduced Su to a wreck, and he eventually made a false confession to the murder of Old Bian. The case was reported to the higher authorities, and Prefect Wu's perspicacity was universally praised. The evidence against Su seemed ironclad, and he lay in prison, awaiting his execution after the Autumn Assizes.

Now, Su may have been a dissolute character, but he was nonetheless an educated gentleman of some repute in the province of Shandong. When he learned that the newly appointed provincial Education Commissioner was none other than Shi Runzhang, a distinguished man of letters, well disposed towards scholars and literary talent in general, Su drew up a petition, protesting in eloquent terms that he had been unjustly treated. Commissioner Shi read the petition, examined the records, and after much reflection he struck his desk and exclaimed, 'This scholar has clearly been wronged!'

He obtained permission from the highest provincial authorities to have the case transferred to his jurisdiction, and questioned Su Jie himself.

'Where did you drop the slipper?'

'I cannot remember. I only remember that it was still in my sleeve when I knocked at Madame Wang's door.'

Commissioner, now Judge, Shi proceeded to question Madame Wang.

'How many lovers do you have besides Mr Su?'

'None,' she replied.

'Are you asking me to believe that a promiscuous woman like yourself has but one lover?'

'Su and I have known each other since we were children, so I couldn't refuse him. Of course other men have tried to seduce me, but I turned them all down.'

She was asked to give the names of these other men.

'My neighbour Big Mao for one. He has tried several times, but each time I have refused him.'

'What prompted you to be so virtuous all of a sudden?' asked the Judge sarcastically, and ordered that she be flogged. The woman immediately began knocking her head on the ground until it bled, protesting that she had never had relations with Big Mao. The Judge changed his mind and decided to dispense with the flogging.

'Tell me,' he went on to ask, 'while your husband was away, did anyone else come to your house on any pretext?'

'Yes, one or two people came to borrow money or to give me presents.'

The men she named were all local loafers, men who secretly fancied her. The Judge recorded their names, five all told including that of Big Mao, and had them arrested. When they arrived, he had them all taken to the City God Temple and made them kneel before the altar.

'The City God has spoken to me in a dream,' he declared. 'He has told me that the murderer is one among the five of you. Now today you are here in the presence of the god and must be sure to speak the truth. If one of you confesses, he will be treated leniently. Anyone caught lying will be severely punished.'

They all with one voice protested their innocence. The Judge ordered the instruments of torture to be brought in – the neck-rack, the hand- and foot-racks – and prepared the men for torture. Their hair was tied up and they were stripped down to the waist. But even when they were ready, they still protested their innocence. The Judge announced that they would proceed without the use of torture.

'Since none of you is willing to confess, I have no choice but to let the god himself identify the murderer.'

He ordered all the windows of the main hall of the temple to be completely blacked out with rugs and quilts, and the suspects to be led, still bare to the waist, into the pitch-dark hall. As they went in they were told to wash their hands in a basin of water, and then they were tied up facing the wall and told not to move, so that the god could 'write something' on the back of the guilty man. After a while, the Judge ordered them to be untied and brought out again into the open. He examined them all.

'That man,' he declared, pointing to Big Mao, 'is the true murderer!'

What the Judge had done was this: first he had given instructions for the wall to be smeared with lime, then for the basin in the darkened hall, in which they had washed their hands, to be filled with a solution of soot. The guilty man among them, fearful of being 'written on by the god', had turned around in the dark and pressed his back up against the wall, thereby smearing lime on it. When he emerged into the light untied, he had tried to cover his back with his hands, leaving sooty marks all over it. That was how the Judge confirmed his suspicions of Big Mao, who was now subjected to the harshest torture and confessed to everything.

The final written judgement was as follows:

'Su Jie: this man, like Deng Tu the famous lecher of old, is a debauched individual whose weakness, like that of Pencheng Guo, all but led to his own death. He knew this woman Madame Wang when they were both young and innocent, and as a grown man refused to abandon their illicit liaison. A chance piece of information about the young girl Rouge tempted him

to make a new conquest, and he scaled the wall, like Jiang
Zhongzi the bold paramour in the *Songs*, posing as a second
Liu Chen in love, and thereby luring her into opening her door.
What a shameful deed, for a gentleman and a scholar thus to
plot against the chastity of an innocent girl! Fortunately he took
pity on her illness and restrained himself at the last moment –
which bespoke some residual virtue of the sort one might hope
to find in a member of the educated class. But then to steal her
slipper as a pledge – was that not a vile deed! He flitted from
her courtyard back to his old flame, and even as his account of
his adventure was being overheard by a passing ne'er-do-well,
he noticed the disappearance of the slipper. This man has been
caught in a double imposture. His is a case of doubly mistaken
identity! First he himself masqueraded as young Li Qiusun, in
order to pass himself off as the girl's suitor; and then, once the
original murder suspect, Li Qiusun himself, had been ruled out,
he, Su, was mistakenly presumed by all to have been guilty of
the father's murder. This Heaven-inflicted punishment for his
own misdeeds nearly cost him his life. His behaviour has
brought disgrace on his fellow scholars and gentlemen. But
nonetheless it would be wrong to convict him of a crime done
by another, and his punishment should be commuted, in view
of what he has already suffered. He is to be demoted to the
rank of commoner, and given a chance to make a fresh start in
a new and humbler life.

'As for the man known as Big Mao: he is an unscrupulous
rogue, the worst kind of street thug. Having been rebuffed by
Madame Wang, his former neighbour, he was incapable of
renouncing his lustful desires. He eavesdropped on her meeting
with her lover, and to his joy learned of an opportunity to
seduce a fair maiden in the neighbourhood, something beyond
his wildest expectations. But Heaven willed it otherwise. He
mistook her father's room for hers, and his amorous adventure
came to a tragic ending. Cornered by the old man, who was
carrying a knife, he struck in desperation and took the man's
life. This was no lover, no romantic philanderer, this was a
monster pure and simple. He should be instantly decapitated,
to appease the righteous wrath of the law-abiding public.

'Then we come to the girl Rouge: she had reached the marrying age but was still unbetrothed. A girl with her good looks
would surely have obtained a handsome husband. But her
infatuation with this one man brought her no end of trouble.
First one scoundrel then another came after her, each posing as
the man she loved, each trying to dupe her. How narrow was
her escape! Who would ever have thought that her passion
would become the engine of her misfortune, and lead to the
violent death of her own father? Thanks to her courage, she has
been able despite everything to preserve her chastity. Therefore
marriage with the object of her affections is still possible, indeed
to be commended, in spite of all that has transpired. Her wish
should be fulfilled, the lovers should be united, in commen-
dation of this girl's brave defence of her chastity against all
odds. Let the County Magistrate act as matchmaker.'

Thus the trial came to an end, and Judge Shi became famous
for his wise judgement. It was thanks to his probing investigation that Rouge came to discover young Li's innocence. As
soon as she knew the truth, she kept looking at the young man
in the tribunal with shame and remorse, her eyes wet with tears.
She seemed to have words to say to comfort him but was too
shy to utter them. Young Li for his part was touched by her
evident sympathy, and, as the case dragged on, he began to
have feelings of affection towards her. He could not help but
be deterred, however, by the fact of her humble birth, and by
her local notoriety as a result of this shocking court case. He
was at first fearful that he might become a laughing stock if he
were to take her as his wife, and pondered the dilemma night
and day, unable to make up his mind. Judge Shi's final judgement, however, enabled him to set aside his doubts. The County
Magistrate took the matter in hand, sent off the betrothal gifts
to Rouge on Li's behalf, and the festive sound of flutes and
drums were soon to be heard all along the road.

98

THE SOUTHERN
WUTONG-SPIRIT

The southern Wutong-spirit is somewhat like the northern fox-spirit. But whereas the northern fox's evil force may be exorcized in a hundred different ways, the Wutong of the Yangtze Valley region is much more vicious and intractable. It possesses and ravishes the beautiful wives of innocent citizens at will, wreaking havoc in the hearts of all. Whole families live in fear and trembling of this powerful and pernicious spirit.

There was a pawnbroker of the southern region of Wu named Zhao Hong, who had a beautiful wife called Yan. One night, a strapping great fellow burst into her room, swinging his sword around him, and her maids and old serving-women fled in terror. Yan herself tried to escape, but the intruder barred her way.

'Do not be afraid,' he said. 'I am a Wutong-spirit. They call me Fourth Brother. I love you; I mean you no harm.'

He took her by the waist, lifting her up as one would an infant. Then he deposited her on the bed, stripped off her skirt and sash and made love to her. His mighty member was more than she could endure and she sank into a trance-like state, groaning and pleading with him to desist. Out of pity for her he did not penetrate her fully, but descended from the couch saying, 'In five days I will return.'

And with these words he left.

The woman's husband was on a business trip, and a maidservant hurried that same night to bring him news of this terrible visitation. He recognized it at once as the doing of a Wutong, and went straight home without asking any further questions. At dawn the following day, when he saw how listless his wife was, how loth she was to rise from her bed, he felt a deep sense of shame at what had happened to her. He gave his household instructions not to breathe a word of the incident. Three or four days later his wife seemed more herself again, but she lived in constant dread of the forthcoming Wutong visit. Meanwhile her maids and serving-women no longer dared to sleep in her apartments, but had all moved out to another part of the house, leaving their mistress alone by her candle, grimly awaiting her fate.

It was not long before the spirit returned, accompanied this time by two other men, fine-looking youths, and a pageboy who laid out sweetmeats and wines. The spirit invited Yan to drink with him, but she bashfully lowered her head, and even when he pressed her she refused, consumed with fearful anticipation that their love-making that night would be the end of her. The three men carried on drinking, pledging each other with many a toast till well past midnight, when the spirit's two young companions rose to leave.

'You, sir, have an assignment tonight with this fair lady. On some other occasion you must invite us to drink with you again.'

They referred to him as Fourth Brother Wutong, and to themselves as Second and Fifth Brothers Wutong. With these words they took their leave.

Fourth Brother Wutong now carried her into the curtained bedstead, and although she pleaded for mercy, he had his way with her again and did not leave until she had begun to bleed heavily and had lost consciousness.

When she finally came to, she lay breathing fitfully on her couch, burning with shame. She resolved to take her own life, but each time she slipped her neck through the noose, the cord always snapped – however often she tried, it was always the same. This means of escape was thus denied her.

Fortunately for her, the spirit left an interval between his visits. To be precise, he always allowed her just sufficient time to recover before her next ordeal. This continued for two or three months, at the end of which time the entire household was at its wits' end.

Now, there was a man from the town of Kuaiji named Wan,

a cousin of Zhao Hong's on his mother's side, a man of great courage and a superb marksman with the bow. He came to visit Zhao one day, and was accommodated in the inner apartments of the house (the usual guest quarters having been taken over by the terrorized members of the family). That night he lay awake longer than usual and, thinking that he heard the sound of a man moving about in the courtyard outside, looked out through his window. Sure enough, he saw a strange man entering the bedchamber of his host's wife. His suspicions immediately aroused, he armed himself with a knife and took up a position in the courtyard from which he had a clear view into the lady's room. He could see the stranger seated next to her, and refreshments spread on the low table beside them on the couch. Unable to contain his righteous wrath, Wan burst into the room and the stranger rose to his feet in alarm, feeling in haste for his sword. But before he could lay hands on it, Wan's knife had sliced its way through his skull, spilling his brains on to the floor. When Wan looked down, he saw that the man's corpse had already been transformed into that of a small horse, the size of a mule. Aghast, he questioned the lady, who told him the whole story of her possession, concluding, 'At any moment his spirit-companions will come for him! What then?'

Wan gestured to her to be silent, extinguished her candle, and lay in wait in the dark, with bow and arrows at the ready. In a little while, four or five men duly alighted from the sky. Wan let loose his first arrow, and the first lay dead. The others bellowed with rage, drew their swords and entered the room in search of the archer. Wan was hiding motionless behind the door, knife in hand, and the first to enter soon fell dead to the ground, his throat slit. Wan stood behind the door a while longer, and when there was no further sound he emerged and went to knock at his cousin Zhao's door and inform him of the night's events. Zhao was greatly alarmed at his tale, and the two of them returned to the scene, where they lit candles and saw the dead bodies of a horse and two pigs. The whole household rejoiced at this deliverance. Out of fear, however, that the surviving creatures might return to seek vengeance, they

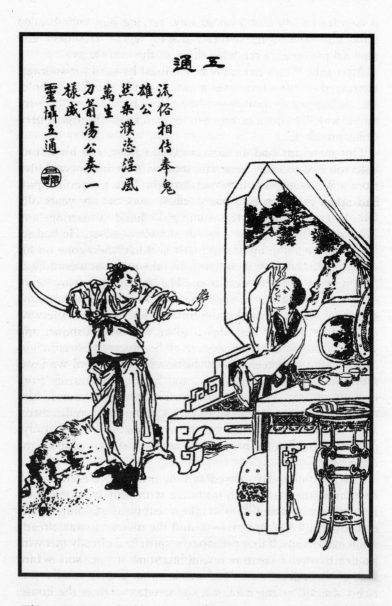

The man's corpse had been transformed into that of a small horse.

persuaded the valiant Wan to stay, serving him with broiled pork and stewed horse-meat, dishes whose freshness and unusual provenance rendered them all the more tasty.

After this, Wan's name became a local byword for courage. He stayed on for a little over a month in the Zhao household, and then, since the possessions seemed to have ceased, he went on his way. By now a certain timber merchant had urgent need of his presence.

This merchant had an unmarried daughter, and his household too had recently been favoured with an unexpected visit from a Wutong-spirit, in broad daylight. This particular spirit had taken the form of a burly fellow over twenty years old, who had come seeking the young girl's hand in marriage and offering the large sum of a hundred taels of silver. He had set the propitious day for the nuptials and had then gone on his way. That day was now at hand, and the entire household was in a state of utter consternation. The merchant, having heard of Wan's reputation in such matters, sent for him urgently, inventing some pressing excuse for fear that he might otherwise prevaricate. He sat Wan down to an elaborate banquet and presented his daughter, arrayed in all her finery, a beautiful girl of sixteen or seventeen. When she bowed before him, Wan was more than a little taken aback, and he rose awkwardly from his seat and returned her courtesy. The merchant pressed him to stay and told him the truth of his daughter's predicament. Wan was at first startled, but being a man who had always prided himself on his bravery, he resolved to stay and see the thing out.

The appointed day arrived and the merchant busied himself decorating the entrance to his house with gaily coloured bunting, while instructing Wan to take a seat inside. By midday the evil spirit still had not arrived, and the merchant was already rejoicing to himself that perhaps the spirit had already met with his death, when a creature resembling some strange sort of bird landed beneath the eaves and was instantly transformed into a richly dressed young man, who proceeded to enter the house. The instant he set eyes on Wan, however, he turned to flee. Wan went after him in hot pursuit. He saw a cloud of black vapour rising from the man's body and, striking out wildly, succeeded in chopping off one foot. The creature continued to flee, letting out a great howl, and the merchant's household saw lying on the ground a huge claw the size of a human hand, part of a strange bird the like of which they had not seen before. They followed the bloody trail left by the wounded bird down to the river. The merchant was overjoyed at the routing of the spirit and, learning that Wan was single, that same evening he gave him his own daughter in marriage, putting at their disposal the very nuptial bed that had been prepared for the Wutong-spirit.

From then on, anyone having trouble with visitors from the Wutong world would invite Wan to spend the night. He stayed on in the timber merchant's home for over a year, and then left with his wife. And thereafter, the sole surviving Wutong-spirit of the Wu region never dared to cause any substantial harm.

SUNSET

A certain gentleman of Suzhou by the name of Jin earned a living as a tutor in the Huai River region, lodging in the garden of a well-to-do local official, where a few rooms were put at his disposal, set amidst a profusion of shrubs and flowers.

Late at night, when his pageboy and servants had dispersed, he was in the habit of pacing up and down in his study, a lonely, irresolute figure, his mood frequently one of profound melancholy. On one such night, towards the end of the third watch, there came a sudden tap at his door. He inquired who it was, and was surprised to hear by way of reply the words 'Can you give me a light?'

The voice resembled that of one of his pageboys. But when he opened the door to let him in, he saw before him a beautiful girl of sixteen, attended by a maidservant. Jin felt as if he had been bewitched, and began asking her all manner of questions.

'You seem such a fine, cultured young man,' she replied. 'I felt sorry for you, all on your own, so I have put aside my scruples and come to help you pass the lonely hours of the night. Please don't ask me too many questions about myself, or I might not want to come at all, and you might not want me to either.'

Jin had a feeling this might be the daughter of a neighbouring family, someone who had run away from home, and, fearful of committing some culpable indecency, he politely declined the girl's proposal. But the next minute she flashed him a soulful glance and he was undone, no longer master of himself. The maidservant at her side understood the situation.

'I'd best be going now, Miss Sunset.'

The girl nodded faintly. 'Off with you then,' she chided her gently. 'And fewer references to the evening sky, if you please!'

The maid departed, and the girl turned to Jin with a smile. 'Since there was no one here other than you, I brought my maid with me. I little thought she would betray my name!'

'You seem so slender and so frail – I fear some ill will come of this . . .'

'I have long known my own mind. I will not be the cause of your ruin or disgrace, of that I can assure you. Do not be afraid.'

They sat down on his bed and she loosened her gown. He saw a bracelet on her wrist, made of jewelled beads strung on gold filigree thread and set with two large pearls. When the lamps were extinguished, the light emanating from the bracelet illuminated the whole room. Jin was more and more bewildered by this strange girl, unable to imagine who she could possibly be or where she might have come from. They made love, and afterwards the maidservant returned and knocked at the window. The girl arose and, using her bracelet to light her way, set off through the shrubbery. From then on she visited Jin every night. Whenever she left him he would try to trail her secretly, but she knew this and covered the light from her bracelet, leaving him stranded in the dense darkness of the shrubs where he could see no further than his hand and was obliged to turn back.

One day, he was travelling in the region to the north of the Huai River when the tie securing his bamboo hat broke and the hat blew away in the wind, leaving him bare-headed on his horse, clutching his saddle. He eventually reached the river and was preparing to cross it on a ferry when, lo and behold, his hat came fluttering down in the wind, only to go bobbing away on the waves. Much bemused, he set off across the river, and just as he reached the other side a strong gust of wind sent the hat whirling up into the air again, after which it descended slowly into his outstretched hand. And to Jin's amazement he saw that the tie was mended. When he returned home to his studio in the garden, he recounted his experience on the river to his strange lady-friend Sunset, during one of her visits. She said nothing, but from the way she smiled he had an idea it was her doing.

'If you are a spirit of some kind,' he said to her earnestly, 'then please tell me. I would be so much easier in my mind if I knew the truth.'

'You have found a devoted companion to cheer you in your solitude,' replied the girl. 'Is that not enough in itself? The things I do, I do out of love. Do you want to kill our love with your questions and never set eyes on me again?'

Jin said not another word.

Prior to all of this, back in the city of Suzhou, Jin had taken on the responsibility for the upbringing of his sister's daughter. When this niece of his came of age and was married, she was possessed by a Wutong-spirit. Jin was most troubled on her behalf, though he mentioned the matter to no one. Now that he had been intimate with Sunset for such a long while, he could keep it a secret from her no longer.

'My father can drive out spirits like that,' she told him when he confided in her. 'But I can hardly go to my father with a private affair of my lover's!'

He pleaded with her to find a way, and she pondered the matter a while.

'There is no real difficulty in dealing with this. But I would have to go myself. And those spirits you mention are base slaves belonging to my family. It would be a terrible disgrace for me to touch such a foul thing like that!'

Jin entreated her again and again, and she finally assured him that she would somehow solve the problem.

The following night she came to him and said, 'I have sent my maidservant to the South to do this for you. But I am afraid she may be too weak to kill it.'

The next night, they had just fallen asleep when the maidservant knocked at the door. Jin rose at once and let her in.

'Well, what happened?' asked Sunset.

'I wasn't able to catch it,' she replied. 'But I did manage to cut off its *thing*.'

Sunset laughed at this and asked for a more detailed account.

'At first I thought I'd find the spirit at Mr Jin's family home.

五通第二

五通神祇一道存婶
子南来炒敛魂绝似
阿雞摩戒體尧從
淫席斬淫根

'I have sent my maidservant to do this for you.'

But I soon discovered my mistake, and went to the house of the young girl's husband. The lights were all lit and there she was, sitting beneath a lamp, leaning on the table as if she'd fallen asleep. I gathered her into a jar, soul and all, and put a stopper on it. In a little while the Wutong-spirit came into the room, but he went straight out again, saying, "I sense a stranger in here!" He had a good look around and, seeing no one, came back in. All this time I was lying in the bed, pretending to be the lady fast asleep. He lifted the quilt and climbed in next to me, then suddenly he cried out "I sense the aura of a weapon here!" I hadn't wanted to dirty my hand by touching such a foul thing, but I knew I didn't have a moment to lose, so I grabbed hold of his member and hacked it off there and then. The creature howled and fled, and I got out of bed and opened the jar. The girl seemed to wake up, so I left.'

Jin thanked her warmly for what she had done, and the maid left with her mistress.

For over a fortnight, Sunset did not return, and Jin feared he would never see her again. Then suddenly she appeared, one day towards the end of the year, when he had already given up his post as tutor and was preparing to leave. He greeted her joyfully.

'You have been away for so long, I thought I must have offended you in some way. Are we never to be together again?'

'The end of the year is an auspicious time,' she replied, 'and it would be wrong of me to part from you without a word of explanation. I heard that you were going home, and have come to say goodbye.'

Jin begged her to let him go with her.

'You do not understand what a difficult thing it is that you propose! No, we must say farewell, and I cannot bear to keep the truth from you any longer. I am the daughter of the Golden Dragon King. You and I were predestined to love one another. That was why I came to you. I did wrong to send my maidservant on that errand to the South, and now word of her exploit has spread far and wide. My people know that for your sake I caused the Wutong-spirit to be castrated. When my father heard about it, he considered it such a great disgrace and was so angry that he wanted to have me put to death. Fortunately for me, my maid took the blame upon herself, and father's anger was somewhat appeased. My maid was given a hundred blows of the bamboo, and now everywhere I go I have to be chaperoned by an old nurse. This time I managed to slip away on some pretext. Alas, I have no time to say all that is in my heart!'

As she made this farewell, Jin held her in his arms and wept.

'Do not be sad,' she said. 'Thirty years from now we will meet again.'

'But I am already thirty years old,' he replied. 'Thirty years from now I shall be a white-haired old man, too old for a beautiful woman like you.'

'Not so,' she replied. 'In the Dragon King's Palace we have no such thing as white-haired old men. And besides, long life has nothing to do with physical appearance. If you wish to retain your youthful looks, that is an easy matter.'

She wrote down a prescription on the margin of one of his books, and departed.

Jin went back to his home town of Suzhou, and his niece told him she had had a strange experience.

'The other night I had a most peculiar dream. Someone shut me up in a jar, and when I woke up there was blood all over my bed and coverlet. Ever since then that horrible creature I told you about has gone away.'

'I prayed for you to the River God,' said Jin.

Now he knew for sure that what Sunset had told him was true.

When he reached the age of sixty, he still had the appearance of a young man of thirty. One day, he was crossing a river when in the distance he saw a lotus leaf floating towards him on the water, as large as a mat. A beautiful lady was sitting on it, and as the leaf floated closer, he recognized the lady as Sunset, the companion of his youth. He tried to jump on to the leaf, but leaf and girl shrank and shrank until they were no bigger than a copper coin, and then they vanished.

The events of this story, and those of the previous one about the pawnbroker Zhao Hong, all took place during the Ming dynasty. I do not know which of the two stories came first in time. If this story about Sunset came after the heroic exploits of Mr Wan, then clearly, thanks to her maidservant's valiant efforts, the sole surviving Wutong-spirit in the southern region of Wu was reduced to half a Wutong, and was thus no longer a serious threat to womankind.

100

THE MALE CONCUBINE

A wealthy gentleman of Yangzhou wanted to buy himself a concubine. He had inspected several women but found that none of them was really what he was looking for. Then an old bawd who was visiting Yangzhou showed him a pretty young girl of fourteen or fifteen, a gifted musician and singer. He found her very attractive, and agreed to buy her for a high price.

The very first night they slept together, he admired the silken softness of her skin and proceeded in a transport of delight to explore her private parts, when to his shock and horror he discovered that 'she' was in fact a boy. He asked 'her' to tell him the whole story. It transpired that the old bawd had bought a pretty young boy, decked him out in all sorts of finery and sold him as a girl – in short she had tricked him.

The next day at dawn, he sent a servant to look for the bawd, but she had disappeared without trace. He was left in a state of great distress, quite at a loss what to do next. Luck had it that an old friend of his from Zhejiang Province came to visit, heard the story and insisted on seeing the boy himself. He was greatly taken with him, bought him for the original price and took him home with him.

男妾

逐臭嗜痂信不誣
雌雄撲朔亮模糊
易將弁晃為巾幗
始信人間有子都

He was greatly taken with him.

101

CORAL

Yue Zhong was a man of Xi'an, whose father died before he was even born. His mother was a pious Buddhist and abstained completely from meat and wine. With the passing years young Zhong, by contrast, grew more and more fond of drinking and eating, and this was often a source of friction between himself and his mother. He regularly tempted her with good things, which she always spat out. On one occasion, when she fell gravely ill and in her delirium craved some meat, Zhong, having no other source of supply handy, cut some flesh from his own left leg and gave it to her to eat. No sooner had she recovered than she was overwhelmed by a sense of remorse at having broken her vow, and resolved to fast until death. In this she was as thoroughgoing as she had been in her lifelong devotions, and finally she breathed her last. Zhong, who was devastated by her death, took a sharp knife and hacked his right leg down to the bone. Members of the household came to his aid, applying an ointment and wrapping the wound in silken bandages, and in due time it healed.

He was unable to drive the thought of his mother's fanatical piety from his mind, and, still grieving at the blind obstinacy that had driven her to her death, he set fire to the Buddhist icons she had been in the habit of worshipping, and in their place set up her own spirit tablet, to which he paid reverence. Whenever he had had too much to drink, he would weep bitterly before this shrine.

When he reached the age of twenty and took a wife, he was still a virgin. Three days after the wedding he said to one of his acquaintances, 'The act of love performed by a man and a woman is surely the vilest thing in the world! I find no pleasure in it!'

Consequently he rid himself of his wife. Three or four times her father, a man by the name of Gu Wenyuan, sent relations of his to plead with him to take her back, but Zhong's mind was made up. Several months later, the father succeeded in arranging a second marriage for his daughter.

Zhong remained single for many years and led a more and more carefree life, seeking his drinking companions from the motley ranks of household servants, yamen-runners, actors and musicians. His generosity became a byword. If a neighbour begged from him, he gave him whatever it was he wanted without the least hesitation. Once, when someone needed a cooking pot for his daughter's wedding feast, Zhong made him a gift from his own kitchen and was later obliged to borrow a pot for his own needs from one of his neighbours.

The local layabouts and ne'er-do-wells constantly took advantage of him. If one of them needed cash to gamble with, he would arrive with some tale of woe, claiming that the bailiffs were after him and that he would soon be forced to sell his children, whereupon Zhong would hand over every penny of the sum he had himself put by for payment of his taxes. And when subsequently the tax-collectors knocked at Zhong's door, he himself had to pawn his own belongings to settle his account. Needless to say, generosity such as this caused his fortunes to go steadily downhill. While he was a wealthy man, his cousins had been only too glad to wait upon him, and he had watched them walk off with countless possessions of his, and never breathed a word of complaint. But now that he was down and out, hardly a single one of them showed the slightest concern for him. Zhong adopted a philosophical view of this, and refused to take offence.

Once, on the anniversary of his mother's death, Zhong was ill and unable to visit her grave as he usually did, so he asked his cousins to take his place. But one cousin after another found some pretext for not going, and he ended up having to pour a libation for her in his own room, weeping before her spirit tablet. The fact of his own childlessness was now beginning to weigh on his mind, and this preoccupation further aggravated his illness. He found himself drifting into a confused and delirious state, in which it seemed to him that someone was in the room stroking him. He half opened his eyes, and beheld his mother.

'What are you doing here?' he asked in astonishment.

'No one from the family came to my tomb, so I thought I would visit you and partake of your offering, and see how you are getting on.'

'Where have you been dwelling all this time, Mother?'

'On the Holy Island of Nanhai.'

With these words, she stopped stroking him. A pleasantly cool feeling permeated his body. He looked around him and saw that there was no one there. And his illness was cured.

When he rose from his bed, his one thought was to go on a pilgrimage to Nanhai. In the neighbouring village, there was a Buddhist community formed for such purposes. Zhong sold several acres of land to raise the necessary funds for the journey, and begged them to let him join them on one of their pilgrimages. They rejected him on account of his reputation as a drinker and eater of meat, but he insisted on following them. Soon, however, they were so repelled by the stench of meat, wine and garlic emanating from him that they seized the first occasion when he was drunk and asleep to abandon him, leaving him to continue the journey on his own. He came to the border of Fujian Province, and there he was entertained by a friend, who had staying with him a famous courtesan by the name of Coral. When she heard that Zhong was travelling on to Nanhai, she proposed accompanying him, an offer he accepted with delight, and when she had packed her things, they set off. They ate together and shared the same bed, but chastely, with no physical intimacy of any kind.

When they finally reached the sea at Nanhai, the members of the Buddhist community, seeing that he had arrived in the company of a courtesan, mocked him heartily and absolutely refused to perform their devotions in his company. Zhong and Coral understood, and let them complete their prayers first. The Bodhisattva Guan Yin was reputed to appear in response to the prayers of the faithful. To the dismay of the monks, their efforts bore no fruit – they were not rewarded with anything in the way of a supernatural apparition. But no sooner had Zhong and Coral knelt on the shore than lotus-flowers with shimmering strings of pearls hanging from them sprang up over the entire surface of the sea. In the lotus-flowers Coral saw the image of the Bodhisattva, while Zhong saw his own mother's face on every lotus-petal. He ran crying towards her, leaping into the water. The assembled company watched as the countless flowers metamorphosed into a bank of spangled multi-coloured cloud, a glistening veil of brocade draped across the sea. In a little while, the cloud dispersed, the sea returned to its normal state and the entire vision vanished. Zhong found himself standing on the shore, perplexed as to how he could have emerged from the water without there being a single drop of moisture on his clothes or his shoes. He gazed far out to sea and uttered a great cry that set the very islands trembling. Coral drew him away and comforted him, and in a mood of great sorrow they left the temple and took a boat back to the North.

During the return journey, a wealthy client took Coral away with him, and Zhong continued on his way alone. He stopped for the night at an inn, where he saw a young boy of eight or nine begging for food. Somehow he did not look at all like an ordinary street-urchin. Speaking to him and learning that he had been turned out of home by his stepmother, Zhong felt sorry for him and, when the boy clung to him and beseeched him to save him, Zhong resolved to take him home. He asked his name.

'Ah Xin,' was the reply. 'My family name is Yong. My mother was born into the Gu family. She often told me that I was born six months after she married Mr Yong, and that my real family name is Yue.'

This gave Zhong quite a turn. Could this poor boy be his own son? But that hardly seemed possible, he reflected, since he and his wife had only once consummated their union. He went on to ask him where the Yue family originally hailed from.

'I do not know,' replied the boy. 'But I have a letter my mother gave me before she died. She told me on no account to lose it.'

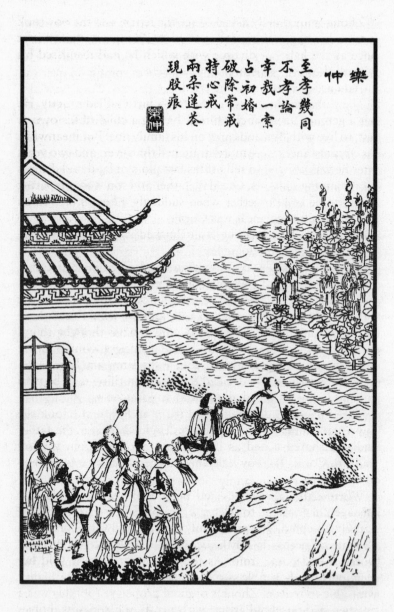

樂仲

至孝幾同
不孝論
幸我一絲
占初婚
破除常戒
持心戒
兩朵蓮苍
現股痕

Lotus-flowers sprang up over the entire surface of the sea.

Zhong immediately asked to see the letter, and the boy took it from his bag and handed it to him. Zhong recognized it at once as the letter of divorce with which he had dismissed his wife all those years before.

'You are truly my son!' he cried.

The year and the month of the boy's birth tallied exactly. He felt a genuine sense of comfort at having a child of his own at last, to live with him and carry on his family line. But meanwhile his circumstances were more straitened than ever, and two years later he was obliged to sell off his last plots of land and dismiss his remaining servants. One day, father and son were preparing their simple meal together when suddenly a beautiful woman appeared before them. It was Coral.

'Where have you sprung from?' asked Zhong in great surprise. 'What are you doing here?'

'You and I once lived as husband and wife,' replied Coral, with a smile, 'in our own fashion. What need have you to ask such questions? I could not stay with you before, because the old bawd I worked for was still alive and she would never have let me do so. Now she is dead, and I have thought things through. If I stay single, I shall be a defenceless woman. But if I marry any man other than you, I shall feel unclean. After much reflection I have decided that the best thing is to be with you. So I have travelled all this way to join you.'

She unpacked her things, and there and then she took the boy's place at the stove. Zhong was delighted. That night, father and son shared a bed as before, and another room was set aside for Coral. The boy called her mother, and she was devoted to him.

When Zhong's relatives and neighbours heard of his new ménage, they wanted to celebrate, a proposition that the couple happily accepted. The guests duly arrived, and Coral produced all that was necessary for the occasion. Zhong did not even ask where it had come from. As the days went by, she sold her seemingly inexhaustible supply of silver and jewellery, and they were able to redeem Zhong's original property. Soon his was a prosperous household again, with maids and servants, horses and oxen.

'If ever I drink too much,' Zhong said to her more than once, 'be sure to keep well away from me. Don't let me near you then.'

She laughingly agreed. But then one day, when he had had more than usual to drink, he called for her urgently, and, far from keeping away, she came in to him dressed in her finest clothes. Zhong stared at her a long while, and then began dancing wildly for joy.

'I am enlightened!' he burst out.

Suddenly he felt completely clear in his mind, and in that instant the world around him was bathed in radiant light and their humble home was transformed into a palace of jade. In a little while the vision faded. From that day on, he never drank save when he was alone with Coral. She, for her part, abstained from meat and wine, and sipped a cup of tea to keep him company.

One day, again when he was already a little tipsy, he asked Coral to massage his legs for him. The old scars, where he had cut them so violently years before, both when his mother was delirious and after her death, had grown into the shape of two tiny crimson lotuses, budding from his flesh. They both marvelled at this strange sight.

'The day these buds open and flower,' said Zhong, with a strange smile, 'our "marriage" of twenty years will be at an end and we will part.'

She took him seriously and believed his words.

The time came for the son Ah Xin to marry, and Coral entrusted the running of the household to his young wife, while she and Zhong lived separately in their own compound. There they received the young couple every few days, offering them advice only if some difficult matter arose. They themselves kept on two maids, one to warm his wine, the other to brew her tea.

One day, Coral went to see Ah Xin and his wife, and stayed with them for some time, discussing household matters. She returned with Ah Xin to see his father, and they found him sitting on his couch barefoot. When he heard them enter, he opened his eyes and smiled at them both.

'I'm so glad that you and your mother have come!'

And with that he closed his eyes again.

'What are you talking about, my dear!' cried Coral.

She looked at his legs. The two lotus-buds were in full bloom. She felt him, and the life force had already gone out of him. Urgently she pressed the petals together again with both her hands, entreating him all the while. 'I came so far to be here with you! It was not easy. I have raised your son and instructed your daughter-in-law. I have done what little I could for us. There were only two or three years left. Could you not have waited a little longer?'

A moment later, Zhong suddenly opened his eyes again and smiled.

'You have your life to lead in this world,' he said. 'Why do I need to be part of it? But so be it, since it is your desire, I will stay with you a while longer.'

Coral took her hands away, and the lotus-flowers were little buds once more. The two of them laughed and chatted together as they had always done.

Three years went by, and Coral was now almost forty years old, though she looked hardly a day over twenty. One day, she said to Zhong out of the blue, 'We must all die sooner or later. And when we do, our bodies will be moved around this way and that at the hands of others – it will be so unclean and undignified! We must make the necessary preparations.'

She gave instructions for two coffins to be made. Ah Xin was appalled and asked her what the meaning of this was.

'You would not understand,' she replied.

When the coffins were ready, she washed herself, put on her grave-clothes, and then she summoned Ah Xin and his wife.

'I am going to my death now,' she said.

'All these years we have depended on you, Mother,' protested Ah Xin tearfully. 'Thanks to your wise advice we have never gone hungry. You yourself have never been able to enjoy a life of leisure. You deserve it. Don't forsake us now!'

She replied, 'Your father by his devotion sowed the seeds of the good fortune that you now enjoy. Your family's servants, maids, cattle, horses, have all been restored. This was the due repayment of the loans your father was tricked into making.

I had no part in it. I am one of the Heavenly Apsaras, a Flower Fairy. My mind became too attached to worldly thoughts, and I was banished into the world of men for thirty years. My time is now finished.'

So saying, she climbed into her own coffin. They cried out, but her eyes were already closed.

Ah Xin went in tears to inform his father, but found him lying formally clad in hat and gown, cold and dead. Weeping fierce tears, he placed his father in his coffin and had both coffins put out in the main hall, delaying the wake for several days in the hope that they might still come back to life. A bright aura emanated from Zhong's limbs and lit up the hall, while Coral's coffin gave off a richly perfumed mist that permeated the whole house. When they finally closed up the coffins, the brightness and the perfume gradually faded away.

After the funeral, various male relatives of the Yue family began eyeing Ah Xin's wealth, and conspired together to disown him of his inheritance, claiming that he was not Zhong's true son and heir. The case came before the Magistrate, who felt unable to reach a decision and proposed as a compromise to divide the property in two, giving half to Ah Xin and half to the relatives. But Ah Xin appealed to the district court, where the case remained a long while unresolved.

Now, many years earlier, as has already been told, after the summary divorce of his daughter, Gu Wenyuan had remarried her – to a certain Mr Yong. A year later, this Yong had moved south from Xi'an to the province of Fujian, and Gu lost touch with them altogether. At the time of Coral's death, Gu was an old man, whose one desire left in life was to see his daughter, his only child, again. He set out for Fujian to find her, only to be told on arrival at the son-in-law's house that his daughter was dead and that his grandson (Ah Xin) had been driven out of the house by Yong and his new wife. Gu informed the local Magistrate of this injustice, and Yong, fearing the consequences, offered his father-in-law a bribe. Gu refused to accept the money, insisting that what he wanted was his grandson, and the two of them sought the boy out everywhere without success. Then, one day, Gu saw a gaily coloured carriage coming down the road, and was just standing aside to let it pass, when a beautiful lady called to him from within the curtains, 'Is that you, Grandpa Gu?'

'It is,' he replied.

'Your grandson is my son,' continued the woman's voice, 'and is now living in the Yue household. Leave your lawsuit here and hurry to your grandson's aid. He has need of you.'

The carriage was gone before Gu could ask any questions. Resolving to accept Yong's money after all, he used it to make his way back to Xi'an, and arrived as the court was in the throes of coming to a judgement on Ah Xin's appeal. Gu went straight to the judge and presented him with all the information he had at his disposal: the date of his daughter's divorce, the date of her remarriage and the date of her son's birth. The facts were conclusive. As a result, the Yue cousins were given a caning and sent packing, Ah Xin was reinstated in his inheritance, and the case was declared closed.

Grandfather Gu went home with his grandson, and told him about the beautiful lady he had seen in the carriage. The encounter had occurred, so Ah Xin informed him, on the very day Coral died.

Ah Xin invited his grandfather to come and live with him, and provided him with quarters of his own and a maid to wait on him. Gu was already sixty years old, and in his old age the maid bore him a son, to whom Ah Xin showed great kindness.

102

MUTTON FAT AND PIG BLOOD

Mi Buyun – 'Cloud-Walker' – of Zhangqiu was an adept of the occult art of spirit-writing known as *Ji*. Whenever his friends gathered together for a social occasion, they would ask him to communicate with some Immortal or other and produce lines of supernaturally inspired verse.

One day, one of his friends was moved by the sight of a subtle cloud formation in the sky to compose a line of verse, to which he asked Mi to 'receive' an 'answer', so that the two lines could form a couplet. The line the friend composed was:

> Mutton-fat-white jade-sky.

The planchette's cryptic response was:

> South of the town, seek out Old Man Dong.

At the time they all thought this was meaningless gibberish.

Some time later, for some reason or another Mi and his friends happened to take a stroll south of the town and came to a place where they noticed that the soil had a strange reddish tinge, like the mineral cinnabar. Nearby they saw an old man with his herd of pigs, and they asked him about the strange colour of the earth.

'Oh that!' he replied. 'That be pig-blood-red mud-earth . . .'

Whereupon they suddenly remembered the planchette reading, and marvelling greatly, asked the old man his name.

'People call me Old Man Dong,' he replied.

The five-word response – *Pig-blood-red mud-earth* – was

'That be pig-blood-red mud-earth.'

certainly no brilliant line of poetry, but it matched the friend's original line word for word and made a good couplet. And the prescience of the planchette in knowing that they would find Old Man Dong south of the town and that he would give them the line – that was something truly extraordinary!

103

DUNG-BEETLE DUMPLINGS

Du Xiaolei lived in the hills west of Yidu. His mother was totally blind, and he looked after her with great filial devotion. Though they were a poor family, he saw to it that she never lacked good things to eat.

One day, he had to go out, and he bought some meat and gave it to his wife, telling her to make some dumplings with it. His wife was an extremely wayward and undutiful daughter-in-law, and when she chopped up the meat she threw in some bits of dung-beetle. Du's mother found the smell of the food repulsive and refused to eat it, putting it aside to show her son on his return.

His first question when he came home was 'Did you like the dumplings?'

His mother shook her head and produced the evidence. Her son opened the dumplings, and when he saw the bits of dung-beetle, he flew into a mighty rage and stormed into the bedroom, intending to give his wife a good beating. But in the end, afraid that his mother might hear, he climbed into bed and lay there brooding. When his wife spoke to him he remained silent, whereupon she became apprehensive and began pacing up and down beside the bed. After a while, Du heard a sort of panting and snorting.

'Can't you go to sleep?' he cried out. 'What are you staying awake for? A good hiding?'

There was complete silence. He rose, lit a candle and there before him he beheld a pig. Looking closer, he saw that it had two human feet, and knew that it was his wife metamorphosed.

When the Magistrate came to hear of this, he ordered the pig

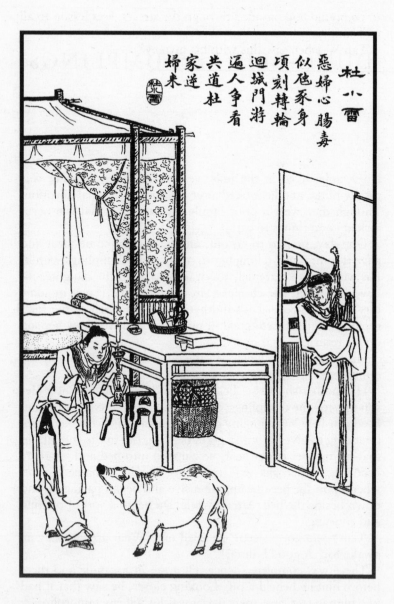

惡婦心腸毒
似砥豕身
頃刻轉輪
迴城門游
遍人爭看
共道杜
家逆子
婦來

杜小雷

There before him he beheld a pig.

to be bound and paraded through the streets, as a lesson to all and sundry.

Tan Weichen saw this with his own eyes.

STIR-FRY

A certain scholar was staying in the provincial capital for the examinations, and returned to his lodgings as night was falling. He had brought back with him some lotus seeds and pieces of lotus root, which he placed on the desk in his room. He also took out a dildo he had acquired, made of rattan, and put it to soak in a bowl of water.

At that very moment, his neighbours, hearing that he was back, came round with wine to spend the evening carousing with him, and he quickly hid the bowl underneath the bed and hurried out to greet them, instructing his wife to prepare some food. After the meal, he went back into his room and shone a lamp under the bed, only to discover that the bowl was empty. He asked his wife what had happened to the contents of the bowl, and she replied, 'Oh *that* – I cooked it just now for our guests, to go with the lotus root. Why, were you keeping it for something?'

When she said this he recalled a dish that had been set before them on the table with something black all chopped up in it, which none of them had been able to recognize. He laughed.

'You foolish woman! How could you think of serving such a thing to our guests!'

'I was wondering why you never gave me a recipe for it,' replied his perplexed wife. 'It was such a nasty-looking thing! I had no idea what it was. All I could think of doing was chopping it up into little pieces and stir-frying it . . .'

He proceeded to tell her what the 'nasty-looking thing' really was, and the two of them had a good laugh about it.

This man went on to become a man of rank. His good friends still joke with him about this story.

Author's Preface

Translator's Note

This is a dense and highly wrought text, a 'crazy quilt of dis-embodied images' (Judith T. Zeitlin, Historian of the Strange: Pu Songling and the Chinese Classical Tale *(Stanford, 1993, p. 50)). Almost every phrase contains an allusion of one sort or another, and every allusion tells a tale. It is in a sense a miniature anthology in its own right, of writers, tales and poems, all of them hinted at obliquely. The standard modern edition (Zhu Qikai, 1989) devotes a single page to the main text, followed by five pages tightly crammed with thirty-two explicatory foot-notes in small type, mostly based on the glosses of Lü Zhan'en (1825). I have consulted these annotations and those of others, including Herbert Giles, André Lévy, Jacques Dars and Chan Hingho, Judith T. Zeitlin, and Chang and Chang. My purpose in translating this Preface has not been to parade the author's learning, but to bring into focus the lineage in which he saw himself, the Chinese pedigree of his tales. We see several things in this self-portrait: a fascination with the supernatural for its own sake, an almost obsessive love of the richness of the Chinese classical language, enlivened by a pervasive and subtle sense of humour, and tinged by an intensely lyrical melancholy, a mood of 'lonely anguish and spleen'. The literary figures the author evokes (sometimes in no more than a couple of words) are his friends and mentors across the ages. At the same time (and this is typical of his extraordinary versatility) in this Pref-ace he is 'performing' in (parodying would too strong a term) the formal, parallelistic style fashionable in his own day. I have broken the prose into lines to indicate something of this formal quality.*

In my annotations I have added fragments by some of the authors referred to, to make the implied literary community more real. Today's reader, unlike the scholar-gentlemen of the late seventeenth century, cannot be expected to understand, from Pu Songling's brief and highly allusive snippets, how this lineage of writers formed a spiritual continuum and how Strange Tales *evolved out of it.*

The second half of the Preface is largely autobiographical. It is worth remembering that in 1679, when it was written, Pu Songling was thirty-nine years old and had only completed a part of the Strange Tales *collection. Modern scholars estimate that he went on adding tales for well over twenty years.*

*

    Ivy-cloak and mistletoe-girdle!
    Thus was the Lord of the Three Wards
    Moved to
    Rhapsodize.
    Ox-ghosts and serpent-spirits!
    Thus was the Bard of the Long Nails
    Driven to
    Versify.
    Each played his
10   Pipes of Heaven,
    Seeking not beauty of sound,
    But music that is what it is
    For reasons of its own.
    My desolate autumn firefly
    Is eclipsed by goblins;
    My insatiable speck of dust
    Is mocked by trolls.
    My talents pale beside
    Those of Gan Bao,
20   Whom I follow
    In his quest for weird spirits.
    My mood mirrors
    That of Su Dongpo,
    Whom I resemble

In his love of strange tales.
Of tales told
I have made a book.
With time
And my love of hoarding,
The matter sent me by friends   30
From the four corners
Has grown into a pile.
Here in the civilized world,
Stranger events by far occur
Than in the Country of Cropped Hair;
Before our very eyes
Weirder tales unfold
Than in the Nation of Flying Heads.
My irrepressible transports
Are an unfettered rapture   40
That cannot be gainsaid;
My far-soaring ideas,
An unbridled folly
That cannot be denied.
Fastidious readers of my book
May mock me,
Just as the tale of Five-Fathers Crossroad
May be baseless –
But who can tell?
The tale of Three-Lives Rock   50
May contain
Food for enlightenment.
My wild words
Should not be put aside
Because of the man
Who utters them.

*

My father,
When I was born,
And the bow hung at his door,
Dreamed of a sickly Buddha,   60

Cassock bare at the right shoulder,
Entering the room,
On one breast
A plaster round like a coin.
He woke from sleep,
And saw on his own newborn child
A black patch.
As a child
I was thin and constantly ailing.
I grew to manhood
Ill-equipped
For the battle of life.
Our home was chill,
Desolate as a monastery.
I earned a living with my pen,
Poor as any priest with his alms-bowl.
Often, head in hand, I would exclaim,
'Could I once
In a previous life
Have been
He who sat with his face to the wall?'
My spiritual failure in this life
Surely stems from obstacles and delusions;
This is
Karma from a previous life.
I have been blown
By the wind,
Driven
Like a flower against a wall,
Falling in the cesspit.
The Six Modes of Transmigration,
Though inscrutable,
Have a reason of their own.

*

Midnight finds me
Here in this desolate studio
By the dim light

70

80

90

Of my flickering lamp,
Fashioning my tales
At this ice-cold table,
Vainly piecing together my sequel   100
To *The Infernal Regions*.
I drink to propel my pen,
But succeed only in venting
My spleen,
My lonely anguish.
Is it not a sad thing,
To find expression thus?
Alas! I am but
A bird
Trembling at the winter frost,   110
Vainly seeking shelter in the tree;
An insect
Crying at the autumn moon,
Feebly hugging the door for warmth.
Those who know me
Are in the green grove,
They are
At the dark frontier.

Written on a spring day,
in the eighteenth year of the Kangxi reign [1679].

NOTES

Lines 1–4 *Ivy-cloak . . . Rhapsodize*: The opening line (the exact iden-
tity of the plants is unsure) comes from 'The Mountain Spirit', one
of the rhapsodic Nine Songs in *The Songs of the South*, written by
Qu Yuan and other poets from the southern cultural region of Chu
in the fourth to third centuries BC (see David Hawkes (trans.), *The
Songs of the South* (Harmondsworth, 1985); also extracts in John
Minford and Joseph S. M. Lau (eds.), *Classical Chinese Literature:
An Anthology of Translations* (New York and Hong Kong, 2000),
I, pp. 237–64). This shamanistic collection ushered in one of the two
main traditions of Chinese poetry – the personal, lyrical tradition, as

opposed to the more folkloric tradition of the ancient anthology
known as the *Book of Songs*, which became a Confucian classic.
David Hawkes speculates that 'The Mountain Spirit' may have been
addressed to the Lady of Gaotang, a fertility goddess whose physical
union with the King of Chu on Mount Wu (Shaman Mountain) in
'the clouds of morning and the rain of evening' gave rise to the
standard Chinese euphemism for sexual intercourse, 'the clouds and
the rain'. The poem ends (in Hawkes's version, p. 116):

> The thunder rumbles; rain darkens the sky:
> The monkeys chatter; apes scream in the night:
> The wind soughs sadly and the trees rustle.
> I think of my lady and stand alone in sadness.

In these very first lines of his Preface, Pu Songling is inscribing
himself in the 'unorthodox' lineage of China's first shaman-
rhapsodist, Qu Yuan, the Lord of the Three Wards (this was supposed to have been his official title), whose poems were always
considered 'strange'. At the same time he identifies himself with Qu
Yuan's melancholy, and echoes his disenchantment with a corrupt
society. According to venerable tradition, Qu Yuan, who had been
a prominent minister of the southern state of Chu, was banished by
his king and committed suicide by throwing himself into the river.
Lines 5–8 *Ox-ghosts . . . Versify*: The Bard of the Long Nails, Li He
(790–816), of the late-Tang period, is often referred to in Western
studies of Chinese literature as the Chinese type of the *poète maudit*
(which can be roughly paraphrased as a 'doomed poet with a vision
so intense the world will destroy him if he does not destroy himself').
André Lévy calls Li a Chinese Rimbaud, while of his English translators, Angus Graham compares him to Baudelaire, and John Frodsham prefers to evoke John Keats. 'He [Li] is half in love at times
with easeful death. He wrote in the shadow of the grave: and no
philosophy, no religion, no consoling belief could quite keep out its
ineluctable cold' (J. D. Frodsham, *Goddesses, Ghosts and Demons:
The Collected Poems of Li He* (London, 1983), p. lviii). In his biography in the *New Tang History* (ed. Ouyang Xiu and Song Qi (1060)),
Li is described as having been 'frail and thin, with eyebrows that met
together and long fingernails'. He loved writing about weird and
exotic subjects, and became known as the 'demon talent'. 'He felt
himself already half way across the boundary between the living and
the dead' (A. C. Graham (trans.), *Poems of the Late T'ang* (London,

1965), p. 90). But he was equally obsessed with the subtle sensuality and fragrance of the living. 'Fine food and wine, music, rich silks and brocades, jewels, and beautiful women figure prominently in his verse' (Frodsham, *Goddesses*, p. xxiv). His fellow poet Du Mu (803–52), in his Preface to Li's *Collected Verse*, places him in the tradition of Qu Yuan and *The Songs of the South*, adding that 'whales yawning, turtles spurting, ox-ghosts and serpent-spirits cannot describe his wildness and extravagance.' The expression 'ox-ghosts and serpent-spirits' came to stand for the supernatural and the fantastic generally. (By an interesting twist, in modern 'revolutionary' times, it came to denote politically 'bad' and unregenerate elements, 'ugly' fellows such as landlords, rich peasants and counter-revolutionaries.)

Among Li's best-known poems is 'Song of Magic Strings', which includes these memorable lines:

> Cassia leaves stripped by the wind,
> Cassia seeds fall,
> Blue racoons are weeping blood
> As shivering foxes die.
> On the ancient wall, a painted dragon,
> Tail inlaid with gold,
> The Rain God is riding it away
> To an autumn tarn.
> Owls that have lived a hundred years,
> Turned forest demons,
> Laugh wildly as an emerald fire
> Leaps from their nests.
> (Frodsham, *Goddesses*, p. 166)

Pu Songling was himself a prolific poet and wrote poems imitating Li's style. He shared Li He's obsessive (driven) interest in the supernatural. Lines 9–10 *Each played . . . Heaven*: Another of Pu Songling's revered mentors, the early Taoist mystic and zany storyteller Zhuangzi (fourth century BC), describes the adept Ziqi of South Wall sitting leaning on a table, breathing slowly, clearly in some sort of a trance: he has heard the Music (literally, the Pipes) of Heaven (or Nature), and is in tune with it. When his disciple asks him what he means by this transcendental music, Ziqi replies, 'It blows on the Ten Thousand Things in a different way, so that each can be itself' (compare Graham's translation in Minford and Lau, *Classical*

Chinese Literature, I, pp. 219–20). In other words, when we hear the Pipes of Heaven, everything sounds as it is by its very nature. It is an inner music that wells up of its own accord.

Line 11 *Seeking not beauty of sound*: In *The Book of Songs*, in one of the Praise Odes of the State of Lu, 'beauteous sounds' are made by the owls in the mulberry trees. According to the traditional didactic interpretation, which would have been standard in Pu Songling's day, the birds are straining to beautify their ugly screeching in order to express their praise of the newly founded college of Lu. By contrast, Pu Songling is seeking to hear (and utter) a sound that arises from within, not one designed to please conventional tastes.

Lines 12–13 *But music ... of its own*: Pu Songling is thinking in Taoist terms. The music must be of itself. We sing the song that we sing because we are what we are.

Line 14 *My desolate autumn firefly*: The feeble firefly's light is a cliché for a man's humble efforts and lowly station in life, compared with the grand achievements of his more famous contemporaries.

Line 15 *Is eclipsed by goblins*: A reference to Xi Kang (223–62), celebrated musician and alchemist and one of the Seven Sages of the Bamboo Grove, that wonderful congeries of medieval Chinese eccentrics (men no doubt after Pu Songling's own heart). Many anecdotes tell of Xi Kang's encounters with spirits while playing his lute. In one he is sitting alone at night, strumming his lute, when suddenly a man more than ten feet tall, clad in black cloth and a leather belt, walks in. Xi Kang looks at him and blows out his lamp, saying, 'How could I venture to emulate the light of a goblin!' (For more on Xi Kang and the Seven Sages, see Minford and Lau, *Classical Chinese Literature*, I, pp. 456–67.)

Line 16 *My insatiable speck of dust*: The unusual word *didi* (insatiable) is taken from *The Book of Changes*, where it is used to describe the craving of a tiger (Richard Wilhelm and Cary F. Baynes (trans.), *I Ching* (New York, 1950), p. 110). Pu Songling seems to be referring to his obsessive and yet consistently unsuccessful attempts to pass the examinations. The 'speck of dust' is another reference to *The Book of Zhuangzi*, Chapter 1, 'Free and Easy Wandering'.

Line 17 *Is mocked by trolls*: The two words Pu Songling chooses for his goblins and trolls can be traced back to an episode in the *Zuo Commentary on the Spring and Autumn Annals*, the first (probably third century BC) work of sustained narrative in the Chinese language and certainly one of the *Strange Tales*' earliest ancestors. *Strange Tales* is strewn with references to it.

All the objects were represented [on the tripods], and instructions were given for the preparations to be made in reference to them, so that people might know the sprites and evil things. Thus the people, when they went among the rivers, marshes, hills and forests, did not meet with the injurious things, and the trolls, monstrous things, and goblins, did not meet with them. Hereby a harmony was secured between the high and the low, and all enjoyed the blessing of Heaven.

(Adapted from James Legge (trans.), *The Chinese Classics*, 5 vols.
(Hong Kong, 1861–72), V, p. 293)

The *Zuo Commentary* itself certainly did not shrink from recording the strange and the supernatural. It is one of the earliest repositories of such accounts. A single episode (dated to the year 680 BC) illustrates this direct line of descent from the *Zuo Commentary* to the *Tales*:

Snakes living within the city and those from outside had engaged in battle in the middle of the southern gate to the capital of Zheng. The snakes living within the city died. Six years later, Duke Li of Zheng returned to the capital. When Duke Zhuang of Lu heard of this, he questioned his minister Shen Xu about it, saying: 'Are there really such things as portents?' Shen replied: 'When people have something they are deeply distressed about, their vital energy flames up and takes such shapes. Portents arise because of people. If people have no dissensions, they will not arise of themselves. When men abandon their constant ways, then portents arise . . .'

(Burton Watson (trans.), *The Tso Chuan* (New York, 1989),
pp. 207–8)

Pu Songling is also alluding here to a story given in the *Annals of the South* (a historical work of the Tang dynasty, 618–907), about a mandarin by the name of Liu Bolong, who, when reduced to poverty and determined to improve his circumstances by engaging in commerce, sees a troll standing by his side, laughing and rubbing his hands in glee. 'Poverty and wealth are matters of destiny,' reflects Liu aloud. 'But to be mocked by a troll . . .' As a consequence he abandons his plans. (The troll's laughter echoes the Confucian contempt towards merchants.)

Lines 18–21 *My talents pale . . . weird spirits*: Gan Bao (*fl.* 320), prominent official and historian, is credited with having compiled one of the earliest and most widely read and imitated medieval

collections of Weird Accounts, entitled *In Search of Spirits* (see
Minford and Lau, *Classical Chinese Literature*, I, pp. 651–65).

Lines 22–5 *My mood mirrors . . . strange tales*: Su Dongpo (1037–
1101), the great poet of the Song dynasty, was fond of ghost stories
and wrote his own. This shared love of strange tales is referred to
in an exchange of poems between the eminent statesman Wang
Shizhen and Pu Songling, dating from 1689, ten years after this
Preface.

Wang wrote to 'his friend Pu Songling, Teller of Tales':

> Bean arbour, gourd trellis, silken rain;
> Idle words, idly spoken, idly heard –
> Like Su the Poet and Teller of Tales,
> Of whom we are both so fond!
> The world's debates disdained;
> We loved to hear the songs of ghosts,
> Issuing from the graves of autumn.

Pu Songling replied:

> Threadbare gown, grey head, silken hair;
> Now my Book of Tales is done –
> An idle jest to share!
> Ten years have I tasted the joys
> Of Su the Teller of Tales and Poet –
> Of whom we are both so fond!
> Nocturnal conversations,
> Cold rain,
> Illuminated by a lamp of autumn.
>   (Zhang Youhe (1962), p. 34)

Actually we know that his 'Book of Tales' was far from 'done' in
1689. It seems that such was Pu Songling's love of the project, he
just kept on adding new items until he was a very old man.

Lines 30–32 *The matter . . . grown into a pile*: Herbert Giles comments, quoting from *The World* on Charles Dickens (24 July 1878):
'And his friends had the habit of jotting down for his unfailing
delight anything quaint or comic that they came across' (*Strange
Stories from a Chinese Studio*, 2nd edn (London, 1908), p. xiii, note
13).

Lines 33–5 *Here in the civilized world . . . Country of Cropped Hair*:
The *Historical Records* of Sima Qian (*c.* 145–*c.* 85 BC) records that

among the 'southern savages' (the then outlandish tribes of southern China) there were men with tattooed bodies and short-cropped hair. Such strange place-names are also to be found throughout *The Book of Hills and Seas* (probably third or second century BC). But Pu Songling can see 'strangeness' all around him. Judith T. Zeitlin comments: 'The cultural categories of strange and familiar, barbarian and civilized, are destabilized and inverted; the "geography of the imagination" has been relocated to the here and now, shifted back to the center. The point is that the strange is not other; the strange resides in our midst. The strange is inseparable from us' (*Historian of the Strange*, p. 47).

Lines 36–8 *Before our very eyes . . . Flying Heads*: A fabulous community, so called because heads were in the habit of leaving their bodies and flying down to marshy places to feed on worms and crabs. A red ring was seen the night before the flight, encircling the neck of the man whose head was about to fly; with the appearance of daylight, the head returned. Some said that the ears were used as wings; others that the hands also left the body and flew away. (Adapted from Giles, *Strange Stories*, p. xiii, note 15.) The story occurs in several early sources, including *Notes from Youyang*, a collection of accounts of curious and marvellous phenomena compiled by Duan Chengshi (*c.* 800–*c.* 863), who 'collected reports on the unseen or supernal worlds from persons who claimed expert knowledge of such places; for instance, he recorded a detailed description of the jewelled surface of the moon, transmitted by a mysterious visitor to the earth' (Edward H. Schafer, in *Indiana Companion to Traditional Chinese Literature*, ed. William Nienhauser (Bloomington, 1986), p. 940). Clearly Duan was another man after Pu Songling's own heart.

Lines 39–41 *My irrepressible transports . . . cannot be gainsaid*: A quotation from the 'Preface for Prince Teng's Pavilion', a much-admired and much-anthologized lyrical essay in elaborate parallel prose written by Wang Bo (*c.* 650–*c.* 676). It celebrates 'a superlative feast' given one autumn day on the estate of a local official in the southern city of Nanchang, in a pavilion named after the Prince of Teng:

> Our joyous songs wafted over the hills, our *unfettered rapture* [my italics] soared through the air. A pure breeze arose to the lively Music of Nature; white clouds loitered to the filigree strains of melody . . . As Heaven spread above us in its height, Earth lay below us in its immensity, we sensed the vast infinity of the Universe; as rapture came to

an end and sorrow took its place, we knew the fated succession of
contraries.

> (My translation, based on Richard Strassberg,
> *Inscribed Landscapes* (Berkeley, 1994))

Lines 42–4 *My far-soaring ideas . . . cannot be denied*: In *Redefining History: Ghosts, Spirits and Human Society in P'u Sung-ling's World, 1640–1715* (Ann Arbor, 1998), Chun-shu Chang and Shelley Hsueh-lun Chang see in this a reference to the poet of ecstasy, Li Bo (701–62).

Lines 47–9 *Just as the tale . . . can tell*: This refers to a 'tale' about Confucius (551–479 BC) and the burial of his mother. Confucius, who should properly have buried his mother in his father's grave, did not know the exact location of the grave and buried her instead at a place known as Five-Fathers Crossroad. Many scholars have chosen to regard this as 'baseless'. How could the great sage Confucius not have known the whereabouts of his father's burial place! But others consider it to be authentic, in view of the uncommon circumstances in which Confucius' father had married his mother (he was already over seventy years old and had nine daughters but only one son, a cripple). Still others have held that there is some profound hidden meaning behind the story regardless of its authenticity. (For more details, see the annotations in Chang and Chang's *Redefining History*.) Pu Songling uses this example to show the relative nature and possible shades of truth of so-called absurd stories.

Lines 50–52 *The tale of Three-Lives Rock . . . enlightenment*: The Three Lives are the previous, present and future. According to certain Buddhist schools of thinking, three rebirths are the minimum necessary to reach enlightenment: one for the planting of the seed, one for the ripening, and one for harvesting and liberation. The rock might be better named the Rock of Reincarnation. The tale referred to here is one of hundreds contained in the vast *Taiping Compendium*, compiled from 475 different sources in the early Song dynasty, in the years 977–8. A glance at the *Compendium*'s range of subjects shows a striking resemblance with *Strange Tales*: 'Taoist arts, feats of magic, Buddhist tales of reward and retribution (karma), omens, predestination, unusual officials and heroes, strange talents and arts, divination, tricks and jokes, immoral acts, dreams, ghosts and apparitions, oddities and grotesques, strange plants, animals and minerals, strange countries' (Edward H. Schafer, in *Sung Bibliography* (Hong Kong, 1978), p. 341). Of course, the

Compendium differs enormously from Pu Songling's work in that it is not the work of one hand but an encyclopedic ragbag of existing materials.

The story referred to, often retold by later writers, goes like this. A monk predicts his reincarnation to his friend, and when they meet again, twelve years later, on a hillside near the southern town of Hangzhou, the monk (now reborn as a boy riding a buffalo) is singing a song which begins with the words 'Here at the Rock of Three Lives, the same old soul . . .'

Lines 53–6 *My wild words . . . Who utters them*: See *Confucian Analects*, XV, 22: 'The superior man does not promote a man simply on account of his words, nor does he put aside good words because of the man.'

Line 59 *And the bow hung at his door*: According to ancient ritual, at the birth of a boy a wooden bow was suspended to the left of the door. Here the Preface changes to the autobiographical mode.

Line 67 *A black patch*: In other words, the child was the reincarnation of the Buddha. 'Black patch' can also be taken to mean Ink Records. The tales themselves are predestined.

Line 81 *He who sat with his face to the wall*: According to legend, the founder of Zen Buddhism, the Indian Bodhidharma, 'a fierce-looking fellow with a bushy beard and wide-open, penetrating eyes', is reputed to have arrived in China around AD 520. (See, for example, Alan Watts, *The Way of Zen* (London, 1957), p. 85.) When his doctrine was not at first accepted by Emperor Wu of Liang, he withdrew to a monastery (some say to the Shaolin Temple near Luoyang) where he sat for many years in meditation facing a wall. Here Pu Songling is referring to the Buddha or Buddhist monk who visited his father in a dream.

Line 83 *Surely stems from obstacles and delusions*: Delusion, *klesa*, is the affliction of troubled passion, the hindrance to enlightenment caused by negative human emotions such as distress, worry, anxiety, desire and fear. Bodhidharma was once asked by Emperor Wu what merit the Emperor had acquired by promoting Buddhism in practical ways, for example by building temples. 'None whatsoever!' replied Bodhidharma, going on to say that such outward acts of devotion still carried within them the seeds of delusion and karma, and that true merit could only be achieved by meditation.

Lines 86–90 *I have been blown . . . in the cesspit*: Pu Songling, in characteristically ambivalent fashion, switches from Buddhism to its opponents, here alluding to a well-known critic of the Buddhist doctrine of karma, Fan Zhen (*c.* 450–*c.* 515), author of the controversial

Treatise on the Extinction of the Soul. A conversation between Fan
and his patron, the devoutly Buddhist Prince of Jingling, is recorded
in the *Annals of the Liang Dynasty* (AD 636). 'If you do not believe in
the process of karma,' asked the Prince, 'how do you account for the
disparities that exist between wealth and poverty, rank and misery?'
Fan Zhen's reply includes many of the words used here by Pu Songling:

> Human life is like the flowers on a tree. Many branches grow on one
> tree. They all produce blossoms which fall where the wind blows them,
> some brushing against woven bamboo screens and falling on soft mats,
> some driven against walls and falling in cesspits. The former are fortu-
> nate men of rank (such as Your Highness), the latter unfortunate com-
> moners (such as myself). What does karma have to do with these
> different paths?

Fan's own philosophy was a Taoist one:

> Creation is a gift of nature, the infinite patterns of which evolve of
> themselves. Impalpably there is being of itself, and imperceptibly there
> is no longer being. When we come it is not because we cause being to
> come, and when we go it is not because we drive being away. We do
> but ride upon the principle of Heaven, and should each act in accord-
> ance with our own nature. Let lesser folk find sweetness in their culti-
> vated acres, and let superior men preserve their quiet simplicity . . .

(Based on Fung Yulan (Feng Youlan), *A History of Chinese Philos-
ophy*, trans. Derk Bodde, 2 vols. (Princeton, 1952–3), II, pp. 291–2.)
Lines 91–3 *The Six Modes of Transmigration . . . of their own*: The
Six Modes of Transmigration are the six modes of the Wheel of
Rebirth. We are back with Buddhism. Fung Yulan (Feng Youlan)
writes:

> The deeds or karma of each sentient being in successive past existences
> determine what he is to be in existences still to come. These rebirths
> take place on several different levels [modes]: that of the beings in the
> various hells, of animals, of human beings, of the divine beings in the
> various heavens . . . In their totality they constitute the wheel of life and
> death.

(*A History of Chinese Philosophy*, II, p. 237)

Line 101 *To The Infernal Regions*: The title of a no-longer-extant
collection of tales of the supernatural attributed to Liu Yiqing

(403–44). Liu was also the author of *New Accounts of Tales of the World* (see Minford and Lau, *Classical Chinese Literature*, I, pp. 665–73).

Lines 104–5 *My spleen . . . lonely anguish*: Here Pu Songling aligns himself with two great writers of the past: Han Feizi (d. 233 BC) and Sima Qian, the Grand Historian, author of the *Historical Records*, both of whom professed to write out of 'spleen'. In his chapter entitled 'Spleen', Han Feizi 'laments the iniquity of the age in general, and the corruption of officials in particular. He finally committed suicide in prison, where he had been cast by the intrigues of a rival minister.' (See Giles, *Strange Stories*, p. xv, note 31.)

Line 115 *Those who know me*: His true friends. See *Confucian Analects*, XIV: 'Alas! There is no one who knows me [for what I am].'

Lines 116–18 *Are in the green grove . . . At the dark frontier*: In a famous poem Du Fu (712–70) dreamed that he saw Li Bo (701–62) appear to him, 'coming when the maple-grove was still green, and returning while the frontier was dark'. That is to say, during the night, when no one could see him; the meaning being that he never came at all, and that those who 'know' Pu Songling are equally non-existent. In *Historian of the Strange* (p. 51), Zeitlin writes: 'His true readers [and his true friends] are wraiths, disembodied spirits, inhabiting the shadowy world of the dead and of dream; it is the writer who is alive and alone, crying out for someone to understand him.'

Glossary

Note: This informal glossary has been provided in the hope that more general readers might like some background on a few of the terms that recur throughout *Strange Tales*. It does not pretend to be either scholarly or original.

Academician Normally this title would imply membership of the elite **Hanlin Academy.**

alchemy Inner or Spiritual Alchemy (*neidan*) is a branch of Taoist self-cultivation using the terminology of Outer or Physical Alchemy (*waidan*), for self-cultivation and development. It has a certain resemblance to Carl Jung's definition of psychic alchemy in the Western tradition, as the 'transformation of the personality through the merging and blending together of the noble and base elements, the conscious and the unconscious' (quoted by Colin Wilson, *The Occult* (New York, 1971), p. 249; see also Joseph Needham, *Science and Civilisation in China*, 22 vols. (Cambridge, 1954–), vol. 5, part 5, section 33, 'Physiological Alchemy', pp. 2–20).

ancestors and ancestral, or spirit, tablets Small wooden boards on which the names and titles of the deceased are inscribed. The soul of the ancestor is widely believed to linger in the tablet, which in wealthier families is placed in a special shrine. (See Wolfram Eberhard, *A Dictionary of Chinese Symbols* (London, 1986), p. 18.)

bedsteads Since beds play such an important part in *Strange Tales*, it is worth pointing out that traditional Chinese bedsteads were large, curtained, live-in structures, somewhat like Western four-poster beds. Some of them even had antechambers. The great German authority on Chinese furniture, Gustav Ecke, refers to them as 'veritable alcove architecture' (*Chinese Domestic Furniture* (Peking, 1944), p. 8). Another authority, the American George Kates, calls them 'rooms within rooms': 'When the bed's curtains were drawn it formed a completely isolated sleeping unit, equipped with all necessaries, not altogether unlike a modern railway compartment' (*Chinese Household Furniture* (New York, 1948), pp. 47–8).

Benevolence and Filial Piety Benevolence, *ren*, has also been translated as Humanity, Altruism or True Manhood. Filial Piety, *xiao*, has sometimes been translated as Filial Submission. They were two key ethical terms in Confucian thought. In the first section of the *Confucian Analects*, the great sage says, 'Filial Piety and Brotherly Respect are the root of Benevolence.' When asked to define what he meant by Filial Piety, he replied, 'Never disobey [your parents].' It was this oppressive weight of obedience, respect and reverence towards parents and ancestors that was later so severely criticized and held to blame for Confucian conservatism and authoritarianism.

Board The traditional Chinese civil service was divided into six Boards or Ministries: Civil Office, Revenue, Works, Rites, War and Justice.

Bodhisattva A being destined for enlightenment who nonetheless postpones his or her own nirvana to save others. Guan Yin, often referred to in English as the Goddess of Mercy or Compassion, is in reality a Chinese female transformation of a male Bodhisattva.

bolus Traditional name for the large pill used in traditional Chinese medicine, often containing several herbal ingredients.

bound feet The tiny feet of Chinese women, mutilated in childhood and wrapped tightly in bandages for the rest of their life, were known euphemistically as Golden Lotuses. Although the custom seems more than strange to Western readers, it does not feature as an observed oddity in Pu Songling's *Tales*. To his fellow Chinese literati, bound feet were taken for granted, indeed they were greatly appreciated and much eulogized. When young ladies in the *Tales* are observed to hobble with some difficulty along the highway, it would be assumed automatically that they did so because their feet were bound.

bow, with clasped hands (*gongshou*) This form of salutation is often referred to in passing in the *Tales*. It involves raising the joined hands (concealed in sleeves, the fingers of the right hand enclosing those of the left, the thumbs meeting in front) to the forehead, mouth or chin, according to the degree of respect to be shown, and making at the same time a slight inclination of the head, as a salute. (Based on Gilbert W. Walshe, *Ways That Are Dark* (Shanghai, 1906), p. 48.)

Buddhism The third of the three Chinese religions, and the only one of foreign extraction. See also **Dharma**.

cap, mandarin This distinctive item of clothing, made of silk, was a little like the traditional Western university don's mortar-board, but with protruding 'antennae' on each side.

cards (visiting cards) Strips of red paper, about seven inches long by three and a quarter broad, bearing the name of the person, and used for formal visits. The servant goes on ahead to announce his master's arrival to the gate-keeper, and to present his master's card, which is taken in and given to another servant. The visitor is carried through several courtyards as far as the first closed gate, where he remains seated in his chair, supported by his bearers, until a servant appears from within, holding the visitor's card aloft in his hand and inviting the guest to enter with the word '*Qing!*' (Based on Walshe, *Ways That Are Dark*, p. 47.)

catty (*jin*) The Chinese 'pound', a basic measure of weight, equivalent to approx. 1.3 British pounds.

censors (*yushi, duchayuan*) These all-important officials (both metropolitan and local) were given as part of their enormous powers the 'responsibility of maintaining disciplinary surveillance over the whole of officialdom, checking records and auditing accounts in government offices, accepting public complaints, and impeaching officials who in their private or public lives violated the law or otherwise conducted themselves improperly' (Charles Hucker, *A Dictionary of Official Titles in Imperial China* (Stanford, 1985), p. 592).

Cinnabar, and Cinnabar Field (*dantian*) Cinnabar is the most important substance used in Taoist **alchemy**, and is the 'elixir' which the Taoist adept distils through his various practices. In Outer Alchemy, purified Cinnabar was claimed to confer actual immortality, while in Inner Alchemy, Cinnabar represented the energy of combined **Yin** and **Yang** kindled in the Cinnabar Field, the tripartite (upper, middle and lower) mid-region of the human body (the lower abdomen, three inches below the navel) through which the vital **energy** *qi* flows. The lower Cinnabar Field is of particular importance in connection with Taoist practices aimed at the prolongation of life, because here not only energy in a general sense but more specifically a man's semen and a woman's menstrual flow are accumulated. 'It is the root of the human being. Here men keep their semen and women their menstrual blood. It houses the gate of harmonious union of Yin and Yang ... It is called the Palace-that-keeps-the-Essence.' (Based on Kristofer Schipper, *The Taoist Body* (Berkeley, 1993), pp. 152–9. See also Ingrid Fischer-Schreiber, *The Shambhala Dictionary of Taoism* (Boston, 1996), pp. 160–62.)

Cold Food Festival Falls on the day before the annual ancestral **Qing Ming Festival**, which is usually around 5 April. Nothing hot is eaten, and no fires are permitted for cooking, out of respect for the dead.

Confucianism and neo-Confucianism This State ideology pervaded Chinese society from the Han dynasty (second century BC) until the early twentieth century. Based loosely on the teachings of Confucius (551–479 BC) and his foremost disciples and successors, it placed social cohesion and loyalty to ancestors, father and Emperor above all other considerations. This was often in conflict with the more subversive and consciousness-centred beliefs of Taoism and Buddhism, but over the years the Confucianists exhibited a remarkable knack for absorbing and co-opting their own 'opposition'.

congee Thin rice gruel popular in many parts of East Asia.

county, department, district The basic administrative units of the provinces were in ascending order: county (*xian*, sometimes called district), department (*zhou*), sub-prefecture (*ting*), prefecture (*fu*), circuit (*dao*) and province (*sheng*). There were hierarchies of magistrates at all levels.

degrees and examinations Pu Songling frequently refers in his tales to the Chinese bureaucracy, and to the ancient and elaborate system of examinations and degrees, of which he himself had fallen victim – what Ichisada Miyazaki calls *China's Examination Hell* (New Haven, 1981). This system was virtually the only channel for success and status in society and for recognition in the intellectual community. The following is a *greatly* simplified sketch of how things worked (and continued to work until the abolition of the system in 1905), to help readers of the *Tales*.

There were three principal stages. The first consisted of the local or district examination, which took place every year in each prefectural city, producing the graduates of the first degree, *xiucai*, literally 'budding talent'. (This was as far as Pu Songling ever rose, despite his extraordinary abilities.) Next came the provincial examination, which was held triennially at the provincial capital, lasted nine days and produced the graduates of the second degree, *juren*, literally 'elevated men'. The third examination, the metropolitan examination, was held triennially in Peking during the third month of the year after the provincial examinations, and was followed a month later by the palace examination, *dianshi*, out of which emerged the crème de la crème, the holders of the third degree, *jinshi*, literally 'advanced scholar'. The three degrees are sometimes approximately referred to in English (e.g. by Herbert Giles) as the Bachelor's, Master's and Doctor's degrees. All the examinations stressed classical literary knowledge and the ability to write formal compositions in eight sections, the so-called **Eight-Legged Essays** or Octopartites.

Sometimes Pu Songling's purpose in depicting the system is satirical, sometimes it is no more than a reflection of what was a universal experience of every educated Chinese gentleman. In the words of the historian Etienne Balazs, China was, and still is in many ways, a 'permanently bureacratic society' (*Chinese Civilisation and Bureaucracy* (New Haven, 1964)).

Dharma At once the Buddhist Doctrine and Universal Law, which are held by Buddhists to be two aspects of the same thing. The essence of Dharma was considered to be the Chain of Causation, the Wheel of Rebirth, from which Buddhism aimed to set men free. Gautama Buddha taught the doctrine of the Four Noble Truths: (1) that suffering exists; (2) that its cause is thirst, craving or desire; (3) that there is an overcoming of suffering through (4) the self-training or self-cultivation of the Noble Eightfold Path.

door-curtains Sometimes called 'portières', this feature of Chinese interiors can often be seen depicted in the illustrations included in this volume.

dragons One of the supreme symbols of Chinese culture. Whereas the Western dragon is often the primordial enemy, combat with which is the ultimate test of virtue, the Chinese dragon is essentially an auspicious and spiritual beast, embodying cosmic energy and representing the **Yang** principle. It is also a symbol of power, and associated with the Emperor.

dreams The identification of dreams with actual excursions of the souls of dreamers is general in China. When the soul of a dreamer is out of his body, it may travel in a short time over enormous distances. (Based on J. J. M. de Groot, *The Religious System of China*, 6 vols. (Leiden, 1892–1910), IV, p. 118.)

elixir The alchemical elixir of immortality, the Inner **Cinnabar**.

energy (*qi*) The word, which occurs throughout *Strange Tales*, has many possible translations in addition to 'energy': spirit, force, atmosphere, tone, manner, aura, breath, pneuma (this last is Joseph Needham's idea). There is a *qi* of Heaven (in modern usage, *tianqi* means 'weather'), and a *qi* of Earth; a *qi* of morning and a *qi* of evening; a *qi* of spring and a *qi* of autumn. There is a **Yin** *qi* and a **Yang** *qi* (their interaction can reinforce or diminish each other). In my home district of France, just north of the Pyrenees, the Yin *qi* is clearly visible when the mists come in from the sea (the wind known as the 'Marin'), bringing with them humidity and rain, and the Yang *qi* can be sensed in the air the instant the wind blows from the hills to the north (the 'Tramontane', known in Provence further east as the 'Mistral'), dispersing the clouds and bringing sun and clear blue skies.

The Tao is made manifest in *qi*. Zhang Jingyue, in *The Contents of the Classic of Internal Medicine Arranged by Subject* (1624), gives some idea of the all pervasive nature of *qi*:

Change, both inception and transformation, rests on *qi*, and there is no being in the Cosmos that does not originate from it. Thus *qi* envelops the Cosmos from without and moves the Cosmos from within. How else than by *qi* can the sun and moon, the planets and the fixed stars shine, can thunder resound and rain, wind and clouds be formed, can all things rise, mature, bear fruit, and withdraw in the Course of the Four Seasons? Man's existence too depends entirely upon this *qi*.

But perhaps an anecdote illustrates *qi* better than any explanation or list of definitions. I copied it down many years ago into a commonplace book from the Introduction to William Acker's *Some T'ang and Pre-T'ang Texts on Chinese Painting* (Leiden, 1954), p. xxix. It could just as easily have come from the Taoist *Book of Zhuangzi*, or indeed from *Strange Tales*:

It was quite natural for the Chinese to conceive of the *qi* flowing about not only within the body but as flowing from body to body, or from the body into material things. In 1934 when I was in Taiyuan in Shanxi to visit the archaeological sites . . . I had the privilege of meeting Mr Ke Huang, then Director of the Provincial Library in that city. He is a distinguished calligrapher and I had the unusual pleasure of watching him write large characters. He stood, feet planted firmly like a fencer, before a large table, on the other side of which stood a servant who leaned across it grasping the top of a large sheet of paper. As Mr Ke wrote, humming to himself and moving the big brush about for all the world like a fencer his foil, the servant kept pulling the paper towards him, so that Mr Ke did not have to change his position. The brush he used was a large one, about four inches thick where the hairs were tied and entered the wooden handle, and I noticed that after plunging it into the ink he would dig his fingers in among the hairs of the brush instead of keeping them on the handle. I asked him why he did so, pointing out that after all it meant that he could never get his hands quite clean, since he was in the habit of writing large characters every day, and he replied that in so doing the *qi* flowed down through his arm and through his fingertips directly into the ink itself, and thence onto the paper where some of it would remain, animating the characters even after the ink had dried. This story provides a good illustration of how concrete and almost tangible a thing *qi* is in Chinese thinking.

Essay, Eight-Legged The core of the Chinese educational curriculum and the most important subject in the official examinations for nearly five hundred years. For a detailed example, and a explanation of the

rhetorical mechanics of writing such things, see vol. IV of the eighteenth-century novel *The Story of the Stone* (Harmondsworth, 1982),
Chapters 82 and 84, and Appendix 2 on Octopartite Composition.

eunuchs In China, when a eunuch was castrated, both penis and
testicles were removed. It is surprising that eunuchs survived this at
all. An interesting account of this question is by Dr Jean-Jacques
Matignon, in his book *La Chine Hermètique* (Paris, 1898). As doctor to the French legation in Peking, Matignon once had occasion
to treat a young eunuch.

fox-spirits (*hulijing*) The fox-spirit or 'were-vixen' has haunted the
Chinese imagination until the present day. What follows are one or
two notes on foxes taken from various sources. See also the relevant
section in the Introduction, pp. xxi–xxiv.

The reason why the fox was credited with special sexual associations:

> must probably be sought for in the combination of two elements. First,
> the ancient belief in the abundant vital essence of the fox. And second,
> its proclivity to play pranks on man . . . When a fox is fifty years old, it
> acquires the ability to change itself into a woman. At a hundred it can
> assume the shape of a beautiful girl, or that of a sorcerer, or also that
> of an adult man who has sexual intercourse with women. At that age
> the fox knows what is happening at a distance of a thousand *li*, it can
> derange [bewitch] the human mind and reduce a person to an imbecile.
> When the fox is a thousand years old, it is in communication with
> Heaven, and is called the Heavenly Fox.
>
> (*Xuanzhongji*, in van Gulik, *Sexual Life in Ancient China*
> (Leiden, 1961), p. 210. Compare de Groot, V, pp. 586–7)

The fox has always been an erotic symbol, and was sometimes
associated with venereal diseases. Many stories tell how a ravishingly
beautiful girl appears one night to a young scholar while he is
studying, and how he makes love to her. She disappears in the early
morning but comes back each evening. The scholar gets weaker and
weaker – until a Taoist informs him that the girl is really a fox which
is sucking him dry in order to imbibe the essence of immortality.
(Based on Eberhard, *A Dictionary of Chinese Symbols*, pp. 117–18.
See for example Tale 54, 'Lotus Fragrance'.)

'Father Mullin speaks of a shrine in Shandong of peculiar structure, with an opening so narrow that worshippers were obliged to
crawl in and out on their hands and knees. Tiny women's shoes
were given as offerings . . . The shrine was built over a spot where

foxes were supposed to formerly have had their den' (Juliet Bredon and Igor Mitrophanow, *The Moon Year* (Shanghai, 1927), p. 417, note 9).

Nicholas Dennys writes that part of traditional fox-lore is the idea that:

> when crossing a frozen river or lake the fox advances very slowly and deliberately, putting his head down close to the ice and listening for the sound of water beneath ... Below the ice is the region of the Yin or female element – the dark world of death and obscurity – while above it is the region of the Yang or male element – the bright world of life and activity. Thus the fox is represented as living on the debatable land which is neither the Earth of life nor the Hades of death. His dwelling place on the earth is among the tombs, or actually, rather, within the tomb, and the spirits of the deceased often occupy his body. Thus he enables ghosts of the dead to return to life or himself performs their terrible behest – visiting upon living men and women the iniquities they have committed against those now dead and by this means bringing peace and rest to the souls of the latter which would else be travelling and troubling for ever.
>
> (*The Folk-Lore of China* (London, 1876), p. 94, quoting the British consular official Thomas Watters, who wrote 'Chinese Fox-Myths')

ghosts (*gui*) In Chinese thinking, the boundary between this world and the world beyond is much more elastic than it is for us, and belief in ghosts and spirits is taken more seriously. (Based on Eberhard, *A Dictionary of Chinese Symbols*, p. 273.) See also hungry ghosts.

'Man consists of the beneficial substances that compose the Heavens and the earth, of the co-operation of the Yin and the Yang, and of the union of a *gui* with a *shen* [see **soul**]; he consists of the finest breath of the Five Elements ... Confucius said: "The *qi* [see **energy**] is the full manifestation of the *shen*, and the *po* is the full manifestation of the *gui*; the union of the *gui* with the *shen* is the highest among all tenets. Living beings are all sure to die, and as they certainly return (*gui*) to the Earth after their death, the soul (which accompanies them thither) is called *gui*. But while the bones and flesh moulder in the ground and mysteriously become earth of the fields, the *qi* issues forth and manifests itself on high as a shining *ming* (light)"' (from the ?third-century BC Confucian classic *Li Ji* or *Record of Rites*; see de Groot, IV, pp. 3–4).

Hanlin Academy Membership of the august Imperial Hanlin Academy (*Hanlin* means literally Forest of Pencils) was the highest literary distinction attainable in China. As an institution it sat at the pinnacle of the whole examination and civil service system, combining the functions of an Academy of Letters (the Imperial centre for Confucian scholarship and instruction of the Emperor and his family) with those of a College of Heralds. (Based on L. C. Arlington and William Lewisohn, *In Search of Old Peking* (Peking, 1935), p. 16.) Numbers were limited to about five hundred, and the higher members were by virtue of their status advisers to the Emperor, and available for appointment to the highest offices, thus constituting an elite of the elite within the Chinese civil service system.

Heaven and Hell Buddhism believes in a horrible and ingeniously cruel series of hells or purgatories (*diyu*, literally 'earth-prison'), where punishment is carried out through long aeons (kalpas, *jie*), before the souls are purged and fit for rebirth. The sinner is sentenced by an infernal judge. In many respects the Chinese hells resemble the hells of Hinduism, but in China a note of more abject terror coupled with a refinement of torture have been introduced. (Based on Karl Ludvig Reichelt, *Truth and Tradition in Chinese Buddhism* (Shanghai, 1927), p. 82.)

hungry ghosts (*egui*) The **ghosts** of those who have suffered a wrong that has not been righted. A class of beings (pretas) with tiny pin-sized heads and huge stomachs, so that, no matter how much they eat, they are in perpetual hunger. The All Souls' Feast, celebrated by Buddhists on the night of the fifteenth day of the seventh month, was for the purpose of appeasing these hungry ghosts by providing food and clothing for them. (Based on Kenneth Ch'en, *Buddhism in China: A Historical Survey* (Princeton, 1964), p. 5, note 1.)

illusion (*huan*) Judith T. Zeitlin, writing about Tale 6, 'The Painted Wall', remarks:

> Pu Songling explores the paradox implicit in the conventional Buddhist wisdom that the phenomenological world is no more than illusion. If the superior mind views everything, both real and unreal, with indifference, then any idea of illusion is eliminated as well. On the other hand, to be guided beyond illusion, images must first be conjured up, and the more seductive and puzzling the images are, the more shattering and profound enlightenment will be.
>
> (*Historian of the Strange*, p. 192)

This theme, a recurring one in Chinese fiction, also pervades the eighteenth-century novel *The Story of the Stone*.

Immortal (*xian*) A transcendent, eternally youthful being, the supreme

Taoist adept, who through occult practice has mastered supernatural and magical skills, and attained physical and spiritual immortality beyond time and space.

Imperial College (*guozi-jian*) The highest government institute of learning, with its seat in a large group of buildings near the Temple of Confucius in the north-east corner of Peking.

incubus 'An *incubus* is a male demon that seeks sexual intercourse with women in their sleep; hence, a nightmare; hence a person or thing that oppresses one as does a nightmare. Etymologically, a person lying *on* another' (Eric Partridge, *Usage and Abusage* (Harmondsworth, 1963), p. 314). 'The name given in the Middle Ages to a male demon which was supposed to haunt women in their sleep, and to whose visits the birth of witches and demons was attributed' (*Encyclopaedia Britannica*, 11th edn, vol. 14 (1911), p. 369). Several of the *Tales* deal with this phenomenon (e.g. Tale 35, 'The Merchant's Son', where the incubus is a fox; Tale 78, 'The Clay Scholar'; and Tale 98, 'The Southern Wutong-Spirit', where the incubus is part of a local cult).

The old Chinese sex handbooks gave advice on the consequences of intercourse with ghosts (see Introduction, pp. xxiv–xxv):

> The after-effects of copulation with an incubus can be cured by the following method. Let the man and the woman have intercourse day and night without cease, without the man ever ejaculating. After seven days of this, the woman will be cured. If the man becomes fatigued and he cannot continue the act, then let him keep his member inside the woman, without moving it – this too is good. If this disease is not treated as indicated here, the victim will die in a few years.
>
> (From a handbook dated to the Sui dynasty (581–618), based on van Gulik, *Sexual Life*, p. 152)

karma The law according to which our thoughts, words and actions in one life produce modifications of our inner being, thus determining the exact nature and circumstances of our next incarnation, and in every way causing us to reap what we have sown and, while reaping, to sow again. (See John Blofeld, *The Wheel of Life* (London, 1972), p. 13.)

kowtow Literally, to 'knock the head'. In *Hobson-Jobson* (London, 1886), Henry Yule and A. C. Burnell write: 'The salutation used in China before the Emperor, his representatives, or his symbols, made by prostrations repeated a fixed number of times, the forehead touching the ground at each prostration. It is also used as the most respectful form of salutation from children to parents, and from servants to masters on formal occasions.'

Lantern Festival The period from the thirteenth to the seventeenth of the first lunar month is called the Lantern Festival, but it is the fifteenth that is the true festival. The origin of this festival, when householders hang lanterns over their doors and put up fir branches to attract prosperity and longevity, is supposed to date from the Han dynasty. The older festival evolved through custom into an occasion of pure enjoyment. Under the Tang dynasty (618–907), some Emperors, not content with looking at the illuminations of their capital from high observation towers like their predecessors, went out into the streets incognito. So did their ladies. Amorous adventures were frequent, and the carnival spirit held sway. (Based on Tun Li-ch'en, *Annual Customs and Festivals* (Peiping, 1936), pp. 6–9, and Bredon and Mitrophanow, *The Moon Year*, pp. 133–4.)

literati (*wenren*) See **scholars and students**.

luck (*fu*) A man born into this world is supposed to have a definite quantity of luck, or predestined happiness, awarded to him for his enjoyment. Some people have more than others. A man whose children die young, or a man who has a beautiful country home but is unable to live in it, is said to have 'no luck to enjoy them'. On the other hand, a man who enjoys too much, or who enjoys inordinately, or enjoys what is not appropriate, as, for instance, receiving a kowtow from an elderly gentleman older than himself, is said to 'curtail his luck' or shorten his life. (Based on Lin Yutang, *The Importance of Living* (London, 1938), p. 448.)

Manchu dynasty See **Qing dynasty**.

palanquins, sedan-chairs The palanquin was the superior (i.e. larger) version of the customary mode of transportation used by upper-class Chinese in traditional times, sometimes described as 'a box-litter'. It is a Portuguese form of a Hindi word, and it was in use throughout India, Malaya, the Dutch East Indies (Indonesia) and China. *Sedan-chair* is the word used for the simpler single-seater, carried by two bearers. There were rules for how many bearers a palanquin could have: sixteen for the Emperor, eight for a Prince of the Blood or a very high-ranking official, four for lesser officials.

piba-mandolin A Chinese musical instrument with four strings, in sound somewhat resembling the mandolin, but larger, and therefore often, though inaccurately, given the conventional English translation 'lute'.

portières See **door-curtains**.

predestined affinity (*yuanfen*) This means the supposed occult and inscrutable chain of causes or attractions that operate to bring together those who have an affinity for each other or who are pre-destined to be joined together. Marriages are predestined. Thus fate reaches down to the home, as into other fields of life. One's family connections are 'recorded and settled by Heaven', in previous existences. They were 'fixed in a former life', on account of the actions and feelings of the couple there. (Based on Calvin Wilson Mateer, *Mandarin Lessons* (Shanghai, 1903), p. 548.) The following related proverbs are based on Clifford Plopper, *Chinese Religion Seen through the Proverb* (Shanghai, 1926), pp. 295–7.

Children, husbands and wives are a retribution for enmities in a former life. (This thread of affinity, running from one incarnation into another, is of course unconscious, as both parties have drunk of the Cup of Oblivion. Where there is this pre-existing relationship, marriages are consummated even though the parties are widely separated, and without it even playmates are nothing to each other.) *When there is a predestined affinity, friends will come a thousand li to meet; and when there is none, they will not become acquainted though face to face.* (Those who have deeply loved in former lives are often permitted to return together and enter again into the same relationship. On the other hand, it is likely to be the doom of enemies to work out the repayment of their former enmities in a marital connection in a succeeding existence.) *Husband and wife were enemies and did evil to each other in a previous life; sons and daughters all come to collect debts.* (Thus is destiny bringing about the just government of the universe, in the marriage union.)

Qing dynasty The Manchu conquerors called their dynasty Qing, or Clear (as their Chinese predecessors had called theirs Ming, or Bright). Thus the two words *Qing* and *Manchu* when used for the dynasty refer to the same period, Manchu being the ethnic designation, Qing the dynastic.

Qing Ming Festival This annual festival usually falls during the first half of the month of April. It is the occasion for sweeping the graves and honouring the dead. Because whole families often went out to the family tombs (including the womenfolk), the festival (like the **Lantern Festival**) is often the setting in Chinese fiction for 'chance' or 'romantic' encounters, with interesting consequences.

raksha (*luosha*) From the Sanskrit. A type of malignant spirit or demon, devourer of men, similar to a **yaksha**. Described as terrifying, with black bodies, red hair and green eyes.

reincarnation This originally Hindu and Buddhist concept, sometimes

expressed in other terms – transmigration, rebirth – plays a very
important part in many of Pu Songling's *Tales*. It must not be
forgotten that by Pu Songling's time, **Buddhism** had already been
absorbed into Chinese culture for many centuries and had come to
exercise a deep influence on the two indigenous creeds of Taoism
and **Confucianism** (and neo-Confucianism). Thus basic Buddhist
ideas such as reincarnation had become an integral part of Chinese
culture. Multi-incarnational plots (as in many of the *Tales*) are
often hard to follow for the Western reader, not accustomed to the
Buddhist idea of the never-ceasing Wheel or Cycle or Round of Life
and Death, *samsāra* (what the Chinese call *lunhui*, literally the
'Turning of the Wheel'). Suffering (and most of the detail of plot
that stems from it) is the consequence of a human's being bound to
this wheel by the continuing action of **karma**. As Derk Bodde,
translator of the modern philosopher Fung Yulan (Feng Youlan),
points out, while true Buddhist thought 'denies the existence of an
enduring entity (soul, ego or *ātman*), which is carried along with
karma into [another] existence ... most Chinese interpreted the
cycle of transmigration to mean that there is an enduring soul which
does not perish' (*A History of Chinese Philosophy*, 2 vols. (Princeton, 1952–3), II, p. 286, note 1).

This rebirth of a soul can happen on or between a variety of levels
(deity, man, animal, hungry ghost and denizen of Hell) and in a
variety of ways. 'A departed human soul may pass into the body of
another deceased person, and thus resuscitate it [usually, but not
always, causing no physical change]. [Or alternatively] an
excarnated soul may obtain a new body by being reborn through a
mother' (de Groot, IV, p. 143).

One of the most common terms for being reborn, *toutai*, is defined
as 'making one's way into a womb, passing into the womb, as the
spirit of a dead person does when sent back to earth for rebirth' in
Herbert Giles, *A Chinese Biographical Dictionary* (London, 1898);
and 'quicken, to be reborn into another state of existence' in R. H.
Mathews, *Chinese–English Dictionary* (Shanghai, 1931), p. 943.
De Groot comments: 'Rebirth may be connected with change of sex'
(*The Religious System of China*, IV, p. 147).

In the light of the widespread acceptance of this doctrine among
the Chinese, De Groot remarks memorably: 'Evangelists in China
must hardly feel astonished at finding that the Lord's resurrection,
which they preach, makes little impression on the reading class, in
the eyes of whom that miracle must appear a very commonplace
event' (IV, p. 124). Of course, the idea of reincarnation has a long

history in the West, from the ancient Greeks (Orphism, Pythagoras) to the present day. Tolstoy, himself greatly influenced by Eastern thought, wrote this in 1908:

> Our whole life is a dream. The dreams of our present life are the environment in which we work out the impressions, thoughts, feelings of a former life. As we live through thousands of dreams in our present life, so is our present life only one of thousands of such lives which we enter from the other, more real life – and then return to after death. Our life is but one of the dreams of that more real life. I believe in it. I know it. I see it without a doubt.
>
> (*Voice of Universal Love* 40 (Moscow, 1908), quoted in Sheila Ostrander and Lynn Schroeder, *PSI: Psychic Discoveries behind the Iron Curtain* (London, 1977), pp. 168–9)

scholars and students In an important sense, the entire mandarin elite in traditional China consisted of 'scholars' and 'students'. But neither word carries with it much of its normal English baggage. The 'scholars' were not necessarily at all scholarly, and the 'students' were usually neither young nor bohemian. But they were all, by virtue of their training, literati, scholar-gentlemen. In that sense, the early Jesuits were right to say that China was Plato's dream come true, a land ruled by philosophers and men of letters.

Passing the various **degrees and examinations** could be a lifelong and frustrating occupation (as Pu Songling knew from bitter experience). Wu Jingzi's brilliant eighteenth-century satirical novel *The Scholars* provides a wonderful gallery of these lifelong 'mature students'. When a character is introduced in *Strange Tales* as a 'scholar' or a 'student' there is no way of telling at first what age he may be. All one knows for sure is that he is part of the mandarin elite. Therefore I have often translated these words as 'gentleman'.

sedan-chairs See **palanquins**.

shadows It is a matter of public opinion in China that **ghosts**, when showing themselves in a human shape, have no shadows. In truth, they are bodiless and mere shadows or souls themselves, and a shadow of a shadow is something hardly imaginable. (See de Groot, *The Religious System of China*, IV, p. 88.)

sing-song girls This all-purpose term, frequently encountered in *Strange Tales*, covers a variety of different types of women who offered their services for hire in traditional Chinese cities. At the top level, they were skilful musicians (their preferred instrument being the four-stringed **piba**), writers and performers of lyrics, trained dancers and geisha-like courtesans, rather than simple prostitutes. Such high-level sing-song girls would be regularly invited to entertain at official banquets. They often had long-standing relations with prominent members of society, and as Robert van Gulik points out in *Sexual Life in Ancient China* (p. 181), they offered their clients not just carnal pleasure but 'a welcome relief from the often oppressive atmosphere of the women's quarters and the compulsory sexual relations' that characterized the typical Chinese upper-class household. (An excellent depiction of this *demi-monde* in nineteenth-century Shanghai can be found in the 1998 film by Hou Hsiao-hsien, *Flowers of Shanghai*, itself based on a well-written novel from the last years of the Manchu dynasty.)

soul (*shen, gui, hun, po*) Of the two souls attributed to man by ancient Chinese philosophy, the *shen* or immaterial soul emanates from the ethereal part of the Cosmos, and consists of **Yang** substance. When operating actively in the living human body, it is called *qi* or 'breath' (energy) and *hun*; when separated from it after death, it exists as a refulgent spirit, styled *ming* (bright). The *gui*, the material, substantial soul, emanates from the terrestrial part of the Universe, and is formed of **Yin** substance. In living man it operates under the name of *po*, and on his death it returns to the Earth. The *jing*, sometimes translated as 'seminal essence', signifies a certain force or fluid that dwells in man, constituting the working energy of his soul, its effective power. (Based on de Groot, *The Religious System of China*, IV, pp. 5 and 10.)

strange (*qi*) Sometimes translated 'rare', *qi* (written with a quite different character from the *qi* meaning 'energy') is really an untranslatable word. Literally it means 'remarkable', 'strange', 'extraordinary', but it has definite associations not fully expressed by the word 'remarkable'. 'There must go with it a subjective love of the unusual, the unconventional and the unattainable by common men. Tired of the humdrum world and the common run of men and things, one is on the lookout for *qi* or rare books, rocks, peaks, flowers, perfumes, delicacies, jewels, curios, etc.' (Lin Yutang, *The Importance of Living*, p. 455).

studio (*zhai*) The Chinese scholar-gentleman's studio is the backdrop to this whole collection, the arena in which these *Tales* take place. Pu Songling has peopled the universe of the studio with the creatures of the scholar-gentleman's mind. It is both highly refined, the home environment of a class where letters and ritual were greatly prized, and also animated by a rich and sometimes violent energy. It is a microcosm of traditional male-dominated Chinese society.

succubus Female demon supposed to have sexual intercourse with men in their sleep; hence, a demon or evil spirit or, metaphorically, a whore; *succuba*, a variant, is rare. (Based on Partridge, *Usage and Abusage*, p. 314.)

tael (*liang*) The common 'Chinese ounce' measure (16 taels make one **catty**). One tael of silver (equivalent to roughly 37.5 grams) was theoretically worth a thousand cash, or copper coins. Silver changed hands in the form of ingots, which had to be weighed to ascertain their value. Here are one or two examples of the value of the silver tael, taken from Craig Clunas, *Superfluous Things* (Urbana, 1991). (Clunas is writing about a slightly earlier period.)

Prime land in the late Ming cost between 28 and 40 taels per hectare. In 1614, the Prince of Fu spent 280,000 taels of silver on the building of a new mansion for himself in the city of Luoyang. A vast chief eunuch's palace changed hands for 700 taels (this, and the following items, are from the novel *Golden Lotus*). The Wanli Emperor paid 150 taels for an unusually large antique ceramic vase of Jun ware. A luxurious lacquered bed inlaid with mother of pearl was valued at 60 taels. A good meal for two with wine in a restaurant cost 0.13 taels. Seven women's silk garments cost 6.5 taels. The official annual salary of a President of a Board was 152 taels (to be greatly magnified by presents and bribes). The annual remuneration of a mercenary soldier was around 6 taels in the 1550s.

Tao, Taoism, Taoist (*dao*) The word is written 'Dao' in the new romanization, and is pronounced like the Arabian boat (dhow). I have preferred to keep the old spelling, which has become familiar in the West and frequently occurs in modern dictionaries of the English language. Throughout these stories we meet Taoist priests and hermits (genuine and not so genuine), we encounter traditions and ways of thinking and living which are more or less vaguely referred to as Taoist, and we hear tell of something ineffable called the Tao. To the initiated reader, all of this is understood; to the outsider, it remains a mystery. To attempt to define or describe any of these terms in a glossary would be a foolishly un-Taoist enterprise. To avoid the issue altogether would be dishonest. One of the best things to do instead is to recommend some of the old Taoist texts, which tend to be in either poetic or storytelling form. The two great early Taoist classics (probably fifth and fourth centuries BC) are *The Way and Its Power* (translated countless times; Arthur Waley's 1934 version is one of the best) and *The Book of Zhuangzi* (Burton Watson's 1968 translation, *The Complete Works of Chuang Tzu*, remains the most readable). Zhuangzi was much admired by Oscar

Wilde, who called his book one of the most 'caustic critiques of modern life' and quoted from it in his 1891 essay 'The Soul of Man under Socialism'. A series of Taoist extracts can be found in Minford and Lau, *Classical Chinese Literature*, I: pp. 202–20 and 226–33 (the third Taoist classic, *The Book of Liezi*); pp. 307–9 (the magnificent poem 'The Bones of Zhuangzi'); pp. 445–73 (the Seven Sages of the Bamboo Grove were archetypal Taoists); and pp. 491–521 and 721–63 (the poets Tao Yuanming and Li Bo).

But Taoism has ramifications far beyond these texts. Indeed, it can be said to permeate Chinese life and thought. Scholars, intellectuals and translators are often less able to communicate the spirit of Taoism than artists, poets and storytellers. One of the most popular exponents of 'living Taoism' of our time was Alan Watts. Another was Lin Yutang, who wrote: 'The object of human wisdom is to fall in line with Tao or the ways and laws of Nature and live in harmony with them. A man who attains this happy state is said "to have attained the Tao" ... One who has found the Tao thereby finds himself also' (*The Importance of Living*, p. 449).

Taoist priests, unlike their Buddhist counterparts, kept their hair long, and in general led far less austere lives. They had a much more liberal attitude, for example, towards drinking wine and sexual intercourse. They also dabbled regularly in alchemical practices.

Troubles The Troubles referred to frequently in *Strange Tales* are the social and political disturbances during the mid-seventeenth-century period of transition from the Ming to the Qing/Manchu dynasty, the chaotic and often violent period during which Pu Songling grew up, and whose excesses clearly made a deep impression on him. See for example Tale 27, 'Wailing Ghosts'.

uncanny (*yao*) One of the most frequently occurring words in the Chinese vocabulary of the strange or weird, used for evil spirits, monsters, demons, fairies, foxes, goblins, magic, sorcery, omens, ill-boding and anything spooky or supernatural. By extension, it is used of seductive women, who fascinate and bewitch.

watches of the night Just as the Chinese have their own lunar calendar, so they have their own traditional system of counting time. A Chinese Hour or *chen* contains two Western hours. There are twelve such double-hours in a day, named after the Twelve Celestial Branches, and falling under the corresponding twelve animal signs. The day 'begins' at 11 p.m., with the Chinese Hour *zi*, the Hour of the Rat; the Chinese Hour *chou*, the Hour of the Ox, lasts from 1 a.m. to 3 a.m.; the Chinese Hour *yin*, the Hour of the Tiger, lasts from 3 a.m. to 5 a.m., etc. Independently of this there are five watches of the night. 'The first watch lasts from 7 p.m. to 9 p.m., and is shown by one blow on the street-watchman's hollow bamboo tube; the second watch is from 9 p.m. to 11 p.m. and is signalled by two beats etc.' (Based on J. Dyer Ball, *Things Chinese, or Notes Connected with China*, 5th edn (London, 1925), p. 664.)

windows, paper windows and lattice-work Wooden frames covered with a semi-transparent paper are used all over the northern provinces of China. In the south, oyster-shells, cut square and thinly planed, are inserted tile-fashion in the long narrow spaces of a wooden frame made to receive them and used for the same purpose. (Giles, *Strange Stories*, p. 38, note 7.)

wine The Chinese wine referred to in these stories would have been a liquor distilled from grain. There were many fine varieties of this, all of them a great deal stronger than our grape wine. Chinese poets through the ages frequently extolled the virtues of the 'thing within the cup'.

yaksha Sanskrit word adopted in Chinese Buddhist terminology, similar in meaning to **raksha**. Malignant, violent demon, devourer of human flesh.

Yama In Indian mythology, Yama is ruler over the dead and judge in the hells, 'grim in aspect, green in colour, clothed in red, riding on a buffalo and holding a club in one hand and a noose in the other' (W. E. Soothill and Lewis Hodous (eds.), *A Dictionary of Chinese Buddhist Terms* (London, 1937), p. 253).

yamen Any mandarin's official compound and residence.

years Dates were traditionally given either in terms of reigns (the fifteenth year of such-and-such a reign) or according to the sixty-year cycle (e.g. the year *gengchen*, which comes after the year *jimao*).

Yin, Yang Since time immemorial the Chinese have divided nature into two great parts, the supreme powers of the universe, one called Yang, embracing light, warmth, life; the other known as Yin, or the principle of darkness, cold and death. The former is identified with the heavens, from which all light, warmth and life emanate; the Yin, on the other hand, with the earth, which, when not directly acted upon by the heavens, is nothing but a dark, cold lifeless mass. (Based on de Groot, *The Religious System of China*, I, p. 22.)

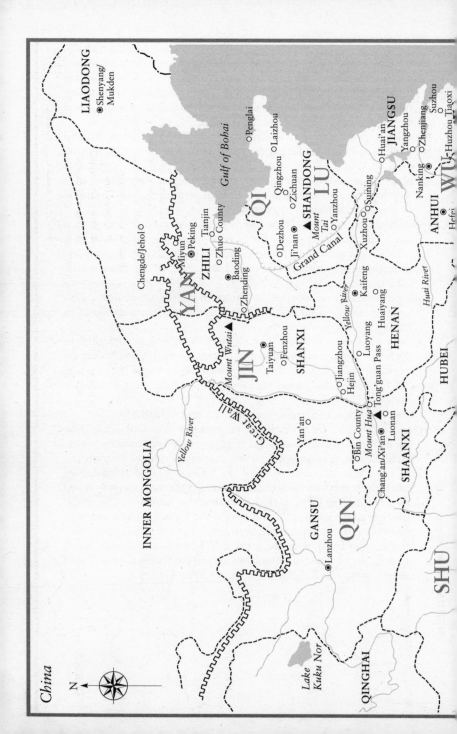

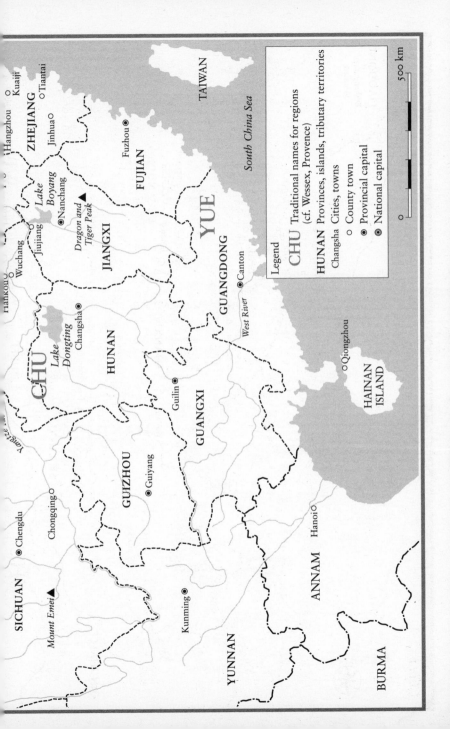

Legend

CHU Traditional names for regions
(cf. Wessex, Provence)

HUNAN Provinces, islands, tributary territories

Changsha Cities, towns
○ County town
◉ Provincial capital
◉ National capital

0   500 km

South China Sea

TAIWAN

ZHEJIANG
○ Hangzhou   ○ Kuaiji
○ Jinhua ○ Tiantai

FUJIAN
Fuzhou ◉

Lake
Boyang
◉ Nanchang
○ Jiujiang
Wuchang ○
○ Hankou

JIANGXI
▲ Dragon and
Tiger Peak

GUANGDONG
Canton ◉
West River

YUE

○ Qiongzhou

HAINAN
ISLAND

CHU

Lake
Dongting
Changsha ◉

HUNAN

Guilin ◉

GUANGXI

Yangtze

○ Chengdu
Chongqing ○

SICHUAN
▲ Mount Emei

GUIZHOU
◉ Guiyang

Kunming ◉

YUNNAN

ANNAM
Hanoi ○

BURMA

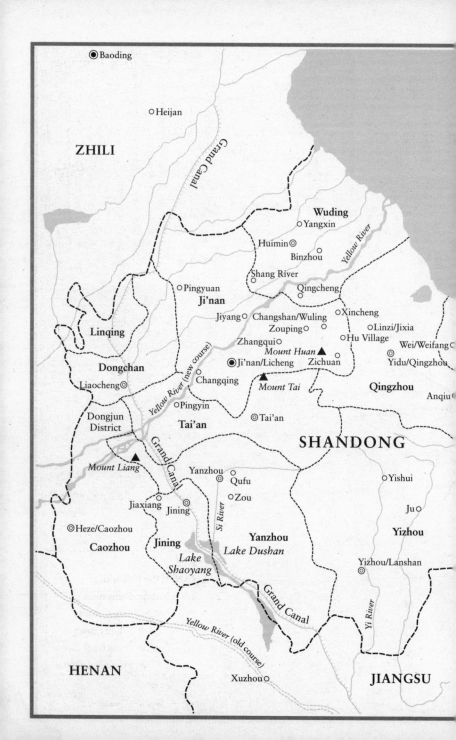

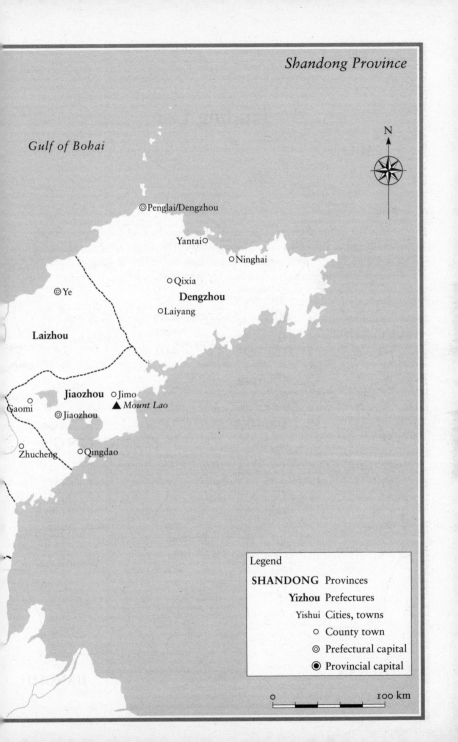

Shandong Province

N

Gulf of Bohai

◎Penglai/Dengzhou

Yantai○

○Ninghai

○Qixia

Dengzhou

○Laiyang

◎Ye

Laizhou

Jiaozhou ○Jimo

▲*Mount Lao*

Gaomi ○

◎Jiaozhou

○Zhucheng

○Qingdao

Legend

SHANDONG Provinces

Yizhou Prefectures

Yishui Cities, towns

○ County town

◎ Prefectural capital

◉ Provincial capital

○ ▬▬▬▬ 100 km

Finding List

This list is for the convenience of those readers who wish to consult the original Chinese texts. The numbers in brackets refer to the listing in Allan Barr's 1984 article, and follow the order in Zhang Youhe's 1962 Variorum edition (see Further Reading).

1	(2)	22	(23)	43	(51)	64	(94)	85	(209)
2	(1)	23	(24)	44	(52)	65	(97)	86	(219)
3	(3)	24	(25)	45	(53)	66	(112)	87	(246)
4	(4)	25	(26)	46	(54)	67	(117)	88	(250)
5	(5)	26	(27)	47	(55)	68	(124)	89	(251)
6	(6)	27	(28)	48	(57)	69	(126)	90	(253)
7	(7)	28	(29)	49	(61)	70	(127)	91	(255)
8	(8)	29	(30)	50	(63)	71	(128)	92	(256)
9	(9)	30	(31)	51	(64)	72	(140)	93	(259)
10	(10)	31	(32)	52	(65)	73	(145)	94	(261)
11	(11)	32	(35)	53	(66)	74	(155)	95	(296)
12	(13)	33	(37)	54	(69)	75	(156)	96	(332)
13	(14)	34	(40)	55	(71)	76	(162)	97	(401)
14	(15)	35	(41)	56	(74)	77	(163)	98	(408)
15	(16)	36	(42)	57	(75)	78	(164)	99	(409)
16	(17)	37	(43)	58	(77)	79	(166)	100	(438)
17	(18)	38	(44)	59	(79)	80	(172)	101	(442)
18	(19)	39	(45)	60	(88)	81	(174)	102	(455)
19	(20)	40	(48)	61	(89)	82	(195)	103	(458)
20	(21)	41	(49)	62	(90)	83	(196)	104	(250b)
21	(22)	42	(50)	63	(93)	84	(199)		

Further Reading

There are now several detailed studies of *Strange Tales* in Western languages to which the reader can turn. I recommend the excellent study by Judith T. Zeitlin, *Historian of the Strange: Pu Songling and the Chinese Classical Tale* (Stanford, 1993), which is both scholarly and lively in its insights. The reader wishing to delve more deeply into the complicated textual history of the book is well served by Allan Barr in his series of articles. A complete annotated French translation by André Lévy will soon be published by Picquier.

IN CHINESE

Modern Editions, Modern Chinese Translations and Works of Reference (arranged chronologically)

Zhang Youhe (ed.), *Liaozhai zhiyi huijiao huizhu huiping ben* (Beijing, 1962; repr. Shanghai, 1978). The standard Variorum edition, with traditional commentaries.

Yan Weiqing and Zhu Qikai (eds.), *Liaozhai zhiyi xuan* (Ji'nan, 1984). Selections.

Liu Liemao et al. (eds.), *Xinping Liaozhai zhiyi erbaipian* (Guangdong, 1985). Selections.

Zhu Yixuan, *Liaozhai zhiyi ziliao huibian* (Henan, 1986). Excellent compendium of materials connected with *Strange Tales*.

Zhu Qikai et al. (eds.), *Quanben xinzhu Liaozhai zhiyi* (Beijing, 1989). Excellent complete annotated edition.

Qiu Shengwei (ed.), *Liaozhai zhiyi duizhao zhuyi xi* (Guangxi, 1991). Complete, with running *baihua* (modern vernacular Chinese) translation, and commentary.

Yu Zaichun (trans.), *Zhengbutou Liaozhai zhiyi de putonghua fanyi* (Shandong, 1991). Complete *baihua* version.

Zhu Yixuan, Geng Lianfeng and Sheng Wei, *Liaozhai zhiyi cidian* (Tianjin, 1991). Excellent handbook, invaluable for the meaning of key terms in the tales.

Yuan Lükun et al. (trans.), *Baihua Liaozhai quanben* (Liaoning, 1992). Complete *baihua* version.

Ma Zhenfang (ed.), *Liaozhai zhiyi pingshang dacheng* (repr. Taibei, 1996). Complete edition, with *baihua* translations and critical comments. Commentaries by Zhang Renrang, Yang Guangmin, Li Chuanrui, et al.

Sheng Wei (ed.), *Liaozhai zhiyi jiaozhu* (Taiyuan, 2000). Complete critical and annotated edition.

IN WESTERN LANGUAGES

Translations of *Strange Tales* and of Related Materials
(arranged alphabetically according to author)

Allen, C. F. R. (trans.), 'Tales from the *Liao Chai Chih Yi*', *China Review* 2 (1873–4); 3 (1874–5); 4 (1875–6).

Bauer, Wolfgang and Herbert Franke (trans.), *The Golden Casket*, trans. Christopher Levenson (Harmondsworth, 1965). An anthology of translated tales through the ages.

Buber, Martin (trans.), *Chinesische Geister und Liebesgeschichten* (Frankfurt, 1927). Partly based on Giles (see below). English trans., Alex Page, *Chinese Tales* (New Jersey, 1991).

Chang, H. C. (trans.), *Tales of the Supernatural* (Edinburgh, 1984). Contains a few tales.

Cohn, Don J. (trans.), *Vignettes from the Chinese: Lithographs from Shanghai in the Late Nineteenth Century* (Hong Kong, 1987). Fine English versions of later descendants of the *Strange Tales* tradition, complete with lithographic illustrations similar to the ones included in this translation.

Dars, Jacques and Chan Hingho, *Comment lire un roman Chinois: anthologie de préfaces et commentaires aux anciennes oeuvres de fiction* (Arles, 2001). Contains good annotated French version of the Author's Preface.

Di Giura, Ludovico Nicola (trans.), *I Racconti Fantastici di Liao* (Milan, 1926). For many years the only complete version in any European language, done by an Italian aristocrat who served as physician to the Italian Legation in Beijing.

Giles, Herbert A. (trans.), *Strange Stories from a Chinese Studio* (London, 1880). A second, revised edition appeared in 1908, which has been often reprinted. Reference is always to this edition. For years this was the standard selection in English. Still worth reading.

Ji Yun, *Shadows in a Chinese Landscape: The Notes of a Confucian Scholar*, trans. David L. Keenan (Armonk, 1999). Translations of a somewhat later collection of 'strange tales'.

Lévy, André (trans.), *Chroniques de l'étrange* (Arles, 1996). First volume in Lévy's excellent (and soon to be complete) French version.

Mair, Denis and Victor Mair (trans.), *Strange Tales from Make-Do Studio* (Beijing, 1989). A selection.

Minford, John (trans.), 'Seven Strange Tales', *Meanjin* 54:1 (Melbourne, 1995). Earlier drafts.

Quong, Rose (Guang Rusi) (trans.), *Chinese Ghost and Love Stories* (New York, 1946). A readable selection.

Rösel, Gottfried (trans.), *Umgang mit Chrysanthemen* (Books 1–4, Zurich, 1987); *Zwei Leben im Traum* (Books 5–8, Zurich, 1989); *Besuch bei den Seligen* (Books 9–12, Zurich, 1991); *Schmetterlinge Fliegen lassen* (Books 13–15, Zurich, 1992); *Kontakte mit Lebenden* (Books 16–17, Zurich, 1992). Complete German translation.

Soulié de Morant, George (trans.), *Strange Stories from the Lodge of Leisures* (London, 1913).

Yuan Mei, *Censored by Confucius: Ghosts Stories*, trans. Kam Louie and Louise Edwards (Armonk, 1996). Another later collection of 'strange tales'.

Critical Works (Concerning *Strange Tales* and Related Subjects)

Barr, Allan, 'The Textual Transmission of *Liaozhai zhiyi*', *Harvard Journal of Asiatic Studies* 44:2 (1984).

—, 'A Comparative Study of Early and Late Tales in *Liaozhai zhiyi*', *Harvard Journal of Asiatic Studies* 45:1 (1985).

—, 'Pu Songling and the Qing Examination System', *Late Imperial China* 7:1 (June 1986).

—, 'Disarming Intruders: Alien Women in *Liaozhai zhiyi*', *Harvard Journal of Asiatic Studies* 49:2 (1989).

Campany, Robert Ford, *Strange Writing: Anomaly Accounts in Early Medieval China* (Albany, 1996).

Chang, Chun-shu and Shelley Hsueh-lun Chang, *Redefining History: Ghosts, Spirits and Human Society in P'u Sung-ling's World, 1640–1715* (Ann Arbor, 1998). A detailed and informative study, if sometimes misguided.

?Gutzlaff, Karl, 'Liau Chai I Chi, or Extraordinary Legends from Liau Chai', *Chinese Repository* 11:4 (1842). Probably the first mention of the work in a Western language.

Hom, Marlon K., *The Continuation of Tradition: A Study of Liaozhai zhiyi by Pu Songling (1640–1715)*, Ph.D. dissertation (University of Washington, 1979).

Huntington, Rania, *Alien Kind: Foxes and Late Imperial Chinese Narrative* (Cambridge, MA, 2003).

Kao, Karl S. Y., *Classical Chinese Tales of the Supernatural and the Fantastic* (Bloomington, 1985).

Minford, John and Tong Man, 'Whose Strange Stories? P'u Sung-ling (1640–1715), Herbert Giles (1845–1935) and the *Liao-chai chih-i*', *East Asian History* 17/18 (1999).

Spence, Jonathan, *The Death of Woman Wang* (New York, 1978). Contains several items from *Strange Tales*, cleverly integrated into Spence's narrative.

Zeitlin, Judith T., *Historian of the Strange: Pu Songling and the Chinese Classical Tale* (Stanford, 1993).

General Interest

A partial list of books of general interest referred to from time to time in the Notes and Glossary.

Arlington, L. C. and William Lewisohn, *In Search of Old Peking* (Peking, 1935).

Balazs, Etienne, *Chinese Civilisation and Bureaucracy*, trans. H. M. Wright (New Haven, 1964).

Ball, J. Dyer, *Things Chinese, or Notes Connected with China*, 5th edn (London, 1925).

Birrell, Anne, *Chinese Mythology: An Introduction* (Baltimore, 1993).

Bredon, Juliet and Igor Mitrophanow, *The Moon Year* (Shanghai, 1927; repr. Hong Kong, 1982).

Cao Xueqin and Gao E., *The Story of the Stone*, trans. David Hawkes and John Minford, 5 vols. (Harmondsworth, 1973–86).

Cass, Victoria, *Dangerous Women: Warriors, Grannies and Geishas of the Ming* (Lanham, MD, 1999).

Clunas, Craig, *Superfluous Things* (Urbana, 1991). An excellent introduction to some of the key concepts of late Ming culture.

Couling, Samuel, *Encyclopedia Sinica* (Shanghai, 1917; repr. Hong Kong). This remains a useful guide to Old China.

De Groot, J. J. M., *The Religious System of China*, 6 vols. (Leiden, 1892–1910; repr. several times in Taiwan). The indefatigable Dutch scholar Jan Jakob Maria de Groot (1854–1921) in this many-volumed work provides a wealth of information on the customs relating to funerals, the dead, spirits and the supernatural in general. He often quotes Pu Songling at length, and his book is a wonderful (if sometimes long-winded) companion to these tales, giving carefully documented descriptions of strange ways of acting and thinking that are taken for granted by Pu Songling.

Doré, Henri, *Researches into Chinese Superstitions*, trans. M. Kennelly and L. F. McGreal (Shanghai, 1914–1938; repr.

several times in Taiwan). This work by the Jesuit Father Henri Doré, like De Groot's work also huge and many volumed, is a wonderful rambling source of information on traditional Chinese beliefs concerning the supernatural.

Eberhard, Wolfram, *A Dictionary of Chinese Symbols* (London, 1986).

Fischer-Schreiber, Ingrid, *The Shambhala Dictionary of Taoism* (Boston, 1996).

Giles, Herbert, *A Chinese Biographical Dictionary* (London, 1898). Still a useful collection of entries, distinguished for the ease with which Giles tells a story.

Giles, Lionel (trans.), *A Gallery of Chinese Immortals* (London, 1948). More tales of strange individuals, translated by Herbert's son.

Graham, A. C. (trans.), *Poems of the Late T'ang* (London, 1965).

Hawkes, David (trans.), *The Songs of the South: An Anthology of Ancient Chinese Poems by Qu Yuan and Other Poets* (Harmondsworth, 1985). A fine translation of the early shaman-poet to whom Pu Songling pays homage in his Preface.

Hinsch, Bret, *Passions of the Cut Sleeve: The Male Homosexual Tradition in China* (Berkeley, 1990).

Ko, Dorothy, *Teachers of the Inner Chambers: Women and Culture in Seventeenth-Century China* (Stanford, 1994).

Levy, Howard, *Chinese Footbinding: The History of a Curious Erotic Custom* (New York, 1966). The classic study by one of the successors to Robert van Gulik.

Lin Yutang, *The Importance of Living* (London, 1938). A book still to be recommended to those wishing to fill in the more everyday background to Pu Songling's strange world.

Luk, Charles (Lu K'uan Yu) (trans.), *Taoist Yoga: Alchemy and Immortality* (London, 1970). One of several modern studies by Luk, delving deeply into a world frequently described by Pu Songling.

Minford, John and Joseph S. M. Lau (eds.), *Classical Chinese Literature: An Anthology of Translations*, I (New York and Hong Kong, 2000).

Miyazaki, Ichisada, *China's Examination Hell: The Civil Service Examinations of Imperial China*, trans. Conrad Shirokauer (New Haven, 1981). Still the standard study of the obsessive system to which Pu Songling and his contemporaries were slaves.

Needham, Joseph et al., *Science and Civilisation in China*, 22 vols. (Cambridge, 1954–). Whereas de Groot and Doré investigate the supernatural, Needham has surveyed the 'natural', often providing information as startling as anything in *Strange Tales*.

Nienhauser, William et al. (eds.), *Indiana Companion to Traditional Chinese Literature* (Bloomington, 1986; vol. 2, Bloomington, 1998).

Reichelt, Karl Ludvig, *Truth and Tradition in Chinese Buddhism* (Shanghai, 1927; repr. several times in Taiwan).

Schipper, Kristofer, *The Taoist Body* (Berkeley, 1993).

Sima Qian (*c.* 145–*c.* 85 BC), *Records of the Grand Historian*, trans. Burton Watson, 3 vols., *Qin Dynasty (221–207)*, vol. I; *Han Dynasty (202–)*, vols. II and III, revised edn (Hong Kong and New York, 1993). The standard modern version of the classic historical text to which Pu Songling often alludes.

Smith, Arthur H., *Proverbs and Common Sayings from the Chinese* (Shanghai, 1914). Often reprinted (e.g. in Dover paperback), this learned and witty collection does much to illuminate some of the darker corners of *Strange Tales*.

Smith, Richard, *Fortune-Tellers and Philosophers* (Boulder, CO, 1991).

Staunton, Sir George Thomas (trans.), *Ta Tsing Leu Lee: Being the Fundamental Laws and a Selection from the Supplementary Statutes of the Penal Code of China* (London, 1810). Reprinted in Taiwan more than once in recent years, this superb translation brings to life many of the byways of behaviour and misbehaviour of Qing-dynasty China, providing an objective counterpoint to Pu Songling.

Van Gulik, Robert, *The Lore of the Chinese Lute* (Tokyo, 1940). Almost any work by the Dutch diplomat-sinologist is

helpful in fleshing out the cultural world of *Strange Tales*.
I have chosen this and the following two books.

—, *Erotic Colour Prints of the Ming Period* (Tokyo, 1951).

—, *Sexual Life in Ancient China* (Leiden, 1961).

Watson, Burton (trans.), *The Tso Chuan: Selections from China's Oldest Narrative History* (New York, 1989). Readable modern versions of an ancient classic often alluded to by Pu Songling.

— (trans.), *The Complete Works of Chuang Tzu* (New York, 1968). The Taoist philosopher, another of Pu Songling's mentors from the past.

Watters, Thomas, 'Chinese Fox-Myths', *Journal of the North-China Branch of the Royal Asiatic Society* VIII (1874).

Werner, E. T. C., *A Dictionary of Chinese Mythology* (Shanghai, 1932).

Wile, Douglas, *Art of the Bedchamber: The Chinese Sexual Yoga Classics* (Albany, 1992). A useful modern supplement to van Gulik's earlier study. Both books are helpful in understanding the attitudes underlying the idea of the fox-spirit.

Notes

In these Notes, matters of general and critical interpretation are dealt with first, followed by brief explanations of detailed terms. The reader is advised that many general terms are described in the Glossary. The traditional Chinese commentators referred to can be found in Zhang Youhe's Variorum edition (1962), while the modern commentators can be identified from the list of editions given under Further Reading.

I

HOMUNCULUS

This is one of several tales dealing with the foibles of practising or would-be practising Taoists (see Glossary), and the pitfalls of spiritual and alchemic self-cultivation. The yogic practice referred to here, *daoyin*, is an ancient one, which combines physical and breathing exercises and self-massage. It is the ancient term for the sort of thing now more commonly known as *qigong*. Joseph Needham, in one of his many extraordinary excursions into Chinese alchemy, has this to say about the physiological side effects of such prolonged breathing exercises: 'There can be no doubt that this technique produced considerable anoxaemia with all its strange effects – buzzing in the ears [the literal title of this tale is "The Man Within the Ear"], vertigo, perspiration, sensations of heat and formication [a sensation as of insects crawling under the skin] in the extremities, fainting and headache' (*Science and Civilisation in China*, 22 vols. (Cambridge, 1954–), vol. V, part 5, pp. 144–5).

In the symbolic language of Inner Alchemy (*neidan*), Cinnabar (*dan*) represents the combined Yin and Yang energy, nurtured in the lower Cinnabar Field (*dantian*, roughly the solar plexus), by means of various meditative and breathing techniques. This Inner Elixir and the Homunculus are one and the same thing. They are the outcome of this

alchemic process, the Taoist 'inner child' or 'immortal foetus', which
takes many months to mature. If the practitioner consciously (and
prematurely) thinks 'with secret delight' of the achievement of immortality, demons may seize the occasion to enter his heart, possessing
him and thereby undoing all his previous progress. (For a famous and
more detailed description of a similar state of possession, see Chapter
87 of Cao Xueqin's *The Story of the Stone* (trans. David Hawkes and
John Minford, 5 vols. (Harmondsworth, 1973–86)), in which the nun
Adamantina has a seizure during Zen meditation.)

He Shouqi (1823) and Dan Minglun (1842) comment that this is
an accurate description of what sometimes happens to unorthodox or
fake Taoist practitioners. Their pretentious vanity exposes them to
strange apparitions, and ultimately they make fools of themselves.
True spirituality is something quite different. The phenomenon is all
too familiar in more recent times in the West, stemming from what
Chögyam Trungpa (1940–87), the modern Tibetan Master, has called
Spiritual Materialism, 'the Ego attempting to acquire and apply the
teachings of spirituality for its own benefit' (*Cutting Through Spiritual
Materialism* (London, 1973)). As Carl Jung (1875–1961) put it, 'Yoga
in Mayfair or Fifth Avenue, or in any other place which is on the
telephone, is a spiritual fake' (Psychological Commentary to *The
Tibetan Book of the Great Liberation* (New York, 1954)). The life of
'the Beast', Aleister Crowley (1875–1947), is a rich source of similar
adventures, examples of esoteric practice distorted by vanity and the
desire for psychic power. It is because this story seems so modern and
universal that I have moved it here from the second place that it
occupies in the author's manuscript.

2

AN OTHERWORLDLY EXAMINATION

He Shouqi (1823) and Dan Minglun (1842) both see this tale as
an allegorical portrayal of virtue rewarded. Feng Zhenluan (1818),
quoting the words of a Buddhist Layman by the name of Half Crazy,
takes a somewhat subtler view: the tale's emphasis on motive, or mind
(*xin*, Song Tao's 'laudable feelings'), belongs to the shared wisdom of
Confucianism, Taoism and Buddhism. Feng is surely right to place Pu
Songling in the grand tradition of Ming 'syncretism', where main-
stream neo-Confucianism was transformed by the spiritual insights of
Taoism and Zen Buddhism, a tradition which reached its climax in
the great philosopher Wang Yangming (1472–1529): 'There is no

object, no event, no moral principle, no righteousness, and no good that lies outside the mind.' Wang, although a neo-Confucian, famously achieved enlightenment and inner peace as the result of a period of Buddhist–Taoist-style meditation in the wilds of south-western China. For Wang, Confucian Benevolence is Compassionate Love, 'the development of an innate feeling of sympathy and commiseration, initially manifested in the love for one's parents'. (See Fung Yulan (Feng Youlan), *A History of Chinese Philosophy*, trans. Derk Bodde, 2 vols. (London, 1952–3), II, pp. 607ff. See also the excellent essays relating to Wang Yangming's thinking in Wm. Theodore de Bary (ed.), *Self and Society in Ming Thought* (New York, 1970).) It is for this love that Song Tao is rewarded in this tale.

examination for the second degree: For the various degrees and examinations, and the formal Eight-Legged Essay, see the Glossary. In this and in many other tales, Pu Songling reflects the lifelong obsession of the Chinese mandarin class with their own bureaucratic system, an obsession which extends well into the Other World. It is no doubt for this reason that he placed this story at the very beginning of the collection, a place it occupies in all extant editions.

Guan Yu: (192–220), the famous general of the Three Kingdoms period, who in 1594 was elevated to the rank of God of War by the Ming Emperor Wanli. His efficacy against demons was recognized by Taoists and Buddhists alike, and his sphere extended far beyond warfare to include (as here) justice and civil administration.

City God: Every town and city had its Tutelary God (*chenghuang*), responsible for the town's welfare, peace and prosperity.

3

LIVING DEAD

recently died: 'Bodily spectres must as a rule be corpses still fresh and undecayed ... They rise especially before burial has hampered their movements by an envelope of solid wood and clay. Even tender women may then rage most fearfully' (J. J. M. de Groot, *The Religious System of China*, 6 vols. (Leiden, 1892–1910), V, p. 734).

a lamp burning: 'This ancient custom is observed by modern Chinese down to the lowest classes ... One of the first cares of the family is to place a lighted candle in an ordinary candlestick near the feet of the deceased ... The disembodied soul, being naturally under the influences of those dark, unseen [Yin] regions, would even in the broadest daylight be quite unable to find its way through them to the corpse and to the sacrifices which are to be offered there every day for its benefit, did not the family remedy the evil [by lighting a candle] ... They strengthen the soul by means of a little artificial Yang, to wit, by light and warmth emanating from the candle or the lamp' (De Groot, *The Religious System of China*, I, p. 21).

the wooden fish: A hollow, fish-shaped block beaten with a clapper by Buddhist monks while reciting sacred texts and liturgies.

inquest: In traditional China this was conducted by the local Magistrate, whose duties included those of District Coroner.

4
SPITTING WATER

Song Wan of Laiyang: (1614–1673), obtained his third (*jinshi*) degree in 1647 and became one of the leading poets of the early-Qing dynasty. Wang Shizhen (1634–1711), a great admirer of Pu Songling and his work, thinks this story apocryphal, because Song lost his mother when he was a mere babe in swaddling clothes. But it is certainly true that Song was nominated to a post in the Board of Finance shortly after 1647, during the disturbed times following the Manchu conquest, when Peking would certainly have been full of haunted and dilapidated mansions. Dan Minglun (1842) comments that Peking was full of spooky houses, and adds a little tale of his own in this connection.

5
TALKING PUPILS

Here, for the first time in the book, Pu Songling adds his own concluding comment, giving himself the mock-grandiose title 'Chronicler of the Strange'. (He does this in almost two hundred of the nearly five hundred tales.) The title clearly alludes to, and gently spoofs, the one adopted by the great Chinese historian Sima Qian (*c.* 145–*c.* 85 BC), who often appended comments at the end of the sections of his *Historical Records*, calling himself the Grand Chronicler or Historian. In this instance, Pu the Chronicler begins by telling another, related story (this was a habit with Chinese commentators):

A certain country gentleman was out strolling with two friends when in the distance he saw a woman leading a donkey. 'Behold a fair damsel!' he said, playfully quoting the *Book of Songs*, and cried to his friends, 'Let's go after her!' They all ran ahead, laughing loudly, and soon caught up with the woman, only to discover that she was the gentleman's own daughter-in-law! He stood there speechless and red in the face with embarrassment, while his friends pretended not to have recognized the lady and began evaluating her looks in the crudest terms. Finally he stammered, 'This lady is the wife of my eldest son . . .' His friends stood where they were, masking their smiles with their sleeves.

Libertines often bring about their own undoing, and end up making themselves a laughing stock.

Was not Fang Dong's blindness a form of retribution inflicted on him by the spirit world? I have no idea which spirit presides over Hibiscus Town . . . No doubt a Bodhisattva incarnate . . . But the little mannikins, by making a new opening, prove that the spirits, however cruel, always give humans a chance to repent and make a fresh start!

PUPILS: The traditional Chinese expression for pupil (*tongren*) means literally 'man in the pupil', from the reflection of oneself that one sees in the eye of another.

Chang'an: The Tang-dynasty (618–907) capital of China, often used in literature to refer loosely to 'the capital', in this instance by implication Peking.

Hibiscus Town: Lü Zhan'en (1825) points out that this is the name for a mythical realm. It is also one of the names for the city of Chengdu, in the mountainous western province of Sichuan, which was planted with countless hibiscus shrubs in the tenth century AD by the second ruler of the Latter Shu Kingdom, Meng Chang (known for his life of debauchery and extravagance).

6

THE PAINTED WALL

The Chronicler of the Strange comments: 'How wise was the monk to say that illusion has its source within man himself! . . . And how regrettable that his words did not inspire Sudden Enlightenment in the Graduate Zhu, that they did not move him to forsake the world and become a mountain-dweller, a hermit with hair flying in the wind!' Judith T. Zeitlin paraphrases Pu Songling well: 'Zhu does not withdraw into the mountains; his heart is too entangled with his illusions,

illusions powerful enough to withstand simple rationalizations or religious truth' (*Historian of the Strange*, p. 193).

Master Baozhi: A Zen monk of the fifth to sixth centuries, renowned for his eccentric behaviour and for his extraordinary ability to appear in two or three places at once. Legend has it that he went roving from village to village, his hair tumbling down abundantly on his shoulders, barefoot and leaning on a pilgrim's staff, to which were attached a mirror, a pair of scissors and two silk tassels. During his peregrinations, he was endowed with the marvellous power of speaking in several languages.

Zeitlin perceptively remarks on the dominant and all-controlling presence of this statue in the monastery (though its existence is only lightly touched on). It directly links the Provincial Graduate Zhu's imaginary journey into the world of the Painted Wall to the process of enlightenment. Both the old monk-guide and the abbot preaching in the painting can be interpreted as manifestations of Master Baozhi, 'come to earth to enlighten suffering human beings' (*Historian of the Strange*, p. 191). It is worth a mention that the Provincial Graduate even shares the Zen Master's family name – Zhu.

Apsaras Scattering Flowers: The Apsaras (*tian-nü*) are Heavenly Maidens, in Buddhist iconography female devas, or angels, to be seen (for example) in the cave-temple murals of Dunhuang. 'Apsaras Scattering Flowers' is a popular motif in Buddhist art, having its origin in the Vimalakirti Sutra.

7

THE TROLL

The *shanxiao* is really more associated with mountains than with our own troll's preferred haunts (caves or subterranean places or the underneaths of bridges). De Groot (*The Religious System of China*, V, pp. 499ff.) devotes several excellent pages to the various descriptions of this creature, commenting: 'The remote, unfrequented mountain-forests are still to the Chinese people a kingdom full of mysterious spectral beings, strange and wonderful.'

11

THE HAUNTED HOUSE

Li Huaxi, President of the Board of Justice: Graduated as a Doctor (*jinshi*) in 1634, during the reign of the last Ming Emperor Chongzhen (1611–44), and rose to high office. He did not become President of the Board of Justice until the Manchu dynasty (1644–1911).
In the seventeenth year . . . Emperor Kangxi: 1678.

12

STEALING A PEACH

The great Moroccan traveller Ibn Batuta (1304–68) provided an account of some Chinese jugglers at the Mongol court in Hangzhou, an account which tallies so extraordinarily with Pu Songling's tale (minus the peach and the baskets), that it is worth giving here in full.

That same night a juggler, who was one of the Khan's slaves, made his appearance, and the Amir said to him: 'Come and show us some of your marvels.' Upon this he took a wooden ball, with several holes in it, through which long thongs were passed, and, laying hold of one of these, slung it into the air. It went so high that we lost sight of it altogether. (It was the hottest season of the year, and we were outside in the middle of the palace court.) There now remained only a little of the end of a thong in the conjuror's hand, and he desired one of the boys who assisted him to lay hold of it and mount. He did so, climbing by the thong, and we lost sight of him also! The conjuror then called to him three times, but getting no answer, he snatched up a knife as if in a great rage, laid hold of the thong, and disappeared also! By and by he threw down one of the boy's hands, then a foot, then the other hand, and then the other foot, then the trunk, and last of all the head! Then he came down himself, all puffing and panting, and with his clothes all bloody, kissed the ground before the Amir, and said something to him in Chinese. The Amir gave some order in reply, and our friend then took the lad's limbs, laid them together in their places, and gave a kick, when, presto! There was the boy, who got up and stood before us. All this astonished me beyond measure, and I had an attack of palpitation like that which overcame me once before in the presence of the Sultan of India, when he showed me something of the same kind. They gave me a cordial, however, which cured the attack. The

Kazi Afkharuddin was next to me, and quoth he, 'Wallah! 'tis my opinion there has been neither going up nor coming down, neither marring nor mending; 'tis all hocus pocus!'

(Henry Yule, The Travels of Marco Polo (New York, 1993), Book I, pp. 316–17)

It is interesting to compare Ibn Batuta's vivid (even over-written) Arabian Nights-style account with Pu Songling's tale. See also the entertaining study by Peter Lamont, The Rise of the Indian Rope Trick (London, 2004).

Spring Festival: Chunjie refers here to the celebrations that took place at the time (normally around 5 February) known as Li Chun, or Establishing the Spring, the first of the twenty-four Solar Terms in the Chinese calendar. It is not the modern chunjie, which refers to the Lunar New Year.

a peach: The fruit of immortality par excellence. Legend places the tree (a Chinese Tree of Life, or axis mundi) bearing these miraculous fruits (which ripened every few thousand years) in the garden of the Queen Mother of the West, somewhere deep in the Kunlun Mountains or some other fabled paradise. In the novel The Journey to the West (attributed to Wu Cheng'en, c. 1500–1582), the mischievous Monkey famously breaks into the garden and eats the lot.

the White Lotus sect: This millenarian Buddhist sect had its origins in the thirteenth century, and was later active in the overthrow of the Mongol dynasty (1279–1368). It emerged again in the late Ming when Xu Hongru led an uprising in Shandong (1622). It became a potent anti-Manchu movement during the Qing dynasty, and was brutally suppressed in the late eighteenth century.

13

GROWING PEARS

This, one of the best known and most often anthologized and translated of all the Tales, is a greatly expanded variation on a brief item in the much earlier collection In Search of Spirits, attributed to Gan Bao (fl. 320). In the earlier story, the magician is called Xu Guang:

Once he was performing his magic arts in the marketplace and begged for a gourd from a vendor, who refused to give him one. So he asked for a flower and planted it in the ground, where it immediately started growing, spreading its tendrils over the ground. First it bore flowers, and then fruits. Xu Guang picked one, ate it, and then began handing the fruits out to the spectators. When the vendor turned to look at his own gourds, they had all disappeared.

(My translation of the extract quoted by Zhu Yixuan, *Liaozhai zhiyi ziliao huibian*, revised edition (Tianjin, 2002), p. 17. For the complete tale, see Li Qi and Liang Guofu (eds.), *Soushenji Soushen houji yizhu* (Jilin, 1997), p. 27.)

For obvious reasons this tale has always been popular with Marxist commentators, and is placed first in the popular selection made by Yan Weiqing and Zhu Qikai in 1984. It has been published many times in cartoon-strip form.

The Chronicler of the Strange appends one of his most trenchant comments to this tale, sharply reproaching the nouveaux riches for their meanness, for the way they turn a deaf ear to needy friends or relations coming to them with simple requests for loans of food or money. In other words, his target is far broader than the country bumpkin who is made to look such a fool in the tale.

14

THE TAOIST PRIEST OF MOUNT LAO

This is another of the most famous and most often anthologized of the *Tales*. The Chronicler of the Strange, in a strongly worded comment, stresses that he is not only making fun of small-town aficionados of Taoism like Mr Wang but also has a wider target in mind: corruption, pretention and ambition in general, all of them nourished by sycophantic hangers-on with fake recipes for success, which eventually cause them to 'hit the wall'.

Everyone bursts out laughing when they hear this story. They do not realize that the world is full of Mr Wangs. When some highly placed nincompoop proceeds with the greatest pleasure to destroy his health, and rejects the idea of taking true medicine, others are only too ready to come along and suck his boils and lick his piles, feeding his vanity, offering him seductive ways to advance his ambition through violence. They thereby win his favour, claiming, 'This Art will take you forward! Abuse the world with it, and you will encounter no obstacle.' At first the Art seems to work and the nincompoop considers himself to be the greatest man in the universe. The sky is the limit. He only learns the truth when he hits the wall and tumbles.

Mount Lao: An extended range famous for its Taoist temples and hermitages, situated on the Shandong coast some twenty-five miles north-east of the port and resort-city of Qingdao.

Chang E: One of the wives of Yi the Mighty Archer, from whom she stole the Elixir of Immortality given him by the Queen Mother of the West (see note on 'a peach' to Tale 12, 'Stealing a Peach'). For this she was banished to the moon.

'Rainbow Skirts': The name of a dance probably performed in feathered costume and almost certainly of Central Asian or Indian origin. It became famous as the dance performed by the ill-fated consort of the Tang Emperor Xuanzong (reigned 712–56).

16
THE SNAKE-CHARMER

The Chronicler of the Strange comments that the snake, although merely a dumb creature, is capable of deep feelings of friendship and devotion, listens to his old master's advice and changes his ways. Human beings, by contrast, are all too capable of betraying their oldest and best friends, and of answering well-meant advice with anger and hostility. Feng Zhenluan (1818) expected the story not to be to his taste, but found himself strangely moved by it.

green: *Qing* is tantalizingly defined in the dictionaries as the colour of nature, a dark neutral tint, green, bluish-green, greenish-blue, blue, grey, black, etc. The precise meaning, the lexicographers tend to say (if precision is intended), must be inferred from the context. See, for example, Herbert Giles, *Chinese–English Dictionary*, 2nd edn (London, 1912); R. H. Mathews' *Chinese–English Dictionary*, American edn (Cambridge, MA, 1943); Lin Yutang, *Chinese–English Dictionary of Modern Usage* (Hong Kong, 1972). When used of bamboo, hemp, peas, plums, moss, grass, olives, dragons, flies and tea, it is green; of the sky, the collar, orchids and porcelain, it is blue; of oxen and foxes, horses, cloth and hair, it is black.

The only snakes I can find that are described as *qing* all seem to be green: for example the *qing-gui she* or Bamboo Viper, *Trimeresurus gramineus*, and the *qing-zhu-si*, a small, green poisonous snake.

17

THE WOUNDED PYTHON

Feng Zhenluan (1818) takes issue with the last comment, as does Qiu Shengwei (1991). For different reasons they both find its simplistic moralizing out of character with what they had expected from Pu Songling.

18

THE FORNICATING DOG

This story does not appear in early printed editions of *Strange Tales*, but is present in the author's manuscript and in early transcriptions. Its absence from the late-nineteenth-century editions explains the lack of an illustration. It is included in both Zhang Youhe's Variorum edition and Zhu Qikai's modern annotated edition (1989).

The Chronicler of the Strange, in his Appended Judgement (on this occasion he actually provides a 'judgement', as opposed to the usual 'comment'), gives a strange extended virtuoso performance in the euphuistic parallel-prose style of which he was a master. (It is longer than, and almost eclipses, the anecdote itself.) In many ways it is similar to his comment at the end of Tale 63, 'Cut Sleeve' (see the note 'Jesting Judgement'). By piling allusion on allusion he succeeds in dwelling graphically on the subject of bestiality, without either passing judgement or being pornographic. It is an extraordinary form of literary bawdy. My version is a free one, and shortened.

> Of old
> Assignations by the River Pu
>   Were frowned upon,
> Trysts in the Mulberry Grove
>   Were decried.
> This merchant's wife had trouble
>   Preserving her chastity,
> She yearned for
>   Carnal pleasure.
> She was a yaksha-demon in bed,
>   A bitch on heat.
> Her pet found his way
>   Down the hole,
> Became her lover

Beneath the quilt.
On the Terrace of Clouds and Rain
His shaggy tail wagged with vigour;
In the Land of Warmth and Tenderness
Their slender limbs writhed with abandon . . .
No law in the Nether World
Covers this case.
Should the dog not be torn
Limb from limb,
And his soul dragged before Yama?

Lingering Death: *Lingchi*, a process of gradual dismemberment sometimes translated as 'cutting into ten thousand pieces' or 'death by the slow process', was the cruellest and most ignominious of all Chinese punishments. By a series of painful but not in themselves mortal cuts, sometimes lasting over three whole days, the offender's body was sliced beyond recognition. The executioner entered ever deeper into his victim's flesh, taking care to avoid the main arteries and life-supporting organs. The head was subsequently exposed in a cage for a period. It was not abolished until 1905.

The Criminal Code of the Qing dynasty was very specific with regards to adultery when combined with murder: 'If the guilty wife shall contrive with the adulterer to procure the death of her husband, she shall suffer death by Lingering Death, and the adulterer shall be beheaded. If the adulterer kills the husband, without the knowledge or connivance of the wife, she shall suffer death by being strangled.'

19

THE GOD OF HAIL

Wang Yuncang: A *jinshi* graduate of 1595, who fell foul of the notorious eunuch Wei Zhongxian and was dismissed from his official post in 1627. He was from Pu Songling's home town of Zichuan.

20

THE GOLDEN GOBLET

Yin Shidan: (1522–82) Took his *jinshi* degree in 1547. He rose to be a member of the Grand Secretariat, but was dismissed in 1571.
the Cowherd and the Spinning Maid: Two stars separated by the Milky

Way – Altair in the constellation Aquila, and Vega in the constellation
Lyra. According to Chinese legend, the stars are lovers who can only
meet once a year, on the seventh day of the seventh month, when the
magpies build a bridge for them across the Milky Way.

21

GRACE AND PINE

The Chronicler of the Strange envies Kong less for his beautiful wife
Pine than for his close friend Grace. The very sight of such a beautiful
friend drives away hunger, the very sound of her voice dispels care.
Spiritual communion between a man and a close woman friend of this
kind is something superior to the carnal love between man and wife.
Modern commentators agree that this is the principal theme of the
story. Instead of marrying his hero to Grace, or portraying him as
harbouring a grudge because he never can marry her, Pu Songling
portrays Kong Xueli as an enlightened friend, reunited at the end with
both Grace (whom he continues to love as a friend) and her brother
Huangfu. They can all carry on playing chess and drinking wine
together from time to time in the garden. It is a poem in praise of
platonic friendship.

   Feng Zhenluan (1818) marvels at the detailed description of Grace's
surgical intervention, which renders the event 'palpable to the reader's
eye'. For him she is the principal character in the story. Dan Minglun
(1842) envies Kong and Huangfu their excellent study routine (a
drinking session every five days, to musical accompaniment), commenting that ordinary drunkards would never be capable of understanding such things.

Kong Xueli: A carefully chosen phrase in the very first sentence
   describes Kong Xueli – *yunjie*, 'of generous spirit and great refinement'. The old Chinese glosses tend to paraphrase this elusive expression with others that are every bit as hard to pin down, e.g.
   kuanhou hanyang, 'broad or generous in spirit'. The idea refers at
   once to aesthetic and ethical self-cultivation, and is picked upon by
   Dan Minglun (1842) to characterize this whole tale. The man is so,
   his wife and friends are so, his words and deeds are so, the whole
   style of writing and subject matter of the tale are so. (One could go
   further and say that the whole *Strange Tales* collection is so.) Subtle,
   contained, cultivated, not showy; poised, poignant, leaving much
   unsaid for the reader to think about.

Kong's poetic accomplishments would have been nothing out of the ordinary. In 1788, in his *General Description of China*, the Abbé Grosier wrote: 'The Chinese say of a man of letters that he has the talent of making good verses, almost in the same manner as if one should praise, in Europe, a captain of dragoons, for being an excellent performer on the violin.'

Tiantai . . . Putuo Temple: The Tiantai range in Zhejiang Province is famous for its Buddhist temples. This one would have been dedicated to the Buddhist 'Goddess of Mercy' Guan Yin, the Bodhisattva Avalokitesvara, whose legendary island home was named Mount Potalaka (abbreviated in Chinese to Putuo).

Jottings from a Distant Realm: An echo of an actual work of the Mongol dynasty, recounting expeditions into fairy realms. Here it is a condensed and elegant way of indicating that Kong has entered an otherworldly (fox-spirit) dimension.

'Bamboo Tears': The ancient sage-ruler Yao nominated as his successor a peasant named Shun, and gave him both his daughters in marriage. At Shun's death these ladies are said to have drowned themselves in the River Xiang, having wept so much that their tears literally 'speckled' the bamboos growing beside their husband's grave.

Speak not of lakes and streams . . . only clouds for me: I have adapted Herbert Giles's version of these famous lines from a poem by the Tang-dynasty poet Yuan Zhen (779–831).

22

A MOST EXEMPLARY MONK

Hell: Lü Zhan'en (1825) remarks laconically: 'For the Nine Dark Places of Hell, and for the Mountain of Knives and the Forest of Swords, see *Journey to the West*.' In its most complete English translation, by Anthony C. Yu (4 vols. (Chicago, 1977–83)), this wonderful novel of the sixteenth century is about 2,000 pages long! A briefer description of the regions of Hell is to be found in 'The Quest of Mulian', an early Buddhist Transformation Text, rediscovered in the caves of Dunhuang in 1908. See John Minford and Joseph S. M. Lau (eds.), *Classical Chinese Literature: An Anthology of Translations* (New York and Hong Kong, 2000), I, pp. 1088–110.

the Mountain of Knives . . . Forest of Swords: The Mountain of Knives is a cliff over which sinners are hurled, to land upon the upright

points of knives below. The branches of the Forest of Swords are
sharp blades which cut and hack all who pass within reach.
gambling and debauchery: Dan Minglun (1842) comments that such
behaviour was all too common among monks. The Jesuit Father Le
Comte wrote in his *Complete History of the Empire of China*
(London, 1739): 'Some [Buddhist Bonzes or monks] abuse the credu-
lous by their hypocritical pretences, others get money out of them
by magical arts, secret thefts, horrible murders, and a thousand
detestable abominations which modesty won't let me mention here.'
the Xingfu Monastery: Possibly the establishment of that name situated at Yetoudian, nine miles from Pu Songling's home town of
Zichuan.

23
MAGICAL ARTS

The Chronicler of the Strange comments: 'How foolish, as I have often
said, to spend money on such consultations! ... And how appalling
for such a man to use the death of others as a way of proving his
own powers!' This story figures prominently in the modern collection
Stories About Not Being Afraid of Ghosts (Peking, 1961), the purpose
of the book being to illustrate Chairman Mao's injunction, 'Do not
fear ghosts, bureaucrats, warlords or capitalists!'

the Chongzhen reign: 1628–43.
fortune-teller: In a note to his *Strange Stories* Giles writes:

The trade of fortune-teller is one of the most flourishing in China. A large
majority of the candidates who are unsuccessful at the public examinations
devote their energies in this direction; and in every Chinese city there are
regular establishments whither the superstitious people repair to consult
the oracle on every imaginable subject – not to mention hosts of itinerant
soothsayers, both in town and in country, whose stock-in-trade consists
of a trestle-table, pen, ink, and paper, and a few other mysterious imple-
ments of their art. The nature of the response, favourable or otherwise, is
determined by an inspection of the year, month, day, and hour at which
the applicant was born, taken in combination with other particulars referring to the question at issue.

hexagrams of the Book of Changes: The hexagrams of the *Book of
Changes*, six-line figures composed of solid (Yang) and broken (Yin)

lines, in sixty-four combinations, have been used for the purposes of divination or fortune-telling since ancient times. The nineteenth-century missionary Justus Doolittle has left a detailed description:

> The fortune-tellers first light incense and candles, placing them before the picture of an old man whom they worship as the deity who presides over this form of divination. They then take [three copper coins of the Tang dynasty] and put them in a tortoise-shell, which they shake once or twice before the picture, invoking the aid and presence of the god. They then empty the cash [coins] out, and, taking them in one hand, they strike the shell gently three times with them, still repeating their formulas. The cash are again put into the shell, and shaken as before three times, when they are turned out upon a plate, carefully observing the manner in which they appear after having fallen out upon the plate. After noting how many have the reverse [uninscribed] side upward, the same cash are put into the shell, and a similar operation is repeated once and again. At the conclusion of the third shaking and the third observation of the relative positions of cash, they proceed to compare the diagrams [hexagrams] with the five elements, according to the abstruse and intricate rules of this species of divination.
>
> (*Social Life of the Chinese* (New York, 1865), pp. 336–7)

dog's blood: Dog's blood has been used in China for exorcism and for the treatment of demon-possession since earliest times. 'Blood of a dog cures catarrh, fever, mental insanity, visions of spectres and spectre-blows, it averts all demonry. Magicians consider dogs suitable for suppressing ground-demons, and capable of averting any evil spectres whatsoever and sorcery' (de Groot, *The Religious System of China*, pp. 1008–9, quoting the sixteenth-century pharmacologist Li Shizhen).

put to death: The Qing-dynasty penal code provided for the execution of sorcerers. 'All persons convicted of writing and editing books of sorcery and magic, or of employing spells and incantations, in order to agitate and influence the minds of the people, shall be beheaded, after remaining in prison the usual period' (Sir George Thomas Staunton (trans.), *Ta Tsing Leu Lee: Being the Fundamental Laws and a Selection from the Supplementary Statutes of the Penal Code of China* (London, 1810), p. 273).

24

WILD DOG

Yu Qi: The Yu Qi uprising in Shandong lasted for much of the first two decades after the Manchu conquest, and was finally suppressed in 1662. Chang and Chang write:

> Over ten thousand of Yu Qi's followers were said to have been brutally slaughtered. Hundreds of innocent people were rounded up and killed by the Manchu soldiers without any evidence of conspiracy. The bloody fighting and massacres finally ended in the early summer of 1662 as Yu Qi led his surviving force to the sea. But the terror continued . . . The Manchu authorities continued to search for, arrest, and imprison anyone who was said to have been slightly acquainted with Yu Qi and his followers. Over one hundred leading families of the gentry were arrested and imprisoned. Stories of horror were heard all over the region; a reign of terror darkened eastern Shandong. The ordeal finally came to an end in 1664 by an order from the Kangxi Emperor.
>
> (*Redefining History*, p. 258, note 12)

Pu Songling grew up in Shandong during this period and must have heard many stories of the 'killing fields'. He wrote in another tale: 'So many were killed – several hundreds a day – the battlefield was soaked in blood and the white bones of corpses were piled up to the sky.'

25

PAST LIVES

The Chronicler of the Strange comments: 'If there are princes and noblemen among our animals, it is because there are animals among our princes and noblemen.' (The modern commentator Qiu Shengwei (1991) takes this to mean that many noblemen are brutes, 'beasts in human clothing'.) The Chronicler goes on to exhort his readers to a life of virtue:

> The man of humble station who leads a virtuous life is like a person who plants a shrub in the hope that it will flower. The man of rank who leads a virtuous life is like a person who cherishes a shrub that has already flowered. In the first case, the shrub will grow and flower; in the second,

its flowering will continue for many years. Those who do not lead virtuous lives, who neither plant nor cherish their shrubs, will become horses, they will have to haul salt-carts and wear bridles; or else they will become dogs, they will eat excrement and be cooked up in a casserole; or they will become snakes, they will grow scales and end up in the bellies of their predators, storks and cranes.

Feng Zhenluan (1818) is much impressed by Pu Songling's rare insight into the inner feelings of dogs concerning their own excrement.

Personally I have always liked the famous anecdote told by Xenophanes (c. 570–c. 480 BC) about that other great believer in reincarnation, Pythagoras (c. 580–c. 500 BC). It reads like a *Strange Tales* miniature.

> Once, they say Pythagoras was passing by when a dog was being ill-treated.
> 'Stop,' he said, 'don't hit it! It is the soul of a friend! I knew it when I heard its voice!'
>
> (Quoted by Bertrand Russell, *History of Western Philosophy* (London, 1946), p. 59)

Soup of Oblivion: This legendary potion for making mortals forget their past lives is administered by an old lady named Mother Meng, who sits upon the Terrace of Oblivion. Perverse spirits may altogether refuse to drink. Then sharp blades start up beneath their feet, and a copper tube is forced down their throats, by which means they are compelled to swallow some. (See Giles, *Strange Stories*, p. 386, note 2.)

the year xinyou: 1621.

26

FOX IN THE BOTTLE

As the commentator He Shouqi (1823) observes, 'Smart woman, stupid fox!'

27

WAILING GHOSTS

The Chronicler of the Strange himself answers the question posed in the last lines of his tale: 'Only virtue can keep evil spirits at bay!' He adds: 'Self-important personages such as Commissioner Wang take note!' Feng Zhenluan (1818) remarks: 'The title Education Commissioner might scare first-degree scholars, but not ghosts!'

Chang and Chang (*Redefining History*, p. 139) stress the political message of this story, in which Pu Songling 'divulges the horror of mass killings by Manchu soldiers in his native district ... The ghosts of the victims of the Manchu slaughter laugh sarcastically at a Ming turncoat, Wang Qixiang, when he tries to scare away the ghosts by mentioning his new official title under the Manchu regime ... The ghosts who died for the Ming cause only laugh at him disgustedly with sarcasm and sadness.'

the Xie Qian troubles in Shandong: Xie Qian's uprising against the Manchus took place in Shandong in 1646–7, during the early years of the reign of the first Manchu Emperor Shunzhi. Zichuan (Pu Songling's home town) became the rebel capital in July 1647, when Pu Songling was a young boy, and the rebels executed large numbers of 'collaborators' (Ming-dynasty officials who had gone over to the Manchus). Xie Qian's men raided Pu Village (Pu Songling's family home outside Zichuan), and one of the Pu family was killed in the fighting. The rebellion was crushed in August 1647, when the Manchu troops took Zichuan using high-powered cannons. In the massacre that followed, more than three thousand people were randomly killed by the Manchus.

Wang Qixiang: Like Pu Songling, a native of Zichuan. He was a second-degree graduate of 1636 and a *jinshi* of 1637, who subsequently went over to the Manchus (thus becoming in the eyes of Xie Qian and many others a collaborator) and went on to be Education Commissioner in Shandong. (There is no information available about the other two Wangs in the story, the visiting gentleman and the gate-man.)

will-o'-the-wisp flickerings of light: These 'were declared by the ancients to be in the main the products of the blood of those slain by steel, that blood having constituted their essential energy while they lived' (De Groot, *The Religious System of China*, IV, p. 80, quoting the *Luncheng* of Wang Chong (27–91)). 'In places where fights are fought and people are slain, the blood of men and horses changes after a series of years into will-o'-the-wisps' (ibid., p. 81, quoting the *Bowuzhi* of Zhang Hua (232–300)).

The British fairy-folklorist Katharine Briggs describes the ignis fatuus, or 'foolish fire', as 'sometimes ghostly in origin, a soul who for some sin could not rest' (*A Dictionary of Fairies* (Harmondsworth, 1976), p. 231), while in Russian folklore, 'these wandering fires are the spirits of stillborn children, which flit between heaven and the Inferno' (*Brewer's Dictionary of Phrase and Fable*, 16th edn (London, 1999), pp. 604–5).

ghosts wailing: In *The Religious System of China*, V (p. 708), De Groot writes of the mysterious wailings attributed by the Chinese to maleficent ghosts, and comments that it was deemed especially ill-omened and dangerous for a man to hear a spectre call him by his proper name (as was the case in our story, with the young gentleman Wang Gaodi).

28

THUMB AND THIMBLE

The foster-mother literally refers to a 'fist-sized mother' and an 'awl-sized baby', the point being that they are both tiny. In the view of Qiu Shengwei (1991), this tale reads like an inconsequential commonplace-book jotting, devoid of any deeper significance. 'After all, there are reports in modern times of such unusual physiological phenomena.' Other modern commentators argue that this tragic story is symptomatic of the oppressive marriage system of China's feudal past, which produced social victims such as this young child-bride.

29

SCORCHED MOTH THE TAOIST

Academician Dong: Dong Na, from Pingyuan in north-western Shandong, was ranked third of the *jinshi* graduates of 1667, eventually rising to be President of the Board of War in the reign of the Manchu Emperor Kangxi (1661–1722).

Under-Secretary Sun: Sun Guangsi is another historical person, also from Shandong (his family origins were in Pingyin, south-west of Ji'nan), who graduated as *jinshi* in 1655, later becoming Vice-President of the Board of War.

30
FRIENDSHIP BEYOND THE GRAVE

The Chronicler of the Strange writes:

> That a man's soul may cleave to a True Friend beyond death, oblivious to death itself – most people will doubt this, but I believe in it implicitly! Did not love enable the spirit of Qian-niang to find her beloved? [For this Tang-dynasty tale, see Minford and Lau, *Classical Chinese Literature*, I, pp. 1032–4.] Do not friends separated by great distances find their way to each other in dreams? How deep it is, the friendship, the predestined affinity between men of letters who spin out their very hearts in intricate webs of words, how deep the friendship between artists and musicians who share inner visions of mountain peaks and rolling streams? [See *Classical Chinese Literature*, I, pp. 231–2, for the famous story 'A Good Listener', about the musician Bo Ya and his friend Zhong Ziqi, who was able to understand his music instinctively. This unspoken 'understanding' is often referred to as a type of true friendship.] Ah! How rare are such encounters! . . . There are not a few men in this world like Ye, men with high aspirations whose lives end in failure! But how few men there are like Ding, friends to whom we can cleave in life and death! Alas!

Feng Zhenluan (1818) comments: 'This moving note by the Chronicler reads like his own autobiography!' Pu Songling himself failed the second-degree examination (crucial for an official career) countless times. After one such failure (in 1687), he wrote an often-quoted lyric, which includes the lines:

> It was as if
> A thousand ladles of cold sweat
> Drenched my gown,
> And my soul
> Left my body;
> And I was numb,
> Felt no pain nor itch,
> But sat listlessly,
> Praying it was all
> A bad dream!

Crane Rider: Ding's name alludes to the Taoist mystics who frequently roamed the skies on their winged steeds.

to purchase for Ye the rank ... for the second degree: In addition to the normal series of examinations, there existed the possibility of purchasing certain ranks, such as membership of the Imperial College, which enabled the candidate to bypass the first-degree examination and become eligible directly for the all-important second-degree examination.

31
KARMIC DEBTS

This tale brings together two recurring themes: the Chinese preoccupation with children and the continuation of the family line on the one hand, and the determining role of karma in key events such as the birth of children on the other. Numerous proverbs drive home the point that virtue (like money) can be accumulated, and that debts (both material and moral) should always be paid. Virtuous sons and daughters are considered to be the visible evidence of previous merit.

> As seed corn is from former years reserved,
> So children are in former lives deserved.
> (Clifford Plopper, *Chinese Religion Seen*
> *through the Proverb* (Shanghai,
> 1926), p. 299)

Wang Xianqian: Obtained his *jinshi* degree in 1570, and rose to be President of the Board of War.
strings of cash: The Chinese traditionally threaded their copper coins or 'cash' on to thongs (usually a thousand coins per thong). The coins had a square hole in the centre for this purpose.

32
RITUAL CLEANSING

Chaotian Temple: The Chaotian (Facing Heaven) Temple complex in Peking was built in 1432, north-west of the Forbidden City, by the Ming Emperor Xuande (r. 1426–36). It was destroyed by fire in 1626. The Spirit Guardians (*ling-guan*) of which the fox-spirit was so afraid were responsible for cleansing temples of all impurities before special days of worship.
tu-na: In these exercises, stale ('dead') air is exhaled as completely as

possible through the mouth, and fresh ('living') air is inhaled through the nose, to fill the lungs to their maximum capacity.

33
THE DOOR GOD AND THE THIEF

Eastern Sacred Mountain: The cult of Mount Tai, the easternmost of the Five Sacred Mountains, situated in Shandong, some thirty-one miles south of the provincial capital Ji'nan, goes back to the very beginnings of Chinese history. During the Qing dynasty (1644–1911), the mountain's sovereign deity (who was judge over the souls of the dead) was officially declared to be 'Lord of this World, Determiner of Birth and Death, Misfortune and Happiness, Honour and Dishonour'. Temples to the mountain are to be found all over China, one of the most famous being in Peking.

34
THE PAINTED SKIN

The Chronicler of the Strange remarks:

How foolish men are, to see nothing but beauty in what is clearly evil! And how benighted to dismiss as absurd what is clearly well-intended! [Is he referring to the Taoist's earlier advice, which Wang ignores?] It is folly such as this that obliges the lady Chen to steel herself to eat another man's phlegm, when her husband has fallen prey to lust. Heaven's Way has its inexorable justice, but some mortals remain foolish and never see the light!

Dan Minglun (1842) comments wryly:

A man who lets a ghost into his own room, ignores his wife's warning, and is blind to the advice of the Taoist priest, is clearly a man in the grip of a serious sexual delusion. The beggar's advice to Wang's wife (that she should not bother bringing her worthless husband back from the dead) is by no means the raving of an idiot, but the wise counsel of an immortal . . .

The contemporary Taiwanese psychoanalytical critic Wang Yijia has some scathing (and rather pertinent) things to say about the way in which the man in the story (a typical Chinese male both obsessed by and terrified of the Chinese femme fatale) has to rely on his wife to save him. 'This is exactly what Sun Longji [the contemporary Chinese-American historian and cultural theorist, author of *The Deep Structure of Chinese Culture* (Hong Kong, 1982)] is referring to when he writes of Chinese males depending on their womenfolk to salvage them whenever things get dirty, whenever the going gets rough, thus helping them to restore the status quo – the Deep Structure of [male-dominated] Chinese culture' (*Liaozhai sougui* (Taipei, 1989), p. 129).

This is one of the most widely read of all the *Strange Tales*. It has been made into a film several times, and continues to be popular for its powerful theme and for the sheer gruesomeness of its detail.

hurrying along . . . with considerable difficulty: She was handicapped by her bound feet. It is worth noting that the binding (mutilation would be a more honest word) of women's feet is itself never something to which Pu Songling draws attention in his work. However strange we may find it today, it was in his time regarded as completely normal.

finding a substitute: If a ghost, especially the ghost of someone who has died from unnatural causes, can find an uncorrupted corpse, the ghost can enter it and make it a substitute for the ghost's own body.

fly-whisk: Originally made from yak's hair, later horsehair or vegetable fibre, fixed to a short wooden handle, the fly-whisk (*chenwei*) was an emblem of purity, detachment and supernatural power, carried by Buddhist and Taoist monks. Its Indian origin (as the chauri or chowry) lies in the Buddhist commandment not to take life, the whisk being used to wave away flies and other insects. In Taoism, it is regarded as an instrument of magic.

the Green Emperor: In one version of legend, the Five Chinese Emperors and their elements and planets comprised the Green Emperor of the East (wood, Jupiter); the Red Emperor of the South (fire, Mars); the White Emperor of the West (metal, Venus); the Black Emperor of the North (water, Mercury); and the Yellow Emperor of the Centre (earth, Saturn).

wooden sword: The sword was one of the principal weapons used by Taoist exorcists. Sometimes they were made of wood (peach-wood, willow, mulberry).

plenty of fine men in this world for you to marry: Pu Songling is having fun putting the venerable words of the *Zuo Commentary on the Spring and Autumn Annals* (?third century BC) in the mouth of the mad beggar. In the original (Duke Huan, 15th Year), a mother, asked by her daughter whether a father or a husband is 'nearer and dearer', replies: 'Any man may be husband to a woman, but she can have but one father.'

35
THE MERCHANT'S SON

The commentators are all loud in the boy's praise. He Shouqi (1823) remarks: 'A treasure indeed, this ten-year-old boy of such courage and intelligence!' When the boy goes to spy on the foxes in the garden, Dan Minglun (1842) quotes Sunzi's *Art of War* (sixth century BC): 'Without entering the tiger's lair, how can one hope to capture the tiger? He is scouting out the disposition of his enemy. "Know the enemy, know yourself, and victory is never in doubt, not in a hundred battles."'

Ho family: Strictly speaking (according to the Hanyu Pinyin system of romanization, the alphabetic system of Chinese words) this family name should be written *He*, but this syllable is open to misinterpretation in English, especially in a narrative.

white liquor: The fiery Chinese schnapps (*baijiu*) distilled from one of several cereals, often misleadingly translated as 'white wine'.

Chen Ping: The famous Han-dynasty statesman (d. 178 BC) who helped restore the imperial family of Liu after the Empress Lü's usurpation of power. As the Grand Historian Sima Qian comments, Chen 'again and again devised ingenious plans, and found a way out of the most perplexing crises' (*Records of the Grand Historian*, trans. Burton Watson, 3 vols., revised edn (Hong Kong and New York, 1993), I, p. 128).

37
A LATTER-DAY BUDDHA

Qiu Shengwei (1991) describes this vivid little sketch as one of Pu Songling's sharpest satirical pieces, a miniature documentary essay (*jishi xiaopin*), exposing the attitudes of a corrupt and perverse feudal society, where eccentricity is elevated to the level of sanctity and excrement to the level of enlightenment. Zhang Renrang and Yang Guangmin (in Ma Zhenfang, 1996) are a little more subtle. They connect the mad monk to the 'crazy Zen' trend of the late-Ming period, as exemplified in such extraordinary individuals and champions of free self-expression as Li Zhi (1527–1602). Despite its absurdity this trend had a 'progressive' dimension, in that it was opposed to Confucian hypocrisy. Pu Songling, as the Chronicler of the Strange, echoes this himself, castigating the behaviour of hypocrites such as Magistrate Nan, who allow their own Confucian temples to fall into disrepair while persecuting 'weirdos' like the mad monk.

Jin Shicheng: The name contains a play on words. The 'mad monk' was, or claimed to be, 'a Living Buddha' (*jinshi chengfu*).
a dhuta: A Buddhist ascetic or mendicant.
Judge Nan: Nan Zhijie was indeed, according to the local gazetteer, Magistrate of Changshan in 1671.

38
FOX ENCHANTMENT

Zhang Renrang and Yang Guangmin (in Ma Zhenfang, 1996) point out the thematic and plot resemblance between this story and 'The Painted Skin'. But whereas in the description of the ghost-seductress and man-killer with the painted skin it is the monster's terrifying, fiendish ugliness that dominates the story, here it is the fatal fox-girl's beauty and sweetly seductive smile.

Tai Su . . . reading the pulse: This method of fortune-telling, practised by traditional physicians, was based on a sensitive pulse-diagnosis (always of primary importance in Chinese medicine). There are at least three pulse points on each wrist and at least twenty-eight recognizable pulse patterns, from which physicians are trained to diagnose the condition of a patient's internal organs and the patient's overall state of health. It is a relatively short step from pulse palpation to the prediction of a patient's lifespan and prosperity. This particular branch of fortune-telling probably dates back to at least the ninth century.
It wasn't your face . . . It was your tail: This is a typical *Strange Tales* use of allusion, the force and humour of which are utterly lost in translation. See p. xvii of the Introduction.
he had ejaculated in his bed: This is one of many tales where the progressive weakening of the male partner is associated with his frequency of ejaculation. One of the prime goals of traditional Chinese sexual practice has always been the conservation of energy, and through the centuries Chinese males have striven to minimize

seminal emission, to 'treasure their fluids'. As Douglas Wile puts it, 'Post-coital enervation impressed the ancient Chinese more than any heights achieved through orgasm ... Ejaculation brings enervation not relaxation, homeostatic holocaust not emotional catharsis. Detumescence of the penis is consistently analogized in these texts with death ... Thus sexual prowess came to be defined not as the ability to expend semen but as the ability to save it' (*Art of the Bedchamber: The Chinese Sexual Yoga Classics* (Albany, 1992), pp. 5–7).

Golden Elixir: The Golden Elixir (*jindan*), which the fox-spirit had been perfecting over the years, is the ultimate goal of the prolonged process of 'nourishment' (*caibu*) by which these succubi accumulate psychosexual power, feeding on the energies of their partners. Another tale, 'Fox as Vampire', by the eighteenth-century writer Ji Yun, describes the process in a very unadorned manner. Ji Yun's beautiful fox-girl finally confesses to her two worn-out lovers: 'I invented that excuse of mine about the man on the mountain, just to give you five days to rest. I wanted to provide you with a chance to recuperate your strength and produce more sperm for my purposes, so that I could nourish my inner force. Now my secret is out. But since your sperm is all used up anyway and neither of you are of any further use to me, I shall be on my way.' In both stories, Ji Yun's 'Fox as Vampire' and Pu Songling's 'Fox Enchantment', the encounter between fox and human can be read as a figurative representation of the sexual transaction between human lovers, in which the one greedily takes and absorbs the essence of the other in order to accumulate her (sometimes his) own strength and life force. Here Taoist techniques of yogic self-cultivation can be seen to merge with the sexual practices of the Chinese Art of the Bedchamber, in a cynical quest for self-empowerment at the expense of one's partner. Here we have in another guise the 'battle of stealing sexual essences', what the Dutch scholar Robert van Gulik has called the 'cruel sexual vampirism of the Taoist male alchemists' (*Erotic Colour Prints of the Ming Period* (Tokyo, 1951), p. 11). In this tale, the fox-spirit plays the role of vampire, treating her partners as mere instruments, human cauldrons and crucibles, in her search for the Golden Elixir. This theme recurs many times in the *Strange Tales* collection, and is developed at greater length in Tale 54, 'Lotus Fragrance'.

40

THE LAUGHING GIRL

Qiu Shengwei (1991) waxes lyrical at Pu Songling's description of the beauty and naive spontaneity of this young girl's pure nature, and praises her aspirations for freedom. He goes on to interpret her ultimate 'taming' as daughter-in-law in the Wang household as a tragic capitulation to feudalism. Her calculating destruction of the young man next door is an uncanny trait (*yaoqi*) inherited from her fox-mother, evidence of Pu Songling's supreme skill as a creator of complex character. Pu Songling himself, as Chronicler of the Strange, suggests a hidden depth of character beneath Yingning's mischievous spontaneity: 'If one considers merely her giggling and silliness, she seems a person without depth. But the nasty trick she plays beneath the wall shows her to be a person of the greatest cunning. And her deep love for her ghost-mother turns her laughter to tears. Beneath our Yingning's laughter lie hidden depths of emotion.' One early manuscript inserts here: 'Our Yingning was not silly at all.'

Judith T. Zeitlin has an ingenious take on the strange twist of the plot, whereby the story invented by Cousin Wu to bring Wang out of his premature decline 'turns out to be true': 'Although the girl proves to be a fox-spirit and the aunt is a ghost, this does not affect the inadvertent truth of the cousin's falsehood. In the fantastic world of *Liaozhai*, there are no real lies, because a lie comes true as soon as it is believed' (*Historian of the Strange*, p. 167).

my own cousin . . . getting married: Marriage between people of the same surname was normally forbidden by law. But a man could marry his cousins on the maternal side.

Year of the Horse: Chinese years are distinguished by the names of twelve animals: rat, ox, tiger, hare, dragon, serpent, horse, sheep, monkey, cock, dog and boar. To the common question 'What is your honourable age?', the reply was frequently 'I was born under the . . .' And the hearer by a short mental calculation could tell at once how old the speaker was. (See Giles, *Strange Stories*, p. 69, note 5.)

your own niece . . . Your sister's daughter: Chinese terms of relationship are very specific, unlike our vague terms *cousin*, *uncle* and *aunt*. In Chinese, it is never open to doubt whether a cousin, nephew/niece, or the cousin's parents (the uncle and aunt) are maternal or paternal, older or younger than the person referred to, etc. When a plot (like this one) depends on the exact nature of the relationship,

one has to make it specific, even if to our ears it sounds a little clumsy.
a shadow like a normal living human: Ghosts were not supposed to
have shadows, and they had very little appetite.
passionately fond of flowers: The word used here (*pi*) means obsession,
mania, 'a pathological fondness for something'. Judith T. Zeitlin
devotes a fascinating chapter of her *Historian of the Strange* (Chapter 3, 'Obsession') to the historical pedigree of this concept and its
rise to prominence in the late Ming as a mode of self-expression and
of self-realization. She quotes a passage from the late-Ming poet
and essayist Yuan Hongdao (1568–1610) that perfectly evokes an
obsession even more extreme than Yingning's passion for flowers:

> In antiquity when someone gripped by an obsession for flowers heard tell
> of a rare blossom, even if it were in a deep valley or in steep mountains,
> he would not be afraid of stumbling and would go in search of it ...
> When a flower was about to bloom, he would move his pillow and mat
> and sleep alongside it to observe how the flower would evolve from
> budding to blooming to fading. Only after it lay withered on the ground
> would he take his leave ... This is what is called a *genuine* love of flowers;
> this is what is called *genuine* connoisseurship.

banksia rose: A fragrant, damask rambling rose producing clusters of
small, violet-scented, double white flowers in April and May. The
plant was named after the wife of Sir Joseph Banks (1743–1820),
the greatest botanist and plant collector of his time (he travelled
with Captain Cook to the Pacific in 1768, and to Iceland in 1772).
Banks, as President of the Royal Society, and founder of what
became Kew Gardens, was instrumental in introducing to England
such Chinese flowering plants as the Yulan magnolia, the japonica,
the hydrangea, the wisteria, tree and herbaceous peonies, many
varieties of roses, chrysanthemums and camellias, all carried back
to London on the tea-clippers of the East India Company. A man
after Yuan Hongdao's own heart!
Nine Springs: This has been a term for the Realm of the Dead ever
since the Han dynasty.

41

THE MAGIC SWORD AND THE MAGIC BAG

When Little Beauty describes her techniques of enchantment, explaining that she uses 'whichever method seems most likely to work at the

time', Dan Minglun (1842) comments: 'If a man is subject to lust, she uses her sensual beauty; if he is subject to greed, she uses gold. In reality it is the man who attracts the enchantment, not the demon who inflicts it.' Feng Zhenluan (1818) comments at the very outset of the story that Ning's uprightness and the single-mindedness of his affections (he only loves one woman) are what make him impervious both to the girl's sexual advances and to the lure of gold.

This is one of several tales that refer to the Martial Arts. Tales of the deeds of sword-wielding *xia*, sometimes translated as knights errant, with lesser or greater supernatural powers, have always been hugely popular with Chinese readers, and in our own times the works of Martial Arts novelists such as Louis Cha (Jin Yong) are best-sellers in Chinese communities all over the world. Cha himself was influenced by *Strange Tales*, and uses one of them to good effect in his novel *The Deer and the Cauldron* (3 vols., Oxford University Press, 1997–2003). The character Wu Liuqi, referred to in the novel as the 'Beggar in the Snow', is taken straight from the tale 'The Mighty General' (Zhang Youhe (1962), p. 220).

Surangama Sutra: A Tantric Buddhist scripture (*Lengyan jing*) translated into Chinese in 705 by the Indian Paramiti. Karl Ludvig Reichelt writes: 'Parts of this sutra are used every day during the morning mass in the temples. Often long sections are quoted in a phonetic transcription of the Sanskrit texts. These parts are said to be of the greatest importance in order to cleanse the heart for the new day. They work almost like a magic formula' (*Truth and Tradition in Chinese Buddhism* (Shanghai, 1927), p. 216).

42
THE DEVOTED MOUSE

Zhang Duqing: (1642–?1716), a poet-friend of Pu Songling's, who like Pu was never appointed to an official position. His ballad, a poem in thirty-six lines, is extant. The contemporary poet and novelist Vikram Seth has retold this tale in verse in his collection *Beastly Tales from Here and There* (London, 1992).

43

AN EARTHQUAKE

Modern commentators note that a massive earthquake took place on 25 July 1668 (which corresponds with Pu Songling's lunar dating), with its epicentre in Shandong. Effects of the quake were felt as far away as the provinces of Jiangsu, Hebei, Henan, Shanxi, Shaanxi, Hubei and Zhejiang. Seismologists estimate that it must have registered 8.5 on the Richter scale.

44

SNAKE ISLAND

Dengzhou: Another name for the town of Penglai, where the northern Shandong coast reaches up towards the Liaodong Peninsula and the city of Dalian, across the Gulf of Bohai. Penglai was always a place associated with magic and the gods. Indeed, it was a name for a fabulous Taoist paradise, home of the Eight Immortals, a place where:

> the houses are made of gold and silver, the birds and animals are all white, and pearl and coral trees grow in profusion. The flowers and seeds all have a sweet flavour, and those who eat them do not grow old or die. There they drink of the fountain of life, and live in ease and pleasure. The Isles are surrounded with water that has no buoyancy, so it is impossible to approach them. They are inhabited only by the immortals who have supernatural powers of transportation.

(See E. T. C. Werner, *Dictionary of Chinese Mythology* (Shanghai, 1932), p. 372, and Plopper, *Chinese Religion Seen through the Proverb*, p. 359.) The indispensable *Lonely Planet Guide to China* (1994 edition) refers to 'the coastal castle of Penglai, a place of the gods often referred to in Chinese mythology, perched on a clifftop overlooking the sea' and to the 'optical illusion' for which Penglai is apparently still famous: 'The last full mirage seen from the castle was in July 1981 when two islands appeared, with roads, trees, buildings, people and vehicles. This phenomenon lasted about 40 minutes.'

45

GENEROSITY

The Chronicler of the Strange observes: 'Generosity in poverty is something found among drinkers, gamblers and drifters. Here it is the innkeeper's wife who is exceptional. How could a man not wish to repay her generosity? Ding's actions were indeed an example of the "kindness of a single meal never forgotten".' This is a reference to Sima Qian's biography of Fan Ju, a statesman of the Qin dynasty (221–207 BC). 'Fan Ju used his private wealth to repay all those who had helped him when he was starving and in distress. Persons who aided him with no more than a single meal invariably received their reward' (*Records of the Grand Historian*, I, p. 145).

Dan Minglun (1842) comments that the innkeeper's wife shows exactly the kind of generosity of spirit appreciated by Ding, who was such an admirer of the chivalrous code of the knight errant.

Guo Xie: One of the most celebrated 'knights errant' (*youxia*) of the early-Han dynasty, who died in approximately 127 BC. His story is memorably told by Sima Qian: 'Guo Xie was short in stature and very quick-tempered; he did not drink wine. In his youth he was sullen, vindictive, and quick to anger when crossed in his will, and this led him to kill a great many people' (*Records of the Grand Historian*, II, pp. 413–18).

censor: In this case it would have been a Shandong provincial censor investigating Ding Qianxi. We are never told what Ding's problem was, or why he had to disappear so fast and was able to return safely so soon afterwards. This laconic style is typical of *Strange Tales*. Censors were often called the Emperor's 'Eyes and Ears', the system through which he was made aware of the true state of the Empire. See also the Glossary.

47

THE GIANT TURTLE

Gold Mountain: Jinshan is a hill north-west of the city of Zhenjiang (written Chinkiang in Treaty Port days), in Jiangsu Province, on the south bank of the Yangtze, near its intersection with the Grand Canal. One imagines that the Zhang family must have travelled south along the canal.

the turtle's strange ways: The species referred to in this tale is the
yuan, translated by Bernard Read as 'the Great Sea-turtle'. It 'comes
from the rivers and lakes of the South, and is from 10 to 20 feet in
circumference' (*Chinese Materia Medica* VIII: Turtle and Shellfish
Drugs (1937), pp. 30–31). It was clearly feared from early times,
since Read also quotes the alchemist and pharmacologist Tao Hongj-
ing (456–536): 'It is said that when this turtle is old it is able to
change into a *mei* (a brownie with a man's face and four legs).' Chen
Cangji of the Tang dynasty comments on the fearsomeness of the
beast: 'It is hard to kill them. When nearly all the flesh has been cut
away it will still bite things and will snap up a bird such as a kite.'

48

MAKING ANIMALS

sorcerer: Dan Minglun (1842) remarks that this sort of sorcery combined with kidnapping was a speciality of people from Sichuan and
Hunan. (Dan himself was a Guizhou man, and apparently had
encountered it there as well.)

died under torture: 'All persons convicted of . . . employing spells and
incantations . . . shall be beheaded, after remaining in prison the
usual period' (*Ta Tsing Leu Lee*, p. 273). In *Chroniques de l'étrange*
(Arles, 1996), André Lévy observes that in this case the Magistrate
most probably caused the man to die on the rack because the normal
course of justice would have been so protracted.

50

DYING TOGETHER

the twenty-first year of the reign of Kangxi: 1682.
Judge Bi: See note on Bi Jiyou, Tale 66, 'Mynah Bird'.

51

THE ALLIGATOR'S REVENGE

The alligator . . . Yangtze River: The Yangtze alligator (*Alligator
sinensis*) has an average length of six and a half feet. Bernard Read
gives interesting information (*Chinese Materia Medica* VII: Dragon
and Snake Drugs (1934), pp. 20–22), taken from his usual Chinese
sources and from the pioneer study written by Albert Auguste Fauvel

(1851–1909), 'Alligators in China', *Journal of the North-China Branch of the Royal Asiatic Society* XIII. According to Chen Cangji of the Tang dynasty, the alligator is 'shaped like a dragon, making a fearful noise; it grows up to ten feet long, and can give out clouds which descend like rain'. Other sources emphasize how hard it is to kill: 'Quite a long time after boiling water has been poured down its throat it dies and is skinned. Its skins are used for covering drums. It is a sleepy animal, lying about with its eyes constantly closed. Exceedingly strong and fierce, it can break down the banks of rivers . . . It can fly sideways but not upwards.'

Chen Youliang: (1320–63), a prominent rebel leader of the last years of the Yuan (Mongol) dynasty, and a rival of Zhu Yuanzhang, who founded the Ming dynasty.

52

SHEEP SKIN

the year xinchou: 1661.

53

SHARP SWORD

Lü Zhan'en (1825) makes the connection between the soldier's sharp sword that cuts clean through (literally 'through the big openings') and the famous blade of the Taoist cook Ding in the fourth-century *Book of Zhuangzi*, Chapter 3, 'The Secret of Caring for Life': 'I go along with the natural make-up, strike in the big hollows, guide the knife through the big openings, and follow things as they are.'

54

LOTUS FRAGRANCE

The Chronicler of the Strange writes: 'Alas! The dead seek life, the living seek death! Is not this human bodily frame the most coveted thing in the world? Unfortunately those who possess this treasure often fail to cherish it; they live with less shame than foxes, and vanish into death with less trace than ghosts!'

In *Redefining History*, Chang and Chang see in this fox-and-ghost story 'profound questions in real life and in this world, [questions about] the meaning of human existence and the metaphysical, physical, psychological and spiritual images of the human body' (p. 44). Wai-yee Li sums up the story succinctly: 'Mutual appreciation and devotion persist through karmic cycles and eventually unite the three characters in a harmonious bigamous relationship' (*Enchantment and Disenchantment: Love and Illusion in Chinese Literature* (Princeton, 1993), p. 127).

embroidered slipper: In *Chinese Footbinding* (New York, 1966, pp. 51ff.), Howard Levy writes:

> The shoe in which the tiny foot was encased flirtatiously suggested concealment, mystery and boudoir pleasures. Well-to-do ladies took pride in their small and well-proportioned 'golden lotuses' [bound feet], designed shoes for them of crimson silk, and wore especially attractive models when preparing for bed. The sleeping shoes, scarlet in hue, were intended to heighten male desire through a striking colour contrast with the white skin of the beloved. These shoes were greatly prized and sought after as love tokens. A woman might secretly give them to her enamoured as proof of love sentiments.

let alone a ghost: Sexual intercourse with a ghost was considered to be a source of extraordinary pleasure, and at the same time usually fatal. See also the Introduction, pp. xxiv–xxv.

sucking the life out of men: See the note on the Golden Elixir in Tale 38, 'Fox Enchantment'. This notion applied as much in the human world as it did to the relations between fox-spirits and men. Man 'regarded woman as the "enemy" because through her causing the man to emit semen she robs him of his precious Yang essence' (van Gulik, *Erotic Colour Prints*, p. 11). See also the Introduction, pp. xxi–xxii.

three Fairy Hills: In Taoist legend, the three Fairy Hills or Islands in the Eastern Sea – Penglai, Yingzhou and Fangzhang – were:

> inhabited by genii whose lustrous forms are nourished upon the gems which lie scattered upon their shores, or with the fountain of life which flows perennially for their enjoyment. Upon the Fairy Island of Yingzhou grows the magic mushroom known as *zhi*, and there is a rock of jade a thousand metres in height, from which flows a spring resembling wine . . . It is called the sweet-wine fountain of jade. Whoso quaffs a few measures of this beverage becomes suddenly inebriated and achieves eternal life.

> (Plopper, *Chinese Religion Seen through the Proverb*, p. 359)

large bolus-like pill: A bolus is a large pill much used in traditional Chinese medicine.

straw burial-doll: Figures buried with, or burned on behalf of, a dead man, to accompany him to the Nether World.

welcoming Sang into her family: It was not uncommon for the groom to 'marry into' the bride's family, especially when he was poorer than they were. Although Sang may have technically become part of the Zhang family, he seems to all intents and purposes to have lived quite independently from them after the marriage.

the swallow of yesteryear: The line is from a well-known lyric poem by Yan Shu (991–1055).

the year gengxu: 1670.

55

KING OF THE NINE MOUNTAINS

first year of the reign of . . . Shunzhi: 1644.

Eight Astrological Signs: These were not 'signs' in our sense of zodiacal signs, but four two-character combinations that represented the year, month, day and hour of the person's birth. One of the two characters was taken from the series known as the Ten Celestial Stems, the other from the series known as the Twelve Earthly Branches, these two series combining to form the basic cycle of sixty used in the Chinese calendar and in fortune-telling. There were many methods of deriving a person's fortune from his Eight Signs or Characters.

Liu Bei . . . the Three Kingdoms: Liu Bei was the Pretender to the throne of the disintegrating Han dynasty, during the period of civil war known as the Three Kingdoms (221–80).

the Dragon Throne: The dragon was throughout the ages the emblem of Imperial power. The Imperial dragon can be distinguished by its fifth claw.

56

THE FOX OF FENZHOU

a fox cannot cross the river: It is part of traditional fox-lore that 'when crossing a frozen river or lake he [the fox] advances very slowly and deliberately, putting his head down close to the ice and listening for the sound of water beneath' (Thomas Watters, 'Chinese Fox-Myths',

NOTES

Journal of the North-China Branch of the Royal Asiatic Society VIII
(1874), p. 51).

57
SILKWORM

Dan Minglun (1842) comments: 'The whole story grows out of the one word "eunuch". But it is handled with skill and ingenuity, with delicacy and elegance, and with a wonderfully expressive style.' Zou Zongliang points out (in Ma Zhenfang, 1996) that in one way this story follows the standard pattern (a recurring one in *Strange Tales* and in much Chinese romantic fiction) of two beautiful women who end up both living with the same man. But unlike many of these romances it broaches the taboo subject of sex, and for this reason has rarely been included in the standard *Strange Tales* selections and has seldom been translated. Zou endorses Dan Minglun's high praise of the story's literary qualities, but goes on to launch a vehement and lengthy attack on what he sees as the story's unnecessary, indeed culpable, obscenity, its gratuitous dwelling on details of matters sexual. This he compares with the episode at the end of Tale 40, 'The Laughing Girl', where the scorpion stings the neighbour's penis. Alas, laments Zou, that such foul dross is to be found side by side with the wonders of *Strange Tales*. Zou recalls in this connection a thought-provoking question once put to him by 'a Japanese friend'. Why is it that in the *Strange Tales*, a girl and a man have no sooner set eyes on each other than they jump into bed? Zou blames the oppressive weight of feudal morality and Confucian prudish hypocrisy, which for centuries prevented normal contact between the sexes and thus created a breeding ground for alienation and perversion, an environment perfect for the growth of such abnormal sexual tendencies. How else, he asks, can one account for the way in which Clever has no sooner opened the door to young Lian than she wants to have sex with him? Or the way in which Auntie Hua, having cured his unfortunate deficiency, locks the young man up and treats him as a sex object? Or the way in which his own feelings of love towards Clever are reduced to base lust? Nonetheless, Zou commends Pu Songling as a progressive element, for having reflected with such accuracy this socially regrettable phenomenon.

silkworm: T. H. Gray writes:

At the time of their birth the worms are black and so small as scarcely to exceed a hair in breadth. Owing to their diminutive size, those in charge of them cut the leaves of the mulberry tree into very small pieces . . . When they have reached the age of thirty-two days they are full grown, each being about two inches in length, and almost as thick as a man's little finger.

> (*China: A History of the Law, Manners and Customs of the People* (London, 1878), pp. 222–3)

cakes of tea: During the Song dynasty (960–1278) a very high-grade 'tribute tea' was made in this form, the leaves compressed into the form of thin circular cakes. Its full name was Dragon Phoenix Cake tea.

not that rude: In the Chinese, she refers by name to a famous ruffian of the Three Kingdoms period, Chen Yuanlong, who had no regard for common courtesy and made his guests sleep on the floor while he slept on a proper bed.

58
VOCAL VIRTUOSITY

Wang Xinyi: An astronomer and mathematician who lived during the reign of the Manchu Emperor Shunzhi (1644–61), gaining his *jinshi* degree in 1647. He was a native of the Shandong county of Changshan.

59
FOX AS PROPHET

shameless greed: The allusion is to a character in a Tang-dynasty story who shamelessly shared his wife's favours in exchange for gifts in cash.

the eleventh year of the reign of the Kangxi Emperor: 1672.

Wang Fuchen: The Provincial Commander-in-Chief of Shaanxi, who in 1674 rebelled against the Manchu Emperor Kangxi, allying himself with the ambitious Satrap Wu Sangui in the south. Wang surrendered to the Manchu army in 1676.

61

FOX CONTROL

Lao Ai . . . Empress Dowager of Qin: Lü Buwei, the powerful Prime Minister of the King of Qin (who subsequently became First Emperor of the Qin dynasty), needed to find a way of satisfying the desires of his sovereign's mother, who despite her increasing age 'did not cease her wanton behaviour'. (She had originally been Lü's own concubine, and showed signs of wishing to renew their relations.) Lü found a man named Lao Ai, gifted with an unusually large penis, and took him on as a servant, instructing him 'to stick his member through the centre of a wheel made of paulownia wood, and walk about with it, making certain that the report of this feat reached the Dowager's ears, so as to excite her interest'. To get himself smuggled into the palace, Lao Ai agreed to undergo a mock castration. He then proceeded to make the Empress Dowager pregnant twice, and she grew to love him greatly. In 238 BC, their clandestine relations were eventually discovered and he was executed, together with many of his relations, including the two sons she had borne him. Three years later, Lü Buwei himself was dismissed and committed suicide. See *Records of the Grand Historian*, I, pp. 163–4.

62

DRAGON DORMANT

Commissioner Qu: Qu Qianqiao, a native of Changshan in Shandong, passed his *jinshi* degree in 1577. He rose to be a commissioner in the Office of Transmission.

63

CUT SLEEVE

the Cut Sleeve persuasion: Emperor Ai, last ruler of the Former Han dynasty (206 BC–AD 9), had a number of boy-lovers, the best-known of whom was a certain Dong Xian. Once when the Emperor was sharing his couch with Dong Xian, the latter fell asleep lying across the Emperor's sleeve. When the Emperor was called away to grant an audience, he took his sword and cut off his sleeve rather than disturb the sleep of his favourite. Hence the term 'Cut Sleeve' (*duanxiu*) has become a literary expression for homosexuality among men. (See Robert van Gulik, *Sexual Life in Ancient China* (Leiden, 1961), p. 63.)

Shao-yin Meridian: The meridian of the kidney, running up from the lower front part of the foot, the meridian associated with sexual dysfunction. 'Anyone who is easily tired, easily confused or upset, is likely to be suspected of some deficiency in this area, and a prolonged depletion of the energy of this function circle [meridian] is thought to result in the disintegration of the personality, total disorientation and insanity' (Manfred Porkert, with Christian Ullmann, *Chinese Medicine* (New York, 1988), pp. 109–10).

pretty boys: Timothy Brook writes:

> The practice of hiring 'singing boys' to entertain at banquets and then letting the guests fondle them after their performance was already known in the most exclusive circles in the capital in the mid-Ming, but few subscribed to this confusing pleasure ... A county magistrate in Fujian paid fifty taels of silver for 'a beautiful boy' in the 1580s, for which his upright provincial governor had him fired.
>
> (*The Confusions of Pleasure* (Berkeley, 1998), pp. 231–2)

Devil's Dance: A dance performed at court by a group of sixteen female dancers, during the Mongol dynasty (1279–1368).

Jesting Judgement: Pu Songling's witty envoi, as I read it, pokes fun at the anti-homosexual lobby, in the form of a brilliant and highly lascivious parallel-prose pastiche of pedantic neo-Confucian prudery. It is roundly condemned as vulgar and obscene by no less a scholar than Zhu Qikai (see his edition, note 85, p. 317), who refuses to interpret its real sense, obliging the reader only to the extent of providing the raw meaning of individual allusions (most of which he takes straight from the nineteenth-century commentator Lü Zhan'en). This strange little piece should surely be seen as a humorous counterpart to Pu Songling's more famous tour de force, the Author's Preface. It is certainly just as crammed with literary allusions. Judith T. Zeitlin calls it 'an amazingly arcane and rather hostile parody in parallel prose on homosexual practices' (*Historian of the Strange*, p. 91). I find it not so much hostile, as a deliberately exaggerated spoof.

A close parallel can be found in the preface to the album of erotic paintings and poems published by Robert van Gulik, in his *Erotic Colour Prints*, 'Variegated Positions of the Flowery Battle':

This preface is a literary *tour de force*. It is composed according to the Chinese stylistic technique known as *jiju* 'assembling phrases', by stringing together various quotations from some ancient literary work. In this case the text consists entirely of quotations from the Five Classical Books. Correct translation is uncommonly difficult because these disconnected phrases are extracted from the Classics at random with a view to fitting the author's particular purpose – a purpose which often completely ignores the meaning the phrase had in the original context.

(pp. 208–9)

Pu Songling's time was one of considerable sexual tolerance. For the extraordinarily rich and ambivalent world of late-Ming/early-Qing erotic fiction, see Keith McMahon's two books, *Causality and Containment* (Leiden, 1988) and *Misers, Shrews and Polygamists* (Durham, 1995). The classic homosexual collection *Tales of the Cut Sleeve* was most probably published during the seventeenth century. While homosexual practices are described in other stories in *Strange Tales*, this is the principal full-length story devoted to the love between a man and a male fox-spirit.

Line 12 *Of Half-Eaten Peach*: Mi Zixia, one of the most celebrated homosexuals in Chinese history and the favourite for a time of Duke Ling of Wei (534–493 BC), 'was strolling with the ruler in an orchard and, biting into a peach and finding it sweet, he stopped eating and gave the remaining half to the ruler to enjoy' (Bret Hinsch, *Passions of the Cut Sleeve* (Berkeley, 1990), p. 20).

Line 15 *bird-track*: This is playing with expressions from the famous poem by Li Bo (701–62), 'The Road to Shu Is Hard': 'West on Taibo Mountain, take a bird road there . . . When earth collapsed and the mountain crashed, the muscled warriors died' (Minford and Lau, *Classical Chinese Literature*, I, pp. 723–5). The Chinese character for 'bird', normally read *niao*, when read *diao*, is a slang expression for the penis.

Line 17 *Peach Blossom Spring*: The title of the famous idyll by Tao Yuanming (365–427), in which a fisherman stumbles upon an earthly paradise. (See Minford and Lau, *Classical Chinese Literature*, I, pp. 515–17.) The relevant passage in Tao's original reads: 'The fisherman left his boat and entered the grotto, which at first was extremely narrow, barely admitting his body; after a few dozen steps it suddenly opened out on to a broad and level plain.' 'Grotto' was one of the standard terms for the vagina.

Lines 25–6 *the up and down . . . manual masturbation*: Here Pu Songling is playfully quoting from the *Zuo Commentary*, where a man questioning a prisoner first raises his hand, then lowers it. (See *The Chinese Classics*, V, pp. 519–20.)

Line 31 *Flowery Pool*: Suggestive of the many expressions for the female genitalia, such as Dark Garden, Jade Terrace.

Line 37 *One-Eyed Marshal*: The One-Eyed Marshal was Li Keyong (d. 908), a famous general of Turkish origin at the end of the Tang dynasty, known as the One-Eyed Dragon. (One is tempted to say One-Eyed Trouser-Snake . . .) This literary and historical reference is full of homosexual double entendres.

Line 39 *Red Hare*: The great horse of Lü Bu (d. AD 198), General of the Eastern Han dynasty. Here it has a sexual connotation, as does the rear gate of the barracks.

Line 43 *to steal the Great Bow*: Another mischievously witty reference to the venerable *Zuo Commentary*, where 'Yang Hu threw off his armour, went to the duke's palace, and took from it the precious symbol of jade and the great bow' (*The Chinese Classics*, V, p. 770). It is not that hard to interpret the sexual innuendo here, bearing in mind that Jade Stalk is one of the many terms for the penis.

Lines 47–8 *Yellow Eel . . . student's thighs*: Lü Zhan'en (1825) refers to a story about the prominent Academician Wang during the Ming dynasty, who had a homosexual liaison with a student in the Imperial College. The young man dreamed of a yellow eel that appeared between his thighs.

Lines 50–53 *The plums sold by Wang Rong . . . posterity*: Wang Rong (235–306), one of the Seven Sages of the Bamboo Grove (see Minford and Lau, *Classical Chinese Literature*, I, pp. 445–6), was proverbially mean and bored holes in his plum stones so that no one else would be able to grow such a delicious variety. Here the plums are being used as a metaphor for childless homosexual relations.

Lines 54–6 *Black Pine Wood . . . Yellow Dragon Palace*: Zhu Qikai (1989) follows Lü Zhan'en (1825) in interpreting these place-names sexually. The (very sketchy) contemporary paraphrase by Yuan Lükun et al. (1992, pp. 288–9), which turns Pu Songling's wit into a heavy moralistic tirade, is extremely blunt here: 'And when the passive male partner suddenly empties his bowels, there is nothing his aggressor can do to stop it.'

64
THE GIRL FROM NANKING

Wang Jinfan (1767): 'Was she a ghost or a fox? There is no knowing for sure. But her coming and going seem more like that of a fox.' Qiu Shengwei (1991) is in no doubt that she is a fox and that she represents the valiant women of the oppressed classes in feudal society.

He Shouqi (1823) analyses the story in terms of an interesting prescription/herb dialectic. A prescription is of no use without its constituent herbs; herbs are no use without the relevant prescription. The two complement each other. If one has the prescription but not the herbs, one must go in search of the herbs; if one has the herbs but no prescription, one must go in search of the prescription. When the girl says she would 'happily be his concubine', He Shouqi comments: 'A prescription in search of herbs.' When Zhao 'pin[es] for the girl greatly', he writes: 'Herbs in search of a prescription.' Zhang Zhenjun (in Ma Zhenfang, 1996) adopts He Shouqi's analysis, adding that the whole story probably evolved as a way of explaining a local folk remedy for warts. Like Wang Jinfan, he concludes that the girl is most probably not a ghost but a fox (from her way of coming and going), but unlike the majority of foxes (who tend to live in abandoned graves), this one lives in the bustling city and helps her father run a shop. Their conjugal love is of a very practical nature, notes Zhenjun, the woman being depicted as performing unromantic household tasks, both in Yishui and in Nanking. She was out on the road in the first place in quest of herbs. Zhao ends up providing them, and is rewarded (for his devotion and for the herbs) with a stock of miraculous remedies.

His luck is thin: Compare the following proverbs, all to be found in Plopper's invaluable *Chinese Religion Seen through the Proverb*:

A man's heart may be lofty as Heaven; but his fate is thin as paper.
If a man's fate is to have only eight tenths of a pint of rice, though he traverse the country over, he cannot get a full pint.
A nine-pint measure will hold nine pints, and will not take an extra pint.
A man fated to receive a certain amount, if he obtains more will not be able to keep it.
Each glass of wine and each slice of meat is predestined.

65
TWENTY YEARS A DREAM

The commentators like the ending. Wang Shizhen (1634–1711): 'The story comes to an end and yet it does not end. Marvellous!' Feng Zhenluan (1818): 'Wang only appreciates this quality in the ending; actually the whole story is like that, fragmentary, inconclusive, loose, delicate, exquisite.' Dan Minglun (1842): 'It is like hearing the sound of celestial music suddenly cease.'

Zhang Zhenjun (in Ma Zhenfang, 1996) praises the description of Locket, who reminds him of Lin Daiyu, the frail and melancholy heroine of *The Story of the Stone*. The platonic relationship between Yang and Locket, their days spent sharing literary and musical interests, is for him reminiscent of a certain genre in Chinese literature (see, for example, Shen Fu's *Six Records of a Floating Life* (c. 1809), trans. L. Pratt and Chiang Su-hui (Harmondsworth, 1983)).

Judith T. Zeitlin comments in her *Historian of the Strange* (p. 154) that in this story Pu Songling has inverted the old 'cliché of the *lebenstraum*', replacing the conceit of 'life as a dream' with that of 'death as a dream'.

refinement and cultivation: *Fengya* encapsulates many of the qualities of the Chinese scholar-gentleman, and indeed evokes the whole cultural universe of *Strange Tales*. *Ya* (elegant, good taste, good form) implies a certain fastidiousness and restraint, an unostentatious distinction, qualities that derive from education and breeding. It is the opposite of *su* (vulgar, bad taste). As Lin Yutang puts it, 'When one drinks tea at a famous spring sitting on a rock with bare feet, it is said to be *ya*' (*The Importance of Living* (London, 1938), p. 444). At one point in this story, Feng Zhenluan (1818) comments that Locket, with her stylish literary and musical accomplishments, is an 'elegant ghost', whereas a little later when the boorish Martial Arts enthusiast Wang starts shouting at her, Feng comments on his 'vulgarity'. The word *feng* (literally wind) brings a touch of glamour to *ya*, a touch of the almost dandyish charm known as *fengliu* (literally 'wind-flowing').

lotus kernels: The allusion here is to the breasts of Yang Guifei, the famous consort of the Tang Emperor Xuanzong, which he described as 'soft and warm as freshly peeled lotus kernels'. (See the tenth-century work *Kaiyuan tianbao yish*, quoted in Zhu Qikai (1989), p. 331.)

'*The Lianchang Palace*': A ballad by the Tang-dynasty poet Yuan
Zhen (779–831) in which an old man recounts the upheaval of the
An Lushan rebellion and describes the abandonment of the Tang
Emperor Xuanzong's palace in Luoyang.

'*trimmed the lamp at the west window*': Li Shangyin (*c*. 813–58),
'Lines to be sent home, written on a rainy night':

> You ask me, when shall I return?
> No date is set.
>
> On the Ba Mountains
> Night rain swells the autumn pond.
> When shall we two trim the lamp
> At the west window?
> When shall we talk about the
> Night rain on the Ba Mountains . . .

66

MYNAH BIRD

Bernard Read's free translations (they are really paraphrases, based
on the drafts of his Chinese collaborators) from that extraordinary
sixteenth-century survey of natural phenomena, the *Materia Medica*
(*Bencao Gangmu*) of Li Shizhen (1518–93), were published in several
issues of the *Peking Natural History Bulletin* (1932–41). Read has
this to say about the mynah bird in China (*Chinese Materia Medica*
VI: Avian Drugs (1932), pp. 65–6):

It loves to bathe in water. It has a timid look, hence the name *qu*. Its
mating habits account for the second name *quyu* [used by Pu Songling].
The name *hangao* comes from its habit of flying in flocks when snow is
about to fall. It nests in magpies' nests or in the hollows of trees, or in the
rafters of houses. The head and body are black. It is spotted white under
the wings. It has a human-like tongue, and when this is cut short with a
pair of scissors it can learn to talk like a man. The young have yellow
beaks which turn white later. According to the *Zhou Li* it never comes
north of Ji'nan [in Shandong]. Its flesh, which is sweet, bland and non-
poisonous, can be eaten to cure bleeding piles. It can be roasted or powdered. It is also taken for stuttering and sighing, and regurgitation. It
improves the mind. For a chronic cough it must be caught on the last day
of the year. The pupils from the eyes of the mynah, when rubbed with

milk and dropped in the eyes, clear the eyesight and enable one to see things at a very great distance.

It is interesting to note that Lü Zhan'en (1825) himself quotes much of this same source in his own note on the tale. Within the huge and timeless domain of Chinese letters known as *biji* or 'notebook literature', history, geography, philology, gastronomy, botany, pharmacology and storytelling were close neighbours.

The Prince: Zhu Qikai (1989) speculates that the princely household in question may have been that of Zhu Rongshun, Prince Lingqiu of the Ming dynasty, sixth son of Zhu Gui (1374–1446), Prince of Dai, who was himself the thirteenth son of the founder of the dynasty, Zhu Yuanzhang. Zhu Rongshun was enfeoffed as Prince in 1424 and set himself up in Jiangzhou (Shanxi) in 1454.

Shanxi . . . Shaanxi Province: These two adjoining provinces in China's north-west have always posed problems of romanization. When they are written in Chinese characters, it can be seen immediately that they mean quite different things. The first province means literally 'Mountain (*shan*) West (*xi*)' or 'Mountainous West' (or possibly 'West of the Mountains', referring to the Taihang range of mountains) – just as Shandong (Pu Songling's province) means 'Mountain or Mountainous East'. The second, on the other hand, means literally 'West (*xi*) of the Pass (*shaan*)', the pass being the celebrated Tong'guan Pass, strategically situated between the ancient cities of Chang'an and Luoyang, where the Yellow River turns eastwards.

But when the two words are spoken, all that sets the first apart from the second is its tone, the fact that its first syllable *shan* is in the first, level tone, whereas the first syllable of the second is in the third, sinking tone. Since the Hanyu Pinyin system does not indicate tones, both provinces would therefore have been written identically. Something had to be done, or administrative chaos would have ensued. In an attempt to mark the difference, it was decided to write the second 'Shaanxi'. This doubling of the vowel is left over from an earlier Chinese romanization system, in which all vowels were tonally spelt, thus: *shan* (first tone), *sharn* (second tone), *shaan* (third tone) and *shahn* (fourth). (The old solution to this problem, before the days of Hanyu Pinyin, was to write the first Shansi, and the second Shensi.)

Bi Jiyou: (1623–93), a native of Zichuan, Pu Songling's wealthy friend and patron, for whom he worked as secretary from 1672 until Bi's death. See Tale 50, 'Dying Together'.

67

LAMP DOG

Han Daqian: A man from Pu Songling's home town of Zichuan. His father had served as Vice-Commissioner in the Office of Transmission, while Han Daqian himself held a minor post in the Imperial Court of Entertainments, an institution loosely supervised by the Board of Rites.

68

DOCTOR FIVE HIDES

Wang Shizhen (1634–1711) also records this little anecdote in his collection *Notes from North of the Pond* (*Chibei outan*).

Chang Tiyuan: A historical person, a local magistrate in the Kangxi reign, mentioned in the local gazetteer of Luonan (Shaanxi), the county where he served. 'Official student' means first-degree graduate.

'Doctor Five Hides' ... Spring and Autumn era: Baili Xi, a famous statesman who served under Duke Mu of Qin (reigned 659 BC), was called 'Doctor Five Hides' because at one point he was ransomed for the price of five ram skins. (See Sima Qian, *Records of the Grand Historian*, I, p. 96.) Lü Zhan'en (1825) gives chapter and verse on Baili Xi, in an extended note several times the length of the tale itself.

tribute student: These Senior Licentiates took a special examination and became eligible for official appointment.

69

BUTTERFLY

doll factory: Literally a 'kiln for baking tiles', girls being traditionally supposed to be content with playing with earthenware tiles, as opposed to boys, who played with jade. See the *Book of Songs*, no. 189.

70

THE BLACK BEAST

The Chronicler of the Strange, in a long note, interprets the story allegorically as a comment on the spineless grovelling and passivity of the people (tiger) towards the corrupt officials who exploit them (black beast). Contemporary Marxist commentators are quick to pick up on this.

Li Jingyi: Grandfather of Pu Songling's friend Li Yaochen (1643–1723). At an important stage in Pu's life (1664, the year after his second failed attempt to pass the provincial examination), he went to stay in the Li family residence, and read widely in their richly stocked library.

71

THE STONE BOWL

drinking game: For examples of more mundane drinking games, see the (eighteenth-century) novel *The Story of the Stone*, especially Chapter 28.

the festival of the winter solstice: This festival, known in Chinese as *la*, goes back into very early Chinese history. See Tun Li-ch'en, *Annual Customs and Festivals* (Peiping, 1936), p. 93.

72

A FATAL JOKE

Sun Jingxia: A holder of the *juren* second degree, who in the fourth year of the Emperor Kangxi's reign (1665) held the teaching post of Instructor in Zichuan, Pu Songling's home town. He went on to become a county magistrate.

75

GHOST FOILED, FOX PUT TO ROUT

The Chronicler of the Strange writes:

I was born too late, alas, to have been able to offer Li the use of my own stick or slippers. But I heard this tale from my elders and am convinced of the great spirit and fearlessness of the man, of which these two incidents

provide ample evidence. When a man has such largeness of spirit, he has
nothing to fear from spirits and foxes!

Wang Jiliang of Xincheng: Feng Zhenluan (1818) states that this Wang
was a relation of the celebrated poet Wang Shizhen (who himself
added certain comments to *Strange Tales*).

76

FROG CHORUS

Wang Zisun: A historical person, the educated son of a poor Zichuan
family, whose life is recorded in the *Zichuan Gazetteer*.

79

FLOWERS OF ILLUSION

He Shouqi (1823) remarks: 'The Taoist was a crafty fellow!' Dan
Minglun (1842) comments, when the man returns empty-handed from
the lake: 'Form is Void, and Void is Form. If we go searching through
Form [the word also carries the meaning of Beauty or Desire] then it
[the object of our search] will be ever harder to find, ever more distant.'
On the blood staining the Intendant's chair: 'If only this punishment
could be meted out for every miscarriage of justice.'

Daming Lake: 'Great Clear Lake', fed by the numerous springs of
Ji'nan, occupies the whole of the northern part of the old inner city,
covering a quarter of the total area within the city walls. There is a
very fine description of it in the second chapter of the late-nineteenth-
century novel *The Travels of Lao Ts'an*, by Liu Tieyun (translated
in 1952 by Harold Shadick). The couplet on the great gate bore the
following inscription: 'Four sides lotuses, three sides willows. A
whole city of mountains, half a city of lake.'
What a pity there are no lotuses . . . gathering: In addition to being
one of the principal symbols of Buddhism, the lotus was greatly
appreciated by the traditional Chinese scholar-gentleman. The love
of the lotus was memorably expressed by the Song-dynasty philosopher Zhou Dunyi (1017–73):

I myself especially love the lotus. It emerges from the mud and remains
untainted. It cleanses itself in the purest water and yet never flaunts its

beauty. It is hollow within and upright without. It has no tendrils or branches. Its scent is the finer for distance. It stands pure and upright. It can be viewed from afar, but not fondled closely. I consider the lotus the true gentleman among flowers.

80

DWARF

He Shouqi (1823) comments: 'In recent years, a similar case to this occurred in Guangdong Province. The Magistrate investigated it, but it is not known if the magician concerned was put to death. The Magistrate of Ye was an admirable fellow.' (He Shouqi was himself of Cantonese origin.) In his *Strange Stories* (p. 139, note 1), Herbert Giles quotes from the Hong Kong *China Mail*, 15 May 1878:

Young children are bought or stolen at a tender age and placed in a *qing*, or vase with a narrow neck, and having in this case a movable bottom. In this receptacle the unfortunate little wretches are kept for years in a sitting posture, their heads outside, being all the while carefully tended and fed ... When the child has reached the age of twenty or over, he or she is taken away to some distant place and 'discovered' in the woods as a wild man or woman.

82

PRINCESS LOTUS

Cassia Palace: A double allusion, to the fairy precincts of the Moon Goddess, in which legend has it there grew a cassia tree; and to the 'plucking of the cassia branch', a figure for the achievement of success in the civil service examinations.

A gentleman cherishes the lotus flower: An allusion to the famous eulogy of the lotus by the Song-dynasty philosopher Zhou Dunyi. See the note to Tale 79, 'Flowers of Illusion'.

And then suddenly he awoke ... sun had almost set: As the commentators Feng Zhenluan (1818) and Dan Minglun (1842) point out, 'Princess Lotus' harks back to two classic dream-tales of the Tang dynasty, 'The World in a Pillow', by Shen Jiji (*c.* 740–*c.* 800; see Minford and Lau, *Classical Chinese Literature*, 1, pp. 1021–4), and 'A Lifetime in a Dream', by Li Gongzuo (*c.* 770–*c.* 848; see Wolfgang Bauer and Herbert Franke, *The Golden Casket* (Harmondsworth,

1965), pp. 102–17). In the former tale, a man dreams of the passage of an entire lifetime while he dozes with his head on a hollow pillow made of green porcelain. He wakes to find that this 'lifetime' of his has 'lasted' less than the time needed to cook a bowl of millet gruel. The latter expresses the same basic idea, but this time the dream world is identified with an ant colony located beneath the 'southern branch' of a nearby tree. Both were turned into lyric dramas by the great Ming playwright Tang Xianzu (1550–1617).

83

THE GIRL IN GREEN

light as silk: Some texts have 'light as a fly'.

84

DUCK JUSTICE

our county town: Zichuan, fifty miles east of Ji'nan.

86

STEEL SHIRT

Steel Shirt: He Shouqi (1823) comments that this style of kungfu was still in existence in his day. And it is still practised today. Wong Kiew Kit writes: 'An established method like Steel Shirt prescribes that you can withstand a weapon attack on your body without sustaining injury if you practise the training procedure for three years' (*The Art of Shaolin Kung Fu* (Shaftesbury, Dorset, 1996), p. 46).

88

LUST PUNISHED BY FOXES

The Chronicler of the Strange points out that whereas most people are aware of the danger involved in storing ordinary poisons (such as arsenic) in the house, few appreciate the havoc that can be caused by leaving aphrodisiacs lying around the place. Men have a healthy fear of the dangers of the military battlefield, but are blissfully unaware of the far greater dangers lurking in the bedchamber.

For a glimpse of the type of thing our gentleman may have been collecting, the reader is directed to Robert van Gulik's excellent study *Sexual Life in Ancient China* (Leiden, 1961), especially pp. 133–4, where the author describes various potions listed in the ancient sex handbook of Master Dong Xuan, such as 'Bald Chicken Potion' ('if taken for sixty days one will be able to copulate with forty women' – this drug was apparently so named after an unfortunate cock who ate it by mistake when it had been thrown out in the courtyard, and copulated with a single hen for several days without dismounting, pecking her head bald); 'Deer Horn Potion' (to cure impotence and involuntary emission); a potion for enlargement of the penis (a mixture of broomrape and seaweed); and a potion for shrinking the vagina (made up of four ingredients, including sulphur and birthwort root). The same text is translated by Douglas Wile in *Art of the Bedchamber*, pp. 112–13.

89

MOUNTAIN CITY

Sun Yu'nian: His father Sun Zixie rose to be President of the Board of War under the Emperor Shunzhi (r. 1644–61).

90

A CURE FOR MARITAL STRIFE

The Chronicler of the Strange warns against the powers of meddling womenfolk (the Six Old Women – bawds, matchmakers, clairvoyants, female quacks, witches and midwives; and the Three Sisters – Taoist and Buddhist nuns, and female diviners). They may be capable of influencing things for the better, turning (as in this tale) antipathy into love, but they can also exercise a negative influence. Such women should be kept from the door.

'venture near the tripod': Literally, 'ask about the cauldrons'. This is a reference to a famous incident in early Chinese history (described in the *Zuo Commentary*), when the Viscount of the southern feudal state of Chu 'ventured to ask about the size and weight of the ancestral cauldrons (or tripods) of the Zhou dynastic King'. This was interpreted as revealing his intention to seize power and usurp the throne. Pu Songling has given the expression a characteristically humorous twist.

erotic scrolls: For a superb introduction to this genre (literally *chun-gong* or *chunhua*, Spring Paintings) as it would have existed in Pu Songling's day, see van Gulik, *Erotic Colour Prints*. The album 'Variegated Positions of the Flowery Battle', reproduced in its entirety in this book, is dated by van Gulik to the late seventeenth century.

moxa: The powdered leaves of mugwort (*Artemisia vulgaris*), used in the healing process known as moxibustion, which is as ancient as acupuncture and uses the same system of points and meridians, or circuits of energy (*qi*), bringing Yin and Yang into proper balance. Moxibustion is especially recommended in all diseases caused by an excess of Yin. The cones are placed on particular spots and ignited; they are extinguished only after they have burned down to the skin and a blister is formed. In the late-Ming novel *Golden Lotus* (first published in 1618), moxa is used as a sexual stimulant during intercourse. The novel's most recent translator David Roy provides a note: 'It was an erotic practice in China to burn cone-shaped pellets of dried moxa on various parts of the female body that were regarded as particularly sensitive, including the breasts, the lower abdomen, and the mons veneris, in order to induce an involuntary writhing that was regarded as sexually stimulating to both partners' (*The Plum in the Golden Vase*, vol. I (Princeton, 1993), p. 500, note 41).

earthworm: Feng Zhenluan (1818) comments that the earthworm, when steeped in wine, can promote conjugal harmony. The commentary to the *Xuanzhongji* of Guo Pu (276–324) describes the creature as 'earth born, an insect without understanding, indiscriminate in its sexual behaviour, having intercourse with locusts' (Read, *Chinese Materia Medica* X: Insect Drugs (1941), p. 171).

as harmonious as . . . lute and zither: The *qin* and the *se* have been emblems of conjugal happiness from earliest times. The two instruments, strictly speaking a seven-stringed and a twenty-five-stringed zither, occur in the *Book of Songs*, where they are played at marriages and other festivities.

92

ADULTERY AND ENLIGHTENMENT

The author's concluding comment (here for once he does not use the persona of the Chronicler of the Strange but speaks directly to his readers) refers to a Zen anecdote, in which a brutal murderer attains instant Buddhahood by throwing down his sword. In Patriarch Luo's case, it was the discovery of the adulterers that triggered off a sudden change of heart and enlightenment. In any case, Pu Songling seems to be poking fun at accepted ideas of sainthood.

Patriarch Luo: According to an informative note in the recent *Liaozhai* edition of Sheng Wei (2000), p. 1249, Patriarch Luo (whose unusual path to enlightenment is described in this story) lived during the reign of the Ming Emperor Zhengde (1506–22), and was originally from Jimo in Shandong. Subsequently he was enlisted in the Miyun garrison (north of Peking). After his enlightenment, he became the founder of the Buddhist sect known as the Luo Sect, a branch of the Linji Zen sect, which spread during the Manchu dynasty and became especially popular among the boatmen on the Grand Canal, eventually merging with the secret society known as the Green Gang (*qingbang*). There were many attempts to suppress Luo's sect, some of which are vividly described in J. J. M. de Groot's *Sectarianism and Religious Persecution in China* (Amsterdam, 1903–4), especially on pp. 180ff. and 285ff. De Groot based his version of the legend (which differs greatly from the one given by Sheng Wei) on 'a parcel of old, dog-eared papers' brought to him by a sect member in Amoy, in the last years of the nineteenth century.

Jade Icicles ... 'transformed': According to Taoist and Buddhist legend, the mucus of certain highly enlightened beings continued to descend from their noses after their transformation or death. This mucus was termed Jade Icicles (literally Pillars) and was regarded as a sign of spiritual perfection.

93
UP HIS SLEEVE

the Prince of Lu: Zhu Tan (1370–90), tenth son of Zhu Yuanzhang (1328–98), founder of the Ming dynasty. Zhu Tan was installed in Yanzhou in southern Shandong as Prince of Lu in 1385. (Lu was the ancient name for the southern part of Shandong.) His father, a ruthless but highly effective ruler (he was described by a Chinese scholar of the eighteenth century as 'sage, hero and robber'), was renowned for his Taoist beliefs and wrote a commentary (in ten days) on the Taoist classic *The Way and Its Power* (*c*. fourth century BC).

he produced a beautiful lady from within his sleeve: The capacious sleeve of the Chinese gentleman's gown, like 'the world within the pillow' of the Tang tale (see the note to Tale 82, 'Princess Lotus'), is 'an alternative world magically enclosed within the Taoist's sleeve' (Judith T. Zeitlin, *Historian of the Strange*, p. 197). For He Shouqi (1823), this microcosmic sleeve-universe recalls the Buddhist saying 'Mount Sumeru [the world mountain of Hindu and Buddhist cosmology] is contained in the tiniest grain of mustard.'

94

SILVER ABOVE BEAUTY

fine grass-script calligraphy: Grass script (*caoshu* – sometimes translated 'cursive script') is the most free and unrestrained of the principal styles of Chinese calligraphy. The two Tang-dynasty masters of this style were Zhang Xu (mid eighth century) and the monk Huai-su (725–85). See Minford and Lau, *Classical Chinese Literature*, I, pp. 750 and 807.

95

THE ANTIQUE LUTE

the Chinese lute: The seven-stringed *qin* is in reality more like a zither than a lute. It is the instrument par excellence of the Chinese scholar-gentleman, producing music of a subdued and highly refined beauty. The cultural ideology surrounding the instrument has been superbly described by Robert van Gulik in his study *The Lore of the Chinese Lute* (Tokyo, 1940).

We 'know each other's sound': One who 'knows the sound' of another is, as William Acker puts it:

a friend whose knowledge of music is such, and whose mind is so attuned to that of the player that he can catch the finest nuances of the performer's thought and feeling, as he listens, and by his speech or by his silence after the playing of a piece shows that he has understood the other's thoughts as though they have been spoken rather than played . . .

(*Some T'ang and Pre-T'ang Texts on Chinese Painting*
(Leiden, 1954), p. 10)

The expression comes from the old story of Bo Ya and Zhong Ziqi, in the Taoist *Book of Liezi* (?third century BC), a story that lies at the heart of the 'lute' legend:

Bo Ya was an excellent lute-player, and Zhong Ziqi an excellent listener. When Bo Ya strummed his lute, with his mind on climbing high mountains, Zhong Ziqi would say, 'Excellent! Lofty as the peaks of Mount Tai!' When Bo Ya's mind was on flowing waters, Zhong Ziqi would say, 'Excellent! Boundless as the waters of the Yellow River and the Yangtze!' Whatever came into Bo Ya's thoughts, Zhong Ziqi always grasped it. Once when Bo Ya was roaming on the north side of Mount Tai, he was caught in a sudden storm of rain, and took shelter under a cliff. Feeling sad, he took up his lute and strummed it. First he composed an air about the persistent rain, then he improvised the sound of crashing mountains. As the music progressed, Zhong Ziqi never missed the direction of his thought. Bo Ya put away his lute and sighed: 'Excellent! Excellent! How wonderfully you listen! What you imagine is exactly what is in my mind. My music can never escape you!'

(Based on Angus Graham's translation; see Minford and Lau,
Classical Chinese Literature, I, pp. 231–2)

A later Taoist text, *The Spring and Autumn of Mr Lü* (c. 239 BC), provides the well-known conclusion to the story: 'When Zhong Ziqi died, Bo Ya smashed his lute and broke the strings, and never played again for the rest of his life. He reckoned that there was no one left in the whole world worth playing to.' Van Gulik comments: 'This story may be said to contain the essence of the system of *qin* ideology, stressing as it does the supreme importance of the significance of Lute music: to express it while playing, and to understand it while listening . . . Perhaps it is an echo of the sacredness of music in ancient China' (*The Lore of the Chinese Lute*, p. 96).

97
ROUGE

The Chronicler of the Strange, in one of his more biting comments, reflects on the prevalence of false accusations in the courts, and on the lack of conscientious and intelligent magistrates. He states that your average mandarin comes to his yamen and whiles the day away playing chess, not caring a fig for the plight of the ordinary citizens in his care, and resorting to the instruments of torture at the slightest opportunity. At the end of his comment, he appends a moving eulogy of his mentor, Judge Shi Runzhang.

Madame Wang: This form of address reflects the Chinese custom whereby married women refer to themselves by their maiden name. She was Mrs Gong, née Wang.

Li Qiusun: His real family name was E, but this is a case where the Hanyu Pinyin system of transcribing Chinese lets us down badly and I have substituted a more easily pronounceable and readable name.

and had him tortured on the rack: Certain forms of torture were legal. These included an instrument for compressing the ankle bones (sometimes called by foreigners the Scotch Boot), made from three wooden boards with grooves; an instrument for compressing the fingers, made from five round sticks; and the bamboo (which was supposed to be planed smooth, and without knots). If the prisoner was beaten to a jelly in the course of his trial, it was technically described as being 'warmly questioned'. But there were also many 'irregular' forms of torture. Samuel Wells Williams writes:

> Pulling or twisting the ears with roughened fingers, and keeping them in a bent position while making the prisoner kneel in chains, or making him kneel for a long time, are among the illegal modes. Striking the lips with sticks until they are nearly jellied, putting the hands in stocks before or behind the back, wrapping the fingers in oiled cloth to burn them, suspending the body by the thumbs and fingers, tying the hands to a bar under the knees, so as to bend the body double, and chaining by the neck close to a stone, are resorted to when the prisoner is contumacious . . . Compelling them to kneel upon pounded glass, sand and salt mixed together, until the knees become excoriated, or simply kneeling upon chains is a lighter mode of the same infliction.
>
> (*The Middle Kingdom* (New York, 1882), pp. 507–8)

Wu Nandai: Obtained his third degree (*jinshi*) in 1633 and served as Prefect of Ji'nan in 1655.

execution after the Autumn Assizes: 'All criminals capitally convicted, except such atrocious offenders as are expressly directed to be executed without delay, are retained in prison for execution at a particular period in the autumn; the sentence passed upon each individual being first duly reported to, and ratified by, the Emperor' (*Ta Tsing Leu Lee*, p. 2).

Shi Runzhang: (1619–83), a celebrated poet and scholar. He was appointed Commissioner of Education in Shandong in 1656, and was the Examiner in 1658 when Pu Songling passed his first (*xiucai*) degree, thus becoming in a sense his mentor. He went on to win a

reputation as a compassionate and incorruptible official, 'affection-
ately known as Shi the Buddha'. (See Arthur W. Hummel, *Eminent
Chinese of the Ch'ing Period* (Washington, DC, 1943), p. 651.)

City God Temple: See note to Tale 2, 'An Otherworldly Examination'.

judgement was as follows: This is another tour de force of allusive
parallel prose (to be compared with the Author's Preface, and the
satirical postface to Tale 63, 'Cut Sleeve'). Pu Songling was clearly
inspired to go to some lengths in honour of his mentor. I have given
one or two hints of this in my notes to the first paragraph, but have
freely paraphrased the remaining sections.

Deng Tu . . . lecher of old: The butt of a rhapsody by the third-century
BC poet Song Yu, where he is characterized as a sexually incontinent
debauchee, who 'although married to an ugly and misshapen wife,
yet had five children by her'.

Pencheng Guo: The philosopher and sage Mencius (*c.* 372–*c.* 289 BC)
said, 'He is a dead man, that Pencheng Guo.' When Pencheng Guo
was put to death, the disciples asked, 'How did you know, Master,
that he would meet with death?' Mencius replied, 'He was a man
who had a little ability but had not learned the great doctrines of
the superior man. He was just qualified to bring death upon himself,
but for nothing more' (*Mencius*, VII, 2, 29).

Jiang Zhongzi . . . in the Songs: 'I pray you, Jiang Zhongzi, do not
come leaping over my wall' (*Book of Songs*, Songs of Zheng, no.
76).

Liu Chen in love: Liu Chen, of the first century AD, once wandered
away with his friend into the Tiantai Mountains to gather herbs.
There they fell in love with two beautiful girls, who gave them
hemp-seed to eat (or in some versions wine to drink); and after a
stay of what appeared to them about six months, they returned to
find that seven generations had passed away.

98
THE SOUTHERN WUTONG-SPIRIT

Wutong-spirit: The expression *Wutong* (literally the Five Penetrating
Ones) is said by some to refer to five brothers who descended from
the sky in human form in a great blaze of light. By the end of the
Tang dynasty there were numerous temples dedicated to them. In
later popular belief, the origins of these five deities were eclipsed by
their sexual and orgiastic associations. In the early years of the
Manchu dynasty, the governor of Jiangsu, Tang Bin (1627–87),

took steps to dismantle the Wutong temples, which were especially common around Suzhou, and to abolish the 'lewd practices' associated with them – drunken rituals, ecstatic dancing and singing. He claimed that whenever a woman displayed acute signs of fever or hysteria, the local shamanesses would say that she had been taken as a bride by the Wutong. Women taken with this condition would rave incoherently, and in the end they usually wasted away and died.

Nicholas B. Dennys (*The Folk-Lore of China* (London, 1876), p. 87) mentions a story in Yuan Mei's eighteenth-century collection *What the Master Did Not Say*, where it is recounted that in a certain village in Sichuan Province the Wutong-spirit required a young girl each year, and that the girl chosen was duly possessed by this evil spirit. In the seventeenth-century *Anatomy of Melancholy*, Robert Burton records a similar story from Japan:

At Japan in the East Indies, at this present (if we are to believe the relation of travellers), there is an idol called Teuchedy, to whom one of the fairest virgins in the country is monthly brought, and left in a private room, in the *fotoqui*, or church, where she sits alone to be deflowered. At certain times the Teuchedy (which is thought to be the devil) appears to her, and knoweth her carnally. Every month a fair virgin is taken in; but what becomes of the old, no man can tell.

(Everyman edition, 3 vols. (London, 1932), III, p. 48)

Recent scholars have suggested a psychological connection between spirit-possession and prenuptial anxiety, and have emphasized the vulnerability of women in traditional Chinese society in the period shortly before and after the consummation of marriage (often to a man they had never seen before). Vivien Ng comments: 'Young women, particularly those on the verge of marriage, seemed to be especially susceptible to the lecherous attentions of malevolent spirits, and they often became temporarily insane as a result' (quoted by Dorothy Ko, *Teachers of the Inner Chambers* (Stanford, 1994), p. 211); while Richard von Glahn writes: 'Feigning union with *Wutong* was a culturally accepted strategy employed by women to avoid sleeping with their betrothed husbands or to escape conjugal obligations altogether' (see 'The Enchantment of Wealth: The God Wutong in the Social History of Jiangnan', *Harvard Journal of Asiatic Studies* 51 (1991), pp. 699–701).

It is interesting to compare these modern explanations with accounts of the incubus phenomenon in Europe. In the words of

Isidore of Seville (*c.* 560–636), 'Satyrs are they who are called Pans in Greek and Incubi in Latin. And they are called Incubi from their practice of overlaying that is debauching. For they often lust lecherously after women, and copulate with them.' The 1486 witch-craft manual *Malleus Maleficarum* describes incubi as 'fallen angels now in devilish shape which have appeared to wanton women and have sought and obtained coition with them' (Maureen Duffy, *The Erotic World of Faery* (New York, 1980), pp. 13–14). The historian Keith Thomas provides a succinct explanation: 'Feelings of guilt evoked by sexual dreams and nocturnal emissions could be assuaged by the reflection that an incubus or succubus must have been at work' (*Religion and the Decline of Magic* (Harmondsworth, 1973), p. 568).

99

SUNSET

such a fine, cultured young man: See the note on refinement and cultivation in Tale 65, 'Twenty Years a Dream', for the full range of meaning of the expression *fengya*.

the Golden Dragon King: A deity revered in the provinces of Anhui and Jiangsu. His origins are supposed to date back to a man named Xie Xu, nephew of the Empress Xie (consort of the last Emperor of the Southern Song dynasty (1127–1278)). Xie Xu was Heir Apparent, and in the last years of the rapidly crumbling dynasty he hid away in the Golden Dragon Mountains near Hangzhou. In order to avoid falling into the hands of the Mongols, he drowned himself in the Tiao River. There was a temple dedicated to him in Suzhou, as a river god.

100

THE MALE CONCUBINE

silken softness: The Chinese expression, a cliché in the vocabulary of beauty, literally means 'smooth and lustrous as lard'.

101
CORAL

The Chronicler of the Strange comments:

> Desisting from meat and wine is but the outward appearance of Buddhist faith. True enlightenment consists in utter childlike simplicity. Yue Zhong saw in his beautiful woman-companion a pure fellow-searcher for the Way, not a partner in sensual pleasure. They slept together for thirty years, in a relationship that combined passion and detachment. Such is the true aspect of Buddhist faith, one that the world cannot fathom!

Feng Zhenluan (1818) several times praises Yue Zhong as a true son of the Dharma, a man combining the qualities of Buddhist, Taoist and knight errant. The whole story is, he says, a veritable *Sutra of Perfect Enlightenment* (*Yuanjuejing*, a scripture translated into Chinese by the Tibetan monk Buddhatrata in 693). Dan Minglun (1842) remarks: 'Let the drinkers of wine drink wine, and the drinkers of tea drink tea! If one has attained the Tao, Buddha is present in both fasting and drinking. If one has not attained the Tao, then Buddha is absent both from drinker and faster', while in *Tales of the Supernatural* (Edinburgh, 1984), H. C. Chang writes that: 'This is one of the very few truly religious tales in *Liaozhai*. On the surface it is about the filial piety of a glutton, but the hero's filial piety leads him to true piety, and his gluttony and drunkenness bring about his eventual enlightenment.'

Devotion to one's parents or filial piety (*xiao*), was one of the cardinal Confucian virtues. Confucius said: 'The duty of children to their parents is the fountain whence all other virtues spring, and also the starting point from which we ought to begin our education' (*The Book of Filial Devotion*, ?fourth–third century BC). Although in this tale Yue Zhong does not necessarily see eye to eye with his mother, in his own way he is extraordinarily devoted to her. The part of the story where he cuts off his own flesh and serves it to her in her delirium echoes some of the more extreme stories of Filial Devotion that were told to Chinese children through the ages, such as the one in the collection *Twenty-Four Examples of Filial Piety* (itself probably a Ming-dynasty concoction), about the Magistrate Yu Qianlu in the Southern Qi dynasty (479–502), who, to oblige the doctor treating his dying father, tasted the old man's excrement.

rid himself of his wife: In traditional Chinese law, a husband could unilaterally repudiate (i.e. divorce) his wife on any one of seven grounds: sterility, lewdness, disobedience to her parents-in-law, loquacity, stealing, jealousy and any repulsive disease. We are not told what the grounds were in this particular instance.

The fact of his own childlessness ... on his mind: In the words of Herbert Giles:

> The importance of male offspring in Chinese social life is hardly to be expressed in words. To the son is confided the task of worshipping at the ancestral tombs, the care of the ancestral tablets, and the due performance of all rites and ceremonies connected with the departed dead. No China-man will die, if he can help it, without leaving a son behind him. If his wife is childless he will buy a concubine.
>
> (*Strange Stories*, p. 39, note 10)

Coral: The young lady's name, Qiong Hua, literally 'beautiful reddish-jade, or agate', has a poetic resonance suggestive of the immortal realms from which she has been banished. He who savours the flowers of the mythical Qiong tree, growing to a towering height on the slopes of the fabulous Kunlun Mountains, is supposed to live for ever.

sea at Nanhai: Pu Songling seems to be more than a trifle vague here about his geography. In ordinary speech, Nanhai can simply mean the Southern Sea, what foreigners call the South China Sea, the stretch of ocean between the provinces of Fujian and Guangdong and the island of Taiwan, in which case it would be perfectly plaus-ible for Yue Zhong to travel from his home in Xi'an (in the north-west) through the province of Fujian to the coast. But the place of pilgrimage referred to here must surely be the Holy Island known as Mount Putuo farther north off the coast of Zhejiang Province, which since the ninth century has been a centre for the cult of the Bodhisattva Guan Yin, the Goddess of Mercy, whose 'special work is to receive the spirit as it leaves the body and place it in a lotus-blossom which opens in the Sacred Lake of the Western Heaven' (Plopper, *Chinese Religion Seen through the Proverb*, p. 156). In this story both Yue Zhong's mother and his companion Coral are linked to the icon of Guan Yin, and to the Bodhisattva's qualities of beauty and compassion. Guan Yin and the lotus-flower are the keynotes of the story. Guan Yin is commonly represented in Buddh-ist devotional art as a beautiful woman seated or standing on a lotus-blossom.

Her island shrine is spoken of in Buddhist parlance as Nanhai or
Mount Putuo, a reference to the Potala Mountains near the southern
coast of India, supposed home of the original male Boddhisattva
Avalokitesvara, of whom Guan Yin is the Chinese female transformation. H. C. Chang, in a long and very interesting note on Mount
Putuo in his *Tales of the Supernatural*, quotes a 1913 eyewitness
account of one of Guan Yin's apparitions by Sir Reginald Johnston
(tutor to the last Manchu Emperor):

At certain times, when atmospheric and tidal conditions are favourable,
a shaft of sunlight streams into the cave through a gap in the roof called
the *tian-chuang* or Heaven's Window, and strikes athwart the flying foam.
The cave then seems to be filled with a tremulous haze, in which the
unbeliever sees nothing but sunlit spray, but which to the devout wor-
shipper is a luminous veil through which the Bodhisattva of Love and Pity
becomes visible to the eyes of her faithful suppliants.

One cannot help but be reminded of Lourdes, and the apparitions
of the Virgin Mary at the grotto.

In a sense, Nanhai, or South Sea, is 'wherever Guan Yin is'. Feng
Zhenluan (1818) quotes the lines:

> That home wherein Guan Yin dwells
> Is a Southern Sea before our very eyes;
> But where men know her not,
> Their prayers are all in vain.

Apsaras: See note to Tale 6, 'The Painted Wall'.

102
MUTTON FAT AND PIG BLOOD

Ji: A Chinese form of spirit-writing or planchette that still takes place in
Hong Kong and Taiwan. Two people, normally the medium and his
assistant, hold a carefully selected wand of peach-wood or willow,
forked or sometimes T-shaped, over a tray of sand. A spirit is called
upon to descend, whereupon the wand traces characters (or marks
which can be interpreted as characters) on the sand. 'Suddenly the tip
comes down, like a hammer it jumps up and down, two, three, even
more times' (de Groot, *The Religious System of China*, VI, pp. 1295–
1322). The marks are then used to predict the future, or to answer some

specific question. Sometimes the exchange between the spirit and the
medium takes the form, as in this story, of an incomplete couplet.
couplet: Literally 'opposites'. Writing these perfectly matching coup-
lets is a peculiarly Chinese pastime. Arthur Smith explains that 'Its
essence is thesis and antithesis – antithesis between different tones
and different meanings, resemblances in the relations between the
characters in one clause and those in another clause . . . The construction of antithetical sentences affords a fertile field for Chinese
ingenuity, a field to which we have nothing in English even remotely
correspondent' (*Proverbs and Common Sayings from the Chinese*
(Shanghai, 1914), pp. 47–50).
Mutton-fat-white jade-sky: Mutton-fat-white jade is one of the most
valuable sorts of jade, a pure white nephrite, which when well
polished resembles congealed mutton fat. It is sometimes known in
the West as Imperial White Jade.

104

STIR-FRY

put it to soak in a bowl of water: Van Gulik (*Erotic Colour Prints*,
pp. 146–7), quoting the erotic novel *Wild Tales of the Bamboo
Grove*, describes another type of dildo, called the 'Cantonese Groin',
which had to be soaked in hot water before use. He thinks it was
filled with the dried stalks of a plant, which swelled when moistened.
the two of them had a good laugh about it: Feng Zhenluan (1818)
jokingly quotes the Taoist sage Laozi, a legendary figure, thought
by some to have been a contemporary of Confucius in the sixth
century BC: 'If they *hadn't* laughed, it would not have been worthy
of being considered the Tao.'

THE STORY OF PENGUIN CLASSICS

Before 1946 ...'Classics' are mainly the domain of academics and students, without readable editions for everyone else. This all changes when a little-known classicist, E. V. Rieu, presents Penguin founder Allen Lane with the translation of Homer's *Odyssey* that he has been working on and reading to his wife Nelly in his spare time.

1946 *The Odyssey* becomes the first Penguin Classic published, and promptly sells three million copies. Suddenly, classic books are no longer for the privileged few.

1950s Rieu, now series editor, turns to professional writers for the best modern, readable translations, including Dorothy L. Sayers's *Inferno* and Robert Graves's *The Twelve Caesars*, which revives the salacious original.

1960s The Classics are given the distinctive black jackets that have remained a constant throughout the series's various looks. Rieu retires in 1964, hailing the Penguin Classics list as 'the greatest educative force of the 20th century'.

1970s A new generation of translators arrives to swell the Penguin Classics ranks, and the list grows to encompass more philosophy, religion, science, history and politics.

1980s The Penguin American Library joins the Classics stable, with titles such as *The Last of the Mohicans* safeguarded. Penguin Classics now offers the most comprehensive library of world literature available.

1990s The launch of Penguin Audiobooks brings the classics to a listening audience for the first time, and in 1999 the launch of the Penguin Classics website takes them online to a larger global readership than ever before.

The 21st Century Penguin Classics are rejacketed for the first time in nearly twenty years. This world famous series now consists of more than 1300 titles, making the widest range of the best books ever written available to millions – and constantly redefining the meaning of what makes a 'classic'.

The Odyssey continues ...

The best books ever written

PENGUIN (🐧) **CLASSICS**

SINCE 1946

Find out more at www.penguinclassics.com

PENGUIN CLASSICS

THE EPIC OF GILGAMESH

'Surpassing all other kings, heroic in stature,
brave scion of Uruk, wild bull on the rampage!
Gilgamesh the tall, magnificent and terrible'

Miraculously preserved on clay tablets dating back as much as four thousand years, the poem of Gilgamesh, king of Uruk, is the world's oldest epic, predating Homer by many centuries. The story tells of Gilgamesh's adventures with the wild man Enkidu, and of his arduous journey to the ends of the earth in quest of the Babylonian Noah and the secret of immortality. Alongside its themes of family, friendship and the duties of kings, *The Epic of Gilgamesh* is, above all, about mankind's eternal struggle with the fear of death.

The Babylonian version has been known for over a century, but linguists are still deciphering new fragments in Akkadian and Sumerian. Andrew George's gripping translation brilliantly combines these into a fluent narrative and will long rank as the definitive English *Gilgamesh*.

'This masterly new verse translation' *The Times*

Translated with an introduction by Andrew George

PENGUIN CLASSICS

THE ANALECTS   CONFUCIUS

'The Master said, "If a man sets his heart on benevolence, he will be free from evil"'

The Analects are a collection of Confucius's sayings brought together by his pupils shortly after his death in 497 BC. Together they express a philosophy, or a moral code, by which Confucius, one of the most humane thinkers of all time, believed everyone should live. Upholding the ideals of wisdom, self-knowledge, courage and love of one's fellow man, he argued that the pursuit of virtue should be every individual's supreme goal. And while following the Way, or the truth, might not result in immediate or material gain, Confucius showed that it could nevertheless bring its own powerful and lasting spiritual rewards.

This edition contains a detailed introduction exploring the concepts of the original work, a bibliography and glossary and appendices on Confucius himself, *The Analects* and the disciples who compiled them.

Translated with an introduction and notes by D. C. Lau

PENGUIN CLASSICS

BUDDHIST SCRIPTURES

'Whoever gives something for the good of others, with heart full of sympathy, not heeding his own good, reaps unspoiled fruit'

While Buddhism has no central text such as the Bible or the Koran, there is a powerful body of scripture from across Asia that encompasses the *dharma*, or the teachings of Buddha. This rich anthology brings together works from a broad historical and geographical range, and from languages such as Pali, Sanskrit, Tibetan, Chinese and Japanese. There are tales of the Buddha's past lives, a discussion of the qualities and qualifications of a monk, and an exploration of the many meanings of Enlightenment. Together they provide a vivid picture of the Buddha and of the vast nature of the Buddhist tradition.

This new edition contains many texts presented in English for the first time as well as new translations of some well-known works, and also includes an informative introduction and prefaces to each chapter by scholar of Buddhism Donald S. Lopez Jr, with suggestions for further reading and a glossary.

Edited with an introduction by Donald S. Lopez, Jr

PENGUIN CLASSICS

THE COMPLETE DEAD SEA SCROLLS IN ENGLISH
GEZA VERMES

'He will heal the wounded and revive the dead and bring good news to the poor'

The discovery of the Dead Sea Scrolls in the Judean desert between 1947 and 1956 was one of the greatest archaeological finds of all time. These extraordinary manuscripts appear to have been hidden in the caves at Qumran by the Essenes, a Jewish sect in existence before and during the time of Jesus. Written in Hebrew, Aramaic and Greek, the scrolls have transformed our understanding of the Hebrew Bible, early Judaism and the origins of Christianity.

This is a fully revised edition of the classic translation by Geza Vermes, the world's leading Dead Sea Scrolls scholar. It is now enhanced by much previously unpublished material and a new preface, and also contains a scroll catalogue and an index of Qumran texts.

'No translation of the Scrolls is either more readable or more authoritative than that of Vermes' *The Times Higher Education Supplement*

'Excellent, up-to-date ... will enable the general public to read the non-biblical scrolls and to judge for themselves their importance'
The New York Times Book Review

Translated and edited with an introduction by Geza Vermes

PENGUIN CLASSICS

RUSSIAN SHORT STORIES FROM PUSCHKIN TO BUIDA

'Light's all very well, brothers, but it's not easy to live with'

From the early nineteenth century to the collapse of the Soviet Union and beyond, the short story has occupied a central place in Russian literature. This collection includes not only well-known classics but also modern masterpieces, many of them previously censored. There are stories by acknowledged giants – Gogol, Tolstoy, Chekhov and Solzhenitsyn – and by equally great writers such as Andrey Platonov who have only recently become known to the English-speaking world. Some stories are tragic, but the volume also includes a great deal of comedy – from Pushkin's subtle wit to Kharms's dark absurdism, from Dostoyevsky's graveyard humour to Teffi's subtle evocations of human stupidity and Zoshchenko's satirical vignettes of everyday life in the decade after the 1917 Revolution.

This new collection of translations includes works only recently rediscovered in Russia. The introduction gives a vivid insight into the history of the Russian short story, while the work of every author is preceded by an individual introduction. This edition also includes notes and a chronology.

Edited by Robert Chandler

PENGUIN CLASSICS

DANTE IN ENGLISH

'All in the middle of the road of life
I stood bewildered in a dusky wood'

Dante Alighieri (1265–1321) created poetry of profound force and beauty that
proved influential far beyond the borders of his native Italy. This new collection
brings together translations from all his verse, including the *Vita Nuova*, his tale of
erotic despair and hope, and the *Commedia*, his vast yet intimate poem depicting
one man's journey into the afterlife. It also contains extracts from many English
masterpieces influenced by Dante, including Chaucer's *Canterbury Tales*,
Milton's *Paradise Lost*, Byron's *Don Juan*, T. S. Eliot's *The Waste Land* and
Derek Walcott's *Omeros*.

Edited by Eric Griffiths and Matthew Reynolds, this anthology explores the
variety of encounters between Dante and English-speakers across more than six
centuries. Its detailed notes enable even readers with little or no Italian to
appreciate translations that range from the hilarious to the inspired. Eric Griffiths'
introduction explains how intricately Dante's work is tied to his own time, yet still
speaks across the ages. This edition also includes an account of Dante's life and a
list of further reading.

Edited with an introduction and notes by Eric Griffiths

and Matthew Reynolds